DRAGONFLY
ESCAPING
NEVER GIVE UP

RAYA KHEDKER

Dragonfly Escaping
Copyright © 2023 by Raya Khedker.
All rights reserved.

No part of this book may be reproduced or transmitted in any form or by any electronic or mechanical means, including photocopying, recording or by any information storage and retrieval system, without the express written permission of the copyright holder, except where permitted by law. This is a work of fiction based on a true story. However, names, characters, places, and incidents have all been altered to protect the privacy of those involved, either living or dead.

The ebook edition of this book is licensed for your personal enjoyment only. The ebook may not be re-sold or given away to other people. If you would like to share the ebook edition with another person, please purchase an additional copy for each recipient. Thank you for respecting the hard work of this author.

EBook ISBN: 978-1-68565-029-2
Trade Paperback ISBN: 978-1-7374037-0-8
Hardcover ISBN: 978-1-68565-028-5
Red Adept, Editor
Cover design by Jeff Yesh, Story Monsters LLC
Cover artwork by Raya C. Khedker
Published by FountKor, LLC
237 Sullivan Place, Brooklyn, NY, 11225
www.fountkor.com
Constanza Ontaneda, Publisher

Join Raya's Ray of Light
at
rayakhedker.com

To Jennifer—My Mother Earth, who picked up every piece of me she found along the way to stick me back together again.

To Olivia—The Enforcer, who said, why are you crawling? Get up and walk, now walk faster!

To Marty—The Nurturer, who cradled me through this entire process.

And to Constanza—The Teacher, who introduced me to the magic of storytelling.

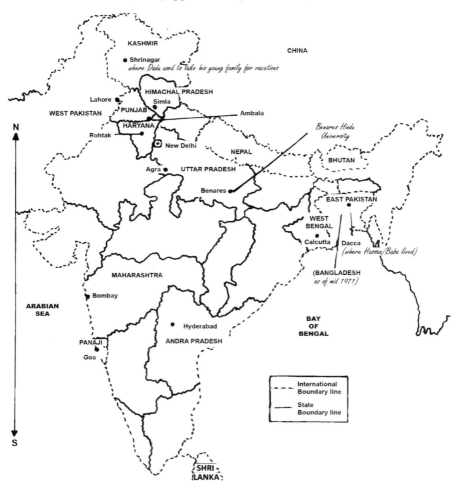

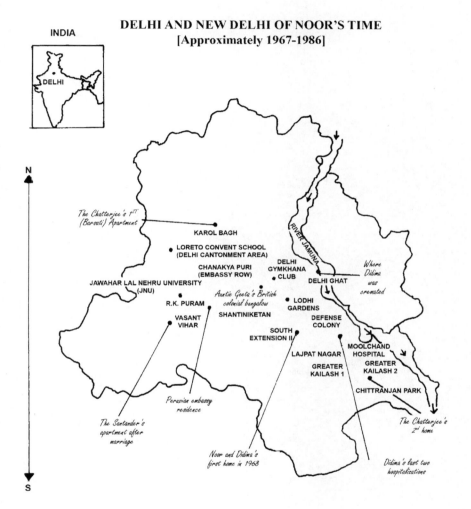

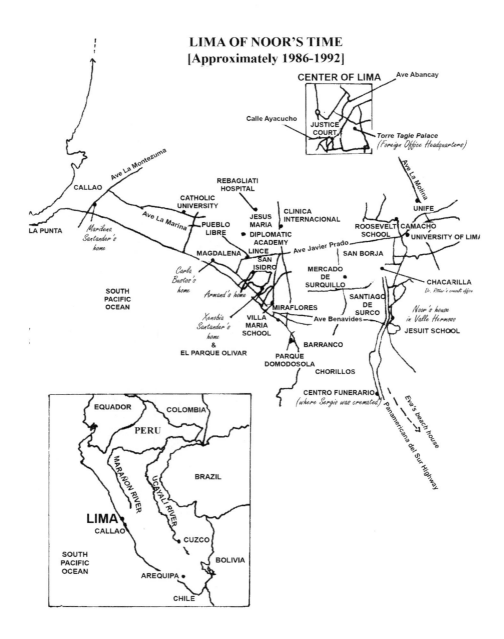

AMARYLLIS

1

New Delhi, 1979

TAKE CONTROL OR DIE. The swollen slit of my right eye stared back at me from the mirror in the bathroom I shared with seven roommates in the Catholic Working Girls' Hostel. An established bruise would stamp my face later. I didn't care, chiefly because I assumed I no longer had to marry Rajat. A splash of cold water soothed my purpling eye. In mute rage, I observed the dried blood caked to my cheeks and upper lip. My face hurt as I washed it, dislodging tiny brown flakes that swirled down the drain of the washbasin. I dressed to go eat breakfast.

Downstairs, the dining hall bustled with girls—girls in the food line, which I joined, girls already seated at the two long dining tables, eating their portions of greasy potato curry out of white ceramic bowls. All, except I, were boarders from out of town who needed a safe place to stay while working in the capital city. Right then, however, the girls shared one more commonality—none of them met my eyes.

Their collective denial of my presence took me back to the previous evening as I burst into their midst through the side entrance of the hostel, jeans and white blouse in disarray, dripping blood from my nose and mouth, panting,

"The mother superior! Where is the mother superior of this place? I must see her."

My entry had scattered every last person, all females, in different directions, like hens fleeing a dog. After a few minutes, it brought forth their mother superior.

"What's the problem?" she asked. Slim and of medium height in her white habit and black wimple, the nun appeared to be around forty years old to my seventeen.

I grabbed her hand, which held a string of wooden rosary beads. "You have to take me in. You have to let me stay," I cried, well aware of how uncommon my behavior must be for her.

South Extension was a quiet, tree-lined, upper-middle-class suburb, therefore not the setting for bleeding girls to badger her for assistance.

"You have to save me from my fiancé," I added to reinforce my case. "He's the one who did this to me." My fingers touched the blood trickling out of my nose, tasting salty on my lips.

"And where is your family?"

"I live with my grandma, who has dementia. She encouraged this beating."

The nun glanced at the crowd of onlookers who had collected around us next to the central stairwell. She took my arm and led me down a gloomy corridor.

Inside her office, she switched on an overhead light, shut the door, and pushed me into a chair across from her desk. "Call me Mother Rosa, and tell me what happened."

"It's hard to explain." I watched Mother Rosa pour me water from a spherical terracotta *ghara* vessel resting on her one windowsill.

"We have all evening." She handed me the glass. "What is your name?"

"Noor. Noor Zulfiker." The events of the last two months gushed out of me in a torrent.

My life had started to unravel as soon as Chirag's letter had arrived. Chirag was the boy I had loved since I was a little girl of ten, but his folks had moved to America, and I had not seen him in years. Then, two months ago, I spotted him in a triangular park near our house, perched on the park railing, a strapping teenager with shoulder-length hair, watching a game of cricket. Ready to faint, I didn't know what to do except beat a quick retreat from the scene.

He showed up at my grandma's doorstep the following morning. We stared at each other, speechless, until he handed me a sprig of jasmine.

"I'm sorry for how I left India without saying goodbye. Can you forgive me? Can I see you later to explain?"

I took the jasmine, touched he remembered how much I loved the scent of the flower, and bobbed my head.

On the day his letter arrived, I walked the fifteen minutes home from the Delhi Polytechnic Institute, where I was a freshman in interior design, lost in my own bubble of happiness for having spent three glorious days with Chirag. Impervious to the gluey smell of tar the road workers were boiling in a metal drum to patch up a part of our street, I daydreamed of how Chirag and I were one. Across continents and seas, no one could penetrate our connection. Above me, the branches of the laburnum trees on the sidewalk were heavy with yellow buds. My steps had a spring to them as I hurried home.

I entered through our back door to see Didima brandishing a stiff, multicolored rectangle folded in two parts. Of course, as my legal guardian and grandma, Didima had the right to open any mail addressed to me. Now she screamed, "Prostitute. I knew it the minute I saw it! Prostitute. Jhummur was one, and you are too. I knew it. I knew it. You deserve to go live with her and her husband."

My stomach tightened at the mention of my mother. She and I had never lived together because she had relegated me to my grandparents' care as a newborn. The two of us also had an ongoing feud regarding my stepfather's behavior from when I was six years old. But Didima was rubbing my mother in my face because dementia had deleted the difference between kindness and cruelty in her addled brain. In her saner moments, Didima also knew how much she and I hated my stepfather, Robu Chatterjee, but right then, she was too crazed to care. Knowing the shouting wouldn't stop, I snatched the stationery out of Didima's hand and ran into Teddy's old room, the only other room in our house.

The mysterious note, with striking snapshots of tulips and windmills, was a folded postcard for first-class passengers flying with KLM Airlines. In it, Chirag, who had convinced me he "never wrote letters," had poured his heart out, writing, *My Darling Noor, I need you back in my arms again…* for Didima to lose her mind over.

Unamused to see her audience disappear, Didima chased me. "What do you see in Chirag? He was a perverted boy even six years ago. How will Rajat marry you now that you're not a virgin? Was it worth jeopardizing your engagement to a full-fledged doctor?"

In India, a girl's virginity was her ultimate treasure to bequeath to a husband on their marriage night.

"Didima, Chirag did not take my virginity, okay?"

"Yes, he did! I'm sure he did!"

I kept quiet, knowing nothing would calm Didima while she was so agitated. If I told her Chirag wanted to marry me, she would have another heart attack, and that would be catastrophic. Poor Didima's thinking had grown disturbingly erratic ever since her son, my uncle Teddy, had left us years earlier to emigrate to Canada. But the dementia diagnosis three weeks ago had led Didima's treating doctor to explain it had been developing in her brain for a long time.

Fifteen minutes later, Didima continued ranting as I penned an urgent letter in the guise of doing homework on our dining table.

Dearest Chirag,

What happened to "I don't write letters"?! The one you sent to my house has pretty much ignited World War III in my grandma's head. As I write this, she's threatening to tell my mother about you. So far, she hasn't mentioned telling Rajat, but I'm sure she'll threaten to reveal your existence to him too. So, <u>please</u> don't mail letters to my house. Write to me at your bhuaji auntie's house in Defense Colony. I promise I'll pick up your letters on alternate days, come rain or shine. Meanwhile, I press this one to my heart. As I read it, your face comes alive in my mind, you talking to me, kissing me...

Over dinner the next day, Didima said, "What will we do now that you're not a virgin anymore?"

I hurled my plate at Teddy's wooden armoire. "Didima!" I yelled. "I *am* a virgin, and I will marry Chirag!"

Didima choked over a mouthful of egg curry and rice. "That's it! I'll send you to live with Jhummur."

"No, you won't. If you send me to live with her, who will give you your injections?"

Didima suffered from advanced diabetes and all its complications. Her failing health had ruled our daily lives since I could remember.

"I don't care!" Didima screamed. "You won't marry Chirag. You will marry Rajat." Didima banged her plate on the dining table so hard it broke.

"Why do you hate him so much? He's a good boy." I got up to collect the shattered pieces of my plate off the floor.

"Good boy? Good *boy*? When he wrote you love letters on the wall at age eleven?"

The argument continued until Didima collapsed into an edema attack and a truce had to be declared. Fight forgotten, I rushed to administer diuretic injections into Didima's vein. When her body calmed down and she could breathe again, I put her to bed. Before I switched off the lights, Didima caressed my cheek, and I kissed her forehead.

For all practical purposes, we lived in South Extension to be close to Didima's youngest brother, my great-uncle Jiten. Uncle Jiten was largely in charge of Didima's healthcare needs, but on a daily basis, the burden of that responsibility fell on my shoulders. In our neighborhood, we were the only poor dwellers who lived in the two back rooms of a large house rented to more affluent tenants, which I deeply resented, having spent my ear-ly childhood surrounded by luxury. I was also the one teenager in the area who took twenty-four-hour care of an ailing adult, a circumstance out of my control.

Didima couldn't know that I hated Rajat, much less why. If she got wind of any part of my secret, her dementia would compel her to shout it to the four winds, then I would be in worse trouble than I already was. I wanted to break my engagement to Rajat on my own terms when he came to New Delhi at the end of April. Being a doctor in the Indian Navy, Rajat provided us with free medicine for Didima's many ailments. That was why, for the time being, I had to keep up the pretense of loving him so as not to upset that balance. Pray God, Didima wouldn't reveal Chirag's existence to Rajat or my mother until I could come up with a plan for how to navigate the future.

Meanwhile, my only solace came from the letters Chirag and I wrote to each other, which I picked up from his auntie's house every other day. Nothing lasted forever, however, and neither did Didima's uneasy peace with me.

One afternoon, in the last week of April, I came home from the polytechnic to Didima sipping a cup of tea on our back patio. Her trembling hand held a green-edged airmail letter.

"Oh my God." I threw down my bookbag and snatched the letter. With shaking fingers, I tore it open. Seeing the incomprehensible Bengali handwriting, I pushed the letter under Didima's nose. "Read it," I insisted. "And don't tell me Baba's coming to India, or I'll have a fit." Baba was my father, whom I had lost a long time ago to his second marriage. I had never forgiven him for it.

Didima shook her bifocals out of her cloth purse. "Hassan arrives in New Delhi"—she glanced up from the depths of her wood-and-canvas easy chair—"at the end of April."

As a child, I had loved Baba's name because many heroes in the *Tales from the Arabian Nights* were named Hassan, and when Didima had read me the stories as a little girl, I would imagine Baba as that hero.

"No!" I shouted. "Write back and put him off. Do it now—what else does the letter say? Is he coming with his wife alone or with his wife and three kids? And what about Rajat? He arrives at the end of April—"

"I can't," interrupted Didima. "April ends in six days."

My eyes welled. "Where will they sleep? I know how this will go… they'll all sleep inside, and you and I will be right out here, on charpoy cots, like slum dwellers."

"They're guests, Noor. My mother-in-law used to say—"

"Didima," I said through clenched teeth, "your mother-in-law was a wealthy widow. You are not. Write back and tell Baba we've gone on a trip. Tell him whatever you want so he doesn't come mooch off us."

"The letter won't reach him in time. Bangladesh is too far away."

I stared at my grandma helplessly, wishing she had a mind to call her own like she used to have even two years ago. Battle lost, I went and threw myself down on Teddy's bed and buried my head in his soft pillow, choking on the lump in my throat. *Does Baba fly dragonflies with his new brood of kids? I am seventeen years old for God's sake… why does the memory of my father always reduce me to the nine-year-old I was when he broke my heart? Does Baba ever remember our Calcutta life together when Dadu, my grandfather, was alive and we were well-off?*

Whichever way I sliced it, Baba was a fair-weather father who lived in the present moment, and I had stopped being his "present" a long time ago. In these past eight years, if Baba had ever regretted abandoning me, I had never seen it. When he visited India, he acted as if I were a relative instead of the beloved only child he had once doted on before he left the country. And his rejection was a permanent knife twisting in my heart.

But that would change once I married Chirag. Chirag would take me to America, and I would live safely, away from Rajat and my stepfather and my baba too. In America, I would also be free to study English, the subject I truly wanted to pursue, and not interior design.

The expensive and modern women's polytechnic where I currently studied had no English honors course. But located in South Extension, what it did offer was the proximity to come home and attend to Didima's healthcare needs during lunchtime. That was yet another unwarranted sacrifice to prevent me from pursuing English. Admittedly, my desire to study English stemmed from a nonstop perusal of English literature anyway. *But who can fault me for reading to escape my reality?*

Six days later, I came home from the polytechnic to find Didima, Baba, his wife, and their five-year-old, Nadir, sharing tea and snacks on our back patio. When I walked in, I wanted Baba to stand up and hug me, but he was too busy assessing the fake smile his wife pasted on at the sight of me.

When he glanced my way, I spat, "How long will you stay?" I didn't bother to greet his overly made-up, overdressed wife or their son clinging to his mother's lap.

"Just like that?" Baba smiled the sunny smile that used to melt my heart as a five-year-old back in Calcutta. "How about a 'Hello,' or a 'How are you?' for your baba?"

"Aren't we past pretending we're a big, happy family, Baba?" Rage lit my eyes on fire. "I'm the one who'll cook, clean, and attend college while you, your wife, and child have fun."

"But I'm here to see you."

"That's such a lie!"

"*Shona.*" Didima used the Bengali word for darling, struggling to her feet from her canvas easy chair. "Come with me to the kitchen."

"Why?" I wiped away angry tears. "So you can talk me out of saying how I feel?"

She took my arm and led me away. "Shona," Didima repeated, "it wasn't Hassan who left you on purpose. It was Jhummur, and you know that, but you always take it out on him."

"I hate them both!" I was crying.

"But they are your parents, and I am not, which makes it horribly awkward because they blame your attitude on me." Didima folded me in a hug.

"Oh, Didima. What a skewed reality we live in. It's so unfair."

"Let it go, my darling. When they leave in a few days, it'll be over."

Within two days, my mood grew even darker knowing Rajat would fly in from Bombay, where he worked on a navy base. Every time I thought of him, I regretted caving to societal pressure and letting Didima force me into an engagement.

That afternoon, I walked home from the polytechnic feeling as if I had swallowed a tablespoonful of hornets. *Will Didima tell him about Chirag?* Poor Didima wanted me to marry Rajat to ensure I wouldn't have to live with my mother and stepfather once she passed away. That possibility preyed upon her so much, she overlooked how Rajat was socially way beneath her, belonging to an uneducated farming family from the rural area of Haryana in the north. It consoled Didima to focus on how Rajat was a doctor, since Didima's own father had been a thriving surgeon in Lahore until the British Government officials had moved him to practice medicine in the Ambala district of the Punjab prior to the Partition of India and Pakistan. Didima knew that in India, as the minor I was, until I reached twenty-one, only a husband could save me from the clutches of my mother after Didima died—and she had been dying little by little for the past five years, always worse after a new diabetic complication.

The last time she became ill, Didima spent two months in the ICU of the Moolchand Hospital until her treating doctor discharged her, saying, "I don't know how she is alive. She should have died a long time ago."

On our back patio, Rajat and my family were having tea. When I came in, he stood and smiled. A little taller than me, Rajat was lithe and athletic, being a marathon runner for the Indian Naval Team. Didima always compared his sports background to that of my grandpa, Dadu, who had been a lightweight boxing and rowing champion for the famous Benares Hindu University while also being a gold-medal-winning academic student. It allowed Didima to ignore how Dadu had belonged to the noble Kshatriya caste, whereas Rajat was a glorified Vaishya villager.

Why did I ever consider him handsome? Rajat's eyes were small and mean behind the expensive rimless glasses.

"Can I see you inside for a minute?" Rajat's voice sounded normal.

Whew! Didima hadn't mentioned Chirag. *What will he do in the room? Kiss me and tell me how much he loves me and missed me? Pretend he doesn't enjoy the power he has over Didima's failing health just because he's a qualified doctor?* If for no other reason, I would never marry Rajat for that meanness alone. Never mind the final humiliation of Didima forcing Rajat to propose to me six months ago.

I dropped my bookbag in our front room and followed him into Teddy's room. *When and how will I break my engagement?* Rajat closed and locked the door behind me. My head whirled as Baba entered through the kitchen-corridor access, followed by his gaudy wife, Didima, and Baba's little son. My stomach dropped as Baba locked that door as well. Both men corralled me.

Rajat slapped my face with one hand and hit my head with the other. He pushed me down on Didima's dressing-table stool and slapped me again. "You slept with Chirag?" he demanded.

I tried to get my breath back.

Hearing Rajat, Baba punched me in the back so hard it felt as if he had punctured my right lung. "You're just like your mother. She cheated on me, too, and I was fool enough to never beat her for it."

My arms shot up to protect my face, and I screamed, "Please! I didn't do anything."

Rajat landed a punch on my right ear.

I couldn't hear myself past the ringing inside my head.

Didima, meanwhile, leaned on Teddy's wooden armoire, chanting in a high, querulous voice, "Don't you see, Noor? Don't you? Don't you? You have to marry Rajat. Otherwise, you'll end up living with Jhummur and Robu when I die."

In between blows—ten, twelve, thirteen, and more—I wept and howled, "Didima, *Didima*, tell them to stop! I didn't sleep with Chirag. I swear I didn't." But the fists rained on my face, hammered on my back, a punch to my jaw, a karate chop to my neck, my hair pulled back for a better angle of my ear.

Rajat swore, "You whore! You think I want you to be the mother of my children?"

I fought the salty taste of blood in my mouth and swore back, "Asshole! I would rather die than have your children, you low-class village idiot. It's Chirag I'll marry, not you. It's his children I'll have, not yours."

I regretted my bravery the second Rajat chopped my right cheek with the edge of one hand. "Oh yeah? Let's see how much he'll want you after I knock your teeth out." He buffeted me off the dressing table stool to land on the floor.

My screams, tears, blood, and mucus blended with the May heat of Delhi as Didima gained a moment of clarity. "Enough! She's had enough!" she shouted.

But no one stopped to listen to her as Rajat kicked me in the kidneys.

Rajat and Baba were busy pummeling me with their feet when I croaked, "Please. Can I please use the bathroom?" If I didn't find an excuse to stop their momentum, both men would beat me unconscious. Neither heeded my request until Didima tottered into their midst, her trembling arms outstretched. "Stop. Please stop! She's had enough. Let her go to the bathroom."

Seizing the opportunity, I charged out of Didima's back door—face bleeding in the evening light—disheveled and crying, running for my life, uncaring of whether our snooty neighbors were at their windows to sneer at the developing drama.

Three blocks down the road, fear of the darkening sky had made me run past my old school bus stop on Ring Road to the metal signboard of the Catholic Working Girls' Hostel, the two-story residence that provided safety for out-of-town girls to live and work in New Delhi.

The shock on Mother Rosa's face told me I had convinced her.

"So here I am. You *have* to take me in because I need a safe place to stay until I figure out what to do with my life. If I go home, my ex-fiancé will beat me to death, and in this country, you know no one will care."

Mother Rosa knew she was cornered. Still, in a weak attempt to save herself from the mess of my life, she said, "We run a working girls' hostel. I can't take you in for free. How will you pay us?"

I patted my jeans pocket. "I have the money. I forgot to pay my polytechnic fees this morning. I'll pay you with what I have. Whatever you decide, please don't send me home."

2

I WAS SO LOST IN THOUGHT, the girl behind me in the breakfast line nudged me to move forward and hold forth my bowl to the young nun who ladled out portions of potato curry. In my life, love and pain had always been two sides of the same coin. I had learned that lesson at five years old, when Dadu, my grandfather, had died and Baba had left me forever to go make a new life. If I loved—I paid. I loved Chirag, which was why I had wanted to break my engagement to Rajat, thus provoking him to beat me. But I would escape the cycle once Chirag married me.

My mind was on Chirag when I walked into my Perspectives class at the polytechnic at eight a.m.

The professor took one look at me and said, "What happened to your eye?" Without waiting for an answer, he gripped my upper arm and marched me, face all puffed up, to the headmistress's office. Relief made me want to hug him for taking charge.

Furious, the headmistress dialed Uncle Jiten's number. She knew him well, since both had been classmates in college at the Konstfackskolan of Stockholm and were thriving artists. "Jiten," she hollered into the phone, "did you know of this beating? Come here immediately."

Uncle Jiten was the main reason Didima had moved us from Calcutta to Delhi. As her only living male sibling, he took care of Didima for the most part, especially when it came to paying for her frequent hospitalizations. Uncle Jiten and their eldest sister, Auntie Geeta, were Didima's two towers of support after she lost my grandpa.

Tall and spare figured, Uncle Jiten arrived half an hour later, head hanging, to take me to his doctor, Dr. Lal. While we waited for him, I attempted to explain my life to the headmistress, but I sensed she couldn't understand the half of what I was babbling.

Didima and I had no health insurance. Therefore, Uncle Jiten paid out of pocket for the five stitches and ten days of antibiotic treatment I required for the gash inside my right cheek. Dr. Lal said the rest of the bruises on my body looked ugly but would heal on their own. His assessment made me want to ask him about my one thousand psychological bruises, but I kept quiet.

Afterward, Uncle Jiten dropped me off outside the hostel gate in his Fiat. "Listen, stay here for now." He patted me on the head. "I'll pay your polytechnic tuition and hire Totini a nurse."

Hearing Didima's first name always startled me, as I never saw her as Totini. Only her siblings called her that.

Uncle Jiten continued, "If I had done that to begin with, she wouldn't have depended so much on Rajat. We'll plan to have you return home once you heal."

"Oh, no!" I slurred out the left side of my mouth, the right side numb from local anesthesia. "I'm never going back home. Once I graduate the polytechnic, help me find a job through your connections in the art world. I will never go back to Didima."

The working girls' hostel provided its boarders breakfast and dinner. With no money left after paying Mother Rosa, I gnawed on my hangnails for lunch.

On Monday, I invested my lunch hour in job hunting. Face swollen, I plodded from one local public school to another within walking distance in the older and poorer sections of Wazin Nagar and Kotla, districts that predated the suburban snobbery of South Extension with its Western-style, middle-class houses, airy windows, and front gardens.

Patiently, I explained to the secretary at each school that I could coach Hindi-speaking schoolgirls for their English exams then wrote down the hostel phone number. "Their families can call me between eight and nine on any night to set it up. Please, *please* help me because I need the money."

I refused to ask Uncle Jiten for food money to show him I could fend for myself and uphold my decision to leave home.

Thanks to the seven schools I visited, I received one phone call to tutor an eighth grader in English every evening from six to seven. Her home was in front of the same triangular park where Chirag and I had spent our first evening together, huddled on a cold park bench, too happy to care we were shivering in the winter cold. The eighth grader's family would pay me fifteen rupees for each class—roughly seven dollars a week. It was enough to buy me a lunch snack.

At dinnertime on Thursday, my eyes popped when Mother Rosa handed me a large box of pastries from the Auto Bakery in Defense Colony.

"Your grandmother came by to see you this afternoon. She looked ill. You should go visit her."

Tears sprang to my eyes. "For what? So she can have my ex-fiancé beat me up all over again? What did my grandma say?"

"She paced our foyer for three hours and shouted about how you have become a prostitute."

My tears spilled. "But if I'm a prostitute, why did she bring me pastries?"

"Because she knew you must be hungry."

I ran out of that busy dining room, bawling. My body slumped on the bottom step of the central stairwell, and the crook of my arm muffled my loud sobs. To calm myself, I wolfed down five chocolate éclairs in a row while stray tears tarnished the glaze on two lemon tarts inside the white container.

Skipping the hostel dinner, I trudged upstairs with my precious pastry box, changed, and hopped into bed. Some part of me wanted to drop it all, jump up, get dressed, and run home to Didima. Despite my bravado to Uncle Jiten about never returning, I felt utterly lost without her. *How is she coping with me gone? Who is administering her medicines and giving her insulin injections twice a day? Yes, Uncle Jiten said he would hire Didima a nurse, but did he?*

I had taken care of Didima since I was eleven years old. Any other reality went so far back in time, I couldn't remember it, except in fragmented snapshots. All I remembered were the numerous hospitalizations Didima had undergone, her coming home a little more dead each time. But the day she really died, I would have to go live with my mother and stepfather—the possibility tensed my stomach and numbed my mind each time I contemplated it.

I plumped my pillow and rolled over.

My roommate to the left whispered, "Settle down already! You're keeping me awake." I pulled my top sheet over my head and scrunched my eyes shut. *Nothing* would persuade me to live with my mother or stepfather, because before then, Chirag would marry me and take me away from India. I had already written Chirag a long letter explaining the new development in my circumstances, but letters took two weeks to reach America.

Meanwhile, during the past few days away from home, I had lived with a permanent sensation of my body not being mine anymore, that the person living at the Catholic Working Girls' Hostel wasn't me because I didn't exist without Didima. We had been a part of the same whole since I was born. But the immediate impediment to my going home was Didima herself. I would have to penetrate the cloud of her dementia so she understood she could not throw me back into Rajat's arms. Yes, within Didima's limited knowledge, Rajat was the answer to the problem of her dying, but Didima had no idea what Rajat had done to me more than two years ago or why I secretly loathed him. Maybe Mother Rosa could talk to Didima. *Yet, do I want to tell Mother Rosa the truth behind why I hate Rajat so much?* It was a moot point, since whether she knew the truth or not, she couldn't tell Didima anything. If Didima found out the facts, all hell would break loose.

In the darkness, my hatred for Rajat was such a physicality, my body tingled with pins and needles.

***

On the day it all happened, in 1976, I had turned fifteen in August, before winter came. Approaching November 15, Didima had already spent an entire month in the Moolchand Hospital ICU, a private hospital located in the older district of Lajpat Nagar. Notwithstanding, I was happy because Didima had finally been transferred into a normal hospital room, which meant she was out of imminent danger. No one was more excited than Didima to have Rajat visit from Bombay to stay three days with us before he headed to his hometown of Rohtak in Haryana to spend four weeks with his parents. On his way back, he would stop in Delhi again for his last week of vacation then fly back to Bombay.

I met Rajat at the Moolchand Hospital's red brick entrance, the wattage of my smile in sharp contrast to my exhaustion. Each morning, I attended school then came to the hospital to watch Didima until Auntie Shalini picked me up in the evenings to go sleep in her extended family home. Dr. Shalini Kale was the daughter of a college friend of my grandpa, Dadu.

In her private hospital room, Didima held up her arms. "Rajat!" She hugged him. I noticed she had put on her dentures for the occasion. "Come, pull up a chair to sit by me."

Rajat squeezed her hand. "Didima, tell me your treating doctor's name. I'll leave you with plenty of medicine before I go."

An hour passed.

"Didima, can I stay at your place even though you're here?" Rajat held Didima's hand.

"Of course! What a question."

"Can Noor come explain the locks and keys to me?"

"Certainly. Please bring me photo albums so I can relive better times."

On the ride to South Extension, I was happy and excited to spend a few minutes alone with Rajat outside Didima's hawkeyed purview. It was too bad we wouldn't have time to walk in the Lodhi Gardens, a favorite haunt of ours from when Rajat used to work in New Delhi and I had just met him.

Inside our house, Rajat kissed me and hugged me nonstop. "Let's go lie in bed for a while. Please. I'm so tired from my marathon practice today and all the travel. Don't refuse me."

I stared at him. *How can I resist his begging?* He'd expressed his undying love for me in every letter from Bombay.

Under the blankets, I kept on my T-shirt and underwear while Rajat pressed close. "Please, this is torture. Please let me rub myself against you."

As though drugged, I let him remove my T-shirt, bra, and panties and his own underwear.

He got on top of me, bearing down hard. "Darling. Open your legs so I can feel you more."

I spread my legs.

"Tell me what you feel."

"I don't know," I whispered. "I'm hot all over. It's the weirdest feeling."

"Ah!" Rajat cried, eyes unfocused.

"Ahhhhhh!" I shrieked, every muscle constricting in pain and panic. "No, Raj, *nooo*, you're hurting me."

But Rajat moaned, a piston moving up and down for at least a minute.

"Raj!" I fought to push him away. "What are you doing? Get off me. You peed on me." I wiped sweat beads off my upper lip.

"Oh, Noor. That was incredible," Rajat panted.

I sat up, chilled by the winter afternoon, yet more sweat beads prickled my forehead and armpits. I touched my burning vagina. White liquid stained my fingers.

"I came." Rajat sounded sheepish.

"Came? Came where?"

"As in, I had an orgasm. You know what that means, don't you?"

"An orgasm is like this? As if you peed on me?"

"It's not pee—it's semen. That's how men come."

"So you took my *virginity?*"

"No. I couldn't go in. You were too tight."

"I think you *did* get inside me, because I hurt. You hurt me."

"Sorry. But I couldn't hold it. You excite me too much."

Oh, so now it's my fault? I pulled the blanket up to cover me, folding knees to chest.

Rajat didn't seem to notice. "C'mon. Let's get going. Didima is waiting for us."

Two days later, Rajat left for his village in Haryana, and Didima came home from the hospital, bedridden. While I attended school, Uncle Jiten's manservant, Mohan Singh, watched Didima, and I took over again in the afternoons.

Back from school each day, I would lie on Teddy's bed to elude Didima's eagle eyes, too distracted to do homework, while I waited for Rajat to return to New Delhi. Often, anxiety made me dwell on what had transpired between us and questioned if that was sex—incredibly painful. But the encounter had been so brief, I wasn't sure. It was far easier to believe Rajat's claim of "you are still a virgin."

In India, as a single girl without my virginity, I would convert to a piece of human refuse in the marriage market. Parents didn't wait for their children to reach adulthood at twenty-one to marry. Girls were "ready" at sixteen, and boys, by eighteen. In fact, if a girl *wasn't* married by twenty-one, she was a spinster. *But I don't have to worry about that, because I'm a virgin. Rajat said so, and he's a doctor.*

Ten days into Rajat's departure, I overslept by twenty minutes on a school day. Running pell-mell to catch the school bus, a piece of buttered toast with sugar sprinkled on top clutched in one hand, my book bag bouncing in the other, I stopped dead in my tracks past Chirag's old home as an unfamiliar spiral of pain jackknifed vertically through my core. So, this is how it hurts if periods come late? Mine had been due four days ago.

For the rest of that school day, each time the spiraling pain occurred, I charged to the bathroom to check for stains.

On day fifteen, the pains continued, but no bleeding set in. *Could I be pregnant? Pregnant with Didima anchored to a bed? Oh my God! But isn't the sign of pregnancy vomiting in the morning?* I wasn't nauseous. No. I would stop worrying like a maniac and wait for Rajat. But Rajat wouldn't return from Haryana for another eight days. I couldn't call him because, like Didima, his parents didn't have a phone. When Didima or I needed to call anyone, we paid our South Indian neighbor, Mr. Guru, to use his telephone.

Who else could I ask? My peers knew as much about pregnancy as I did. Besides, they would become suspicious. If one of them mentioned my questions to their parents, or worse, reported me to our headmistress, Mother Theresa, she would seek out Didima. But in India, once my pregnancy showed, people would stone me on the street if they discovered I wasn't married. *What am I going to do?*

During my afternoons home from school, too upset to binge-read the novels that held me spellbound in lieu of homework, my mind jumped from solution to solution. *If I am indeed pregnant, what if Rajat marries me and we have this baby? No!* I would be expelled from school. *Hadn't Great-Grandma Panaeker given birth to Dadu at age fifteen?* Yes, but unlike me, Great-Grandma Panaeker had been *married*. The ramifications from that simple word were mind-boggling. If Rajat and I were to keep the baby, we would have to marry like a pair of thieves, and once the child was born seven or eight months later, no one would believe it was premature. Moreover, Rajat was the eldest Talwar son, the apple of his parents' eyes. They wouldn't settle for a hasty wedding. Rajat was the first member of their extended farming family to ever receive a college degree. To them, he was a god. *Stop! I have to stop. My mind is jumping to conclusions all over again. I'm not pregnant, because I'm not nauseous.*

Another week passed.

On one school morning, I hacked up a thin drool of bile, frighteningly nauseous. After that, I couldn't avoid the truth. I *was* pregnant. In school, all nine classes passed in a haze of queasiness I couldn't confess to classmates. Worse, I couldn't fathom Didima's humiliation in front of Delhi society. My mother would have a field day condemning poor, sick Didima for "the kind of mother she is." *Oh, why did I lie down next to Rajat and let him remove my clothes? Why did I trust him?*

Neither I nor my hapless, unborn baby would live down the shame of my conduct in India. God forbid, if it was a girl, my daughter would carry the shame of being conceived out of wedlock until the day she died. On top of that was the stigma of my checkered Hindu-Muslim parentage, where my Hindu mother had eloped to marry my Muslim father. *Who would marry such a daughter? What can I do in the face of all this? Rajat never said it, but he'll marry me, won't he? Yes!* Rajat loved me, and he was ten years older. He would never abandon or harm me.

All I had to do was talk to him. He would have the solution to whatever the problem was.

At last, Rajat arrived.

I smiled through an interminable lunch with Didima until I could drag him to the Lodhi Gardens so we could talk alone. He hadn't yet switched off the ignition of his rented Lambretta scooter when I erupted, "Raj, I'm pregnant."

Rajat's head swung. "What?"

I repeated my suspicion as we entered the exquisite gardens through the West Gate.

"Are you sure of this?" Rajat gazed at the paved path stretching ahead instead of into my eyes.

"Well, my period is two weeks late, and I'm nauseous every morning. You tell me. You're the doctor."

"I suppose I'll have to marry you now."

My head spun to stare at him, but he evaded eye contact.

"Wait a minute. You're saying that as if it's the worst option in the world."

Rajat looked at the ground. "Well, isn't it?"

He sent a stray stone flying with the pointed toe of his leather boot. The pebble bounced against a eucalyptus tree trunk and fell on the grass below.

"What will happen to your schooling?"

"*My schooling?* I'm telling you I'm pregnant, and you're talking about my schooling?"

"Won't you have to quit school if you're pregnant?"

"Yes," I said tightly. "I'll get expelled if my mother superior finds out, and I can't let that happen. School is the only anchor I have. I can't lose it."

"Then wouldn't it be better if you got an abortion?" That time, his eyes met mine.

Again, I said yes since he wasn't giving me any choice. Old as he was, he knew I couldn't remain unmarried and pregnant in our country, yet he wasn't proposing to me.

What could I ask except "When can it happen?"

"Soon. I'll talk to my doctor friends here." Rajat sounded so casual he could have been discussing yesterday's lunch.

3

AT MIDNIGHT, I LAY IN my bed beside Didima's, so daunted by my predicament that I couldn't even cry. In the other room, Rajat snored on Teddy's bed. *Had Rajat ever loved me?* If he had, he would have proposed to me because that was what any decent man would have done. Instead, he had cornered me into an abortion since he knew I was at his mercy. I burned with rage, but if I wanted to survive, I would have to swallow my ire. No matter how I assessed it, I had no solution to my problem without Rajat.

At dawn, Rajat left for his usual thirty-mile marathon-training run. At seven thirty, I waited for him on our back patio with a smile glued on my face and a customary pitcher of fresh lemonade.

The following two days, he attended reunions at the houses of former coworkers, avoiding the "solution" explanation. On the two occasions I asked, Rajat said, "I'm arranging it." Yet he was leaving for Bombay in three days.

The next afternoon, stranded and desperate, I came home from school and phoned Auntie Shalini from the house of Uncle and Auntie Guru, our South Indian neighbors next door. Auntie Shalini was the only doctor I knew other than Didima's doctor, Dr. Lal, and of course, Rajat, the root cause of my predicament.

"Auntie Shalini, can I see you alone?"

Auntie Guru sat "reading" on a sofa in front of me, but her eyes remained fixed on the same spot on the page.

An interminable conversation later, Auntie Shalini suggested we meet outside the Mehra & Sons jewelry store in the South Extension Market. "We'll grab an ice cream and talk."

In the confines of Auntie Shalini's brand-new four-seater Fiat, she and I licked soft-serve strawberry ice cream cones.

I took the plunge. "Auntie Shalini, you'll hate what I have to say."

"What is it? You know you can tell me anything." Auntie Shalini smiled. My gaze dropped.

"Is it Auntie Totini?" She loved to involve Didima in everything.

"No, it's me. I'm pregnant." I looked up, seeking mercy.

"Pregnant?" Auntie Shalini's eyes widened. "How did that happen? Or should I say, when did that happen?"

In that split second, I watched the affection in Auntie Shalini's eyes harden into derision. My eyes grew teary. "Auntie, I can't have this baby out of wedlock."

"I presume Rajat is the culprit?" Auntie Shalini's face resembled a mask, so I couldn't tell what she was thinking.

I nodded.

"And what does he say?"

"He said he would see to it, but he's leaving in three days, and he hasn't taken me to see a doctor friend."

"No!" Auntie Shalini's hand shot up, palm out. "Don't go to his friends. I don't trust Rajat, but it's hard to interrupt Auntie Totini when she's on the subject of him marrying you."

"That's because she doesn't want me to live with my mother and stepfather once she's dead," I interjected.

"Right. Can you be at my home office at ten tomorrow morning? I have clinic duty in the afternoon."

"But it's a school day."

"Noor, how can we deal with this on a weekend, when my younger siblings are all home? Pretend you are going to school so Auntie Totini won't worry, and have Rajat drive you over. It's the least he can do."

I agreed to do as she said.

Rajat, however, didn't. "I can't drop you off at ten. I have a farewell party at the Cantonment Base Hospital at nine, and Greater Kailash is in the opposite direction. My old boss is retiring. I can pick you up at one, if that helps."

The following morning, with no money or even the knowledge of which public bus to catch, I set off from home at seven a.m. to hurry across the fashionable suburbs of South Extension and Defense Colony, the older and less safe district of Lajpat Nagar, until I could reach the posh security of Greater Kailash 2 on the other side. On that walk, I passed large, affluent houses with front gardens, tight city housing, a slum, and cramped government apartments until I got back into the refuge of a neighborhood like Greater Kailash. Grateful it was winter and not a boiling summer day, for the first time, I gained enough perspective to reflect on how trees and space were only the privilege of the rich in Delhi, while slum dwellers lived with piles of stinking, open trash at each street corner, exposed sewers, and dirty, ill-dressed children played the best they could amidst strewn rubbish on filthy streets, some paved, others not. Yet despite assimilating this to be the reality of my country, I couldn't control a flinch at the sight of a dead dog, so decomposed, its entire surface was writhing in maggots. These images forced me to face how I wasn't technically poor. But in India, even the poorest of the poor would pity me if they discovered I was half-Hindu and half-Muslim, because being a half-caste made me worse than belonging in the *Shudra* caste of *untouchables*.

Of course, I had my mother to thank for my mixed birth. Born into an affluent and politically conservative family, as a young woman, my mother had been a rebel without a cause—a pseudoleftist who married a Pakistani national when she could have had the pick of Calcutta high society. She did so at age eighteen, more to prove how conscious she was of social justice than out of any real love for my light-spirited, happy-go-lucky, not-too-intelligent father. Of course, as soon as her marriage began to fail, she had a child upon the advice of the family doctor, realizing too late that she didn't want it. And I was the result, left to face the consequences of her magnanimous gesture.

I sprinted the last thousand yards to Dr. Shalini Kale's large, three-story family home and rang the doorbell. My hands clapped over my warm cheeks as Auntie Shalini unlocked the door.

"Please tell me I'm not late," I panted.

Auntie Shalini glanced at her wristwatch. "It's nine fifty. I said ten. Why are you puffing? Where's Rajat?"

"He had a previous engagement."

"Then how did you get here?"

"I walked."

Auntie Shalini's eyebrows arched. "From South Extension?"

"Yes. I left home for the school bus stop three hours ago and never stopped."

"Once we're done, I'll give you money for a taxi. You won't be in any condition to walk."

"You won't have to. Rajat said he'd come for me by one."

Auntie Shalini glanced at the ceiling, grimacing. She led the way through their home into her obstetrics and gynecology office.

I hurried behind. "Is anyone here?"

"My mother, but she's having a bad day. I told her to stay in her room on the third floor and watch TV."

Old Mrs. Kale had Alzheimer's.

Auntie Shalini locked her consulting office door behind me. "Remove everything from the waist down, and go lie on my examining table."

Her words got my heart pounding. Close to tears, I squirmed out of my maroon school cardigan, pulled off my dark-green tie, unbuckled my Mary Jane shoes, unhooked my maroon-and-green plaid uniform skirt, and stood in my white cotton blouse, green knee-high woolen socks, and pink cotton panties. "Do I remove my panties as well?"

"What do you think, Noor?"

Auntie Shalini's sarcasm stung like a slap in the face. Following directions, I climbed the stepladder and lay prone on the examining table. My bare skin adjusted to the shock of cold steel on my exposed buttocks in the chilly consulting office while Auntie Shalini clanged metal instruments as she took them out of a metal sterilizer. The room acquired a curious rotten odor, making me want to throw up, but I swallowed and lay still under the glare of two white operating lights.

Auntie Shalini approached the examining table. "What was the date of your last period?" Her tone was a hundred percent businesslike.

"October 23."

"Hmm. You're over five weeks. I'll have to scrape you."

"What does that mean?"

"You'll see."

With the tip of her tongue clenched between pressed lips, Auntie Shalini hoisted my right leg to a stirrup and strapped in my calf and green-socked foot.

"What are you doing?" I experienced a new degree of unprecedented nakedness.

"Preparing you. Grip the sides of this table, and bite the piece of gauze I give you. It'll hurt."

With both legs strapped, I felt as skinned as the chickens dangling from wire lines in the butchers' shops at the INA Market. *Did those chickens feel like I do right now? Of course not, they had their heads chopped off before this part happened to them. Why hadn't someone sliced my head off?* I yelped as Auntie Shalini inserted the cold, broad instrument into my vagina, and a giant scissor yawned inside me, hurting on so many levels, I had to bite my lower lip hard to not scream. Immediately, the stagnant air woke up and infiltrated my gaping vagina, making me cold and paper-dry to a core I never knew I possessed.

From down below, Auntie Shalini said, "Bite the gauze."

I let out an earsplitting scream as Auntie Shalini introduced another ice-cold instrument into my vagina and gripped something. A pointy instrument speared my insides. In my mind, my fifteen-year-old brain splattered in a bloody mess on the white ceiling above. I pulled at my braided hair, shattering the air with screams.

"Bite the gauze, and stop screaming." Auntie Shalini's voice sounded far away while her infantile mother banged on the door, hollering, "Shalini, open the door. Shalini, Shalini, Shaliniiii, open the doooor. I'm having a baaaabyyyy!"

"I'll be out in a minute, Mamma!" Auntie Shalini shouted back. "Be a good girl and go sit in the drawing room till I come get you."

The different cries collided and circled into huge red whorls as Auntie Shalini scraped a wall inside me. I regained consciousness as a terrifying whoosh of cold liquid sloshed into me, swished around, and drained out, wetting my entire backside. I cried for Auntie Shalini to "Stop, please stop" through a sea of cramps ebbing and flowing through my lower back and abdomen. Auntie Shalini untied my legs while I panted on that shiny metal table—hair, face, and chest drenched in sweat and tears.

Auntie Shalini came around with a stainless-steel kidney tray and directed her chin toward floating chunks of liverlike maroon meat in red water. "You should be okay now."

Her matter-of-fact statement was the opposite of how I felt. I sobbed out a hiccup. "Could I please have two Baralgan tablets for the pain?" I sought Auntie Shalini's eyes for some glimpse of reprieve but saw none.

"As soon as you dress." She handed me two sanitary pads. "Check your pad every hour. You'll bleed more than during your normal period."

Ten minutes later, I hunched alone on a sofa in the huge Kale family drawing room, hugging my aching abdomen, shivering, and praying for the painkillers to kick in. In their kitchen, Auntie Shalini's voice soothed her own puerile mother, promising the old lady all was well. Did she want a drink of water? The question made me thirsty, but I kept quiet.

When Rajat knocked, Auntie Shalini showed me out, thin-lipped and glaring at him but avoiding a confrontation. I hobbled to Rajat's Lambretta scooter and sat sideways, unable to bear the prospect of parting my legs for any reason. Without a sound, I put my right arm around Rajat's taut and lean belly, keenly conscious of the pain he was *not* experiencing. As the scooter jumped forward, I craved a kind word, a word of affection, or even an acknowledgment, but Rajat remained silent. Through the din, motion, and fumes of the midday traffic, I vowed not to succumb to sex with Rajat again until he married me. *But would he marry me?* My free hand convulsed around the pleated plaid of my school-uniform skirt. As much as I hated Rajat, if he didn't marry me, and some different husband discovered I wasn't a virgin, then *he* could kick me out and make a juicy scandal of it.

The waiting game began as soon as Rajat left for Bombay. After two days, I checked our letterbox four times a day. A week passed, then two, and no letter arrived. I bit my hangnails. In school, teachers yelled at me twice for inattention during class.

Eighteen days later, when I came home from school, Didima said, "Raj wrote to you. I put both letters on your pillow."

I devoured those letters.

Darling Noor,

Just got back from a three-day fishing trip on a friend's boat. Do you know if you get seasick? Why haven't I received a letter from you? Are you in the middle of exams...?

No apology, no explanation for his silence. No question asking how I was doing. Rajat was pretending the abortion had never happened. To continue with him, I would have to remain the amusing teenager of eleven weeks ago, write funny letters, and say I couldn't wait to see him next May. Meanwhile, in between writing him letters, I was so angry with what had happened, I got lost in rage hallucinations where I stuck a knife into Rajat's groin or strangled him or held his head underwater until he drowned for making me deal with the consequences of his actions.

Two months after the abortion, I was at my most depressed when the Hollywood movie, *Love Story*, arrived in India, years after it had been aired in America. The book, by Harvard professor Erich Segal, had been the talk of the town for years, but in my school, only seniors were allowed to borrow it from the school library, as it was considered too risqué for the lower grades. Excited we could watch the movie, even if we hadn't read the book, twenty girls from my ninth-grade class arranged to meet at the Chanakya movie theater to see what was so forbidden about the film.

Watching *Love Story*, I wondered if the story was changing my classmates' inner horizon like it was mine, but of course, I didn't dare probe too deeply, since no one could discover my secret. For me, beyond the collective tears we shed for the impossible and truncated loves of Oliver Barrett IV and Jennifer Cavilleri, the film became an anthem of the freedom that could have been mine if I had been born in America and not in India. America had no caste system, and social mobility was considered a birthright instead of an impossibility, like it was in my country. Eager to read the actual novel, I scrimped on the grocery money Didima gave me for two months to purchase the book. At home, I covered it in brown paper so Didima wouldn't discover I was reading it.

And the more times I read it, the more convinced I became of how different my life could have been outside India. In my daydreams, I fantasized about attending a university such as Radcliffe despite being poor. I stretched the dream further, fantasizing that my uncle Teddy would pay the tuition, even though he hadn't come to India once to see Didima or me since he had emigrated to Canada.

With the advent of *Love Story* in my life, in my head, I began living three separate realities. The first as a young girl in America, free to do as I pleased and live unjudged by society. The second as my reality of life with Didima, being her daily caretaker. And the third was the toughest to accept, because I recognized I had no choice but to marry Rajat.

Thus trapped, I complained to Didima because she was all I had. A week before Rajat was to arrive, I served Didima her afternoon tea. "Didima, I am so angry with Rajat, I could cry."

Didima's gaze became anxious. "Why, what did he write to upset you?"

"His younger brother got married in their hometown last week, and he only met this girl seven months ago. But here I am, waiting for Rajat to propose to me, and we've known each other for over two years."

Didima remained silent after my outburst, giving me no relief. Finally, she said, "Leave it to me."

"Why, what can you do?"

"You'll have to wait and see." She sounded like the grandmother she used to be years ago, when she had really been my caretaker, rather than the other way around.

However, I didn't attach too much meaning to her declaration, since in any marriage negotiation, Didima was severely handicapped by my half-caste status.

On May 1, when Rajat arrived in New Delhi for his vacation, to receive him, I wore jeans and a high-neck top to cover as much of my body as I could. I never wanted him near me again, but of course, I couldn't say that and continue to pretend I loved him. Instead, I obsessed over how best to avoid being alone with him as he walked through our back door and put his suitcase down.

"Mmm. Didima, I can smell your chicken curry. It's incomparable."

Without smiling back, Didima answered, "I didn't make it. Noor did."

I reassessed Didima's face. Lately, Didima had become alarmingly unpredictable. She seesawed from amicable to intractable in midsentence. Last Friday she misquoted her favorite poet, Percy Shelley. "*We look before and forward and pine for what is naught.*" When I corrected her, Didima sobbed, "Now you'll correct my *English*?" As a doctor's daughter, Didima had attended the Sacred Heart Convent School in Ambala. Her English was flawless.

"Shall we have lunch?" Didima led Rajat into Teddy's room, where our dining table was cramped next to Teddy's bed.

"How are you doing, Didima? I got you lots of free medicine from Bombay." Rajat pulled out a dining chair, scraping the floor.

But Didima gave him a hard look. "Rajat, I won't allow Noor to see you anymore without being engaged. You've known her for two years, while your younger brother met and married his girlfriend within seven months. It's high time you proposed to Noor. She's sixteen years old—old enough to be married."

I glanced at Rajat.

He drank water to stall answering Didima's directive. Eventually, out of options, he said, "Fine, Didima. Let's plan for it in December, shall we? It's the soonest I can ask for leave again."

My gaze dropped. Two years ago, I hadn't believed Dr. Lal when he had predicted failing health would render Didima senile. Even six months ago, Didima would never have confronted Rajat. But the deed was done, and Rajat and I would get engaged in December. In the confused recesses of my mind, a part of me was thrilled Didima had defended me so fiercely, but my overriding feeling was a deep, horrible misery that I had to marry Rajat at all.

***

Lying in the darkness of the Catholic Working Girls' Hostel, I became aware of my fisted hands when I switched sides on my narrow bed, fearful of disturbing the roommate who had yelled at me. The memory of how poor Didima had defended me convinced me more than ever that I just wanted to go back to her. In the morning, I would request Mother Rosa mediate between Didima and me. Thank God, tomorrow night I would sleep at home, where I belonged, next to Didima. Whatever my lessons, God had also sent me Chirag. Like Oliver from *Love Story*, Chirag would rescue me from India once Didima died. Until then, I had to take care of the one person who had been my mother since I was born.

4

At six a.m., my blotchy blue-black face in the hostel bathroom mirror only stoked my anger toward Rajat because I knew I was powerless to inflict any revenge on him. In India, even if Uncle Jiten had reported Rajat's beating to the police, both he and I would have become objects of laughter and taunts, while Rajat would have gone scot-free. I imploded with the impotence of knowing that in this country I had no means to seek justice. Regardless of how "modern" India turned, where women like Didima's eldest sister, Auntie Geeta, could become the chief minister of Uttar Pradesh, the largest agricultural state in the country, and Indira Gandhi had risen to the post of prime minister, basic and age-old social rules and judgments remained unchanged. At the grassroots level, men could beat women whenever they pleased, and I would always be a social pariah for being a half-caste.

I had more than discovered that bitter truth during my engagement ceremony to Rajat, when his country bumpkin, village oaf of a father insulted Didima in a loud, condescending voice. "Madam, you must be so happy my doctor son is willing to marry your half-caste granddaughter."

I had watched Didima's face crumple, forced to swallow the slight, unable to refute him, furthermore stigmatized by the lack of money. Somehow, I had controlled the mad urge to jump up and slap the old man, but of course I, too, had to be grateful Rajat was marrying me.

Yes, indeed, sick and addled as she was, Didima had encouraged Rajat to beat me, but Rajat, by contrast, had revealed the sadist in him when he enjoyed each blow he had inflicted on me, confident that his physical violence would translate into mental domination as well. And my father's participation in it just added insult to injury. He had stopped loving me years ago. And as the shallow character he was, he had used the occasion to pro-cess an old grudge against my mother. Baba had always had a chip on his shoulder that my mother had a

BA in art from the famous Calcutta College of Arts and Crafts, whereas he had embarrassed his own overeducated fa-ther by dropping out of the University of Dacca as a freshman. He could also never forgive that my mother had grown bored with him, which was why she had cheated on him then divorced him. So Rajat's beating had been Baba's perfect opportunity to join in the fray and rid himself of old venom.

Yet men like Rajat, Baba, and my stepfather were the common denominator in India. If I wanted a different reality, I would have to leave the country, and Chirag was my one shot at doing that. When I returned home to Didima, I would use my tutoring money to send Chirag a telegram that evening.

Downstairs, I intended to find Mother Rosa to beg her to talk to Didima for me so I could go home. As I tapped a roommate's shoulder to request she save me a spot in the breakfast line, someone else tapped my shoulder.

Behind me stood Uncle Guru, Didima's South Indian neighbor. He shook his head and wrung his hands as he always did. "Noor! Come home."

I pointed to my face and opened my mouth to explain my plan, when Uncle Guru blurted, "Your didima is dead."

A brick rammed into my chest. I choked. "That's not possible!" *Didima couldn't be dead. Not today. Not while I'm not there...*

"Come." Uncle Guru grasped my hand. "Let me take you home."

Outside our back entrance, a stranger of ten days, I jumped off the passenger seat of Uncle Guru's blue Vespa scooter and ran into the house. On our patio, in terracotta flowerpots, Didima's riot of amaryllis bloomed in trumpet-shaped splashes of red, white, and pale pink, as if greeting me.

In our bedroom, Didima lay in bed, wearing her usual white nightdress. She had never worn any other color but widow's white since Dadu had died. Then I saw her face. In the throes of death, Didima's eyes had all but disappeared into the left side of her forehead while her lips had contorted to the right, exposing naked gums. One agonized hand had frozen en route to the protruding tendons in her neck, while the other lay in a fist on her distended stomach, holding a severed tuft of her own gray hair, as if she had wrenched it out from pain.

Probably the expression on my face made Uncle Guru take my arm as though I were the child he had met eleven years ago. He sat me down on my own bed, opposite Didima's. "Your Uncle Jiten will come soon." He shook his curly-haired head like a dancing wooden toy.

"When did she die?" Something in my stomach settled like a one-ton weight.

"I don't know." Uncle Guru wrung his hands again. "My wife found her when she came to check on her. I have to leave. I'm late for work."

Alone with Didima, I sat as motionless in life as Didima lay in death. Light poured in through our bedroom windows. Our hand-sewn curtains were always open, except on blistering summer afternoons. A breeze touched Didima's uncombed hair, emphasizing her stillness. Next to her head, Dadu's writing desk sported my novel collection, neatly lined up.

If I had come home last night, Didima would be alive right now. That fact stared me down like Dadu's eyes from his framed black-and-white photograph inside a niche in the left wall. *Are they together now—Didima and Dadu? Why did they leave me behind?* For me, no reality had existed without them. Beneath Dadu's picture stood our coffee table, a trip hazard parked out of poor Didima's way.

In the middle of that table sat our copper ashtray, its edge forever dented from when my mother had hurled it at the wall on the unforgettable morning of my dressing-down when I was six years old. No one had mentioned that failed sleepover at my mother's and stepfather's house in years, yet for me, it dwelled in plain sight each time I noticed the dent in the ashtray and the gash it had made on the wall. To that day, the damaged wall shed brick residue on the pages of my novels, causing my teeth to grit whenever I licked a finger to turn a page.

My thoughts floated out in disjointed fragments—*Plants too dry. I'm missing classes. Where's Didima's wedding ring? And her pearl ring?*

Hearing a skirmish outside the east window, my eyes cut to the left. The wife and son of our new front neighbor peeked in, holding empty cardboard boxes. Seeing me, they dropped the boxes and ran. *Is that where Didima's rings disappeared to?* I wanted to get up and yell, "Thieves!" but I couldn't move.

Time stood still until Uncle Jiten came into the room with my mother. She was beautifully dressed in a pale-green sari even on the occasion of her mother's death. *Why did Uncle Jiten have to bring her?* It was my curse that people said I resembled my mother. We shared almond-shaped eyes, the similar upturned nose of the Panaeker women, heart-shaped faces, and long, silky hair. It came as little consolation that I had inherited Baba's square eyebrows and full lips because I hated him as much as I hated her.

Uncle Jiten gave me a nervous hug but looked at my mother. "Jhummur? Could you change Totini into a sari?"

My mother obeyed, missed her footing, and practically fell on me, toppling my novels on Dadu's writing desk sideways. She straightened to access an unfinished wall enclosure partitioned by a curtain, where Didima stored her saris. As soon as she parted the curtain, the piney, winter rain fragrance of Ma Griffe by Craven, pure sandalwood, and Sunlight laundry soap brought Didima so sharply back to life, my breath caught. My fingers curled as my mother rummaged through Didima's neat pile of white saris and yanked one from the middle, uprooting the ones above it. *Why didn't she pick the top one? They're all white, aren't they?*

Sari in hand, my mother stared at Didima. She attempted to lift Didima by her shoulders—they didn't budge. Next, she grabbed Didima's stiff right leg but dropped that too.

I sprang to my feet and snatched the sari out of my astonished mother's hand. "Leave her alone. She was my didima. I'll dress her." The weight in my stomach rose to my throat.

An angry frown surfaced on my mother's forehead. "No, you won't—"

But Uncle Jiten intervened with placating arms, separating us both. "Jhummur—let her dress her didima."

Hearing him, that weight in my stomach came right up my throat to spill out of my mouth in an indescribable sound. My torrent of salty teardrops along with my runny nose soaked through the front of Didima's nightdress as I lifted Didima's dead shoulders two feet off the bed to roll the sari under her body. When I was done dressing her, I sat down on her bed, beside her, laying my head on Didima's chest to hug her.

Within the hour, our two-room house filled with people I hadn't seen in years. Most stole furtive glances at Didima and me when they assumed I wouldn't notice. Not even my mother's effort to pry me away from Didima's body could crack my grip. Tranquility shrouded Didima and me as we lay there together, my beating heart against her still one. I broke that reverie only once to beg to ride in the funeral hearse with Didima, when the black van arrived. Its arrival told me that was it. Didima would be cremated that day, since the very heat in India sabotaged the possibility of holding long, drawn-out wakes.

Inside the hearse, I put my head on Didima's white-sari-covered chest and wrapped my arms around her inert stomach, knowing I had maybe one more hour of Didima's presence in any physical form. In the midday heat of May, Didima's lifeless body burned so hot against the bruises on my face, I couldn't believe she was dead. Instead, her heat comforted my swollen right cheek.

Enclosed inside the windowless metal box, I heard the earsplitting blasts of horns, felt the stops and starts, but it was as if we were protected, Didima and I. Didima's sari smelled of sandalwood underneath the stridence of Sunlight detergent soap. *Why can't we ride forever, with me cocooned on Didima's warm chest in a moving coffin?*

The engine died, but I didn't stir. Behind me, the doors scraped open, and I sensed an assortment of eyes touch the back of my head.

Uncle Jiten said, "Noor, come out."

I obeyed like a sleepwalker, avoiding the eyes of my mother, my stepfather, and the van driver while I blinked to acclimate to the blinding afternoon glare. In the cloying heat were people, parked cars, flower vendors, and other funeral vans. To the right, more people milled under a row of pavilions. The air smelled of stale flowers, incense, and grilled meat from burning bodies, since Hindus burned their dead and didn't bury them like Christians or Muslims.

The guests who had gathered at Didima's house poured out of arriving cars and assembled around us in groups. I sniffed the air. *What is that water smell?* I glanced around. Beyond the concrete pavilions flowed an imposing river. *The Jamuna? Where is the electric crematorium?* This wasn't the place where Didima's eldest sister, Auntie Geeta, had been cremated. *Perhaps the crematorium is around the corner?* But no corners were in sight.

The driver and three other dhoti-clad males surprised me when they pulled out the bier Didima lay on and hoisted it onto their shoulders. Didima's body had gone from stiff to lax, judging by the unnatural way it moved as opposed to theirs. Marching in step, the bier-bearers passed through the pavilions to stop short at a cement rectangle by the riverbank, piled waist-high with seasoned firewood.

Suddenly, I understood there would be no electric crematorium for Didima. This was the River Jamuna Funeral Ghat, where the Hindus burned their dead on pyres, native-style. They did it next to the river because, after-ward, they floated the ashes in the flowing water in accordance with Hindu customs. Thus, Hindus believed, a person became one with the universe while their soul wandered free until it claimed another body to be reborn in. No one from our family had ever been cremated in such traditional style. *Why is poor Didima the exception? Who decided this kind of native ending for Didima?*

Next to the cement slab, the River Jamuna flowed, a muddy, understated turbulence stretching at least three-fourths of a mile to the other bank. The blazing one-o'clock sun cast our stunted dark-brown shadows on the roasting ground. To me, everything felt surreal—the musky water smell, the odor of the previous day's smoke, the haze of that day's smoke, scattered ashes, whiffs of sweat, withered plant debris, clove, sandalwood, and the pungence of charred flesh. Even the men who lifted Didima's body off the bier to lay her on the woodpile bed didn't register with me.

I noticed how my head pounded only when my mother said, "Uncle Jiten, Robu should light the funeral pyre. He is the one Brahmin male among us."

Uncle Jiten said, as if pacifying a child, "Of course, Jhummur, but I'm Totini's sole living brother. Let me light the pyre."

Surprising myself, I said, "I'll light her pyre. She was my didima."

"Sorry." My mother made a dismissive hand gesture. "Women don't light funeral pyres."

"Oh, but I will," I repeated softly.

"No, you won't." My mother's nostrils flared. "Robu will."

"Over my dead body." My hands curled into fists. "Didima hated him, and you will not dishonor her."

My mother directed an incredulous look at me, sensing my reference. Defeated, she stalked off to speak to her haloed, upper-caste, Brahmin husband.

The ghat pallbearers adjusted Didima on the firewood bed with both her feet pointed in the same direction, free from the alignment of the living. They piled logs *on top of* her, as if to suffocate what little presence remained. My hands spasmed, but I clasped one over the other, biting my lower lip. As a last log obliterated Didima's contorted face, I fell to the ground, nails clawing at a riverbank covered in other people's ashes, hard-packed with other people's tears.

I lurched to my feet as a disapproving and muttering ghat pundit thrust an ignited fire log into my hand, shaking his shaven head because women didn't light funeral pyres. I clutched the fiery log, terrified to face the conical mound that was Didima. Through a lens of tears, I stumbled, causing the flaming stick to fly out of my hands and land right onto the ghee-saturated pyre surface.

The resultant combustion startled me so badly, I screamed and lunged at the fire to pull out logs until a pair of arms lifted me up and away. In Uncle Jiten's embrace, I howled, "Uncle Jiten, pull her out! Pull her out of the fire, or else she'll burn. Please. *Please rescue her.* She can't burn like this. She can't!"

Tearing up himself, Uncle Jiten held me tight as the sound of the fire's crackle and pop gained momentum. He couldn't, however, prevent the river breeze from blowing the searing heat our way. As the roar of the fire under the scorching sun and its glowing incandescence devoured the mortal remains of Didima, my sobs converted into coughing while I clutched Uncle Jiten's shirt front.

"I can't watch this," I gasped.

"Then just go, my dear. I'll see this through," Uncle Jiten said.

"She can't leave!" My mother latched a heavy hand on my forearm. "She has to stay till the end."

I wrenched free and ran. I ran past the concrete pavilions, past the cars and funeral vans, past the ground debris, and past a large funeral ghat entrance gate I did not know existed.

Outside, life met me as abrasively as the fire consumed Didima inside the ghat. In my eyes, the pedestrians, buses, bicycle rickshaws, and horse-drawn *tongas* shimmered in an orange blaze until I boarded the first bus that stopped.

Daylight had waned when I walked into our house for the second time that day, my whole life undone in nine hours. Again, I sat down on my bed, the silence a scream in my ears, the stillness agonizing. In those last years, Didima had descended so far into senility, even before the dementia, she talked nonstop. Whereas once I would have given anything to have her stop talking, right then, I wanted to hear that high, reedy voice just one more time. My eyes grew hot, and I rubbed them, but I had run out of tears. *This whole thing is my fault. If I hadn't left home, this wouldn't have happened.*

As if waking from a dream, I understood why Didima had refused to die through all her hospitalizations. It was because, during each of those times, she had had me to live for. But with me gone, she had lost her reason to live. *Yes. I failed Didima when she needed me the most.*

Slowly, the reality of Didima's death spun around me in a spiderweb. *With her gone, where will I live?* The girls' hostel seemed like a mirage, even though I had stayed there for the past ten days. The truth was, as soon as the month was over, I would have no money to pay for the hostel, and Mother Rosa would be forced to kick me out. Then, as a minor, I would have no choice if my mother and stepfather decided to participate in my care.

5

PANIC MADE MY EYES DART to our copper ashtray sitting on Didima's teak coffee table. The memories it held would soon overtake my life if my mother claimed custody of me. The only way to escape that fate would be to marry Chirag. But of course, I hadn't been able to send Chirag that telegram, and Didima, my one protector from my stepfather, was gone. The next morning, I would miss my Perspectives class to send that telegram. Meanwhile, for me, the dent on that copper ashtray marked a milestone to register how a predatory adult had destroyed my childhood.

* * *

In 1967, I was six years old when Didima, Teddy—whom I had never called uncle since childhood—our servant boy, Agya, and I arrived in New Delhi from Calcutta soon after Dadu had died. In those days, Didima cried a lot, not just because she had lost Dadu but because his best friend had swindled Didima out of Dadu's entire land inheritance in Maharashtra and left us penniless. When she cried, I cried, too, and I didn't know what "swindled" meant, but if I petted Didima's hand, she stopped crying sooner.

Didima's life was already miserable enough when my mother started complaining I was a stranger to her, making Didima's life even worse.

My mother had recently become the new art teacher at the Loreto Convent School, my school.

To pacify her, one day, Didima said, "Noor Shona, why don't you visit your mother during lunch break?"

Knowing how much it would mean to Didima to have me obey her, I did my best. In school, I dropped my habit of eating my butter-and-sugar sandwiches hidden in the school gardens to avoid socializing with rich peers who might ask to visit Didima's two-room home in South Extension and discover how poor we were. Instead, I went straight upstairs to the cluttered confines of the art room that smelled of linseed oil and turpentine. There, my mother brought me a hard-boiled egg to eat with salt while she talked to me of silly nonsense that didn't even make me laugh.

Those conversations must have irked my mother, too, because soon after, she said, "Come spend a night with us in Karol Bagh. We can practice living as mother and daughter until Uncle Robu and I marry. Then we'll become a real family."

Uncle Robu wasn't my uncle, but that was what my mother insisted I call him. He and my mother were old friends from the Calcutta College of Art, where he had been a senior when she joined as a freshman. Once my mother decided to divorce my baba while we lived in Calcutta, Uncle Robu had invited my mother to come live with him and a few of their mutual art-college friends in New Delhi, saying they would find her a job and help her rebuild her life.

Therefore, whenever my mother suggested I go visit them overnight, I would nod to appease her, but behind her back, I would run to Didima when I got home from school and tremble, "Didima, you won't send me away to live with them, will you? I don't want to live with them. I want to live here with you."

"I know, shona." Didima hugged me on one such afternoon. "But maybe you could sleep over at their place one night? Otherwise, I'll keep hearing how I've stolen you from her."

At dinner at our house the next Saturday, I struggled past my reluctance and volunteered to spend the night at my mother's and her fiancé's on the upcoming weekend.

Ma and Uncle Robu lived in a *barsati* flat in the old and faraway neighborhood of Karol Bagh, miles and miles in distance from Didima's two-room home in South Extension.

Barsatis were a clever invention of Indian landlords to use otherwise useless flat rooftops and convert them into a rent-earning option. They consisted of one or two rooms, a bathroom, and a kitchen, and lo and behold, the rooftop became an income producer.

Therefore, Uncle Robu's particular barsati had two tiny rooms at opposite ends of the roof of a sprawling, old five-story apartment complex, with a kitchen and bathroom thrown in at one corner. He had transformed the rest of the elevated basketball court into a spectacular rose garden, an island of silence in an otherwise frenetic city setting. Each time I visited them with Didima, I smelled the sweet and rich elixir of each rose, reminded of Baba tending to our Calcutta flower garden.

On the afternoon of my sleepover, I climbed the six dark flights of stairs to Uncle Robu's barsati, hoping each new step might magically transport me home to Didima. In my stomach, a leaf trembled, caught in a permanent breeze. At least Uncle Robu's hundred roses bloomed strong under the October sun. *Maybe if I smell each rose for two minutes, time will go by faster?* Otherwise, the inky cave of the night ahead loomed in front of me, making me want to cry.

My mother went off to change from street clothes into home clothes.

Uncle Robu strolled out of his studio room to greet me. Dressed in a white Indian-style cotton lungi wraparound and a sleeveless *bunyaan* undershirt, he pressed their new pet, a calico kitten, to one cheek. "Do you want to pet her?" He smiled. But the tiny kitten only made his bushy, wavy hair stand out and his hooked nose enormous.

I shook my head.

"Then come, draw with my crayons."

Whenever Didima and I visited with them, Uncle Robu let me use his crayons, although for him, they were work ones, not play ones, because he was a graphic artist.

I controlled a flinch when his fingers touched my right shoulder, urging me toward the studio. At its door, I halted once my eyes fell on Uncle Robu's work stool. To color with his crayons, Uncle Robu insisted I sit on that stool and use his special inclined drawing table with a guard lip "so the crayons don't roll and get lost." But whenever I perched on the stool, he would place an arm around my shoulders and press his lungi front to the side of my thigh. Then a soft thing other than his legs would rub against me, making me squirm away. But whichever way I shifted, Uncle Robu followed with the squishy, lurky thing behind the folds of his wraparound touching my body.

I ran back toward the middle of the roof. "I don't want to color right now." Thank God my mother had come back from changing her clothes.

"Are you sure?" Uncle Robu smiled. "I have chocolates for each drawing you complete."

I shook my head. *Why can't I just go home?* But Didima had made me promise to be a brave girl. *"Remember it's only one night, shona…"* she said inside my head. *Was that only this morning?*

I jerked as Ma said, "I'm tired. Shall we go nap? It's this terrible afternoon sun."

Too overwhelmed to protest, I headed to the other end of the roof, navigating around the rose pots. The cramped room had a ceiling so low it was impossible to have an overhead fan. As a substitute, a squat cream-colored table fan stood on top of an old, scratched-up dresser. Facing it, two beds intersected at the opposite corner of the room.

Ma stepped in and grabbed a rolled-up straw-and-bamboo-cane chatai mat propped behind one door panel. She let it fall to the polished cement floor and pointed for Uncle Robu and me to climb onto a bed each to free the floor space. Her dirty bare foot unrolled the chatai mat, and she dropped on her knees with difficulty since she was fat.

"Robu, throw me a pillow, will you?"

I lay down, wound up like a jack-in-the-box, balancing at the edge of my chosen bed, forcing a smile at Ma on the floor.

"When I wake up, I'll make you a *cheenee ka paratha*," Ma promised.

That was a whole-wheat Indian flatbread stuffed with granular sugar and fried to caramelization.

I rubbed my hungry stomach, contemplating the rough, whitewashed plaster ceiling.

Soon, Ma's breathing deepened, and the whir of the table fan swerving from side to side became a roar inside my head. Each time it crossed my vision, I imagined the grimy dust mites on its concentric grills to be a pack of migrating geese, all flying in the same direction. My God—it was hot in there. I wriggled to pull down my frock and threw my arms back in despair. My cheeks hurt from so much smiling. At home, in South Extension, right then, I would be having lunch with Didima. *Will this day never end?*

On the floor, Ma snored, her head to one side, mouth ajar. Her exposed calves resembled those huge melons the fruit vendors sold in the marketplace. *Had Uncle Robu caught me staring?* I stole a glance.

"You look restless," he whispered. "Let me pet you, as your ma does."

My mother and I had an arrangement where we each caressed the other's arms, legs, or back with the gentlest brush of our fingertips. *Wouldn't that help time go by faster?*

"Okay." I threw my arms backward and closed my eyes as Uncle Robu's hand caressed my forearms then my arms. I attempted to experience the sleepy happiness my mother's fingers evoked in me, but all I felt was a mounting dread. *Maybe how a man did it was different?* But it was too late. If I complained, Uncle Robu would report it to Ma.

Uncle Robu's fingers moved up, up to touch my collarbone. I lay there, trapped like a butterfly pinned to a board in a curio shop with its wings nailed down, unable to move, cry, or protest. I wanted to tell Uncle Robu to stop, but the words wouldn't come out. On the floor, Ma snored louder as Uncle Robu's hands traveled right through the huge armholes of my frock, home-sewn by Didima. Like some gigantic, hairy spider, his fingers touched the dark spots on my chest, pinched them between his index and middle finger. He did it again, and again, but I couldn't move or even flinch.

At last, I pictured myself escaping my body. The trick of imagining I was outside my physical body calmed me a lot. From that new place, I commanded myself to wriggle downward in real time, away from Uncle Robu's groping fingers.

He whispered, "Didn't you love that?"

I shook my head, hugging my shoulders as I swung my legs off the bed. Emboldened by success, I jumped over the supine body of my sleeping mother and ran out of the room onto the rough brick-and-cement rooftop.

Outside that room, the sun-cooked bricks scalded my bare soles, and I hopped and scampered until, at last, I knelt to trace a dusty X by the rose pot in front of me.

Pot by pot, I cupped each flower with my hands, sniffed the bloom, and counted them. I was on my forty-fourth pot and ninety-eighth rose when I exploded into tears. My sobs caused the pigeons dozing on the broad cement parapet to glare at me as they flapped up into the air in an uneven flurry of gray-and-black stripes. It reminded me of how Uncle Robu collected their droppings in a paper bag to fertilize his roses, two teaspoons per flowerpot, and I cried even harder.

The sound of my crying brought Ma out in drowsy confusion, hair tumbling down her back. Uncle Robu followed.

"*Ma shona?* Did you hurt yourself?" Ma bent to my level.

"N-n-n-no," I stuttered between panting gasps.

"But what upset you?"

"I want to go home. Now!"

"But you're staying the night, remember?" She said it as if it were a new concept instead of one that had been tormenting me for a week.

The argument escalated until my rib cage hurt so much from crying that I crumpled to the brown scorching rooftop, curling into a ball between the rose pots.

At last, Ma said, "Okay. Enough is enough. Uncle Robu will drive you home right now on his motorcycle."

The statement panicked me worse as Uncle Robu smiled.

"No!" I cried. "You bring me home."

"Oh, stop being so impossible." My mother lifted a hand as if to slap me then dropped it, changing her mind.

At ground level, I watched, teary-eyed, as Uncle Robu kicked his Royal Enfield motorcycle off its stand from in between two similar models. He flung a leg over the vehicle and motioned with his head for me to climb on behind him.

I approached the two-wheeled transport, dreading that Uncle Robu would request I hug his midsection for safety's sake during the ride. That day, no power on earth would make me obey him, no matter what he said. I climbed on and absorbed how he held still, waiting for my arms to go around him.

After a minute, I said, "I'm holding the back grill. We can go now."

Without arguing, Uncle Robu accelerated with a jerky blast. Soon, two wet streams flowed from the sides of my eyes into the hairline above my ears. Uncle Robu drove a lot faster and crazier than usual.

When we arrived in South Extension, Didima was sipping on her cup of afternoon tea in her canvas recliner on the patio part of our garden. Her eyes policed our servant boy, Agya, as he watered the rest of the garden. Agya was our only servant boy who had refused to leave Didima's service when we had moved to New Delhi from Calcutta nine months ago. He loved Didima because his own mother had died and his father had remarried. He hated his stepmother.

"What happened?" Didima rose to her feet as I leapt off Uncle Robu's motorcycle and engulfed her snow-white sari in a hug.

Uncle Robu shrugged. "I don't know. She began crying out of nowhere, asking to come home. Perhaps she should visit us more?"

I shook my head hard and clung tighter to Didima.

"Why, of course." Didima's voice sounded awkward.

He hadn't yet blared away when I spilled my guts. "He touched my chest, Didima. Why did he have to do that? Ma never touches or pinches my chest to pet me. You say I'm a big girl now, and I have to hide my chest from all men. Was I bad, Didima?"

"No, *shona mona*, of course you weren't." Didima appeared close to tears.

"What if he does it again?" I wrung my hands.

Didima unclenched her fists to hug me. "I promise you'll never be alone with him from now on. This is my fault. I shouldn't have sent you to Jhummur's alone."

"So I don't have to sleep over at their house anymore?" Relief made me cling to Didima harder.

"No, never." Didima smoothed my hair. "Now be a good girl, and go play out front with your friends. I need to talk to Teddy." Teddy had been in the shower since I'd arrived home.

I was playing an intent game of marbles with my new neighborhood playmates on the dusty footpath, when Teddy strode up to pull me to my feet.

"Ma shona, come home right now and tell me what happened at Jhummur's."

"What—again?"

"Just once more, ma shona. C'mon," said Teddy more gently.

As I finished my story, Teddy said to Didima, "Ma, I can kill Robu. That's what Baba's guns are for."

I convulsed into another fit of blubbering, afraid if that happened, my mother would definitely take me to live with her.

The next morning, Teddy whisked me away to watch *Neel Kamal*, the Hindi movie my neighborhood girlfriends were swooning over. Late in the afternoon, I skipped into the house through our back entrance, holding Teddy's hand. It took me a couple of seconds to notice how Didima was hunched at a curious angle on our plastic imitation-cane chair, a broken doll. Then I saw Uncle Robu sitting next to my mother on Didima's bed, gazing out of the east window, and my grip around Teddy's fingers tightened.

My mother screamed, "Why are you telling Didima such disgusting lies about Robu? You're a Muslim liar, like your father. Why else wouldn't you appreciate the oodles of chocolates Robu buys you or his expensive Winsor & Newton crayons he lets you play with in our house? Tell me. Why did you lie to Didima?"

"I didn't lie." My knees wobbled.

"Oh, yes you did! You invented this lie so you don't have to come live with me." Uncle Robu nodded, the picture of injured innocence.

"You were sleeping." My lips puckered as I let go of Teddy's hand to sidle up to Didima. My trembling fingers crept around Didima's sagging shoulders as I pressed close to my support system.

"Jhummur," Teddy said. "Leave. Go home for now. Go."

Teddy's chilly voice snapped Didima out of her trance. She put an arm around me. "Both of you." She pointed to the door. "Get out of my house this second."

In a slow dream, I watched my mother struggle off Didima's bed and swipe up the copper ashtray from our coffee table. Two of Uncle Robu's half-stubbed cigarette butts smoldered inside it. I cowered to shield my face in the folds of Didima's sari, convinced the ashtray was coming at me. In-stead, the ashtray hit the wall above Dadu's writing table and fell on it with a loud, denting thud. I smelled the scattered cigarette ash. Then I lowered my elbow a fraction to see my mother grab her fiancé's hand and storm out of our house. His motorcycle came alive and roared off into the distance.

***

I observed the copper ashtray, colorless in the gloom of a dusk Didima would never see again. Yet, the lavender light outside the windows of our little home tricked me into believing Didima was still alive, just out of sight, while the reality and silence reported otherwise. Caught between these two feelings, my heart felt like a hummingbird trapped in a cage.

Whatever happened next, I would run away before I succumbed to living with my mother and her husband. Bone-tired, I rubbed my eyes. To run away, I needed a plan and money, and that evening, I had neither one. Right then, all I could do was force my fingers to lock up after myself and return to the working girls' hostel. The next day, I would formulate an escape plan.

ROSES

6

At seven the following morning, on the outside, I stood in the breakfast line, smelling Friday's usual potato curry. On the inside, I floated without direction, like a boat whose mooring had been cut loose.

My one link to reality was Chirag, but I hadn't had the wherewithal to write to him the night before. Meanwhile, time marched on, objective, inexorable, and dispassionate, unmoved by how shattered I felt about leaving Didima to die alone or the hole in my heart she had left behind. A hole that constantly felt cold, as if no one could ever warm the space again.

In the breakfast line, I inched forward to receive a portion of greasy curry. My steaming bowl plummeted out of my hands when someone tapped me on the back.

"A man out front asked for you." A young nun gestured toward the lobby.

"Who? Rajat?" My heart began to pound while I registered the yellow curry splattered on my shirtfront and the white tablecloth of the serving table.

"I didn't ask his name."

I scuttled out, panicked about what I would say to Rajat when all I wanted to do was kill him, my fantasy as unattainable as reaching the moon.

The foyer at the working girls' hostel was a large room lined with mismatched vinyl chairs overlooking Ring Road through four French doors. Its one claim to glory was a Steinway grand piano. But in place of Rajat, lingering by the grand piano was a muscular stranger with slanted eyes and a wispy black mustache. His face resembled a pen-and-ink sketch from my old Indian history textbook of the fearsome Mongolian conqueror Timur Lane.

"You asked to see me? Who are you?" My voice came out trembly.

"I'm here to arrest you. Don't let my plain clothes fool you. I'm Officer Shushanto Das," he announced.

Arrest me? I grasped the covered grand piano keyboard. "Are you Anup Das's brother?" Anup Das was my stepfather's student from the Delhi Art College, and he shared the same last name. I had met Anup twice.

"Ma'am, you didn't listen. I'm here to arrest you. For associating with a Chirag Jagdev."

"But he's in America."

"Don't I know it." Shushanto Das launched full sail. "The Jagdevs are known smugglers of girls for prostitution. We suspect you're their new contact in India."

Felled by the accusation, I stuttered, "No, they aren't. They export medical goods."

Officer Das sneered. "Did you know their medical goods have two legs and a destination? As soon as I can prove your connection to that operation, you'll go to jail."

"Th-then I-I want a lawyer," I said verbatim from the Perry Mason thrillers I read nonstop.

Officer Das's face hardened. "As a minor, you're not entitled to one."

"So w-what will you do to me?"

In answer, Officer Das clanked a pair of handcuffs around my wrists in front of me and marched me, crying and curry-stained, to his police vehicle.

Inside the vehicle, I was so intimidated by the sheer electronic paraphernalia on the dashboard, blinking lights, and radio calls that all I could do was stare out the window. Conscious of my handcuffs, I was too scared to ask where we were going. Panic gave way to numbness as my mind shut down to a total blank.

At last, it became obvious we were headed to my mother's and stepfather's new home in Chittranjan Park. They had moved to the bourgeois neighborhood soon after my stepfather made tenure at the Delhi College of Art.

I disembarked from the police car, perforated by the naked stares of their neighbors.

In full view of the ogling neighbors, Officer Das explained my house arrest to my parents. "Please supervise her closely until a full inquiry can either absolve her or indict her. Your daughter is in a lot of trouble because the family she is associating with has been on our radar for years. But the Jagdevs are criminals at so many levels, we don't want to prosecute them for one crime so they can go unscathed on all the other counts. You're lucky Noor is a minor and we're letting her spend her arrest time with you. However, whenever we wrap up the Jagdev case, if we discover her involvement, she will go to a juvenile jail. I'll be back tomorrow to conduct a formal interrogation."

Anger rearranged my mother's expression, making my cuffed hands over the mess of potato curry on my shirt front feel like lead weights. Officer Das undid my handcuffs and shoved me so hard I stumbled in my mother's direction.

Inside their home, my mother motioned me to sit in the armchair in their bedroom. I blinked at the floor, too frightened to glance at her or my stepfather as they settled on their comfortable king-sized bed. Their staring eyes converted me to the goldfish my baba had kept in an old wood-framed aquarium in our Jodpur Park home in Calcutta. At age three, I used to place sticky palms on that aquarium glass, gaze intently at the fish, and wait for each one to emit a bubble. I would watch the precious bubble rise to the surface, wanting to hear it pop, but I never could.

At last, I dared to address my mother. "Did you know of the arrest?"

Uncle Robu rarely gave me a direct answer or met my eyes if I spoke to him.

My mother responded with dead silence. Inside my head, another bunch of goldfish bubbles burst. Finally, my mother smiled a nasty smile. "I'm sorry that you'll now have a permanent felony charge attached to your name. It'll be that much harder to arrange a decent marriage for you. No Indian boy will want a girl with a criminal record."

"I won't marry Rajat."

"No. We'll find someone more civilized and more qualified."

Her words made me desperately aware of how Chirag would never find me, let alone marry me. I didn't believe Chirag was guilty of anything. Maybe his family was criminal, like the officer claimed. I had no basis or means to prove or disprove otherwise. However, I would never swallow that Chirag, my Chirag, had ever intended to harm me. We went back too far, and I would marry Chirag without a second's doubt. But for the time being, as a minor, I was trapped. If I wanted to survive, I had to play whatever game my parents played until I could find a way to escape them.

That night, Uncle Robu rolled out a straw chatai mat on the floor next to my mother's side of the bed, *sans* sheets or pillows. *Is this the chatai mat from my horrible sleepover at their barsati eleven years ago?* Back then, I'd had Didima to run back to. Today, I was utterly lost. I hoped they couldn't hear me weep in the dark. The scent of yellow jasmine drifted in through the window to remind me of Chirag and how I might never see him again.

The next morning, Officer Das came to my mother's house before seven o'clock. He observed the dark circles under my eyes, appearing satisfied. "Good morning. Are you ready for your interrogation?"

Complete silence. I didn't dare open my mouth.

He placed his face so close to mine, I breathed in the warmth of tobacco and fried eggs. He raised my chin and administered a cracking, backhanded slap.

"You answer me when I speak to you! You understand?" he shouted.

I jumped, eyes watering. "Yes." Thank God he hadn't hit the cheek Rajat had split open.

"Mrs. Chatterjee?" He looked straight at my mother. "Please give me privacy. No one can come into the drawing room at any point in my interrogation. Understood?"

"Yes, Officer." My stepfather nodded.

After they left, Officer Das gave my left forearm a rough tug. "What drugs do you use?"

"I don't do drugs."

Another stinging slap across the other cheek. *Did he split the healed stitches?* My hand shot up to stem the agony of jagged pain as I let out a sob.

"I don't believe you. I bet you have drugs hidden on you right now. Take your clothes off."

"What?"

"Remove everything except your bra and panties."

I complied with convulsive movements, tears spilling. *Can't my parents hear him? How can they sit there and allow this?*

For me to stand in front of a stranger in my light-blue brassiere and mismatched cotton panties was a mental territory hitherto unexplored. I crossed my arms over my chest, emitting shallow gasps.

Officer Das cracked three more resounding slaps across my face, and I tasted blood all over again.

"Lower those arms unless you want another slap." He inspected my body inch by inch for needle marks.

When he touched my inner thighs, I bit my lower lip until it hurt, while he stretched portions of my unexposed skin between his thumb and forefinger. I knew if I protested, he would hit me and tell me to shut up.

He stood and brushed his hands. "What do you smoke?"

"I don't smoke." I received a whacking slap across my buttocks.

Shushanto Das sized me up and down and tugged on the diamond pendant above my cleavage. "Where did you get this cheap glass trinket?"

"From Chirag. It's not glass. It's a diamond."

The officer bared his teeth, wrenched the chain off my neck, and threw it to the floor. "I have a present for you too." From a briefcase, he pulled out the snow-white Valentine booklet Chirag had mailed me in February. The booklet landed at my feet. "Here, keep this rubbish."

Instantly, I knew he had been to the working girls' hostel and confiscated all my belongings. *What horrible things did he invent to Mother Rosa about me?*

Watching me hug the card's bright-red bow to my chest, he shook his head, picked up the chain and diamond pendant off the floor, and dropped it into his pocket. "He doesn't love you, you stupid fool. He recruited you. Such generic mementos are standard recruitment methods for dumb girls like you. When I read the letters he wrote you, I'm sure I'll find concrete proof of that." Chirag Jagdev, he added, had likely romanced three or four other girls for the same purpose, and all were mooning over their identical Valentine cards, touching their glass trinkets, thinking how important they were to Chirag. "Get dressed." He flicked aside the curtain between my parents' drawing room and bedroom. "Mrs. Chatterjee? I'm done here. Please watch her. Undercover police are surveilling this house. I won't hesitate to put your daughter in jail if she steps one millimeter out of line."

"Can she finish her semester at the polytechnic?" I heard my mother's high, little-girl-like voice.

"No, ma'am. You'd better terminate her enrollment there. I interrogated her college professors and peers. Many of them confirmed how your daughter planned to marry Chirag Jagdev and leave the country. She's not allowed to leave this house unless I say so."

7

From that beating on, my life was reduced to a series of moments instead of days. Like a rock climber, I clung from one instant to reach the next. I had gone from student and girlfriend to prisoner in two hours. My head spun every time I reflected on it. Only Chirag could save me, but he wasn't around. Instead, I had to endure the presence of my mother and stepfather minute by minute, taunting me, accusing me of being a criminal, policing my every move. And I had to take it with my mouth shut because they would report me to Officer Das, who could then beat me. Therefore, day after day, I obeyed my mother's commands to remake beds, dust bookshelves, clean the pantry in complete silence.

I swallowed that reality for ten whole days until, one morning, I woke up on the chatai mat next to my mother's side of the bed, gripped by a new idea. Suffering the stifling heat of May, my eyes converted to laser beams as I obeyed my mother, mind focused on one objective—how to end my life. Chirag would never find me, and I refused to live in India, let alone with my parents.

Three interminable days later, my fingers wrapped around a tangle of parachute rope while I reorganized the second-bedroom closet. That was what I needed for my purpose. My heart became a ticking time bomb as I covered the rope with a torn plastic bag full of rusty nails and glanced around like a robber. I hid the nails under dusty twine, two bottles of rancid castor oil, and a tin of thick turpentine.

That evening, I sat in my parents' bedroom reading a *Woman & Home* magazine short story, my mind obsessing over the rope I had found. Parachute rope was the strongest kind of rope available. It wouldn't break when I hung myself with it. I wished I could hang and die right then, but that was impossible with my parents haunting every minute of my existence. Yet, if I was patient, sooner or later, the opportunity would come. My mind already flew free knowing I would escape the Chatterjees.

I reigned in my anger, refusing to let the infuriating cacophony of their new television set disrupt the story I was reading, when Uncle Robu asked, "What time did you rent the truck for?"

"Ten o'clock." My mother didn't take her eyes off Farmer's Advice on the black-and-white screen.

What are they talking about? My ears pricked up like the ears of their pet calico sharing the wicker armchair with me.

Uncle Robu raised his voice. "I told Officer Das to double surveillance for tomorrow."

My hearing sharpened as I bent my head. *What does he mean? Will I be home alone?* To hide my anticipation, I picked up the cat and buried my face in its fur, but I wasn't fool enough to ask questions. I didn't even wince when the cat dug a sharp claw into my knee. Try as I might, I couldn't quell the hope bubbling inside me. Just maybe, I could end the misery of my existence once and for all. The possibility was so thrilling, I didn't even mind the television noise anymore. Soon, I gleaned from my parents' subsequent remarks that they had three days left to vacate Didima's and my precious home in South Extension. What a miracle they didn't plan to drag me along.

That night, hope had me falling asleep as soon as my head touched the chatai mat. In my dream, Dadu woke me up, his narrow, tanned face looming over mine. Springy grayish-brown hair flopped past his wide forehead—lion-yellow eyes crinkled in the corners.

"Ma shona, I'm back! Are you ready for our color cognition game?" Dadu smoothed the sleep-tousled hair from my four-year-old forehead. "If you name your gemstones right, I'll buy you six gas balloons at the lakeside instead of three."

As a geologist, Dadu prized his gemstone collection as much as I did. On each birthday, Didima and I got to select gemstones that Dadu's jeweler later fashioned into earrings or a pendant for us.

Dadu bundled me in his arms and carried me to our vast dining table, where his two shoeboxes full of precious and semiprecious stones waited for our game. The CC Game was the best game in my world. I rubbed the sleep from my eyes as Dadu plunked me on a dining chair, scooped my long hair into a jumbled ponytail, and hurried to unfold the nearest wax-paper packet of gemstones.

Outside the dining room picture window, dozens of wild parrots shrieked in our vegetable garden, feasting on plate-sized sunflower heads. Peridot-green feathers flashed in the morning sun as cornelian-red beaks tweezed out fresh sunflower seeds to gobble up in one continuous swallow.

Ignoring the birds, I stared at the cluster of pink gemstones lying in front of me. "Trumaline?" I yawned.

"Not 'tru,' *tou*rmaline. Say it after me."

"Toormaline."

"And what do they remind you of?"

"Phlox. The first phlox in spring."

Dadu smiled. "And what other color do tourmalines come in?"

I hesitated. "Green?" Greens were difficult, as Dadu's collection contained many green gemstones.

"But, shona, what *kind* of green?" he insisted.

"The dark, dark green of the mango tree leaves by Jodpur Park Lake."

"That's right, my darling. You're such a smart girl." Dadu kissed the top of my head. "And these?" Dadu unfolded another packet of medium-green gemstones.

"Peridot?"

"Come on. This is easy."

"Like those parrots?" I pointed an index finger toward the garden.

"I knew you'd say that." Dadu grinned his schoolboy grin, catching my finger midair. "And these?"

"Jade. Like the lotus leaves in the library pond." I squared my shoulders, gaining confidence.

"Okay, you might fail this because you've only seen it once." Dadu unfolded a pale-pink faceted gemstone the size of his thumbnail.

I stared. "Morga? Morgan…?"

"Morga*nite*," Dadu finished. "But that was a great try. We'll count it as a point."

"I want it, Dadu. It's beautiful. Give it to me…"

I woke up before Dadu could reply, nearly making me cry. That dream reinforced my resolve to die. In the dining room, I touched a sunray sparkling reflections on my parents' sandstone dining table, hyperaware of being alive. The aroma of frying onions wafted from the kitchen, and it felt as if I had never experienced the smell. A cup of coffee. That was my last wish. My mother brewed coffee all weekend long, since caffeine enhanced my stepfather's capacity to illustrate children's books for freelance income. Observing him drawing pictures of children for hours, one day, it dawned on me he was no longer a sexual threat to my person. His predilection lay in children under the age of ten. My suspicions strengthened as I watched him browse his collection of children's photographs every Sunday morning, claiming he was studying their muscle movements for accurate illustration rendition. And he had hundreds of photographs of ragged children, half-dressed children, naked children, and well-dressed children. The hours never passed when my stepfather perused those photos. It was one more reason to escape living with him.

To enjoy my coffee, I dragged a chair from the back veranda across the drawing room to the front porch. I parked it next to my stepfather's Royal Enfield motorcycle, smelling oil vapor and petrol fumes.

No cup of coffee had ever tasted so good as I memorized the front garden patch. In my mind, the cosmos bobbed like rubies and tourmalines in a warm diamond of sunlight. *Do people remember colors in heaven?*

As my parents departed, my hands developed a tremor. I wiped them on my nightdress. A peek outside from behind the drawing room curtain revealed no surveillance. *But what if they knock?* I couldn't imagine the trouble I would be in if they caught me in the middle of hanging myself.

Fifteen minutes frittered by while I waited for a knock. I switched off the drawing room fan. My knees shook as I hurried to the second bedroom and collapsed in front of its closet. Rusty nails scattered to the floor as I pulled out the tangle of parachute rope. My fingers converted to inert candle stubs as I tried to unravel the length I might need. On my wrist, Didima's watch hammered out the seconds as if to highlight that I didn't know how long I had to complete my mission. Ready to cry, I dropped the rope and zigzagged back to the drawing room. I dragged a pine bench to place it right under the ceiling fan.

Once on the bench, I balanced on tiptoes to touch the motionless fan blades. They hung inches above my fingers. I ran back to fetch my stepfather's drawing stool and grabbed the untangled end of the rope. It trailed behind me, a confused snake, as I placed the stool on top of the bench. Suddenly, I realized that to jump and hang, I needed to be high enough and close enough to the fan to string the rope but *nothing below could obstruct me.*

Underarms soaked with perspiration, I cursed the absence of a second fan. My eyes kept straying to the drawing room door as I anxiously dreaded a knock.

I tried to fashion a noose that would work while all I thought of in the boiling heat of May was my last Christmas in Calcutta with Dadu, when I was too young to understand what my religion was. As devout a Hindu as Dadu had been, his childhood had been too steeped in English culture for him to forego Christmas celebrations, despite his fervent support of the Indian independence movement as a young college student in the 1930s. I supposed that last Christmas season had been like any other Christmas for Dadu, but it was the first one I could remember, as a four-year-old and, for me, the final one with him. I remembered a family party at our home on Christmas Eve and Dadu entering our Jodpur Park townhouse wearing a dark-blue blazer, his arms loaded with presents, boxes of pastries, and paper bags of meat patties. Later at the same party, I recalled a chocolate cake decorated with three pink marzipan roses and me eating a rose on Dadu's lap, falling in love with the taste of marzipan.

Truly, life had never been the same without Dadu. Yes, I had loved Didima, but after Dadu had died, my life with her became one long scene of watching her slow decline from diabetes, during which I had morphed into her caretaker instead of she taking care of me. And with Didima gone, my one remaining hope had been Chirag, but of course, our relationship was an impossibility. *So, what is there to live for? A life with Jhummur and Robu Chatterjee? Or married to a stranger of their choice? Is that why I want to live to see tomorrow?* I tightened the noose around my wrist to see if it worked. *Should I change out of my nightdress?* No. My mother could have the pleasure of dressing my dead body as I had dressed the body of Didima. I bunched my nightdress around my waist and climbed the pine bench and the stool. On the stool, I couldn't stand straight because I was too tall. Without warning, my knees knocked as I realized the fan blades resembled rapiers that close to my face. Contorted as I was, sweat trickles snaked down my sides, but I couldn't wipe my armpits.

It took five minutes to harness the ceiling hook because my fingers shook so much. In my mind, I saw the pinks and maroons of the cosmos as I eased the noose over my head. That action brought such a rush of blood to my nose, and caused so much pain, I could smell the difference. The noose lay slack around my angled neck, but I loosened it further just to accommodate the freight train inside my chest.

I had to calm down. Say a prayer. Death couldn't be that awful when it was supposed to be a release. I closed my eyes in an effort to breathe, but my heart wouldn't allow it.

Then, unbidden, an electric jolt zapped right through me, and I saw Chirag's long-lashed eyes in the flash—*I want to live!*

My whole body felt pinpricks, refusing to die, refusing to give up, refusing to fail. Eyes sprang open. The floor swirled far, far below. My hand grabbed a fan blade. Designed to glide, the blade slid forward, and my noose constricted.

Poised between life and death, choking, I prayed, *Lord, please don't kill me.* Somehow, my right foot helped me regain my balance. The relief was so huge, I just stood there, even though my throat was half-choked. My body raced from warm to cold, and I shivered while my icy fingers fumbled to loosen the noose. Lungs flooded with air. Shaking all over, I slipped the noose over my head. Wobbly and frightened, I climbed off my self-fashioned pedestal of death. Seven more minutes passed on the wall clock until I collapsed on the terrazzo floor, a jellyfish throbbing on a beach.

When my parents came home, they found me in my usual armchair in their bedroom finishing the *Woman & Home* short story I had started the previous day.

I said, "I cooked you *khichiri*."

Khichiri was a goulash of rice, lentils, vegetables, and turmeric Didima would cook a lot, since it was the only one-step meal she could deliver until I assumed the role of cook in our lives together. My parents exchanged a quick glance as if to share how they had tamed me. They would discover their mistake when I found Chirag and escaped them.

8

CHIRAG AND I MET IN the autumn of 1971, when I was ten years old. His entry into my life was all the more poignant because of the way Baba had shattered my heart into a million pieces during his first visit to New Delhi that same spring. Newly married to his second wife, Baba had been too mesmerized by his own happiness to pay attention to a little girl whose whole world had revolved around seeing him again after five years of separation.

Soon after Baba's visit, Teddy left Didima and me to work in Alberta, Canada, and Didima suffered her second heart attack from the shock of his departure. To make things worse, Didima sent our servant boy, Agya, back to his hometown because she couldn't afford his salary anymore. So there we were, six months later, Didima and I, all alone, unclear as to who took care of whom. Yet, despite all my worries, I was happy because that day was the morning of the Diwali Light Festival, my favorite Hindu religious celebration, even though I was not technically a Hindu.

I knew if I lit candles in the correct spots, the Goddess Lakhsmi would visit us and bless Didima with health so she would never fall sick again. As it was a school holiday, after breakfast, I warmed candle bottoms and stuck them ten inches apart on our windowsills and the tops of our outer walls. Then all I had to do was wait for dusk to fall, so I, and the rest of India, could gild our homes to guide in the goddess and light fireworks to ignite the very firmament.

By afternoon, however, fed up with waiting for the sun to set, I ran out front to see if my neighborhood playmates were around. The street was deserted. *What will I do for the next six hours? Maybe I could persuade Mrs. Gulati to cut me a dozen of her precious chrysanthemums blooming crimson, white, and bronze right inside the family's forged-iron gate, standing wide-open?* To gather the courage to ask, I hopped onto the Gulatis' gate, my two-o'clock shadow blocking its geometric patterns on the dirt road. In India, gates were a source of contention between adults and children. Given the opportunity, we mounted them and swung back and forth, sagging the gates, snapping their hinges, or both. I began to swing. *Could I convince old Mrs. Gulati to cut me chrysanthemums?* If I succeeded, Dadu would have a vaseful in front of his photograph in the niche of the left wall in Didima's room. Dadu had loved the pungent and salty smell of chrysanthemums.

I stepped off the gate, lungs inflated to call out to Mrs. Gulati, when two boys ran toward me. Ganju was a regular playmate. The other boy, tagging behind, was Chirag, a newcomer to our neighborhood. Chirag had the longest lashes I had ever seen on a boy, and his parents had to be rich because they rented the largest house two streets over. The bridge of my nose wrinkled in alarm. *Will they report my gate swinging to Mrs. Gulati?*

The boys panted to a halt so close to me, I stepped back and clutched the gate grill with both hands. Ganju looked his usual neat self, but Chirag's hands and knees were mud-stained, his gray sweater caked with bits of grass, and his hair stood on end.

"Noor," huffed Ganju, "choose a boyfriend. It's either him or me."

Phew! Thank God this didn't concern my gate-swinging. Of course, Ganju said what he did because he knew no adults would overhear us. Girls in India weren't allowed to have boyfriends. Neither could boys have girlfriends. Those were Western ideas we learned in our Catholic schools. At home, our Hindu parents prohibited any close associations between girls and boys.

"Noor, didn't you hear me?" Ganju's voice rose.

"I heard you." I focused on my scuffed Mary Jane shoes. *Would Ganju say this to me if he knew I was half-Muslim?*

I remembered, at seven years old, playing a game of Chinese checkers in Nita Malhotra's home. Nita's mother had thrown me out of their house after she'd asked me what my last name was and discovered it was a Muslim one. Tears streaming, I had run all the way until I'd reached Didima tending to her amaryllis bulbs in our back garden.

"Didima, why is my last name Zulfiker and not Panaeker?" I had cried.

And Didima had hugged me hard. "Because, shona, Panaeker is your mother's last name. If you have your mother's last name, people will think your baba never married your ma, then they'll call you illegitimate. In our country, an illegitimate is worse than a Muslim."

Ganju waved a hand in front of my face. "Hello? Why aren't you choosing?"

"Because I'm half-Muslim." I hung my head.

"So?" Chirag spoke at last. He wiped his runny nose and streaked his left cheek with mud.

"So don't you care? Auntie Malhotra"—I pointed to a pistachio-green house—"doesn't let me into their home anymore since she found out I have a Muslim father. Auntie Chibb heard it, and she doesn't let me into their home either." I unclutched the gate to rub the burn in my eyes because I didn't want to cry in front of the boys.

"I didn't know that." Ganju scratched his snub nose.

"Know what? That I'm half-Muslim or that Auntie Malhotra and Auntie Chibb now treat me like an *untouchable?*" My eyes stung again. I didn't know if being an untouchable was better or worse than being an illegitimate child or a Muslim in a Hindu world. The sweepers who cleaned our bathrooms were untouchables. If they brushed against us by mistake, we had to take a bath. It was hard to remember all the rules we had to follow to be proper Indians.

"What's the other half?" Chirag cut in.

"Hindu."

"Show me your hands."

I stuck them out.

Chirag took both and inspected each one. He faced my palms up. "Can you tell which one is Hindu and which one Muslim?"

"You're making fun of me."

"No, I'm serious. Can you tell?" Chirag stared at me with his shiny, dark eyes from under curvy eyelashes.

"Of course not."

"Neither can I. So, will you be my girlfriend?"

I bobbed my head, speechless.

My answer must have surprised Chirag. "Why are you choosing me and not Ganju?"

"I don't know. Should I choose him?"

"No, no. Don't forget I am your boyfriend from now on." Chirag smiled, showing steel braces. The boys ran off as abruptly as they had come.

That night, no fireworks blazed as brightly as those inside my heart. *Why couldn't more people think as Chirag does? Indeed, which of the hairs on my head are Hindu, and which ones Muslim? Why are Auntie Malhotra and Auntie Chibb so mean to me, considering I have no choice in who my parents are?*

The following morning, Didima watered her rose pots late. The noise from the Diwali fireworks hadn't let her sleep, and low blood sugar had caused her to wake up dizzy. Beside her, I cut roses for the vase in front of Dadu's portrait. Right then, Chirag's face peeked over our garden wall and disappeared. In sailed a white paper plane to land on top of Didima's jasmine bush.

"Didima," I said, "go check Dadu's vase. Tell me how many roses you want me to cut for it so we'll have fresh ones on the bushes for the weekend." With Didima busy, I dashed to rescue the paper plane, heart racing as I bolted into our bathroom. The plane had a neat newspaper package taped to it with a red rose. I smelled the rose. My present contained six gorgeous stamps with images of birds and animals and a note: *A bird told me you like stamps. Meet me out front at two p.m.*

I showed early, but Chirag was already balanced on a blue bicycle by the Gulatis' gate.

He smiled. "Want a ride? I have to go play cricket afterward, but I'll leave you my bicycle to play with while I'm gone."

"No, no, you keep your bicycle. I don't know how to ride a bike."

"You don't?" Chirag sounded nonplussed. "I guess I'll cancel my cricket game to teach you how. Come on. Sit on the carrier seat behind and pedal. You'll learn to balance if your feet can touch the ground."

"You want to teach me right now?"

"Sure."

I mounted the carrier seat and wobbled down a hundred yards.

Chirag clapped. "Now ride back to me."

"This will take time." I wavered.

"It's okay. We have the whole afternoon." Chirag squeezed my hand clutched around the bicycle handlebar. "Maybe my dad can buy you one. I'll ask."

I shook my head. "Don't bother. My grandma wouldn't let me accept it. She's too proud. What does your father do? He must be rich, because your house is huge."

"He is. He exports medical stuff to America." Chirag smiled proudly.

"What medical stuff?"

"Hospital bedsheets, doctor's coats, you know, the white ones? Surgical instruments and those steel utensils they use during operations. It's our family business. In America, one uncle manages the distribution. Another one is a hospital administrator. He started the business."

"Wow. Have you been to America?"

"For vacations. Maybe, one day, we'll go there together. It's fun. You'd love it."

***

The spring of 1972 gave way to summer at lightning speed. While Chirag raided neighbors' gardens to hand me bouquets, late summer heralded the monsoon rains. Children in New Delhi assessed the sky, willing the steely rain clouds to materialize. We loved the dark clouds because the heavier the rains, the more fun we had trolling inside uncovered rain drains, dancing in the rain, or watching it come pelting down, venturing wild guesses as to how long the weather would remain cool.

On one such Friday afternoon, when the rain clouds looked so heavy an extra-long stick could puncture them into rainfall, Chirag waited, poised on his bicycle with one foot balanced on the raised barrier of a covered culvert at street level.

"I have a surprise for you."

"Where?"

His hands on the handlebars were empty, and his shorts pockets flat.

"It's far away. We'll have to go for a ride."

"Now?" I took in the roiling sky. "We'll get drenched. Can't you smell the rain?" My prediction was confirmed by a zigzag of silver lightning and a rifle crack of reverberating thunder.

"Are you scared of a drenching? It *has* to be like this for me to give you the surprise."

"Be like what? Near rain any minute?"

"Get on the back of my bike before my surprise is ruined."

After fifteen minutes, I shouted, "Are we there yet?" My cheek was squashed to Chirag's bony back as wind rushed over his shoulders.

"Nearly. You've never seen such a sight." His sneakers scraped the dirt road to slow the bicycle wheels.

Ahead, a gated stone wall towered over us in the old district of Mote Ki Mashjit, behind South Extension, where I wasn't allowed to go since it was considered a poor and dangerous area. But even I had heard of the Jain temple, though I had never seen it.

Above the wall flared the canopies of trees, beautiful, outstretched, and ancient, their greenness greener against the luscious curves of the pewter sky. The monsoon clouds grumbled and rolled, panicking the crows, pigeons, and sparrows hidden amid the tree leaves into deafening debate over when the first raindrop would fall.

"I love it already." I clasped my hands.

Chirag ran to the gate, peeked in, and ran back, startling two squirrels chasing each other on the parched ground.

At the wooden gate, he grabbed my arm. "Cover your eyes. Don't be afraid to trip. You'll be on grass in a minute, but walk slow, okay? Ten more steps. Ready?"

I uncovered my eyes. We stood in a garden in front of a yellow sandstone temple with a roof sloped to form a four-sided cone. Two drab peahens perched on the flat edge around the base of the cone. The peahens stared down at six peacocks dancing on the grass next to Chirag and me. They dazzled the peahens with their iridescent splendor of royal blue, indigo, green, and purple, oblivious to all but the prospective approval of their two mates. Putting on a show of sways and teeters, runs and swishes, they brushed feathers as they misjudged the sheer circumference of their tail fans, bridling when they did, embarrassed in their own way to have bungled the dance that would decide whom the peahens chose from among them.

"What do you think?" whispered Chirag. He encircled my waist from behind.

"How did you know they'd be dancing?" I whispered back.

"Because peacocks do that before the monsoon rains."

"How did you find this place?"

"Ganju. Did you know his family is Jain? The temple priest told him of the peacocks. His sister got married here. This is the only Jain temple for miles around."

"I want to get married here."

"Do you want to marry me?"

"Yes!"

"Let's go in and do it."

"What? Get married? How?" All the marriages I had seen in our neighborhood were elaborate ceremonies.

"We'll light oil lamps. I brought matches. Ganju says Jains light oil lamps like Hindus paint orange *tikas* on their foreheads. After that, people are married."

"How did you know I would say yes?"

"I figured you would because this temple isn't Hindu or Muslim."

"Oh, Chirag. You're so smart. If we light the lamps, we'll be married?" My heart felt it would burst with joy that Chirag wanted to marry me.

"Yes. It'll be our secret."

At the end of August, when the monsoon season dovetailed into the second part of the broiling summer, I ran out front. It was the eve of my eleventh birthday.

"Did you draw a red heart on my back door?" I panted.

Chirag grinned his lopsided grin. "Guess."

"Well, I love it, but you shouldn't have used a crayon—not today. Today is a horrible day for us because my grandpa died on this day seven years ago. Now my grandma is sad and hopping mad that she'll have to boil soap and water to scrub it off."

"But I don't want her to scrub it off. I want that heart to remain forever. Why can't she leave it alone?"

"Why are you such a clown?" I rubbed the hotness in my cheeks. "Promise me you won't do it again."

But Chirag drew hearts pierced with arrows wherever they were visible and tossed gifts tied to a stubby-stemmed rose attached to a paper plane into our courtyard after peeking over the sidewall of our garden to ascertain Didima was out of sight.

Our luck ran out one September evening when Didima caught Chirag writing *I love you* on our outer wall with his mother's pink lipstick. I was gone to buy eggs when Didima dragged him into our house and shouted at him. I witnessed Didima throwing Chirag out of our back door, saying, "And we'll see how your parents like that—"

Chirag ran down the road while I ran into our house to yank Didima's *sari pallu* on our back patio.

"Didima, what did you say to him? I know him. What did you say to him?"

But Didima wouldn't budge from her answer of "Nothing."

The next afternoon, Chirag didn't reply when I addressed him. Soon, he ran the other way if he spotted me on the street, making me cry because his behavior was so opposite of what I was used to.

***

On the day of the Diwali Light Festival, a year since Chirag had asked me to be his girlfriend and four months since he had talked to me, I knocked on Ganju's door.

"Ganju." My chin wobbled. "Do you know why Chirag hates me so much now? It wasn't me. It was my grandma who screamed at him."

"Aww, Noor. You mean you don't know why?"

"Of course I do. I came home right as my grandma finished screaming at him. But couldn't he have spoken to me once to say goodbye?"

"Is that all you know?" Ganju dug his big toe into the ground outside his house.

"I know she didn't scream at him twice." I scratched my eyebrow.

"She did a lot worse." Ganju stared at me.

My intestines twisted. "Did she speak to his parents?"

Ganju's ears reddened. "She complained to the Jesuit headmaster of our school. She said Chirag was a delinquent who drew hearts with lipstick on your door. The headmaster summoned his parents and ripped Chirag apart. He had to promise never to speak to you again."

My shoulders shook. "Oh, Ganju, will you tell Chirag I'm sorry?"

"Yes. Noor—shhh, it's okay. Stop crying. People will think I'm making you cry. Come here. Take my hankie and wipe your face. Will you come out to light firecrackers with us?"

I shook my head, chest aching. "I'll tell my grandma I'm sick. I don't want to be around with Chirag ignoring me." I walked home, head hanging. *Had Chirag ever loved me?* He could have talked to me on the street anytime, without any adult knowing, but he never had.

Two months later, at the end of December, Ganju asked me if I had been invited to the lawn tea party Chirag's mother was organizing for Chirag's and his elder brother's friends.

I shook my head.

On New Year's Day of 1973, it was Ganju who told me Chirag's family had left for America to join the family business there, breaking my heart completely.

9

But six weeks ago, when Chirag had seen me again, his first gesture had been to apologize for how he had left India without talking to me. And I wouldn't rest until I found a way to contact him. *Yet how can we run away with Officer Das and his surveillance people watching me?* I didn't know the answer. However, that wouldn't stop me from fighting for my happiness. I would never marry any boy except Chirag.

Meanwhile, the confinement of my house arrest, the hundred-plus-degree weather of June in Delhi, and my complete inability to find a way out of my hellhole drove me crazy. By then, Chirag must have written me at least twenty letters to his bhuaji auntie's house, which Officer Das had to be collecting and reading. Das knew that address since confiscating my belongings at the working girls' hostel.

As if to mock my secret resolve to find Chirag, each evening, I also enjoyed the drama of my stepfather getting drunk. And when he drank, he sought me out to listen to him. In answer, I would lock myself in my bedroom. Then he would ramble, and shout, and speak to people who weren't there, and my mother would reason with him until their exchanges ended in fighting.

The next morning, my mother would pretend the evening hadn't happened, like she pretended the pending court case involving my stepfather's drunken driving had nothing to do with maiming a teenage boy into a wheelchair.

Largely to escape listening to my parents, one evening, I poured myself a quarter glassful of the imported alcohol Teddy hadn't been able to take with him to Canada. It was poetic justice that the alcohol was stored in my very bedroom, inside the same cupboard where I had found the parachute rope. My stepfather didn't drink fancy gins and vermouths or Campari or the sweet liqueurs Teddy had enjoyed. He drank straight whiskey to hit oblivion quickly.

Within a month, my quarter glassful became a glassful of mixed alcohol each evening. With the cunningness only alcohol drove, I would sneak up to my stepfather's incomparable rooftop rose garden, where the noise of my parents' voices receded in the face of my own quiet stupor. In the fading evening light, roses zoomed in and out of my vision as I confused them with overripe, blooming cabbages. *But wait, my stepfather doesn't grow cabbages, or is it roses he doesn't grow?* God, I was drunk, as drunk as a skunk. *What is a skunk, anyway?* India didn't have skunks. I knew the expression from a Hemingway novel. *Or is it Steinbeck? Or maybe Rudyard Kipling? No, no, that's a mongoose. What's the plural of mongoose, mongeese?* At least Steinbeck wrote about America, unlike Hemingway.

In drunken glee, I would laugh at my own jokes. But too often, my laughter dissolved into tears. Then tears blurred the roses—or cabbages—to amorphous blobs. Dizzily, I would close my eyes. My head was a large green watermelon. With great care, I would lean the fruit back on the terrace wall of Uncle Robu's roof garden. If I moved, it would drop and split, red and pulpy, and I would be headless. Again, I would giggle or cry until I passed out. Late at night, when the mad people downstairs had gone to bed, I would stagger into the second bedroom and let sleep take care of one more night.

By the third month of that behavior, one day, my iron will to survive reasserted itself. The mindless drinking wouldn't help me escape my parents. It would only prolong my life in their company. What I needed was a real, viable plan, *right in their view*, as obvious as the Trojan horse. I had no clue what that could be, but the hope of it materializing kept me from drinking anymore.

Without the alcohol-induced sleep, however, all I did each night was stay wide-awake and think—think of how to contact Chirag, yet I never found a way to do it. Sooner or later, my parents would arrange a marriage for me to a backward, biased, "educated" man of their choice because remaining a single woman in my country was a stigma no parent wanted to face. The perceived stigma enticed even erudite Indian men, who had lived abroad for years, to come home and select a bride who would obey them, cook their meals, and bear their children. That would be my fate, too, unless I found a way to escape it. I shuddered.

Free from the palliative of alcohol, during the autumn of 1979, I almost welcomed Officer Das's random, twice-a-month check-in visits to relieve me from the company of my parents.

But each time he visited, he told us stories about how Chirag's father and uncles lured young women to sign up for modeling jobs in Arab countries, all expenses paid. After that first prostitution stop, the survivors were funneled to America and sold into prostitution rings. Of course, Das's implication was that this had been Chirag's main reason to contact me, but knowing Chirag since childhood, I couldn't believe that. Yet gradually, Das was mining my faith in what Chirag's family might be involved in because I had no way to refute him. As a child, I had rarely seen Chirag's parents and had never directly talked to them.

Thus caught up in the snare of my reality, the last person I ever expected to see again stood at the door of my parents' home when I answered a knock one afternoon in the middle of June.

All I could do was stare while, from within the kitchen, my mother said in her high voice, "Noor? Who is it?"

"Noor, darling!" Rajat held his yellow helmet in his hand in a familiar gesture. "I love you. I want to marry you."

Perhaps it was the heat or my rage and frustration and the heat combined that exploded a bomb inside me. "Asshole!" I screamed. "You killed my didima. Now you want me back to beat me whenever you want?"

"Noor, I'm sorry about—"

The ring of my slap on his cheek broke his apology. "Get out of here!" I shrieked in lunatic frenzy. "Get out of here, or I'll stick a knife into you!"

"Auntie Jhummur." Rajat looked past me at my mother standing behind my shoulder. "Please tell Noor to listen to me. We are still engaged."

I pushed Rajat in the chest. "Out! *Leave.* And don't ever come back. I have never hated anyone as much as I hate you, and I'll die before I marry you."

My mother and I watched Rajat mount his rented scooter and ride away.

In his wake, my mother said, "I know he beat you, but he is a doctor, and he wants to marry you. Couldn't you have forgiven him?"

Tears flooded my eyes. "Of course you would say that! You stood by while Officer Das beat me, too, because a man beating a woman is the norm here. But this is what you *don't* know. Rajat made me have an abortion when I was fifteen. Try selling *that* to the next groom you find me." I charged up the stairs leading to my stepfather's roof garden, the only place to afford me privacy in my no-win existence. There, I hunched in the shade of the stairwell and cried and prayed I would succeed in finding Chirag again soon.

Downstairs, an hour later, my mother's voice emerged subdued. "Who did your abortion? Rajat?"

"Yes," I lied, knowing if I mentioned it was Auntie Shalini who had saved me, my mother would immediately seek out the gynecologist to attack her, thereby avoiding her own gargantuan incompetence as a parent.

In that fashion, the months passed, and I was no closer to finding any way out of my house arrest. Outwardly, I played my mother's willing slave while inside, I seethed on a slow burn, as determined as ever to escape my parents and find Chirag.

At last, November came, and the weather cooled a little, making me feel saner. On one such day, Officer Das dropped in for a random check-in visit.

Throwing caution to the wind, I asked, "Officer, could I run in the mornings? You know, for the exercise." I knew if I didn't find relief from my parents' company, I would try suicide again.

Shushanto Das smirked. "Fine. The surveillance people will catch you if you try to abscond."

The next morning, I awoke at sunrise. Determined to practice *Kunjal Kriya*, the yoga exercise Didima's doctor had recommended as the one foolproof method to thwart diabetes, I began to drink the first of eight glasses of water on an empty stomach. Vomiting the water out would train my pancreas to produce the right amount of insulin.

I was drinking my fifth glass of water when Niagara Falls gushed out of my mouth, to my astonishment. After that, I went for a run, schooling myself to go a hundred yards farther each morning. How ironic that I was doing something Rajat loved, but running was the only activity that provided me with an illusion of freedom when the wind hit my face. I had never asked Rajat why *he* ran, so his motivation would always remain a mystery.

At the end of November, on a Sunday, I was bent over in front of my parents' gate to stretch my hamstrings after a forty-minute run. Hearing me, my mother waddled out of the house and waved an outstretched *Times of India* newspaper. I cursed under my breath because, apart from my run, I never had a minute's peace.

"Look." My mother pointed to an article as if I could read newsprint from four feet away.

"What?" I straightened to stretch my arms, resisting an eye roll.

"You'll study Spanish."

My stomach muscles tensed. "Why? You know I want to study English. I always have—except it didn't fit in with my taking care of Didima." I itched to add that should have been *her* job, not mine. *But why pick a fight I can't win?* Not while Officer Das could appear whenever he pleased to beat me up. That constant fear kept me from doing anything that might incite his wrath.

"It won't serve us in the marriage market. English graduates are a dime a dozen." My mother waved the newspaper again.

Is that *what this is about? Are they already reviewing grooms to marry me off to?* In India, hundreds of girls got PhDs simply because the degree would raise their eligibility in a marriage negotiation. For a girl's parents, higher education was a bargaining chip to pay less dowry to the groom's family. The payment of dowry in money or assets was so crippling, every prospective mother preferred to give birth to a boy rather than a girl. Dowries were why beggar women wearing silver jewelry walked the streets. All Indians understood that the poor woman couldn't sell those valuables. She had to save them to pay the dowry of a daughter she had been unlucky enough to have.

In India, marriage only happened for those who could pay the right price. Western people simply couldn't and didn't comprehend how our cultural rules dominated our decisions and how bound we felt by those rules. Regardless, I attempted to defend myself. "What use is Spanish in India? Why can't you let me study English? It's a language, the same as Spanish is, isn't it? Who cares which one I study?"

"Because the United Nations declared Spanish their fifth official language." My mother waved the newspaper in my face. "English is useless. Too many girls study English in India," she repeated. "You need to study Spanish."

I wanted to scream, "I hate you! You're crazy," but I kept quiet.

My mother would have her way. And the more I begged to study English, the more my mother would ram Spanish down my throat. It was her thousandfold revenge on me for how I had treated her when Didima was alive and I had had the power.

I forced myself to take a deep breath. "Fine. I'll study Spanish if that's what you want. What do I have to do?" But in that moment, a seed of an idea germinated in my brain, and I dropped my gaze, lest my mother should spot the idea in my eyes. *What if learning Spanish could become my Trojan horse? My way to escape my parents by leaving for Spain?* It was worth the consideration. I could study English once I married Chirag and lived in America. Yet for the time being, Spanish just might become my ticket out of India and my parents' clutches.

My mother's expression denoted triumph, as it always did when she got to thwart me. "You'll go to Jawahar Lal Nehru University tomorrow with Robu and fill out an application form for their Spanish degree career."

10

ATTENDING COLLEGE IN THE NEIGHBORHOOD of R. K. Puram for the better part of each week during January 1980 was a bittersweet reprieve. To get there from my parents' home, I had to take two public buses and ride in them for more than an hour, constantly racked by fear that the surveillance crew was following me in a car.

Notwithstanding, on my first morning at the Jawahar Lal Nehru University, or JNU, on the outside, I was one more student in the eyes of my collegemates. *Yet what would these teenagers say if they knew I had a criminal record and surveillance watching my every move?*

Two weeks into school, I ran around the entire perimeter of the cafeteria building to try to identify my surveillance but spotted no one. The exercise further convinced me of how good they were. That was what my mind told me. My heart, however, daydreamed from Monday to Friday of writing to Chirag and persuading a classmate to post the letter.

I waited all the way until March to know my classmates better. One afternoon, I approached the youngest student in our class after everyone else had vacated the hallway. "Suresh, can you post this letter for me whenever you go to the post office next? I don't know where the post office is near here."

Sadly, my reason for choosing Suresh was despicable, but I knew it would work. He was from out of town, which meant he would know where the post office was located, but more importantly, he was an untouchable. Poor Suresh never hid that he was in our Spanish program, given a special political campaign to uplift the profile of his people. He would be flattered *anyone* was asking him for any favor, even a half-caste like me.

For the next fifteen days, I walked around on a cloud, expecting Chirag's reply, as I had explained the whole surveillance operation to him in detail. *Maybe a cousin or friend of his will bring me a letter at JNU.* The anticipation alone acted as my happiness drug.

I came home on a Friday at the end of March to see Officer Das's police car outside my parents' home. When I walked into the living room, he stood up and waved my opened letter in my face. Abruptly, I understood what novels meant when they said the blood drained from their protagonist's face.

"Can you explain this to me?" Officer Das's voice was mild, which frightened me more.

My eyes shifted then met his, my heart converting to a beating tom-tom. "Chirag is innocent." But the anticipation of violence didn't mitigate the slap that swung my face sideways.

"Come on." Das dragged me to his police car. "You need a reality check. All the freedom you received went to your head, didn't it?"

Das drove for an hour, leaving New Delhi behind, while I didn't say one word. At last, he parked his car in front of Tihar Jail, an institution I had only ever heard of. With me in tow, he checked in, holding a whispered conversation with a lady jail official. While I processed how the dingy, ill-lit facility was probably my new home, the lady official escorted us into an inner area, unlocking the door into a large, dim hallway with tiny cells on both sides. What horrified me was how silent the inmates fell as soon as that door opened.

Without sparing a word, Das dragged me to the end of that urine-and-sweat-smelling corridor and back, and for the first time, I smelled fear as the lady official locked up that hallway again, with me miraculously outside a jail cell.

In Das's police vehicle, I learned I was more terrified of Das's silence than of him yelling at me or beating me. At my parents' place, he said to them, "Now she knows where she's going next. So let her tell you what she saw."

After Das left, if I hadn't been scared out of my mind, I would have laughed at the sight of Rajat walking through the gate. My mother hurried out to meet him.

"Auntie Jhummur, can I talk to Noor?"

"About what, Rajat? The abortion you made her undergo at age fifteen?"

I couldn't see my mother's face as I stood behind her, but I did see the color drain from Rajat's face.

"Get out of my sight, and don't ever come back here. We know a police officer who can contact your boss if you ever come near my daughter again. That will take care of your medical career."

Despite the show of solidarity from my mother, over the weekend, I took to the bottle again. Only alcohol blurred my memory of that jail corridor, which swept over me without notice. Yet even drinking couldn't blind me to how, more than ever, my ticket to freedom was to learn Spanish well, in case it served as a way out of my parents' clutches and the country.

But *deciding* to study Spanish proved a lot easier than studying it. Used to a lifetime of passing from grade to grade just by paying attention in class, I had shirked homework whenever possible in the Loreto Convent School. At home with Didima, during any free time available to me, I had gobbled fiction to escape my life.

Throughout my teens, my three drugs had been fiction, food, and flowers. Fiction and flowers transported me out of my reality, and food enhanced the experience. Purplish-blue jacarandas flew me to South Africa. Roses transported me to Mediterranean Europe. Phloxes, gladiola, dahlias, nasturtiums, and countless others metamorphosed the dusty New Delhi suburbia of South Extension into the English countryside described by Enid Blyton, Agatha Christie, Emily Brontë, Daphne du Maurier, and Henry James. Therefore, actually studying Spanish came as a rude shock.

Within three months, even the memory of that jail Das had shown me couldn't compare to how much I detested Spanish. Gone was the relief of fiction from my life while I spent my evenings deciphering grammar, a beast I had happily never met on the English country paths I roamed in my mind. In the Loreto Convent School of New Delhi in the 1970s, all English grammar had been taught by example, not memorization or definition. Therefore, passing school exams had never required me to know even simple animals such as adverbs or adjectives, never mind complex creatures like the plus quam perfect I had to deal with in college-level Spanish grammar. My life had been reduced to memorizing verbs, adverbs, and adjectives, yet the more words I crammed, the less sense they made. Learning a foreign language became a puzzle consisting of the whole Oxford dictionary chopped up into itty-bitty pieces, where none of the pieces added up to any word I recognized. Notwithstanding, I studied late into each night, until I was ready to drop from exhaustion.

The brightest feature of all the studying was how much my new academic zeal pleased my mother and stepfather. Not once did they guess why I studied so hard. And each night, without exception, I would drink myself into a haze and take refuge in the black-and-white photographs of Madrid and Barcelona in my history textbook as windows through which to glimpse the freedom that could be mine if I kept up my degree of perseverance. I had to believe in my escape plan and keep going because it was my road to Chirag. In bed, waiting to fall asleep, I would close my eyes and see him as I had seen him last.

***

In December 1978, I had been engaged to Rajat for a month when I graduated high school at seventeen years old. On the surface, I had to pretend I was happy Rajat would marry me soon. Inside, however, I wished I were dead because, with every passing day, I hated Rajat more, yet I couldn't tell anybody that detail. Only my unruly mind never stopped dreaming of how my life might have been if I were an ordinary girl in America, like Jennifer Cavilleri in *Love Story*. I imagined I was an English honors student at Radcliffe or Harvard, whereas in reality, I didn't even have the freedom to study English in India.

During my first semester at the polytechnic, after coming home on an early-February afternoon, I headed out again to buy milk from an iron cow, a concrete refrigeration unit that stored fresh milk accessible with a metal token sold by a person inside a booth. The iron cow was located next to a triangular park, where my childhood playmates were playing cricket.

But in India, from puberty onward, children had to ignore the opposite gender. Therefore, milk can swinging from one hand, I cast the briefest glance in my old friends' direction to see one teenage boy perched on the park railing, watching the game. My body lit on fire. I remembered his face peeking over the sidewall of our house with Didima in plain sight. I relived the thrill of watching his glee as he launched a paper plane tied to a stubby-stemmed rose to land inches behind Didima tending to her rose pots. Yet I approached the lady behind the iron-cow window, pretending I hadn't noticed him. His shoulder-length hair and a wiry body didn't disguise the impish tilt to his head I remembered so well. Heart hammering, I hurried away, wondering if he had seen or recognized me.

At eleven o'clock the next morning, a knock on our back door had me face-to-face with Chirag, the physical materialization of Oliver Barrett IV from *Love Story*. He was certainly as handsome, and we both stared at each other, at a loss for words. *Did he notice the splinters of blue paint flaking off our door where he had drawn that heart with a red crayon?* After years of harsh sunlight, the blue had all but peeled away. The door resembled a piece of driftwood, like my life.

"Do you know who he is?" Ganju had accompanied Chirag.

I nodded shyly. "I recognized him last night while you guys were playing cricket."

"I owe you an apology." Chirag held forth a sprig of jasmine.

"For?" I smiled. He had remembered how much I loved jasmine.

"For treating you the way I did before I left India. I should have talked to you. I—"

I placed a finger to my lips. "Don't." I looked at Ganju. "Ganju told me what my grandma did. It's her diabetes." I raised the jasmine sprig to my nose. "She's a hundred times worse now. She forgets words and phrases. The doctor diagnosed her with dementia two weeks ago, though she's only sixty-five years old. He said it's been developing in her brain for a long time."

"Either way." Chirag rubbed the back of his neck. "All these years, I've dreamed of how I would apologize to you."

"Apology accepted." I smiled again. "But please don't remind me anymore of how sick my grandma is."

"Can we come in?" Chirag gestured with his hand.

I hesitated. "Er, are you sure you want to? I can't predict how my grandma will react."

"Yes, I do. To forgive her."

I showed them in, chewing on my lower lip. "Didima, it's Chirag. He's visiting from the States. He came to say hi to us."

"Oh. Would you boys like a cup of tea? Noor, don't slouch like an alley cat. Straighten up and stand tall. If you don't behave like a lady, who'll believe you are one?"

Chirag smiled at me. "Sure, Auntie. I'd love a cup of tea."

I rushed away.

Chirag was midsentence "…we live in Virginia Beach, Auntie…" when I darted back in and lied, "I can't serve them tea, Didima. The milk curdled." I had no other excuse to hustle the two boys out of Didima's unpredictable presence. By the doorway, I muttered, "Wait for me by the milk booth at four sharp."

That evening, the winter sky darkened as Chirag and I huddled on a cement bench in another park, hands intertwined, impervious to the cold while our breaths intermingled in cloudy puffs.

"What grade are you in?" Chirag placed an arm around my shivering shoulders. "If we sit close, we'll be warmer."

"I'm not in school. I study interior design at the women's polytechnic. It's right across from my old school bus stop by Ring Road. And you? Are you in college? You're a year older than me."

Chirag shook his head. "Not yet. I'll graduate high school in May."

"How come? Shouldn't you be in college already?"

"Not in the States. Out there, high school goes up to the twelfth grade, not like here, until the eleventh." Chirag took my chin. "What's all this I hear about you and a fiancé? Is it true?"

I nodded. "It's my grandma's plan, not mine. She wants me married before she dies." I explained Didima's rationale to save me from my mother and stepfather.

"Can you break it?"

"Why would I do that?" I had to be cautious about Chirag's intentions after my Rajat experience.

"So we can be together. Why else? Can I kiss you?"

I fidgeted with my shirt collar, so happy I wanted to jump up and hug Chirag but scared to appear too eager. *Yet would Chirag want to be with me if he knew I wasn't a virgin? I wouldn't learn the answer to that question because I would never tell him. I would not lose Chirag again. Not over Rajat.*

"Will you refuse me?" Chirag bit the inside corner of his mouth, the same as he used to do ever since I had known him.

"I've kissed my fiancé, and I don't enjoy it."

"Can we change that?"

I leaned in, lips parted, and gazed into Chirag's impossibly thick-lashed eyes. Instantly, I knew Chirag and I would connect in a way I had never connected with Rajat. Chirag pulled me close, smoothing my hair back.

"Mmm, you smell good." I burrowed my face in his neck. "Nutty and lemony. What is it?"

"Vetiver by Guerlain. I never use any other cologne." Chirag kissed my shoulder.

"You know what I wish?"

"What?" He played with my hair.

"That you would have kissed me in the Jain temple. Remember?"

"Take a guess." He pressed his lips into mine.

As our kiss deepened, I felt as if Chirag had plugged into my soul, and suddenly, I knew I couldn't lose him. When that fear grew too intense, I pulled back. "I have to go." Thus, regaining some control, I added, "My grandma thinks I'm visiting a girlfriend. Heaven help us if she wanders out into the cold to search for me."

But Chirag pulled me back into his arms. "When will I see you again?"

I wanted to say, "See me forever," but I said, "I can skip classes tomorrow."

"I'll wait at your old school bus stop on Ring Road."

Chirag was already waiting when I arrived at seven a.m. In the morning light, the memory of the previous night's kiss was visible in his eyes. "Would it scare you if we went to a hotel?" My eyes widened, but Chirag raised his right hand. "I swear, not to make love." His eyes bore into mine. "You're the girl I'm going to marry. We'll save lovemaking for our wedding night."

Nonetheless, the anxiety of the Rajat experience caused me to blurt. "You will keep your promise, right? You won't try to make love to me or anything?"

"Noor. You've known me since we were kids. You don't trust me?" Chirag's eyes held hurt.

"I dooo. I swear I do." I touched his hand. "I'm sorry I sounded like I didn't."

"So? Can we go to a hotel? It's too cold to sit on a park bench all day. Moreover, this is India. You want to be caught kissing at a park in broad daylight?"

"No." I shuddered. "They'd stone us or beat us or both."

"Hotel? Yes, no?"

I nodded, wanting more than ever to experience our connection from yesterday one more time.

Chirag hugged me and hailed a passing taxi.

At the reception desk of the Hotel Oberoi Sheraton, near the neighborhood of Nissamuddin, which I didn't know well, Chirag mesmerized me with his polish and suavity to book us a room. But soon, my apprehension of spending time alone in a hotel room with a boy converted to shame for never having *seen* a hotel room. I gawked at the beige-and-blue woven floor-to-ceiling curtains, the matching bedspread, nightstands, and desk, and stopped myself from sniffing the faintly flowery-smelling air. *Did Chirag notice my gauche behavior?*

"Will you worry if I take my sweater off?" Chirag's eyelashes blinked in question.

"Worry about what?"

"I don't know. Like I'm maybe undressing?"

I placed my hands on my warming cheeks. "Of course not. I have to take my sweater off too. This room is boiling. Why is it so hot in here?"

"Central heating. Five-star hotels around the world require central heating, even though no one in India has it in their houses. Otherwise, they lose their operating license."

I filed away that piece of information as Chirag kicked off his brown leather American boots and climbed under the covers of the king-sized bed. He patted the space beside him. After a pause, my head landed on a plumped pillow.

We huddled under the covers for half the day, kissing and cuddling, where Chirag didn't once suggest we remove our clothes, making me trust him more.

"Are you hungry? Let's order food." Chirag twirled the end of a swath of my long black hair.

While we waited, I crossed my hands under my head. "Remember the day you and Ganju came and asked me to choose a boyfriend?"

"I remember your face when I asked which of your hands was Hindu and which was Muslim."

"How did I look?"

"As if you'd just woken up to how nuts it was to be called half of anything."

"I fell in love with you in that instant."

"Why?"

"Because, to you, I wasn't a freak."

Chirag emitted a guttural sound and pulled me to him. "You will leave this fiancé of yours, right?" His brow knit in a frown.

"Whenever he comes back from Bombay, in April or May."

"Do you love him?"

I shook my head. "I accepted only because it was a better option than ending up with my mother and stepfather."

"Well, screw him and screw your mother and stepfather too. What was your question?"

"Oh, yeah. On the day you and Ganju came to me, Ganju was all neatness, and you looked as if you'd been pulled out of a dumpster. Why was that?"

"Oh, didn't I ever tell you? I fell in love with you the minute I laid eyes on you. You were playing hopscotch on the street, and an older girl reproached you because you were playing it wrong. From then on, I couldn't get your woebegone face out of my head. The day we came to you, I had told the boys I intended to be your boyfriend, and they jumped all over me. 'Why?' they said. 'Why you? You're new here, and she belongs to our neighborhood. She's ours.' So I said, 'Okay, let's have a boxing match. Whoever wins can have Noor.'"

"And you won?"

"Yes—no." Chirag laughed. "I won against ten guys until only Ganju was left. Then Ganju said, 'Chirag, I know you'll win this fight. It's in your eyes. But what if Noor doesn't want you? Why don't we go ask her to choose instead?'"

"Jesus! Tell Ganju to become a lawyer."

The next day was our last day together. Chirag would fly home to Virginia Beach that night. "Hotel?" Chirag stood at the bus stop.

"I guess." *Would he keep his promise and not make love to me?*

But in a different room in the same hotel, Chirag kissed my face and neck, repeating how much he loved me. "I'll talk to my dad tonight. I'll tell him I want to marry you as soon as possible."

"Does he know it was my grandma who got you into trouble?"

"Yes, but he doesn't mind, because I explained your grandma's diabetes and dementia."

"Well, thank God." I nestled in the crook of his arm, dreaming of becoming Mrs. Noor Jagdev in America.

That evening, Chirag met me in the darkness of a back alley close to Didima's house. We hugged in the dry winter chill, delaying our inevitable separation. "I have a present for you." He handed me a postcard-sized box wrapped in newspaper and taped to a paper plane.

"Sorry, I have no rose for it. They're hard to find in the winter."

"What is it?" I smiled in the dim light of the lamppost he leaned against.

"Open it and see."

Inside was a bottle of perfume, Diorissimo, by Dior.

"You'll know why I'm giving you this the minute you smell it."

"It's jasmine." I teared up.

"Yes. For the flowers I didn't give you all these years. And I have another present." Chirag fished into his jeans pocket and dangled what appeared to be a silver chain near my face.

Its pendant reflected the lamplight and flashed an elusive fire.

"What gemstone is it?" I grabbed it. "I love gemstones because my grandpa was a geologist."

"It's a diamond on a white-gold chain. Promise me you'll wear it until we marry for real this time around." He unclasped the chain and encircled my neck with it. "Turn, so I can fasten it." He kissed the back of my neck.

"Are you proposing again?" I teased, knowing how serious he was by the expensiveness of his gift.

"Could I marry anyone but you? I've loved you since I was eleven years old."

"Will you write to me?" I ran my fingers over his face to memorize the shape.

"I'm not a letter writer."

"Then how will we keep in touch?" My fingers angled the diamond pendant to catch the glow of the streetlamp.

"Expect me here by the end of May. I'll fly back after graduation."

"I'll fly back after graduation" had been Chirag's last words to me.

In the darkness of my parents' second bedroom, I opened my eyes. We had kissed one more time and parted without words because words couldn't describe how we felt. I had to remember that kiss and keep studying Spanish. I closed my eyes on my narrow bed, hoping to see Chirag in my dreams.

PERIWINKLE

11

I HAD ALREADY TURNED TWENTY BY October of 1981 when Teddy wrote to inform my mother he was coming to visit from Canada. I digested the news, recalling how many times Didima had implored Teddy in letters to come see her one last time, but he never had.

"Why is he coming?" I asked. "I don't know," replied my mother.

"Will you tell Teddy of my criminal record?"

Teddy had never liked problems. I was sure he wouldn't want to see me if he found out I had issues with the law.

"No. I see no point in it. He won't be here long enough for it to matter."

"Where will he sleep? In the drawing room?"

"No. He's too snooty to stay with me. He'll rent a bungalow at the club."

By "the club," my mother meant the Delhi Gymhkana Club. It was one of the oldest, pre-independence institutions in Delhi, and Teddy was an automatic club member, thanks to being Dadu's son.

On a crisp autumn morning, I skipped college to visit Teddy. He answered my knock on the porch door of a courtesy bungalow for members of the Delhi Gymkhana Club. Coming to the stately, old area always reminded me of Didima's oldest sister, Auntie Geeta, and our six-month stay in her beautiful home when Didima, Teddy, and I had first come to live in Delhi. In those days, at six years old, I hadn't understood how poor Didima had become after Dadu had died and his best friend had swindled Didima out of Dadu's entire land inheritance.

"Ma shona!" exclaimed Teddy. "Look at you! So thin and beautiful." He greeted me with a kiss and a hug. "Why, people who don't know us would assume you're my daughter, not Jhummur's. How do you do it? What perfume is that? It's divine."

"Oh, it's Diorissimo by Dior." My heart winged back to a dark South Extension alley on a winter's night. "It's the scent of jasmine."

"India sells Dior now?"

I changed the subject. "So, what brings you to India?" I wanted to add, *Because you never did come for Didima or me. Did you love us? Did you ever regret letting Didima down so badly? Would it have been so hard for you to send for us from Canada?*—but I let it go. Antagonizing Teddy wouldn't alter the past. It would only stop him wanting to see me. And any change from my parents' company was a welcome one.

"The club," Teddy replied. "The gymkhana's new board is opening its doors to riffraff. Since I've been away too long, they threatened to terminate my membership, as I don't live here anymore."

The club? You came all the way back to India for your club membership, but you couldn't come visit your own mother? I forced myself to say, "You look terrific. Your hair resembles Dadu's more than ever because you have so much gray in it." Teddy had always been tall and light-skinned with Didima's huge, dark eyes that even his prescription tortoiseshell glasses could never dim. Those, the aquiline nose, his soft, springy hair, and a sportsman physique had never failed to procure Teddy any girl he wanted, but there he was, single at forty-five.

"Don't talk of how gray my hair is, shona." Teddy ran a manicured hand through his mop. "My Panaeker genes got me graying at twenty-five, like Baba."

"Would you prefer to be bald?"

"You're right, ma shona. You always were wiser than your years. But let's focus on you. How do you stay so thin? I gained weight the minute I turned forty."

"I run every day."

"And do you speak Spanish? Jhummur said you did."

"Fluently."

"Tomorrow I'll put your Spanish to a real test. I have a midmorning cocktail party at the Colombian ambassador's house. Be here at nine. You'll come with me."

"A morning cocktail?" I tilted my head. "Don't cocktails happen in the evening?"

"Ma shona, you do have a lot to learn, don't you?"

I couldn't believe I would attend a party. "How do you know the Colombian ambassador?"

"I met the president of Colombia on a job. He said if I ever came to New Delhi, I should contact his niece. She is the ambassador here."

My parents didn't object to my missing college or attending the party, since Teddy would be present. For it, I left my henna-tinted hair loose, accentuating my high cheekbones and sharp jawline by a mere hint of pink lipstick.

Teddy told guest after guest, "Please speak to her in Spanish. She says she speaks it, but I want to know for sure."

His insistence was so annoying that at one point, I asked, "Why does it mean so much to you whether I speak Spanish or not?"

"Because I am dating a rich widow from Uruguay in Canada. If she ever meets you, I know your Spanish will impress her."

I wanted to ask him if he could still consider taking me to live with him in Canada, but I didn't bother. Teddy didn't inconvenience himself for anyone else. *Haven't I learned that yet? Why am I letting the brief glitter of his presence blind me to my actual reality?* It was best to enjoy the moment, an interlude spent with people to whom I meant nothing and whom I would never see again.

Nevertheless, under the late-morning sun of October, I couldn't help but smile when Peruvian Ambassador José Santanilla and his wife, Angela, from Long Island, New York, said *hola* to me.

The cheeriness of the introduction inspired Angela Santanilla, with her Ava Gardner looks, to lapse into her native English. "You must meet our daughter, Isabel. She'll be here in two weeks." Angela chose a salmon and caper hors d'oeuvre from a passing tray.

"Where is she coming from?" I followed Angela's example and took an hors d'oeuvre, impeccable in my social graces from a lifetime of Didima's training on how to behave like a lady even when we were at our most impoverished.

"Spain. The poor girl lost her husband two months ago." Angela bit into her chosen snack as José Santanilla hurried off to say hello to another newcomer to the gathering.

My ears burned so much at the mention of Spain that I touched them, hoping no one would notice if they reddened. "I'm so sorry. How old is poor Isabel?" *Could Isabel become my contact in Spain if I manage to escape my mother?* I couldn't control my racing thoughts. And they all led to Chirag.

"She's thirty-four, and my granddaughter five."

"What a tragedy. Will she be here long?"

"I hope so. We'll have you and your uncle over as soon as she arrives. You'll meet our son, Tikku, too. He comes from Nice to celebrate Christmas with us."

I pictured the flower-sprinkled French Riviera described in James Bond thrillers while my heart hammered. *If I could become friends with Isabel, my parents would perhaps let me go to Spain to visit her… then nothing would stop Chirag from meeting me in Spain and marrying me.* "Has Isabel ever been to India?"

"Oh!" exclaimed Angela. "She probably knows India better than you do. Isabel and her husband spent two years in the seventies traveling through India as hippies."

I laughed. "That's not hard. I haven't traveled at all, neither in India nor abroad."

Angela's periwinkle eyes widened to appear bluer than a second ago. "But your Spanish! It's unbelievable. How do you do it?"

"I study all the time." I diluted the bitterness threatening to surface on my face with a smile.

"Practice your Spanish with Isabel. She speaks it better than I do because I never received formal instruction in it. I can't wait to have you over."

Two weeks later, Teddy was smoking a Dunhill cigarette, relaxing on the porch of his gymkhana club member's bungalow when I arrived. "Ma shona, tell Jhummur when you go home tonight you'll sleep over here on Friday. We're invited to a private cocktail hour at the residence of the Peruvian ambassador."

"Where do they live? In the Diplomatic Enclave?"

That was the famous stretch of avenue in the district of Chanakya Puri, where foreign countries had purchased land for a song after the Indian Independence. The embassy complexes were spectacular.

"No. Their residence is in Shantiniketan." In the social hierarchy, Shantiniketan was less upscale than Chanakya Puri, but it was pompous enough for many countries to have their embassy residences there, including the Colombian ambassador, whose place we had visited the other morning.

At home, I purposely praised the Peruvian ambassador and his wife and their upcoming invitation, emphasizing how much Teddy appreciated and respected them. I wanted the name "Isabel" to register in my parents' psyche in case Isabel and I became friends. My manipulative behavior sickened me, but that was what house arrest, and all the beatings I had received, had done. Slowly, even my temper was going from hot to cold and calculating. As the French saying went, revenge was a platter best served cold.

On the evening of the Santanilla's invitation, I discovered the Peruvian residence was a mansion perhaps fifteen houses down from the Colombian residence. At its doorstep, Angela Santanilla greeted us, every bit her bubbly, Italian-American self. I extended one cheek to be kissed in greeting, South American style.

"Come in, my dear. Our son, Tikku, arrived last night. He's eager to meet you after all I've told him about you."

In their chic drawing room, Tikku stood when he saw me. His windblown bronze hair and long-lashed green eyes immediately brought Chirag to my mind, though Chirag's hair and eyes were dark. Upon closer scrutiny, the real similarity between Tikku and Chirag was their noses. They both had strong, straight noses with the slightest convexity to the bridge. And they were both tall and slender yet muscular.

Within half an hour, I was deep in conversation with the French Riviera paragon regarding the flowers that grew in Nice, where he and his girlfriend lived on a hillside cottage overlooking the sea.

"Come visit Nice once Papá retires—" Tikku said.

Right then, Angela exclaimed, "Ah, here comes Isabel!"

I stared at the willowy blonde possessing a Madonna-like grace who had stepped into the drawing room.

She wore a leopard-patterned full-body leotard. To enhance the feline effect, Isabel had jammed a furry leopard-ears hairband on her flowing curls. The whole outfit contrasted starkly with her natural poise. "Hola." She had a Spanish-from-Spain accent. "My mamá can't stop talking about you. We must meet for coffee. Right now, I'm off to a Halloween party with Sergio."

"*Cuando quieras.*" My eyes shifted to take in the gentleman standing head-to-head beside Isabel. His hair and half his face were hidden behind a corn-colored lion's mane.

"*¿Dónde aprendiste a hablar un Español tan perfecto?*" His smile exposed large, even teeth.

"I study Spanish honors at JNU."

"*¡Niña!*" exclaimed José Santanilla. "This is Sergio Santander, the counselor at our embassy. Congratulations are in order—he was promoted from first secretary to counselor this morning."

That night, I went to bed on a sofa in Teddy's club bungalow, too wound up for sleep. Finally, I had caught a break. *But will Isabel follow through and invite me to have coffee with her? What is my surveillance reporting to Officer Das? What if he decides to squash my new social life? Right now, Teddy's presence is endorsing all this unfamiliar activity. What will happen once he leaves?*

12

To my utter relief, Isabel invited me to coffee the following week while Teddy was still in town.

After much debate, I told my mother, "I'd like to be her friend because she just lost her husband." I made sure Isabel sounded saintly, when in reality, I was unsure if she was dating that Peruvian counselor, Sergio.

"How old is she?"

Inside, I cringed as my mother gave me a noncommittal power-trip glance. If she vetoed the idea, there would be no further discussion.

"Thirty-four." *Will Isabel's age help or hurt my mother's decision?* "She has a daughter of five."

"Fine," my mother said. "But I'm going to discuss this with Officer Das. You can't be friends with her if he has any objections."

"Right." I lowered my eyes, lest she saw how much I hated her.

For the coffee invitation, Angela baked an American apple pie, which I fell in love with. While Isabel, Tikku, Angela, and I chattered in English and ate apple pie, I found out that Isabel was not dating Sergio Santander. She was very much mourning her late husband, who had been a Basque from Barcelona, where she would live once her trip to visit her parents ended. I asked her when that would be. "By August next year, when Papá retires."

"Yes," Tikku said. "Remember I said come visit us in Nice? Papá and Mamá have a villa near where I live."

I left that intimate coffee party with my head in a whirl regarding all the possibilities on how and when I could leave India. Yet try as I might, I couldn't discount how quickly my mother and her best friend, Das, could foil any plan of mine.

But up in heaven, God did rule, because my parents and Officer Das did not squash my budding friendship with Isabel once Teddy left town. By March of 1982, my mother even agreed to let me sleep over at Isabel's.

The contrast between that reality and my parents' home was so great, I learned to compartmentalize. Notwithstanding, whenever my mother refused to let me sleep over at the Peruvian residence, I obeyed because angering her would be stupid.

I finally revealed Chirag's existence to Isabel in April, when I knew she trusted me and I trusted her. Skipping the whole house-arrest saga, I said, "You're my one excuse to go to Barcelona. You won't ditch me, will you?"

"Nope. Come anytime you want. We'll determine the Chirag angle when you arrive."

Soon. I will see Chirag soon.

Without meaning to, I came to depend on the Saturday nights when Angela baked her anchovy pizza napolitana from scratch to be accompanied by ice-cold cans of Heineken. The familiar meal always ended with Angela's ice cream fruit cake—yellow pound cake sides filled with homemade mincemeat pie filling folded into vanilla ice cream. During the summer of that year, it was my most favorite dessert in the world.

For me, Isabel's company was truly novel because she thought completely outside the little box of my Indian upbringing. Unlike me and my sheltered school and college friends, Isabel disregarded the acute segregation of class and castes so completely, her daughter's nanny was an untouchable. From Isabel, I learned it was perfectly okay to hug Lila, the nanny. No one vaporized. No lightning bolt from heaven cooked us, nor did anyone die. The one thing that died was my own inhibition, and with every minute I spent in Isabel's healing presence, I rejected my country more—the country that had condemned my own half-caste existence throughout my life.

Arriving for one such weekend sleepover on a Friday afternoon, I pushed the side door into the Santanilla's home, when the door was pulled out of my reach. My arm was at half-mast when out came Sergio Santander, slipping a folded piece of paper into the left pocket of a dark-blue suit.

"Noor? Hi! Isabel praises you all the time. We should get together soon."

"Hi, of course—" I raced indoors to avoid further conversation, miserably embarrassed by my disheveled hair and casual jeans-and-sneakers attire, standard college clothes to wear all week. I caught Angela hurrying out of the kitchen. "What was Sergio doing here? He saw me looking like a ragbag."

"Oh, sweetheart—wait till you're fifty. Then you'll know what 'ragbag' means without the help of fancy clothes and makeup."

"What did he want?" I dropped my heavy book bag on the main-floor foyer.

"He and I exchange recipes all the time. Today, he wanted my salmon mousse recipe. I don't mind, except when he cooks my recipes to taste better than I can."

That evening, at the Santanillas' dinner table, I munched on the sharp taste of anchovy slivers on my bite of pizza. "So, what's the deal with Sergio?" I asked Isabel. "Is he married? Divorced? Single—"

"Oh, he's bi." Isabel giggled.

I paused in my chewing. "What does that mean? Does it mean—"

"Shhh," whispered Isabel. "Later."

"Isabel," admonished José. "Stop being a rumor mill. Sergio is like a son to me."

Upstairs, in Isabel's bedroom, I exclaimed, "What did you *mean*—is Sergio bisexual? He's into boys *and* girls? How do you know this?"

"Because we are best friends, and a week ago, we spent ten days together visiting Dharamshala and the Ajanta and Ellora caves. We shared a king-sized bed for Christ's sake, to cut costs."

"So you slept with him?" My eyes goggled in excitement.

"Yes, but not in the way you mean it. Did I think of it? Absolutely. Especially when he didn't mention the subject three nights in a row. But on the fourth night, he brought up the topic himself. He said, given a choice, he enjoys men more... something about the depth of the mind connection."

"So he's gay?"

"No. He likes women too. He's had many girlfriends."

"Well, as Oscar Wilde said, it doubles his chances of finding a date."

"Not in South America. Peru is rabidly homophobic."

"But what about his housemate, Jorge?" I had met Jorge Alvez at several cocktail parties. "Jorge is so outrageously gay. Each time he speaks, I can't tell if he is prouder of his two sons or of being homosexual."

"Jorge isn't South American. He's Portuguese," Isabel corrected. "Europe is a lot more liberal regarding sexual preferences. I'll bet Sergio's family has no inkling he's attracted to men too. Lima is the epitome of a hypocritical, tight-knit provincial society. I should know. I spent from fifteen to eighteen there, after being born and raised between Amsterdam, Frankfurt, and Paris."

"But don't Peruvian diplomats serve six years abroad and three at home?"

"Not back when Papá was young. I had never even seen Lima until I turned fifteen. I hated it."

At night, in Isabel's king-sized bed, which we shared during my sleepovers, my last waking memory was of how dashingly handsome Sergio was in a conquistador, old-fashioned sort of way. His reddish-brown hair, mustache, and goatee offset his green-brown eyes. He didn't appear bisexual. But how would I know what bisexual looks like? Until attending JNU, I had never been exposed to a homosexual person like our oldest Spanish professor, Andres Verona, who was outstandingly effeminate and flirtatious with his male stu-dents. Sergio wasn't effeminate at all, and he was as handsome as Chirag but in a different way.

13

I GREW SO ACCUSTOMED TO SHARING quality time with the Santanillas and participating in Angela's tea parties that their company became a mental refuge I craved constantly.

Come July of 1982, the New Delhi lawns were scorched to a yellow-brown when I tripped into the air-conditioned relief of the Santanillas' home one Friday afternoon for yet another sleepover.

I dropped my schoolbag on the Persian rug of the dayroom floor and slipped off my shoes, ready to attack Angela's apple pie, when Angela said, "Remind me to mail off an invitation for you to our national day cocktail party. I hope your parents will allow you to spend that weekend with us."

"But, Mamá," interjected Isabel, "I want Noor to sleep over the following Thursday night, before I leave. Noor's mother is always a pain about allowing two sleepovers too soon in a row."

"Whoa, whoa." I raised my arms. "Slow down! Where are you off to, and when is this national day?"

"Right, you don't know, do you?" Angela addressed me but glanced at Isabel over the top of her gold-rimmed reading cheaters.

"Come sit." Isabel patted the paisley-patterned plumpness of the sofa she sat on. "I'm leaving for Barcelona."

"For how long?" I forgot how hungry I was.

"I'm afraid for good. A friend of mine opened a jewelry shop in downtown Barcelona. She's offered to hire me as manager and buyer because I know all the gemstone centers in Delhi and Goa. I don't have a choice. With Papá retiring in August, my freeloading with them out here is over, and with Giovanni dead, I have no recourse but to work to support Tata and me."

My stomach felt hollow. I wished Isabel had warned me, but she had no way of doing so since my parents didn't have a phone. She depended on me to call her to set up any of our get-togethers.

I addressed Angela. "Ange, when are you leaving? August is around the corner."

"I leave for Nice a week after Isabel. I don't want José around for any part of setting up our new home. He'll drive me crazy. I'll do it with Tikku's help. José can join us once he's done here."

On July 28, the Peruvian national day, Isabel laid aside a pale-green linen dress of hers for me to wear. She said, "You look lovely in green."

At six o'clock, the summer evening was bright when I stood close to a blooming jasmine bush on the residence porch. In front of me, the familiar diplomatic crowd milled in elegant splendor. That night, I was still the smiling, amusing, intelligent Noor who spoke fluent Spanish. *Will I ever see these people once Angela and Isabel leave? For that matter, will I ever see Angela and Isabel again?* I couldn't let that hope go. My whole thesis of reencountering Chirag rested on visiting Isabel in Barcelona. Yet inside me, a tiny voice whispered, *How? How will any of that materialize?*

"*¿Tan sola, tan temprano? Qué piensas?*" A hand landed on the thin shoulder strap of my linen dress.

I spun around. "Sergio! *Hola. ¿Cómo vas?*" I didn't *know* Sergio, despite Isabel and I discussing him in detail several times. I scrutinized his face for effeminate ways and didn't see any.

That day, Sergio's hazel eyes appeared lion yellow, like Dadu's used to, in the light of the setting sun. He looked incredibly sophisticated in a gray pinstripe suit and a claret woven silk tie. His clothing accentuated the red glints in his wavy brown hair and goatee.

Unaware of my scrutiny, Sergio spoke to me in Spanish. "Tell me, why did you choose to study Spanish when most Indians are such Francophiles?"

"If you must know," I replied, also in Spanish, "I wanted to study English, not French or Spanish. But my mother had her way. Spanish was her dream, not mine." We continued to converse in his language, but Sergio kept interrupting to correct my sentence constructions.

"Jesus, Sergio!" I exploded in English. "I don't want to speak to you in Spanish anymore! Your constant corrections are causing me to make mistakes."

Taken aback, Sergio protested. "But you're *not* making mistakes. You could just say it differently."

My cheeks warmed in annoyance. "Oh yeah? Let's see how you would react if I interrupted you constantly and told you how to say this or that differently in English."

My outburst brought José Santanilla to my rescue.

"Are you harassing her, Sergio?" José approached us with his birdlike gait, smoothing back his silver hair.

"Yes, he *is*," I complained.

"God, Sergio. You're such a bore." José clasped my elbow. "Come on, child. Come meet the Argentine ambassador and his wife. They met your uncle Teddy, so they're curious to meet you."

Later that evening, Sergio cornered me again. That time, he addressed me in faultless English. "Do you always have such a temper?" His grin took the edge off his words.

I grinned back. "Why? You want to give me more Spanish lessons?"

"To tell you the truth, I wouldn't mind. Would you? You do have a gift for language."

"And how would you know that?" But his praise thrilled me.

"Because I speak four myself. How many do you speak?"

"I can communicate in Hindi, Bengali, Punjabi, and Urdu, but my favorite language is English. You won't want to hear this, but I detest Spanish. It was an absolute misery to learn—plus, my mother forced me into it when all I craved was to go to college for English."

"Let's go out for coffee sometime. I'd like to get to know you."

I remembered my surveillance. "Sure. You, Isabel, and I can go out anytime."

After the cocktail party was over, Isabel spread a dhurrie rug on the terrace beside her room for us to lie on.

I was admiring the silver of the moonlight on Isabel's blond ringlets when she said, "You should consider Sergio once I'm gone. He thinks the world of your Spanish and the way you conduct yourself."

"What does Sergio know of how I conduct myself?"

"Well, he knows because he is super observant. He told me he has watched you for months, anytime he sees you at my parents' parties. Apparently, you avoid all the known diplomatic bachelor scavengers and focus your time on practicing Spanish with the older Latin American ambassadors and their wives.

That behavior impressed him. Get together with him. He's a great guy. I don't know this for sure, but I'm guessing he wants to date you."

"Date me? How old is he? He looks old, and I'm only twenty! Besides—my heart is stuck on Chirag."

"Noor, how do you know Chirag's heart is stuck on you after all these years?"

"I don't, but I refuse to give up on him until I reach Barcelona and contact him."

"You should see Sergio if he asks you out. He has been intrigued by you since the day he saw you because of how perfect your Spanish is."

"Even though he's bi?"

"So what? Bi means he likes girls *and* boys. He's a year older than me, which means he's thirty-six. I know he wants to marry and dreams of having kids. If he calls you, go out with him… what do you have to lose? If Chirag comes through for you, great. Otherwise, if your parents don't let you come to Barcelona, do you want to marry an Indian your parents choose for you? Wouldn't Sergio be the better choice?"

"No! I love Chirag. I can't… I won't marry anyone else. I'll get my degree and come stay with you in Spain." But I was secretly pleased to know Sergio liked me.

14

Too soon, Isabel left for Barcelona, but the vivid memory of that silent Tihar Jail walk prevented me from giving her a letter to post to Chirag from Spain. A week later, Angela left for Nice, making me feel utterly abandoned.

In the relentless heat of August, I resumed traveling back and forth from home to school, school to home, on unending public bus rides.

What if Isabel was right about Sergio's interest in me? I shook my head. I hadn't heard a word from either José Santanilla or Sergio. *And why would I?* I wasn't linked to the Peruvian embassy in any way. My friendship with Angela and Isabel had been strictly private.

At home, in total desperation, I brought up the subject of my possible trip to Barcelona after I was to receive my BA degree that coming January. "Can I go visit Isabel during my summer vacation?"

My mother's expression was inscrutable. "Go to Spain once you graduate, but I'll let your husband take you there. Maybe the groom of our choice can take you for a honeymoon."

By the end of August, I was at my lowest. As I arrived home from college one evening, my mother handed me an already-torn-open, handwritten invitation from Sergio Santander. The gist of it read:

My housemates and I will host a final but informal farewell party for my dearest boss and colleague, Ambassador José Santanilla. I hope you'll come to it. Please RSVP as soon as you receive this.

He remembered me! I fingered the embossed card paper, unsurprised my mother had already opened the letter but touched Sergio had written the invitation in English. My heart thudded. "Sergio is the counselor at the Peruvian embassy. Can I attend this party?"

I couldn't read my mother's face as she replied, "Yes, but don't take my consent for granted." *Of course. Of course my mother had to include the threat component so I never forget who is the boss. But one day, I will find a way to escape her.* That possibility was my constant companion.

Without Isabel's wardrobe to borrow dresses from, I wore a sky-blue *Chanderi* gauze sari to the gathering. I loved that sari because Didima had worn it on her first date with Dadu.

At the party, as soon as I spotted Sergio, I asked, "Hi, can you drop me off at school after this ends? I don't want to be out alone after dark."

"Of course." Sergio spoke in English. "But why would you go to school at that hour when I can drop you home?"

"No, no. My parents live far away. I'll stay the night in a friend's room at the JNU Hostel."

Throughout the evening, I waited for Sergio to talk to me more, but he was so busy as the host that conversation never happened. Whenever he was near me, others joined us, making the conversation general. The status quo really disappointed me, since I didn't want to go out with Sergio alone and have Officer Das rain on my parade. However, I also wasn't willing to come across as a floozie chasing him by seeking him out.

Sergio was finally free to give me a ride at midnight. "I heard you mention to three people you want to go to Spain. Mind if I ask why?"

"I have to escape my parents."

"But why?"

"Because they'll marry me to some Indian slob, and I hate the idea." I wished I could add, *I detest all Indian men for everything they've done to me. Chirag is different because he doesn't even look Indian, let alone behave like one.*

"Do they have someone in mind?" Sergio's glance was quizzical in the gloom within his car.

I flicked my hair back from my shoulders, breathing hard. "If they did, they wouldn't tell me. I have to find a way to escape to Spain as soon as possible."

"You sound desperate."

"I am."

"Then marry me instead."

"What did you just say?" I pitched forward to grab the passenger-side door handle.

"What are you doing?"

"Getting ready to jump out of the car!"

"Why?"

"Because you're either drunk or crazy or both."

"No, I'm not."

"But you hardly know me. Besides, don't you prefer men to women?" *Yikes. I shouldn't have said that.*

"What?" exclaimed Sergio. "Who told you that?"

I looked at Sergio unhappily but couldn't see a way out. "Isabel did."

"She's wrong." Sergio ran a harried hand through his mop of wavy hair. "I told Isabel that because I'm not into blondes and I didn't want to hurt her after she just lost her husband. Besides, aren't same-sex experiences common in India? Boys and girls can't date here. My Indian friends tell me most Indian adolescents have at least one such experience before they are married off. It doesn't mean they're gay."

"Errr, I suppose not." I felt confused and uncertain. *Yet why would Sergio lie to me?* I peered at him in the dark. "Would you wait for me until I came back from Spain?"

"Nope. It's now or never. I won't wait, like the Elvis Presley song goes."

"And if I don't marry you, will you tell the Spanish embassy to refuse me a visa?"

"What? Why would you say that?"

I shrugged uncomfortably. "I don't know." *Because I have a criminal record maybe?*

"I'm thirty-six. I won't wait another year."

"But you're so old. I'm only twenty."

"I'm *not* old." Sergio brought his car to a smooth halt by the JNU's Hostel Complex curbside. "You're very young."

"So, why do you want to marry me? You don't know me."

"Because I'm a great judge of people. I can see a good person from a bad one a mile away. Besides, in India, I couldn't date you even if I wanted to, now, could I? I know enough about you to be willing to take that risk."

Oh, Sergio, would you propose to me if you knew I wasn't a virgin, have had an abortion, and have a healthy and existing criminal record? The secrets we hide behind a pretty face!

He leaned in to kiss my lips, but I kept my mouth shut, remembering Chirag.

Seeing my reaction, Sergio said, "Don't answer me now. Answer me in a week."

As Sergio's car purred away, I walked through the hostel gate, beset by the new twist in my circumstances. In the darkness, I hitched up my sari to save the hem from getting muddy and trudged uphill toward my friend's dorm entrance. I could always tell Sergio the truth—all of it—and have him run in the opposite direction in no time. *But do I want that?* Good question. *And where does Chirag fit into this puzzle? He doesn't,* answered a voice inside my head.

And what would Officer Das say about me marrying a foreigner if I said yes to Sergio? But why am I even considering this? I barely know Sergio, much less love him... how could I marry him? I rubbed my eyes in the darkness and stared up at the starry summer sky, thinking of Das and his taunts whenever he came over. Taunts like "Are you behaving yourself? Or would you care for a vacation at the women's jail?" while I listened to him in agonized silence.

Either way, I couldn't untangle the silk skein of Sergio's proposal that second. I needed time to process it *without* my parents' interference. *But what if the surveillance people tell Officer Das about Sergio kissing me and he brings it up with my mother and stepfather?* I stopped in my tracks and let go of my sari. The surveillance people couldn't have seen Sergio kiss me in the dark nor heard him propose in the privacy of his car. Sergio had said to answer him in a week. I would take the week. I opened the dorm's main door, making it groan in protest.

15

My first action the next day was to write to Isabel. *Can you think of why Sergio wants to marry me so quickly? He barely knows me...*

Scared to death of Das, I asked my friend Suresh to write Isabel's address in his handwriting and write his name and address as the sender. The subterfuge was threadbare, but hopefully, the only flagged address at the post office was poor Chirag's.

Meanwhile, a day passed, then two, then three, and I knew I wasn't in love with Sergio in the slightest. Yes, he was attractive, but I didn't experience any magnetism toward him as I had with Chirag. Yet marrying Sergio would provide me with a way to leave my parents behind forever, along with India and Indian men. It would also give me access to Isabel and Angela again. Plus, outside my wretched country, with a different last name, no one would ever suspect my Hindu-Muslim origins, much less insult me for them. *And Chirag?* insisted the voice in my head. Marrying Sergio would annihilate that dream.

On day four, I woke up certain I would never escape alone to Spain with my mother in the mix. Spain was a mirage. My mother would never relax her power to let me flee. She enjoyed her domination over me too much. *Yet could I marry someone I don't love?* The answer was no because I wanted to marry Chirag.

By day five, I couldn't handle the pressure. I called Sergio during lunch break. I was heaving with anxiety as I dialed Sergio's number. "Sergio? I can't marry you!"

Silence.

"Sergio, are you there?"

"Yes."

Is he sniffling? "Are you crying?"

"Sort of."

"Why?"

"Because I've never proposed to anyone in my life."

"Well." I gulped. "Isn't it better to know now than tomorrow?" *Why can't he be reasonable about this?*

"On the telephone? I don't even deserve a face-to-face turndown?"

"But what good would that do?" He was pulling me into his vortex, and I couldn't stop it.

"I don't know. I guess I want to see you."

Loath to deny such a minor request, I consented "Okay, I'll come to the embassy tomorrow. I finish early on Fridays, but I won't stay long. I have loads of homework to finish."

I entered the Peruvian embassy on reluctant feet, torn between a desire to run away and the guilt of hurting Sergio more.

Sergio, however, greeted me with a wide smile.

"You aren't mad at me?" The corners of my eyes crinkled tentatively.

"Nope, I'm over it. Can we be friends anyway?"

"If you don't hold it against me that I won't marry you."

Sergio changed the subject. "Do you receive a lot of written work?"

"Of course! It's my third year. I'm buried in homework."

"I could do some of it for you."

"You didn't just say that! Did you mean it?" My eyes widened.

"Sure. Your teachers won't ever know. As a Latin American diplomat, I'm always curious to see how Spanish is taught abroad. This will be my perfect chance."

Over the next two weeks, Sergio did two of my written assignments, which I left with his secretary. Not seeing Sergio was a relief because it lessened my worry about repaying his kindness. A lifetime of Didima's strict Victorian upbringing had ruined me for ever receiving presents. Throughout my life, whenever I got a gift, Didima would wait until the giver was out of earshot then say, "Don't feel so happy! Now I'll have to decide how to reciprocate. That present has a price tag."

After completing the fourth assignment, Sergio put his foot down. "Either you wait to explain it to me in person, or I won't do it." The following time, once I explained the assignment, Sergio said, "I'm off to the Taj Hotel to do embassy paperwork. Want to accompany me for ice cream once I'm done?" He sensed my hesitation. "Oh, come on! It's Friday, so you've got the time."

I didn't have the heart or the voice to refuse after all the novels I had gobbled during the absence of Spanish homework. If the surveillance people reported me to Officer Das and he told my parents, I would deal with the challenge when it happened. I already spent too long worrying about my criminal record. That day, I would have fun. "I have a better idea. Have you ever seen Humayun's Tomb?"

"No."

"Take the afternoon off, and let's go see it. It's my favorite Mogul monument."

The astonishment on Sergio's face was my best reward.

Inside the tomb grounds forty-five minutes later, I gripped Sergio's forearm. "Stop. Look at the monument, and picture it with four towers on the corners of its platform."

Sergio did what I asked. "Wow. A bunch of towers would change everything. They would frame the monument like a painting."

I smiled. "That's the exact rationale the architect of the Taj Mahal had. That's why Humayun's Tomb is just another Mogul monument in India, whereas the Taj is a wonder of the world. And here's the cruelest irony of all—Humayun's Tomb was the Taj architect's biggest inspiration."

"And you know this how?"

"Before Spanish, I studied a year of interior design. I learned that in my Perspectives class. When we enter the tomb, you'll see how insanely gorgeous the inlay work is. But few people associate this tomb's beauty or similarity to the Taj, nor do they care."

Half an hour later, literally the only visitors to the tomb on a blistering summer afternoon, Sergio and I sat on the marble floor of the tomb's main chamber to escape the August afternoon heat. Clearly, a large green dragonfly shared our idea, because it landed on my printed orange dress sleeve, iridescent wings delicate yet taut, glimmering despite the shady light surrounding us.

Sergio grinned a lopsided grin. "It likes you better than it likes me."

"No. It thinks my orange dress is some kind of flower. When I was a little girl in Calcutta, my family had an enormous garden. In it, my father would catch me dragonflies and tie a long section of sewing thread around its tail and hand it to me to fly like a live kite. In time, in my mind, I became the dragonfly. You know, a fairy princess with those unbelievable wings."

"Then why do you sound so sad telling me that story?"

We both followed the dragonfly with our eyes as it took off.

"Because my father ditched me after I turned five. Once my mother divorced him, he went home to East Pakistan, married again, and moved on to a new life. He broke my heart into a million pieces."

Sergio laced his fingers through mine. "I don't know if that story is more or less sad than my father dying when I was four years old."

"What?" My fingers tightened around his. "I didn't know that!"

"Why would you? You never stay a minute more than you need to after you explain your homework assignments to me!"

"I'm sorry. I promise I won't do that anymore." I freed my hand from his, put my arm around his shoulders, and squeezed. "So, how did it go for you after he died?"

"Worse, I guess. My mother was overwhelmed with four kids, where I was the oldest. She distributed us among my father's relatives and took off to Panama to seek her fortune. Don't ask me why."

"Did she ever come back?"

"Yes. Six years later. Broke and humbled. But I continued in the care of my paternal aunt because she was a schoolteacher. Living with her provided me with free schooling in an amazing school in Callao."

"I've studied Callao. It was Peru's main seaport during colonial times, wasn't it?"

"Yes. And you wonder why I like you. It's because you are such a bright bulb. Come on. Let's go have ice cream."

On our second outing, we visited the Red Fort in Old Delhi. "Do you chew cardamom?" I asked Sergio, curious.

He smiled sheepishly. "Yes."

"But I never see you chewing it! Why do you?"

"Because I love how my breath smells afterward. I'm too self-conscious to come across as a gum-chewer type, however, so I eat some before any meeting."

"How wonderful! Cardamom is such a noble Indian scent."

Soon, the after-homework outings with Sergio became a ritual. Mostly, we frequented Humayun's Tomb, because Sergio's passion was photography and he was mesmerized by the exquisite inlay work in the interior of the underappreciated monument once I had woken him to it.

He introduced me to his second passion one afternoon, sneaking in a Peruvian chicken salad he had prepared especially for the occasion since he delighted in cooking well. We munched on his delicious salad with walnut bits and celery folded in homemade mayonnaise in the main chamber of the tomb.

"I feel as if I'm a dead Egyptian princess in a pyramid enjoying a feast!" I said.

Sergio laughed. "Thank you for converting an ordinary salad into a banquet."

To reciprocate, the following time, I brought Cadbury chocolates to our secret picnic. "These are my favorite chocolates." I handed him my stash after we ate roast beef sandwiches.

And the more time we spent together, the more I trusted him while we shared life stories.

One day, he said, "I hope you meet my mentor, Jaime León, someday. He urged me into the diplomatic career. And if I hadn't become a diplomat, I would never have met you. Jaime persuaded me to study law and apply to the diplomatic academy while I served the Peruvian foreign office as their youngest stenographer yet. I often wonder what direction my life would have taken if he hadn't rescued me."

"How can I meet him? He's in Peru."

"You could marry me!"

"Hey. Back off. I'm not going to marry you, because I hope to go to Barcelona after I receive my BA degree."

But Sergio never tired of bugging me about it, and eventually, it became a joke between us. Meanwhile, to remain alive in the minds of my parents, he mailed diplomatic invitations to their address for me to be his invitee whenever the occasion called for a partner.

On September 7, Suresh thrilled me with a reply from Isabel. It read:

Jesus! How awesome Sergio proposed to you. His haste might have to do with the rumors Mr. Portuguese, Jorge Alves, is spreading about Sergio being a homosexual. I heard from mutual friends that when Papá retired, Sergio moved out of Jorge's tenancy and now lives in the residence until a new ambassador arrives, and Jorge is livid. He is also vindictive and cruel, so I suspect Sergio fears if these rumors reach whoever the new Peruvian ambassador will be, the word will significantly hurt his career. Remember I told you how homophobic Peruvians are? But all these are just my conjectures. Beyond any of them, Sergio really likes you. You should seriously consider his proposal.

16

SEPTEMBER IN NEW DELHI WAS the second phase of the summer, after the blessing of the monsoon rains. On the evening of the day I received Isabel's letter, I came home hot, sticky, and thirsty. In the drawing room, I dropped my book bag at the sight of my parents, who seemed to have morphed into a pair of thunderclouds as they waited to ambush me.

I sighed. "Now what have I done?"

"Who is this Sergio Santander?" interrogated Uncle Robu. He waved an invitation card in the air.

"You know who he is. He's the counselor at the Peruvian embassy."

"Why does he invite you out so often?" attacked my mother.

"How should I know? Maybe because he likes me?" *What you don't know is he wants to marry me—I'm the one who refuses. But I haven't told you two about it because I hate you, and I don't want to deal with what you would do to me.*

"Well, you won't accept any more of his invitations," concluded my stepfather. He tore the invitation in two.

"Yes, I will."

"No, you won't." My mother advanced upon me like a steamroller.

"Yes, I will, because I'm going to marry him!" I clapped a hand over my mouth as soon as I said it, but I'd done it, and I would stand by it. Marrying Sergio would be better than spending one more minute with my parents.

Why hadn't I agreed to marry him yet? Of course, it was out of loyalty to Chirag. But Chirag was long gone, and waiting for him would end up in a marriage to a groom of my parents' choice. At least marrying Sergio would be an act of my own will. I would stand by my unwitting declaration.

"That's it. I'll call Officer Das right this minute. He can straighten you out for romancing a stranger behind our backs." Uncle Robu strode to the door to go use the neighbor's phone.

"Call him," I challenged. "His surveillance people will confirm that Sergio is just a great friend."

"Enough!" My mother pushed me toward the second bedroom and locked the door behind me. "You'll stay in there either until Officer Das arrives or we decide what to do with you. You may have just ended your college career."

I threw myself on my bed, tears of fear and rage falling in a helpless stream on my pillow. My mother could and would terminate my education if she so desired. She never tired of the ecstasy of wielding her power over me any more than I had ever disguised my hatred of her while Didima had been alive. In an overwhelming wave of sorrow, I remembered my sixteenth birthday, when Didima had been alive to protect me. Sick and ailing as she had been, Didima and I had had an unbreakable bond that no one had ever been able to penetrate—until I had committed the ultimate treason of abandoning her and Didima had died from the shock of it. That was why I was there, as punishment for killing poor Didima, swallowing my mother's tyranny one gulp at a time with no way out.

***

The night before my sixteenth birthday, after three hours of sleep, I woke in a panic to the sound of Didima gasping for air.

"Shona, I can't breathe—"

Grabbing Didima's shoulders, I sat her up in bed, yet Didima continued to pant. *How can I run to Uncle Jiten's house, eight city blocks away, at two in the morning?*

Clad in pajamas, I dashed out of the house to knock hard on Uncle Guru's door. "Uncle Guru," I heaved. "Sorry to wake you up, but my grandma can't breathe. May I call my uncle Jiten? I'll pay you tomorrow."

While we waited for Uncle Jiten to arrive, I rubbed Didima's back but to no avail. *What is taking Uncle Jiten so long? At this hour, the traffic is almost nil. Please, God,* I prayed. *Please don't kill Didima. Not tonight. Not on my birthday. Isn't it enough that Dadu died today? Is that why Didima's so sick… because she can't handle that memory without distress?*

When Uncle Jiten arrived with Dr. Lal, Didima was doubled over between her knees, struggling for one gasp at a time.

"Jiten." Dr. Lal administered five injections in a row. "You have to hire a nurse for this. Your sister is having a pulmonary edema attack, and she'll get worse because her kidney function is deteriorating."

I noticed Didima trying to speak. "Listen. Dr. Lal, my grandma's talking." I shook the doctor's arm.

"What is it, Mrs. Panaeker?" Dr. Lal placed an ear close to Didima's mouth.

"No money," wheezed Didima.

Uncle Jiten rolled his eyes. "Totini, I'll take care of it. Your health comes first." Of course he would say that. He didn't understand how it felt to *become* poor. He was a leading interior decorator and textile designer, famous throughout India. His life had been charmed since he had received a full scholarship to study arts and crafts in Sweden thirty years ago.

"Dr. Lal." I put a hand on Didima's back. "Can you teach me to administer intravenous injections? I know how to give regular ones."

"Let's practice right now," Dr. Lal said. "She needs two more diuretics. Here, tie this rubber strap around her upper arm while I fill the injection. Mrs. Panaeker, please ball your fist." His finger traced a line down the crook of Didima's arm. "See how the vein bulges?" He handed me the syringe. "Pierce the skin two millimeters at a slant to reach the vein. You'll know you've succeeded once blood backtracks into the syringe… yes, that's it. Now push the medicine in with your thumb."

I was taken aback at how tough it was to pierce skin near a vein. *Or is Didima's skin harder due to diabetes?*

In the morning, I went to school after Uncle Jiten's manservant, Mohan Singh, arrived.

My mother had already phoned Uncle Guru to say, "Poor Robu isn't well. We'll bring you your birthday present on Sunday." That meant my stepfather had gotten drunk. But my mother never faced the obvious.

When I came home in the afternoon, Didima lay propped in bed, her preferred resting place.

"Hi, Didima. Have you eaten lunch yet?" I kissed the top of her head.

"No, but I'm thirsty, shona. Please pour me a glass of water."

I tossed my book bag on Teddy's old bed and flicked the fan switch to combat a smidgen of the September heat. Then I yanked open the fridge door, anticipating its delicious blast of cold air. As I grabbed a bottle of chilled water from the door, my jaw dropped. Each shelf of the fridge held boxes and containers of my favorite snacks. On the top shelf rested two earthenware containers of white *rasgulla* cheeseballs and reddish-brown *gulabjamun* balls immersed in their own syrup. The second shelf displayed a large yellow cardboard box with a transparent lid to show a selection of twenty-four Indian pastries. On the third shelf sat two paper bags, color-coded brown and white for meat and chicken patties from the Auto Bakery in Defense Colony. Even the shelf over the vegetable drawer contained a white box brimming with chocolate-and-fresh-cream éclairs, lemon tarts, mille-feuille, and rum balls.

"Didimaaaa!" I bounded back to her room to hug her. "Have you gone crazy? What did you do? Rent a taxi? You can't afford this. This is *nuts*. I love you. Thank you."

Didima laughed and gripped my forearm lying across her white-sari-covered bosom. "A belated happy birthday, my darling. But don't thank me. Thank Jiten. He came to check on me and showed up with all this."

"Did you tell him it was my birthday today?"

"No. He noticed it circled and jotted on my calendar."

"Oh, I'm so lucky." I danced in front of our teak coffee table.

The next day, a Friday, I ran home from the school bus stop. In my book bag were four Alistair MacLean thrillers borrowed from the school library. Once I heated the patties and got into bed with a book and snacks galore, I could read and read until Sunday evening. Reading provided the best escape from my reality, and escape was the best birthday present anyone could offer in my life as Didima's caretaker.

I knocked on our back door, smiling in anticipation of a delightful afternoon. My smile grew rigid as my mother, and not Didima, opened the door.

"Hi." I paused. "Didn't you say you'd come on Sunday evening?"

My mother looked resplendent in a bright-yellow sari with a magenta *teep* dot the size of a black grape on her forehead. Even obese, she was beautiful at thirty-six. *And why wouldn't she be?* She didn't worry Didima might die during sleepless vigils. I touched my flat stomach. *I wouldn't gain weight from the snacks I was eating, would I? Especially if I skipped dinner.*

"Because Robu is better, I came to say happy birthday."

Of course you did. I avoided her overture for a hug and skirted past the sunflower sari, catching a whiff of rose attar, my mother's favorite perfume. *Because my birthday is never about me. It's about how your alcoholic husband is doing. Can't you tell him to stop drinking for two days before my birthday? Oops, I forgot. He can't last a day without a drink.* If only I had the courage to say that out loud, but thank God I had my snacks and the thrillers to escape into.

I threw my book bag on Teddy's bed. My whole afternoon was ruined. If I ate my snacks, I would have to offer them to my mother too. I pulled out the four Alistair MacLeans, choosing *When Eight Bells Toll.* Maybe if I read that one without snacks, the afternoon would go by faster. My teeth bared. My mother wouldn't leave her precious husband alone after dark. But I was so hungry. Darn it.

From the front room, I heard Didima say, "You should have come for her birthday."

"We couldn't," replied my mother. "Robu was too sick the day before."

I went to the front room in an attempt to please my mother. But to avoid her touch or caress, I sat close to Didima. "So, where is my present?"

"Robu hasn't bought it yet."

Wonderful. I stood up. "I should go do homework. I have two tests on Monday."

"But I came here to see you." My mother's voice changed from cheery to bellicose. "Can't you sit and be civil for a change?"

No one asked you to come, I wanted to shout, but I bit back the retort. "Ma, I have a lot of homework to do. I'll sit with you guys at four, when I serve you tea, okay?"

Cornered by my lie, I pulled out my English language notebook. I might as well finish the graded essay I'd begun in class. Maybe homework on a Friday afternoon wasn't the world's worst idea. I would sneak one chocolate-and-cream éclair from the four I had left and read a chapter of *When Eight Bells Toll.* Hunger would stymie decent writing.

I eased the fridge door open and pulled out the Auto Bakery pastry box. My stomach gnawed harder at its sugary aroma. I raised the lid. "Didimaaaa!" I wailed.

"What, shona?" Didima asked from her room.

I ran to her, pillaged pastry box in hand.

"She ate it all." I burst into tears. The éclairs were gone. One remaining mille-feuille was cut in half, and a solitary rum ball gazed at me like a giant black pupil.

Didima pinned her daughter with an accusing glance.

"So?" challenged my mother. "They were to share with everybody."

"You mean as in *you*, you glutton!" I screamed. "That's why you came over, to raid our refrigerator the same as you always do."

My mother pointed an index finger at Didima. "See? This is who you have raised since you stole my child."

"*Stole* your child?" Didima sat up, back stiffened to a ramrod. "You came home from the hospital in Calcutta and handed your newborn to Vasant in our drawing room, saying, 'Baba, I have to sleep, otherwise I'll fail my midterm exam at college tomorrow.' And you know why I remember that? Because I was right behind you, carrying your luggage."

"Yes, for my exam week. You and Baba weren't supposed to fall in love with your grandchild and keep her sleeping in between the two of you for the rest of her life. I never had a chance."

"Enough!" I yelled. I impaled my mother with a glare. "Don't come back on Sunday because I. Hate. You. Keep whatever lousy birthday present you have for me." I stormed out of the room to land on Teddy's bed, the looted pastry box a wounded wingman to flank my torso. My sobs shook the soft mattress.

"Noor Shona, my darling." Didima limped up from behind. "I'll give you money to walk to Defense Colony right now and buy more pastries." Her hand on my calf felt warm and protective.

"Spoil her. Spoil her more," my mother said. "As if she isn't bad enough already."

"Jhummur." Didima subsided on the bed, next to my legs. "Please leave my house right now. You've done enough damage for one day."

"Apologize to me." My mother tugged on my ankle.

I flipped over like a released spring. "Apologize?" I sprang up on Teddy's spongy mattress. "Apologize for what? For you ditching me when I was born? Or for every dime you haven't paid in school fees, doctor's visits, school uniforms, school shoes, or any shoes? Or for your husband molesting me when I was six? Where should I start?"

My mother thumped Teddy's wooden armoire so hard it shook, clinking the imported alcohol bottles he hadn't taken with him to Canada. "You're a consummate liar. You lied about poor Robu. On that afternoon, he lay so far away from you his hands couldn't have touched your head, let alone your body."

I folded my legs underneath me, and my mouth twisted. "Believe what you want to, Ma," I spat. "But I'll never forgive you for disbelieving your husband molested me. You aren't fit to be called a mother. I'm sixteen now, not six. You think I don't hear you when you complain to Didima he doesn't have sex with you? Of course he doesn't! Uncle Robu doesn't want to have sex with a land whale like you. He wants to have sex with children—" A ringing slap struck my cheek. My eyes stung with fresh tears as my hand shot up to alleviate the pain.

"Get out!" shouted Didima. "I said leave my house right now, Jhummur." Didima placed an arm around my shoulders, and suddenly, I was six again, engulfed by her love.

***

I wiped my tears, the sorrow of Didima's death overwhelming me. From my parents' backyard, the scent of yellow jasmine drifted in through my one bedroom window to remind me of Chirag and the jasmine that used to grow in Didima's South Extension garden. I got up and gripped the grills on the window until my hands hurt. "Goodbye, Chirag," I whispered. "I waited for you as long as I could. If I wait any longer, only I will pay for the consequences, and I have already paid too much for too many consequences."

With ice in my heart, I knocked on my bedroom door from the inside. When the door opened, I held my mother's gaze. I said, "*A*, I'm not having an affair with Sergio. He's just a great friend. *B*, why can't you consider him a future son-in-law when you'll marry me off to another stranger anyway? *C*, don't for one minute forget how I am not a virgin anymore. If an Indian groom or his family discovers that, they will crucify you for peddling damaged goods, and you will never live down the shame. And *D*, if you won't let me go to school tomorrow, tell me now. I won't bother to study for my midterm exam."

My mother shook her fist. "Go study. I'll let you know in the morning whether you'll go to school or not."

17

AT FOUR A.M., MY MOTHER woke me up with a loud, knockless entry since I wasn't allowed to lock my door at night. She towered over my bed. "Go to school, but on the way back, inform this Sergio Santander that if he is serious, he needs to come by *this evening* to ask for your hand in marriage."

Instantly, I knew my abortion argument had helped my case.

Without comment, I catapulted out of bed and substituted my Kunjal Kriya yoga exercise of vomiting water to prevent diabetes and my morning run for a quick shower. If the buses cooperated, I needed to see Sergio *right then*. My whole plan of escaping my parents depended on him, and I couldn't wait eight more hours to determine if he was on board.

At six forty-five, the Peruvian residence's huge wrought iron gate was locked and its wooden guard post vacant. I figured the young Gurkha guard must be on a bathroom break. Without further ado, I climbed over the ornate gate and raced to ring the side doorbell.

Silence.

I rang the bell again. *Oh my God. Is Sergio not home?*

More silence.

The residence had servants' quarters, but they didn't live in them, choosing to commute to work. I checked Didima's wristwatch. Seven a.m. My exam began at eight. Thank goodness JNU wasn't too far away from Shantiniketan. *Would the guard have a key to the house to let me in if Sergio is around? Where the hell is he?* I dropped my book bag and ran to the front.

Since Sergio had moved into the residence as acting ambassador, he'd preferred Isabel's old bedroom upstairs rather than Angela's master bedroom suite downstairs. I searched the façade for exposed pipes I might climb to his balcony. Seeing none, I lumped a handful of compost from a nearby flowerbed and threw it hard at Sergio's balcony door. The loamy dirt disintegrated on the glass surface without making any noise. *Fifty-two minutes to go.*

I grabbed another fistful of soil.

Sergio yanked open the balcony door and rubbed sleepy eyes. "What do you think you're doing?"

"I'm going to marry you," I announced.

"I thought you were a thief."

"Did you hear me? I said I'd marry you."

"What?"

I cupped my dirty hands around my mouth. "I'm going to marry you!" I shouted.

"Can you come to the side door? I'll come down."

Lord above. Sergio hadn't jumped for joy to hear my news. *After the production of yesterday, what if Sergio had changed his mind? What would my parents do to me now?*

At the side door, Sergio tied a broad sash around a blue-and-white striped kimono, his hair tousled, face unshaven. "What is going *on*?" He appeared twice as annoyed as he had five minutes ago.

My heart sank further. "It's okay. You don't have to marry me." I swung my book bag onto a shoulder.

"I didn't say that. I asked what's the matter." Sergio ran a hand through his spiky hair. "And don't stand there pouting like a naughty schoolgirl. Come in and explain this to me."

I glanced at my wrist. Seven twenty. "I don't have time to sit and chat. I have an exam at eight. Do you have the key to the gate? I climbed over it."

"What? Where was the guard?"

"How do *I* know? Please unlock the bloody gate so I can leave."

"No. I want an explanation."

"No! I'll miss my exam, and I can't because it's a midterm. Unless you'll drop me off at school after we talk?"

Both of us spotted the Gurkha guard strolling out from behind the back corner of the house. Seeing Sergio, he loped over, stood to attention, and saluted. "Good morning, *sar*." His round Mongolian face beamed brighter than the slanting rays of the morning sun.

Sergio's eyes rolled. "Ramdas, why aren't you at your guard post? What do I pay you for?"

"Bathroom break, sar." He beamed us another smile.

I literally experienced Sergio's frustration as he pointed to the guard post. "Go guard the gate. Now! And you." He grabbed my arm. "Come explain to me why you want to marry me at seven in the morning."

"It's not seven. It's seven thirty." I tapped the face of Didima's wristwatch. "I have an exam at eight. Will you drop me to school or not?"

"You're so impossible! I'll go get dressed for work then drop you off. Tell me what this is about on the way to JNU, and it better be good."

Fifteen minutes later, in Sergio's blue Datsun four-seater, he had a cut on his right cheek from shaving in haste, and he didn't look happy.

I said, "Serg, you don't have to marry me."

"Stop *saying* that, and tell me what really happened! What changed your mind?"

"Basically, my parents threatened to never let me see you again." I told him of my stepfather tearing up his latest invitation card and the ensuing fight, skipping the reasoning about my abortion and Chirag and Didima dying.

"And how do you feel about that?"

"Their threat made me conscious of how attached I've grown to you. I don't want to lose you."

"So, what's their solution, to let you keep seeing me?"

"They are demanding that if you are serious, you have to come ask for my hand *this very evening*."

"What? They can't be that unreasonable! Today is a Tuesday, and I have a cocktail and dinner I am already committed to attending. Make them understand that, as a diplomat, my evening engagements are for work, not fun. I'll come ask for your hand on Saturday."

"Fine. Then forget about seeing me ever again."

"That's so ridiculous!"

"How many times have I told you my mother and stepfather are psychos? I can't control that they're crazy! This will go ten times worse for me than for you. Now that they know you exist in my life, they'll hustle me into marrying an Indian jerk even faster." I wiped away angry tears.

By the JNU campus curbside, Sergio pressed on the brake. "Can you come to my office when your classes finish? Let me think this through."

"So, in short, you're telling me you're not sure you want to marry me." I opened the passenger-side door.

"No. All I'm asking for is some time to digest the bomb you detonated under my butt pretty much while I was asleep."

Throughout my midterm exam, my brain feverishly imagined how the evening would unfold. If Sergio backed out of his desire to marry me, I really had cooked my goose.

That afternoon, when I arrived at the embassy, Sergio was in a work meeting. The receptionist instructed me to wait in the reception room as if to emphasize how I was always the last person in charge of my fate.

An hour later, Sergio showed me into his office without a smile, tanking my heart completely. Behind closed doors, however, he pulled me to him and folded me in a hug. He disengaged and smiled. "This is not my formal proposal, but will you marry me?"

I teared up, nodding as I snorted in a runny nose.

Sergio hugged me again. "Come on. Let's go to your home and sort this out with your crazy parents."

"And what about your evening engagements?"

"I had to cancel everything in honor of your parents."

We kissed for the first time in Humayun's Tomb the next afternoon. I was struck by how different kissing Sergio felt to the smoldering passion Chirag and I had experienced kissing each other. Sergio's kiss tasted staid, comfortable, and reassuring. And that kiss transitioned me from girlhood into womanhood.

18

SERGIO AND I GOT ENGAGED in November of 1982, after Officer Das said he would drop all charges against me if I married Sergio and behaved myself in the future. I wanted to lash out, say I had never behaved badly in the first place, but fear and prudence kept me quiet.

From the engagement onward, March 25, 1983, the day I would marry Sergio, became the official date of my liberation from my mother and stepfather. Whenever I argued with my mother, I charged to my room and pulled out a pocket calendar hidden among a jumble of clothes inside Didima's corrugated steel armoire. "Ninety-eight days. Ninety-eight days more, and these two will have *no power* over me," I would mutter, puffing like a steam engine until I calmed down.

Fittingly, Sergio and I had our first serious argument inside the Humayun's Tomb, that being the center stage where our relationship had deepened from casual to serious.

In the middle of December, we were parked on the main tomb floor, eating ham and cheese sandwiches, when out of the blue, Sergio declared, "Quit college as soon as you can. As my wife, you'll have a hundred duties to perform. You don't need a second-rate degree from a third-rate Indian university."

"Hey, JNU isn't a third-rate university," I fought back. "It's where Indian diplomats have to graduate from."

"Yes, but you didn't study to become a diplomat," argued Sergio. "You studied Spanish, and you already know Spanish. Let this go."

"Will you let me go back to school for English once we are settled after a few years?"

"Yes! Go back to school for Swahili for all I care."

I didn't argue with Sergio any further. However, I also wasn't convinced by him. Being a great student was such a novel development in my life, I wasn't sure

I wanted to lose the sense of control and accomplishment it gave me. Thus, I was unable to make a decision.

Behind Sergio's back, Uncle Robu argued, "Don't drop out of school three months shy of a BA degree. What harm can it do to attend school for three more months until you finish?"

Knowing my parents' wish was reason enough to do the exact opposite, but my fate was decided for me right after the New Year of 1983. The day college reopened, on January 3, JNU's oldest Spanish language professor, the one who was flamboyantly gay, was found dead in his college-housing apartment.

Andres Verona's body escaped discovery for ten days, thanks to the holidays, but once the cat was out of the bag, every leading newspaper splashed headlines about the twenty-five stab wounds in Professor Verona's decayed chest, indicating attacks long past death. Lengthy front-page articles reported the professor's blatant homosexual behavior, speculating on how much that might have contributed to his murder.

At the peak of the scandal, Sergio waved the latest newspaper article in my face when I went to the embassy after college one afternoon. "Look, just quit. Okay? I can't sit here and stress over your safety all day while I concentrate on work." Sergio dropped the open newspaper to the floor.

"But, Serg," I protested, "Professor Verona probably got murdered because he was so flirtatious and lenient toward his young male students. What does that have to do with me and my safety when I don't even live on campus?"

Sergio shook his head. "Aren't you scared some crazy Hindu or Muslim fanatic on campus will want to harm you because you're marrying neither of those but a Catholic?"

"I don't have any evening classes, and I leave campus as soon as my classes end. How am I in any danger?"

"Noor, give me a break, okay?" insisted Sergio. "I *promise* you can rejoin university once we leave India."

In my heart, I knew I wasn't protesting enough because studying Spanish had never been *my* dream. Plus, the added lure of defying my parents was too hard to resist. Knowing I could thwart them was such sweet revenge. The following day, I informed Dr. Dey, the head of the JNU Spanish department, I was dropping out.

"Why?" Dr. Dey asked. "You're such a good student. Why would you do that?"

"Because I am getting married, and those are my husband-to-be's wishes."

A week later, I smiled triumphantly into the mirror as I put on makeup for a cocktail party in a guest bedroom at the Peruvian residence. My plan to escape my parents was in full sail.

I started as Sergio barged into the room and plunked himself on its queen-sized bed.

"What's wrong?" I set down my mascara brush.

"I'm so mad I could punch somebody." Sergio crossed his hands under his head.

"About what?"

"Our Catholic wedding in Lima. I've researched the rules and regulations, and the timing is a mess. I planned the Catholic wedding for two weeks after the Indian one, while we pass through Lima on our honeymoon. Now it can't happen unless I do six months of paperwork for special permission from the Vatican because you're not a Catholic. I'm losing it."

For me, it was a huge overkill to have two weddings, but my parents wouldn't let me leave India with Sergio without a Hindu wedding ceremony, and Sergio wanted a Catholic wedding celebration for his family and friends in Lima. "So this problem wouldn't exist if I were a Catholic?" I stared at Sergio.

Sergio nodded.

"Then why don't I become a Catholic? Can I?"

"You're kidding, right?"

"Of course not. As a kid in my convent school, I dreamed of being a Catholic. Each Christmas, I felt desolate when the Christian kids chattered nonstop about how much fun they were having decorating their Christmas trees, so secure in where they belonged, whereas I belonged nowhere. My happiest school memories are of singing hymns and Christmas carols, irrespective of our religions. Did I ever tell you the only prayer I know is the 'Our Father'? I've believed in Jesus and Mary since I met them in first grade."

"Yes, but your parents will disagree," Sergio pointed out.

I paused by the bed. "Serg, I'm twenty-one. By law, I'm an adult, though my mother loves to pretend otherwise. And we're already engaged. If we both stand firm, they can't stop us."

"I'll call the archbishop at the nunciature on Monday."

"No," I urged. "Go call him right now. It isn't five o'clock yet." My hands bunched into fists. "If I can become a Catholic and escape my stupid Hindu-Muslim past *forever*, don't wait on it."

My eyes clouded at the memory of a yellow-sandstone Jain temple, my beloved Chirag lighting an oil lamp and holding my hand, his pupils shining in the lamp's glow despite the sunless gloom of a monsoon afternoon.

"Don't you wish we were peacocks?" he had asked. "Then we wouldn't have to worry about this religion nonsense."

I lassoed my mind back to the present, unclenched my fingers, and smiled at Sergio. "If I can become a Catholic to marry you, it'll be the best wedding present you could give me. Go see to it." *Nothing in the world would displease my parents more.*

With the plan in motion, my only routine to follow during January and February of 1983 became the catechism classes I attended twice a week. For Sergio, I had no other responsibility. And I loved those classes because, for the first time, I would formally belong within the religion I had loved since I was a child.

Furthermore, with no college to attend, I lounged in bed with my next novel, convinced all my reading would pay off when I went back to school for English someday. Words were art in thought, each syllable a feather touch, each phrase a brushstroke. Sentences melted on the tongue of my mind like chocolate, warm, caressing, and enveloping. They embraced my senses in a woolly blanket until they shaped the formless, physicalized the invisible, causing me to laugh, cry, hurt, or fly at the behest of a mere page. Each day, I snuggled in bed with the best in literature and the worst in junk food, giving my mother free rein to do whatever wedding shopping she pleased. Either way, she would impose her will on what I wore. *Why do I need to shop with her if, instead, I can escape into the magic of yet another unread book?*

On the day of my baptism, February 28, in the century-old brick-and-stone Sacred Heart Cathedral of New Delhi, I excused myself from the cluster of Sergio's diplomatic friends and kneeled alone at the main altar. Christ stared at me from a huge wooden crucifix hanging high above.

I genuflected to him and whispered, "Thank you, Jesus, for letting me 'belong' with you at last. From today onward, my past is dead. This is my new beginning under your wing."

19

With twenty-four hours to go until my wedding day, I danced on air as I decorated my hands with henna paste for the ceremony the following evening. I had long since suppressed my misgivings about my lack of attraction to Sergio in exchange for the elation of escaping my mother and stepfather forever.

What does it matter if I'm not physically drawn to Sergio? Don't Indian girls have sex with their husbands once their parents arrange their marriages? Whenever I pictured my actual marriage night and sex with Sergio, I balked. *But what is the alternative? Marrying an Indian stranger of my parents' choice, where he inflicts sex on me?*

The setting sun poured in and splashed on the edge of my parents' sandstone dining table as I rested my elbows on its smooth red-and-white stippled surface. Dust danced in the shaft of sunlight, joining my heart in song. I admired the henna patterns on my hands and forearms. To cure the henna stains to a darker shade of rust, I had massaged in a generous amount of mango-pickle oil. The dining room reeked of tart pickle spices. *My God, I have less than a day left until freedom!* By that time tomorrow, my parents would *never* control me again. The concept intoxicated me. "Thank God I'll never see Das again, from now until eternity," I remarked as my mother swayed out of the kitchen and leaned on the doorframe.

"Of course you will. He's coming to the wedding with his family." My mother smiled happily.

"What? Why? I don't want him there!"

"Because you pretty much owe him for your wedding to Sergio."

"Why would I owe *him* for that?"

My mother looked uncomfortable. "I didn't mean that."

"Yes, you did! You'd better confess what you meant." Now I could hear my heart beating.

"We owe him for straightening you out about the whole marrying Chirag nonsense."

My voice came out grim. "Ma, either explain this to me, or I'll call Sergio to cancel this wedding... so talk."

"We requested Shushanto Das to engineer your house arrest because he *is* Anup Das's brother and a real policeman. We knew he could pull it off."

In my stomach, a boulder settled. "So no criminal charges ever existed against me?"

"No. But look how far you've come! You were out of control when Didima died."

"So the beatings, that jail visit, it was all a lie?"

My mother giggled. "Yes. Das was always struck by how innocent and gullible you were. He believes Sergio is the right age to take care of you. Otherwise, you are too headstrong for your own good."

Inside my head, Chirag's face flared. Chirag on the day we reunited after six years, him standing by the rickety leaf of our age-stained back door, sunlight streaming on his blackish-brown hair, the taste of his lips as he kissed me in a triangular park near the South Extension Part 2 Market Place. His lips on mine had transformed us into one being. I saw his perfect smile, his waiting by my old school bus stop, the bitter winter wind blowing through his hair, the outline of pectoral muscles underneath a white cashmere sweater. His waiting under a street lamp in a back alley near our house, eager to give me the diamond pendant on a white gold chain as a promise to marry me.

My vision blackened, and I tasted a warm rush of bile as I rose to my feet. Forgetting my pickle-oiled hands, I grasped the dining table edge. My mother still talked, wagging a fat index finger in my direction as I inched toward the staircase leading to my one refuge in my parents' home. Tears blurred my eyes while my feet fumbled up to Uncle Robu's rooftop rose garden. I stumbled and fell after I locked the terrace door behind me.

Sobbing, I crawled to a rose pot and buried my face in an overgrown bloom, lemon topaz in the golden evening sunlight. Three years of paranoia, second-guessing my every action, while the entire time my mother, stepfather, and Officer Das had laughed themselves into stitches behind my back. I could have written to Chirag anytime. Run away with him anytime. Fresh tears doused the yellow rose cupped in my hands. I let it go and lay down on the dusty roof floor, staring at the sky.

What can I do? Cancel my wedding to Sergio, whom I now consider a trusted friend? Could I hurt him and embarrass him as I surely would if I canceled the wedding? Besides, like Isabel said—how do I know Chirag hasn't moved on? And what would the canceled wedding get me—more time in my parents' clutches and an Indian groom?

I got up and wiped my tears with my T-shirt front, feeling like I had aged ten years in twenty minutes. *Yes, my mother has won the battle of subjugating me to her will, but tomorrow, I will marry Sergio and win this war. In time, Chirag would fade to what he really was—my teenage fantasy of happiness.*

TUBEROSES

20

On my wedding day, I woke up numb and puffy-eyed from crying, deeply conscious of how Chirag was out there but that day I would forego my last chance to marry him. Once I swore to be true to Sergio, his presence would influence my every remaining decision for the rest of my life.

I approached the mirror of Didima's teak dressing table in the far corner of the second bedroom where I slept. From that day on, I would belong to Sergio and have to sleep with him. I would have had to sleep with Chirag, too, if it was him I married, but I *loved* Chirag. Passionately. *And where had love led me?* To a cliff edge I had to jump off every time I trusted love. But that day, my mind wouldn't listen to reason. I kept remembering how Chirag's kisses had consumed me, as if he had plugged into my body and mind to take over my soul with an electricity that had coursed through both of us.

Sergio's kisses, instead, felt masterful, but no life, no current flowed through them. And I responded equally puppetlike. *God above! What was my crime, other than being born in a country which didn't accept me? Then losing Dadu, the one person influential enough to protect me from the societal consequences of my mixed-blood birth? Would Dadu have lived if I hadn't loved him as a father?* I stared out of my window at the blooming jasmine creeper.

"Noor?" My mother banged into the bedroom without a knock. "Oh, good. You're awake. I didn't want you to oversleep." A happy grin wreathed her face.

I excavated a smile. Eight hours to freedom.

"It's nine o'clock." My mother pointed at the wall clock as though I couldn't see it too. "Shower and do your nails. Sergio's driver will be here at eleven. Don't be late, because after he drops you off, he comes back for us."

The wedding ceremony and reception would take place at the Taj Hotel, a location Sergio had chosen. As the acting head of the Peruvian embassy and consulate, he had invited all his diplomatic friends and colleagues, and therefore, he'd paid for most of the expenses. My parents were responsible for both of our wedding attires, the flower arrangements, and the Hindu priest's stipend to conduct the religious marriage rites.

Secretly, I had grinned in glee when I'd overheard my mother forbidding my stepfather from confessing my conversion to Catholicism to anyone because the conversion would embarrass them in a Hindu society.

Thus relieved of the financial burden of the marriage, my mother, who had been denied a wedding ceremony the first time for eloping from India with a Pakistani national and thwarted the second time around by Uncle Robu's desire for a simple civil marriage, was determined to restore her truncated dreams of how a real wedding should be. For my wedding, jasmine and tuberose garlands had been flown in from Calcutta.

Sergio had booked a hotel room for me because, once my hair was coiffed, all he wanted was for me to be ensconced in that room, dressed and ready at five in the evening. Excited and happy as he was, he was still the consummate diplomat who didn't want the show to go wrong. In his opinion, Indians were notoriously bad time managers, and he distrusted my parents' word to have me there punctually. He planned to arrive in his Indian wedding attire of silk *churidaar* pants, brocade achkan jacket, and hand-embroidered *nagra* shoes. To tie Sergio's ritual turban, his prince friend, Aditya, would accompany him. Other than that, my parents could use his car, as they didn't have one, complete with the embassy chauffeur, to do whatever they pleased to uphold their end of the arrangements.

At three in the afternoon, I walked into a hotel room for the third time in my life. I paused at its familiar, flowery smell. *Does Chirag remember me when he walks into hotel rooms?* My feet gravitated toward a floor-to-ceiling curtain. I draped the maroon flower-patterned curtain around myself and closed my eyes.

On our first morning together at the Oberoi Sheraton, I had come out from using the bathroom and Chirag had disappeared.

"Chirag?"

No one answered.

Panicked, I eased my shoes back on, frightened I would lose my way leaving the hotel all alone.

Right then, Chirag jumped out from behind a curtain and came running to hug me. "Sorry! I'm so sorry I frightened you." He had kneeled to hug me around the waist and buried his face below my breasts. "I swear I'll never scare you again. Ever. How did I forget how naïve and trusting you always were, even when we were kids?"

Now, I came out from behind the curtain to observe the turquoise brocade sari my mother had chosen for the wedding alongside its matching blouse and petticoat. Thank goodness, as an artist, my mother had exquisite taste in clothes. That thought made me rub my puffy eyes. If they didn't unpuff in two hours, I would look as ridiculous as Garfield the cat getting married in a sari.

What will I do in this room for two hours? Why didn't I bring a book to distract me from my jumbled thinking? Maybe if I visit the garden where the ceremony will be held, time will go by faster?

The rear garden of the Taj Hotel was abloom with colorful bushes. That day, however, its beauty was highlighted by a hut-sized pavilion in its center. White jasmine and milky tuberose garlands covered every inch of the coned structure supported by four poles. I touched the delicate jasmine and sturdier tuberose petals. One blink, and the pavilion could float away on its own heady scent. *Why can't I sit in it and travel back in time to my childhood in Calcutta, when Dadu was alive and life had been one safe and endless playfield?*

"Noor?"

My head swung.

My mother charged up the paved path to the pavilion like an oil tanker, followed by her fleet of bobbing Bengali girlfriends. "What are you doing in the sun, getting darker by the minute? Go rest in your room."

"I can't lie down." I tried to control the raw irritation in my voice and pointed to my head. "Not with my hair done up."

"Well, go to your room. I don't want people to see you in faded jeans and flip-flops."

In the hotel room, I fumed as I chose a banana from a fruit basket on a desk, when my mother blew in. I peeled the banana, taking a sizable bite.

"Stop eating. You're supposed to fast."

"I'm hungry," I said through a mouthful of banana. *Moron.* "Sergio isn't a Hindu, and neither am I, so it doesn't matter."

"Yes, it does. It isn't auspicious." My mother admonished.

"Should I throw it up?"

She ignored my spurt of impertinence. "I forgot your wedding veil in my closet, so Robu's gone home to fetch it. Be dressed when it arrives."

"Why? Sergio won't be here for over an hour."

"Do it." My mother banged out of the room.

I clenched my hands and emitted a lengthy sigh. Time wasn't ticking by any faster or slower. It just felt never-ending.

In the bathroom mirror, my face registered young and pretty, almond-shaped eyes unpuffed. It was so contrary to the spaced-out sensation inside me, I slapped my cheeks and wiggled my nose. As eager as I was to marry Sergio, it felt as if someone else, and not I, was in my shoes. Hopefully, "someone else" would make love to him that night too.

I fastened the last of Didima's five precious gemstone-encrusted necklaces at the base of my neck as my mother swung into the bathroom, veil outstretched. My God, the veil was beautiful, with its tiny brocade flowers on pale-turquoise Chanderi gauze. As my mother draped it over my bejeweled head, its sheen, transparency, and weightlessness reminded me of dragonfly wings glinting in the sun of my childhood.

I picked up a hairpin, took in the veil's shimmering reflection in the mirror, and glanced away. *What utter irony to realize I'm my own dragonfly, flying, always flying, but trapped by a thread tied to my tail for another person to pull. Could I ever break free?*

"Oh, shona, how beautiful you look." My mother's gaze softened, and I knew she was thinking of the weddings she had never had. She placed a hand on my shoulder. "Don't make my mistake. Accept Sergio for who he is, and learn to be happy with him."

Through the mirror, I nodded. *Poor, poor Jhummur. Always impulsive, always too headstrong to control her actions. She had relegated me into my grandparents' care when she didn't want the responsibility of a child at age twenty, and now she demands instant motherhood. Instant love. As if I am a doll she can play with.* I covered my mother's hand with one of my own. "I'll do my best, Ma." *But how is it my fault that the word "mother" only conjures up an image of Didima?*

"Come on, hurry," my mother urged. "Sergio's already here."

"Then he's early, Ma. I have to put a hairpin through this veil without ripping a hole in it. Can't you see it won't stay on my head? Can you please leave? I have to pee. I swear I'll be out at the garden entrance in five minutes."

At the garden entrance, I saw my stepfather, Officer Shushanto Das, and my mother deep in conversation. Ready to gouge Das's eyes out, I glanced away. *What would he say or do to me if I stopped right now and asked him to give back Chirag's diamond necklace he stole?* But I didn't pause as I hurried onto the pathway to the pavilion. The sooner I got married, the sooner I would escape India. Chirag was just my immortal fantasy, a dream and a memory to live inside me forever.

Outside, knots of guests chatted over the subdued volume of *shehnai* music permeating the salmon-hued evening air. In the distance, my groom talked to a group of four with his back to me. For those seconds, I daydreamed he was someone else.

Nudged by his companions, Sergio turned around, and the dream ended. He smiled, arms outstretched to receive me, the sun accentuating the green in his hazel eyes. It was no traditional Hindu wedding—*But who cares?* My freedom walk had commenced.

The guests lined up to form a human corridor as Sergio kissed my henna-patterned hands. He appeared proud and happy enough to burst under the folds of his starched red turban tied to Rajput distinction. Sergio was the right choice. He was so nice and kind and dependable. Once we married under the fairy-tale canopy of that flower pavilion, Sergio would protect me forever.

Isn't that what I have most sought since Dadu had died? To be happy and safe in my home life and have the stability of knowing tomorrow will be taken care of? It was within my grasp, and I would seize it.

21

Late in the evening, as the embassy chauffeur drove the two of us, newly wed, to the Peruvian embassy residence, Sergio took my hand and whispered, "Hi, Mrs. Santander."

Could I stall sex until tomorrow? I resented that my worry was marring my relief of escape from the Chatterjee Alcatraz.

A week ago, when Sergio had brought up the subject of birth control, I had panicked. *What if that abortion had rendered me incapable of conceiving?* I knew how much Sergio wanted a child. *Would he leave me if he knew I maybe couldn't have one?* I had to postpone the discovery. "I don't want to become pregnant until I get to know you better. Let's wait a year or two?"

"That long?" Sergio exclaimed. "Then I'll be forty by the time we have a child!"

"Well, how long can you let me wait?"

"I hate using condoms, so how about you get an IUD?"

"Fine." I smiled, relieved that an IUD would hide whatever my true state was much more than a condom. I had one inserted two days before the wedding.

"Alone at last." Sergio eased the unfamiliar turban off his head and put it away in what I still considered Isabel's closet in the upstairs main bedroom of the Peruvian residence. Our honeymoon would begin at dawn, once we boarded a plane to Germany. The trip included visits to friends and family in Frankfurt, Madrid, Lima, and Nice. Our only alone time would be the side tours to Cuzco and Arequipa in the highlands of Peru.

"Aren't you tired?" I faked a yawn, praying Sergio would follow my lead. "I'm dead."

"Then, let's make love once we're both less tired."

I suppressed my sigh of relief behind a smile.

Forty-eight hours later, however, I awoke in a Frankfurt hotel room with no excuse to avoid the inevitable. "Hi." *Would Sergio detect the strain in my voice?*

He put an arm around my waist. "I promise I'll be gentle," he said in a flash of understanding.

"I should go brush my teeth." I tried not to dwell on my first and last encounter with sex.

"And I'll dig out this lubricant I have." Sergio shrugged out of his pajama top in front of me.

As he bent over his suitcase, I exclaimed, "Who gave you those scars on your back?"

"Oh, those." Sergio didn't react to the sound of my surprise. "They're from my childhood. Forget they exist, will you? I have."

"How? They crisscross your whole back. How can I *forget* they're there?"

"Noor. I don't discuss them. Please don't ever ask me that question again. Understood? And no, I won't change my mind, so drop it."

I had never heard my new husband's voice so dry. I let the subject go. *Perhaps he could pretend they weren't there because he couldn't see them, but how could I, when they were in plain sight, latticing his back, so obviously the size and width of the whip used to inflict them?* Those scars had to have bled when he received the lashings. "I'm sorry." I bent my head. "I didn't mean to pry." *How would I react if he were to discover the secrets I had to hide?*

"No, I'm sorry. It's not your fault. I should have mentioned them." His face softened into a smile.

We engaged in another passionless kiss. Sergio paused to rub on his lubricant, and I parted my legs as if readying for execution. *Would I have felt this reluctant to have sex with Chirag? Probably not.* But Sergio was Sergio, not Chirag.

I kept my tears at bay. "Serg, I know this will hurt, so just do it, okay? I mean, don't do it little by little. Just go for it so the pain part is over."

But the tears escaped once Sergio entered and the pain reminded me of Rajat. To deal with getting through it, I shut my eyes, as tense as a drum, waiting for the semen part. *Perhaps it's my imagination, but is Sergio taking a lot longer than Rajat?* And through the whole horrible pain of it, I wondered, *Will he realize I'm not a virgin?*

Five, six, seven minutes later, when Sergio panted to a finish, I opened my eyes, dreading what he would say next. But he lay back on the bed, smiling. "I've never been with a virgin. It's true what they say about their tightness."

I smiled a watery smile, relieved on too many levels to reply.

But on the third day of intercourse, Sergio said, "Why can't you relax? You would dilate more if you weren't so tense every time we make love," and I knew I had a problem.

On the fourth day, when we flew to Madrid to visit a diplomatic couple who were friends of Sergio's, at night, I learned to shut my eyes and travel to a place in my head with Chirag so Sergio could make love to me. It was my only way to respond to Sergio's bodily needs and ignore the pain he provoked.

We arrived in Lima ten days after leaving New Delhi. By then, we had already had sex a hundred times until my period rescued me. Like the majority of men from the third world I had heard of, Sergio didn't want to have sex with a bleeding chicken.

By the fourth day of my period, I drenched two sanitary pads per hour. "Serg." I subsided on his mother's living room sofa. "I can't go to your aunt's tea party. I'm dizzy." As much as I wanted to avoid staying home with my frosty mother-in-law, worse would be to faint during an outing.

"Could you be pregnant?" asked Sergio's sister, Nila, strikingly blond and gray-eyed compared to Sergio's brown hair and hazel eyes.

I gave her a hollow glance. "Don't women stop menstruating when they're pregnant? This is the eighth pad I've used today, and it's already my fourth day, when I usually stop bleeding altogether."

"What?" Nila looked sympathetic. "You don't bleed this much normally?"

"No. My period peters out by the third day."

Nila shook her head. "We need to address this now. Or else you'll pass out during the wedding the day after tomorrow."

"What do you have in mind?" Sergio took my hand and squeezed it while he stared at his sister.

"Let's take her to an ER. No regular doctor will see her at such short notice."

In the emergency room of the Clínica Americana of Lima, an angry doctor demanded, "What butcher put an IUD inside this young girl?"

"A gynecologist in India," Sergio said.

"She'll bleed to death if I don't remove it. Were you in pain before your period?" The doctor placed a hand on my brow.

"Yes! Yes, I was," I gasped, vindicated despite the predicament it would put me in. So my pain wasn't psychological reluctance. It was real after all. *Yet pain or no pain, without the IUD, if I fail to get pregnant, maybe Sergio will suggest I undergo tests to see why? Could a doctor tell upon examining me I have undergone an abortion?* I shivered. *What explanation will I offer Sergio if matters progress that far?*

Meanwhile, the doctor rubbed my hand. "IUDs are for women whose uterus and cervix have already experienced childbirth. I want you on absolute sexual rest until your next menstrual cycle is over."

I covered my face and coughed to hide my smile.

But two weeks later, alone with Sergio in a fancy hotel suite just outside the famed Inca ruins complex of Machu Picchu, it was impossible to ward off Sergio's amorous overtures. "I don't want to get pregnant," I protested with what sounded like an old excuse to hide that I might *never get pregnant*, never mind the sex part.

"Good God, Noor. It's our honeymoon for heaven's sake." Sergio faced away and switched off the lamp on his nightstand.

"Fine. Fine. Let's do it." I pulled him to me in the darkness.

Making love to Sergio would be a regular part of my life. I might as well work on getting used to it rather than concocting excuses to avoid it. As an Indian wife, it was my job to satisfy my husband's wishes. At least that was what Didima would have told me with her no-nonsense, Victorian-age education. But that would have been easy for Didima to say. Dadu and she had had a textbook college romance. Both were madly in love when they defied all societal rules to marry each other in the early 1930s.

Maybe sex will become more pleasant in time? Would Sergio let up on sex if I were to get pregnant? But the million-dollar question is… can I get pregnant?

22

Upon our return to New Delhi after the two-month-long whirlwind honeymoon, the glitter of our intercultural marriage, celebrated twice over on two continents, was all but extinguished by a vile attack of the flu. When my flu morphed into dreadful morning sickness, a new worry besieged me. *Clearly I'm pregnant, meaning I surmounted the main hurdle, but will my child be born normal after that abortion?*

Sergio immediately consulted with his doctor friend, Ashwin Chopra, to recommend us a good obstetrician. Ashwin was a gastroenterologist, but Sergio trusted him so much, he consulted Ashwin for everything health-related first.

On my first visit to the obstetrician, Dr. Usha Khosla, a week later, Sergio glowed like a firefly while I drowned in a fit of tears, unable to confess my real worry. Instead, I complained to the doctor, "Why do they call this morning sickness when I vomit all day and night long? I can't even *think* I'm so nauseous all the time!"

Yet sick or well, I was obliged to attend diplomatic parties, which were a required part of Sergio's duties as an official representative of his country abroad. His absence was unconscionable because it meant Peru's absence from another country's national day, commercial agreement, or whatever else the party commemorated. And I complied, a pale specter hovering close to the nearest bathroom, always well-dressed, with my hair and makeup impeccable—worried silly I would give birth to some monster.

That was when Isabel wrote to me from Barcelona:

What? Pregnant already? I heard the news from my mom. We'll talk once I arrive in India on June 5th to buy gemstones. Can I stay with you guys?

Before Isabel's arrival, Sergio rented us a flat in Vasant Vihar because he received word a replacement ambassador was on his way to fill the vacancy José Santanilla's retirement had created. Vasant Vihar was suburbia, the same as South Extension only newer, so it had more green areas and bigger houses. Sergio picked that neighborhood since it was close to Shantiniketan, where the Peruvian embassy was located. Personally, I was so worried about my baby being born normal, the move didn't even register on me.

What did register was Sergio asking me, "Do you want a house in Lima or an apartment?"

"You mean you don't have a house already? You're thirty-seven!"

"Hey, no need to sound so judgmental. I didn't think of a house because I wanted to travel and show my mother a good time. She had a rough life."

"I would prefer a house with a garden."

"Fine. I'll ask Carlos to buy land, then, so we can build to our specifications." Carlos was Sergio's youngest sibling.

When Isabel arrived, she asked, "How do you feel about becoming a *mother*?"

I wished I could tell her my *real* worry, but Isabel had been friends with Sergio a lot longer than she had been friends with me. I couldn't put her in a position where she would have to question and decide where her loyalties lay. Instead, I said, "I'm so sick, I hadn't thought that far ahead." I gagged. "I have to go vomit." I came back to rasp, "Were you sick all day, too, when you were pregnant with Tata?"

Isabel's daughter was seven by then.

"You'll hate to hear this, but I wasn't." Isabel bit into a samosa patty. "I didn't suffer a day of nausea."

"I do hate you." I smiled wanly. "I go out every single evening, sick as a dog. I'm so resentful of the nausea, I want to throw up all over the person standing next to me, but of course, I choke it back with a hankie and dash to the bathroom."

Isabel shuddered. "I swore I'd never marry a diplomat after watching my mom go from party to party while she was sick, we were sick, while facing a crisis… fighting with Papá… It was all the same—she had to look fantastic and attend parties beside Papá as if she had no other purpose on earth. My entire childhood, I vowed that wouldn't be *my* life. Call me stupid, but I live happy as a hippie, where my days are my own and I do as I please with my time."

For the first time, I couldn't agree more, but I had chosen to marry Sergio, so I had to live it. In life, everything had a price, and that was the price of escaping my parents as soon as possible.

One afternoon, in the middle of my sixth month, I vomited a trail of pure blood from the bathroom of our flat to the old-fashioned, black-box telephone located near the pantry door.

My phone call caught Sergio in the throes of a formal luncheon to support his newly arrived ambassador at the Peruvian residence.

"Sergio Sar, Noor Madam in house, very blood," announced a frantic waiter.

Sergio rushed home, calling me ahead to be dressed and downstairs to race me to the doctor's. In the car, after ten minutes, I said, "Hey, this isn't the way to Usha's." Obstetrician, Dr. Usha Khosla, had her consulting office in Jor Bagh.

"We aren't going to Usha's. I'm taking you to Ashwin."

"Why? Ashwin is a stomach doctor. Why are you taking me to him for a pregnancy problem?" My eyes widened.

"Ashwin said your vomiting is a gastro issue. If it was a pregnancy issue, you'd bleed from the vagina."

I resisted an eye roll, knowing that no one could shake Sergio's faith in Ashwin.

At Ashwin's two-doctor consulting office on Safdarjung Marg, which he shared with his twin brother, a cardiologist, Ashwin stuffed an endless tube called an endoscope the thickness of my ring finger down my unhappy throat. On an attached TV-like screen, he pointed out my esophagus, torn beyond the half point, where it met my stomach. "You need complete bed rest and a clear liquid diet until this heals," he said. "But your pregnancy is in no danger." He put a stethoscope to my stomach and we all heard the baby's heart beating along steadily like a little choo-choo train. That's when I fully grasped why Sergio believed so much in Ashwin Chopra's professional competence.

At home, I resigned myself to stomach aching starvation, plus the constant nausea, until one morning, two weeks after my consult with Ashwin, I woke up to *no nausea* at seven months pregnant.

From then on, whenever I woke up hungry at night, Sergio would wake up, too, and prepare me anything I desired. On some nights, it was a simple grilled cheese sandwich with fresh tomatoes. Other nights, he would fry me eggs served on toast with French spinach sauce mixed in with béchamel, which he knew I loved, and his attention to my needs thrilled me into believing I loved him.

But all the extra attention and the expectation I knew Sergio attached to the birth of his first child ratcheted my fear about giving birth to an abnormal child.

Therefore, without the nausea to deal with, I quelled my worry in quantities of fried plantain chips or Indian sweetmeats or English pastries. To act like a normal Indian girl would under the circumstances, I rummaged through Didima's old *Woman & Home* magazines stored in a cardboard box, searching for patterns to knit for my baby as Didima had done for me.

If I didn't knit, I sewed self-fashioned baby garments on Didima's old Singer sewing machine I cherished as a reminder of Didima. Didima had never taught me how to sew, but I had learned the basics from watching her, and the more garments I sewed, the better I got at it, much to Sergio's delight. For him, my sewing had a sentimental meaning, since his mother had supported herself and her children as a seamstress once her husband had died and her trip to "seek her fortune in Panama" had ended in failure.

Sergio understood sewing wasn't easy or cheap, so he loved that I did it as a hobby because it saved him money from having to constantly replenish my wardrobe, given our hectic social life. In any remaining free time I had, I lost myself in the world of Dadu's favorite author, P. G. Wodehouse. When I read, I didn't worry.

I had been thirteen when I unearthed the English author's works stashed in shoeboxes under Teddy's bed. The novels, covered in Dadu's college-issued brown paper, had smelled old as I ran my fingers over Dadu's bold and decisive handwriting, which registered the novels' titles and the date on which he bought them. I dove into the pile of impossible stories to rediscover Dadu in Wodehouse's outrageous satires, as deliciously eccentric as I recalled my grandpa to be. Our two rooms in South Extension rang with my laughter as I identified Dadu's stiff-upper-lip forbearance and his Victorian chivalry, the same qualities that Didima had fallen in love with during their college days together.

Observing me, Didima would remark, "You couldn't pay Vasant to watch tragedies like *Gone with the Wind*," when I begged her for one more story about Dadu. "For him, real life was the drama he sought to escape. Wit, he said, was for the rich, and buffoonery for the poor, but P. G. Wodehouse was pure humor, which helped him laugh off the worst humdinger of a day."

By my eighth month, I realized Sergio didn't particularly approve of my reading when he came home and said, "You could have been ready for this evening's engagements if you'd stopped reading on time." Or "I wish I could stay home and read all day." Or "Maybe I should read P. G. Wodehouse to see what you like so much about him?"

But since I couldn't believe he was serious, I didn't pay any attention to the warning signs until one evening when Dadu's novels were stacked high on my nightstand and Sergio spotted me stuffing wool socks into a large white purse to attend a cocktail party.

"What're you doing?"

"Giving the bag shape."

Sergio snatched the purse from my hand. "Then why can't you keep your name cards in there or your wallet that's lost in your closet? And the day planner I gave you or the address book you've yet to open?" He yanked my closet door, hooking a snarl of handbags, silk scarves, pantyhose, and knitting wool to toss them on the bedroom floor. "Why, Noor? Tell me, why?" He pulled his hair and kicked the pile. "Why can't you be like other wives, who help instead of hinder? Those books are your demons. That's why you act possessed. One day, they'll disappear. Maybe that'll wake you up."

I stared at him in silence because my multiple beatings had taught me to remain silent. But I began obsessing about how Sergio would disappear my last link to my beloved grandpa, and that fear became a new worry. Outwardly, however, I finished dressing and accompanied Sergio to his evening commitment since we couldn't be late.

The next day, I drowned my anxiety in quantities of junk food and hid my novels under the mattress before Sergio came home. Between the stress of the former and my worry about my due date approaching in less than a month, my water broke ten days later, on a Thursday afternoon in early March.

"Come to the clinic immediately." The obstetrician sounded worried. "A dry birth is a nightmare."

Sergio rushed home from work, and we both had scared eyes when we arrived at the clinic in Jor Bagh forty minutes later. The obstetrician hastened to place me on a Pitocin IV, fearing my water would run out. She encouraged me to walk up and down a corridor so the baby would come sooner. And neither she nor Sergio guessed that my real fear was the actual condition of the child, not the giving-birth part. Within half an hour, however, the Pitocin accelerated my contractions to such a pitch, I forgot all my fears and shrieked and howled in pain as I shouted out the "Our Father" prayer, needing to anchor my thoughts.

Thanks to being an athletic twenty-two-year-old, my baby was born literally on my second push after the doctor laid me down on the delivery table. Everything happened so fast, I was dimly aware of Sergio holding my hand, the doctor screaming, a baby screaming, and a huge hollow space inside me as I lay there drenched in sweat.

The doctor came around to my side with a screeching bundle in her arms. "It's a girl." She smiled.

"Is she normal?" I croaked.

"Of course! Why wouldn't she be normal? You are twenty-two years old. Your baby is perfect."

Weakly, I squeezed Sergio's hand, meeting his eyes.

He had tears streaming down his face. "Thank you," he whispered. "I never knew having a child was so painful."

And I had my own tears, but they were tears of gratitude to God that my child was no monster. The obstetrician handed my baby to the waiting pediatrician.

I said, "I have this crater of pain inside me. Please. I need something for pain."

"In a few minutes. We have to wait for the placenta to come out. "Do you want to hold your child?"

"No." I rubbed my eyes. "Just please give me a painkiller."

Sergio left the clinic after I was settled in a patient room, and I fell asleep despite the truck-hit-me sensation. The following morning, a nurse woke me while I wondered how village women in India gave birth and resumed tending to their fields two hours after. Then I discovered how my small breasts had been replaced by two gigantically painful rocks.

"That's good," the nurse said. "It means your milk descended."

She hurried out and brought in a pink bundle that now had a name. Pia. Awkwardly, I held Pia to my breast, seeing my child for the first time with her thatch of golden hair, little red face, and squinting blue eyes. I wasn't prepared for an avalanche of love when Pia tugged at my nipple hungrily.

Overwhelmed by the new love, the gulf between my mother and me grew wider because I doubly didn't understand how she had relegated me to her parents upon my birth.

In the evening, Sergio showed up with a present.

I opened a blue velvet box to see an exquisite, eight-strand river-pearl choker with a moonstone clasp. "And this?" I looked at him.

"For giving me the most beautiful child in the world."

At home two days later, one glance into the full-length mirror made me burst into tears.

I had gained so much weight, I looked just like my mother. Also, Sergio and I hadn't found a nanny yet. Therefore, as the expert parents we were, Sergio had imported me twelve soft linen diapers from China.

That very day, we found out how a newborn needed around ten to twelve diaper changes *a day*, and Sergio raced to order more cloth diapers. We had both decided we didn't want to use disposable ones because they were expensive and we didn't know what chemicals they contained. That meant a frantic race to wash the diapers while Pia slept in two-hour chunks, but both Sergio and I were so entranced by Pia, we didn't care.

All too soon, we found a Bengali nanny through the reference of a fellow diplomatic couple, and I had no excuse to stay home with Pia anymore. Hating my fat, jiggly body, I continued to wear my maternity dresses, mortified to attend parties in them but with no choice.

To add insult to injury, Pia, since the day she was born, received formal invitations to diplomats' children's birthday parties. I began to loath my social engagements, which interrupted Pia's nap time and my precious alone time with her. I fantasized about ditching going to parties that, in real life, I had no means to refuse to attend. Meanwhile, each dawn, after feeding Pia, I drove to the Nehru Park in Chanakya Puri, five miles away, to run its three-mile perimeter, desperate to lose weight.

My favorite part of the day became nine o'clock, when Sergio left for work and Pia got to nap on my chest as I gobbled the relief of reading P. G. Wodehouse while she slept. But forty days after Pia was born, I had yet to lose a gram, and I came up with a new plan. That night, during a formal dinner at the Argentine residence, I ate a five-course dinner of consommé, cheese soufflé, a cauliflower salad, baked chicken in orange sauce with rice, and caramel pudding. Unable to avoid a single bite with only twelve people around the dining table, I ate it all. While waiting for coffee and liqueurs, I calmly visited the guest bathroom, drank five glasses' worth of water from the tap, and vomited out the entire dinner. At last, I experienced some control over my life.

Thus drowning in my own troubles, I failed to relate to the battles Sergio fought at work. All I understood was that, once again, Sergio became head of mission when his new ambassador died of a massive stroke in June 1984. I hated it that he was gone at all hours. The only time I saw Sergio was when he came home in the evening to change and we had to head out to social engagements. Our dysfunction peaked when I let rot four roasted chickens the night before Peru's national day reception on July 28.

"It's your fault!" Sergio shouted. "You should have put them in the fridge."

"No!" I shouted back. "I didn't roast them. The cook did. *He* should have put them in the fridge before he left for the evening. I was out all afternoon at a ladies' luncheon. How could I know about the chickens?"

"Because all responsible housewives check the kitchen before they retire for the night!"

"Well, I can't play wife *and* mother *and* your perfect social companion *and* cook monitor too!"

"Of course you can't! You're too busy reading! You think I don't know you hide your novels under your side of the mattress?"

"What? Have you been spying on me?"

"It's not spying, Noor. It's feeling completely crazy with a nutjob for a wife whom *I* have to manage on top of my work, which goes on around the clock."

"Then you better get ready for more, because I want another child."

"*Another child?* Are you crazy? Pia isn't even a year old yet. So why would you want a second child when you have trouble maintaining Pia's social calendar?"

"Because Pia will *not* be an only child like I was, catching my crazy family's windblast because they had no other victim to torment."

"Not going to happen! I refuse to add a second child to this madness."

Meanwhile, our shouting match had reduced Pia to bawling so loudly in the arms of Rani, the nanny, she waved her arm, trying to interrupt us.

"What?" I shouted, turning on her.

"Can't you see what you're doing to Pia?" She pointed to Pia's face. "Give me money so I can get her out of here and go buy more chicken with the driver. That's what this fight is about, isn't it? Shhhh." She wiped Pia's tears, hiding the child's face on her ample shoulder.

"Let's wait a few years to have another child." Sergio fished out his wallet from his trouser pocket. "You may be less stressed by then, better able to handle the pace of diplomatic life in time." He handed Rani a hundred rupees.

"Why? So I get to have a child alone in Peru, where you tell me your salary won't even afford us a nanny? It's either now or forget about a son."

I became pregnant again within forty days.

23

Perhaps my sixth sense should have warned me all was not well with my second pregnancy, but it didn't. Instead, during one minute, I would be fine, focused on knitting baby garments, delighted that my condition came without nausea, then in the next minute, I would punch my stomach in fits of vicious rage to be pregnant at all. Without notice, I would drown in insane bouts of anger and fear about the responsibility of two children instead of one. Afterward, I would sob for a good hour. But the last emotion was always shame—ugly, berating, crucifying shame that kept me from ever confessing my fits to Sergio or my obstetrician because I attended all my doctor's appointments with Sergio present. Thus, each time I went to the doctor's, I came away pacified by the doctor's examination that the baby was doing well.

In the end, isn't it all that matters? That my child is healthy?

In the aftermath of my panic attacks, only junk food calmed me. Junk food and a book to lose myself in for a while, go to another country, become another person, lead another life in between the lines on a printed page. It was my reprieve from dressing for the next diplomatic engagement where I had to chat with friends and acquaintances or spending my precious home time struggling to plan our next guest list without repeating a recipe within six months.

One night, Sergio approached me. We exchanged a preliminary kiss, and I knew what would follow.

"What, again?" I exclaimed, too late to take it back. *Christ.* My job was to provide Sergio with as much sex as he wanted. "Sorry I said that."

"No, you're not." Sergio's voice rose. "You meant it. I'm not blind. I see how you lie there and close your eyes as if you're not there at all. You don't enjoy sex. Do you think I don't notice? You're one of those frigid types."

I wanted to say, *No, I'm not. I loved it when Chirag kissed me... I'm sure I would have loved to make love with him too. It's you. Your kisses are dead, and when you kiss me, I feel dead too. Besides, you don't care about me. You just make yourself come.* But out loud, I said, "You're right. Maybe I *am* frigid. Maybe it's not my fault, because I'm pregnant."

"Oh, please. You were frigid since day one. You appear young and sexy, yet you're an iceberg—" He yanked his pajamas back on.

In bed, he didn't say good night as he switched off the lights. In the darkness, I chewed on my lower lip, convinced I had put my foot in it since Sergio already had so many complaints regarding my shortcomings as a wife.

From the next day on, Sergio demanded to know why the furniture wasn't dusted or the grocery list up to date or our clothes back from the dry cleaners. He also demanded to know why it was his job to track the week's social calendar and remind me of my engagements when I was the stay-at-home wife. I brushed aside his criticism, too busy dressing for our next evening engagement.

During my fourth month of pregnancy, on a Sunday afternoon, an acerbic remark from Sergio to tidy my closet "so the doors don't fall out" escalated into a roaring fight.

"Of course!" I shouted. "It's my job to tidy closets on top of everything else I do."

"What do you do, Noor, except stay home, dress up, and play pretty?"

Trapped between us on our bed, Pia cried, staring at us with frightened eyes. Sergio picked her up, saying, "Shhh, *amor*, it's okay."

"*Okay?*" I screamed. "I'll show you okay!" I bounced off the bed and galloped to the telephone by the pantry door and dialed my obstetrician's number. "I want an abortion right *now*!" I screamed, satisfied to see Sergio's eyes round as he followed me.

He couldn't stop me, because abortions were one hundred percent legal in India.

"What's wrong? Are you bleeding?" I imagined pretty Dr. Khosla's forehead creasing in alarm.

"No!"

"Well, tell me what the matter is, or else how can I proceed?"

"What do you care as long as I pay you?" I shook with a fury I couldn't control.

"If it's not an emergency, don't ruin my Sunday. Come to my office tomorrow morning, and we can do whatever you decide."

"What time?" I punched the wall.

"Eight thirty. I have appointments from nine on."

After I hung up the phone, Sergio said, "It's best you *do* get an abortion. You're not equipped to be the mother of *one* child, let alone two."

I wrenched a howling Pia from his arms and locked myself in the second bedroom, where Pia had her crib.

The next day, unlike ever before, Sergio sent me to see Dr. Khosla alone with the chauffeur. "Do whatever you please," he said. "I'll pay for it, but I won't support you through it."

At her clinic, Dr. Khosla didn't smile as she gestured to an inner door. "I have to do an ultrasound so I can decide on how to abort."

Prodded by the ultrasound probe, my fetus put its thumb in its mouth. It moved a tiny leg and scratched its huge head with a diminutive hand, and my throat choked from a rush of completely unexpected emotion.

"Should we do it tomorrow?" Dr. Khosla watched me.

I glanced at the lady doctor in dumb pain. I could not kill this baby who sucked its thumb inside of me with no notion I lay here planning its death. My eyes swam in unshed tears.

"I knew you'd come to your senses, you silly girl." Dr. Khosla smiled. "Go home and eat something wonderful." Yes. Junk food would calm me. I had to buy a lot of it on the way home.

At lunch time, Sergio came home. "So, when is the abortion?"

"There isn't going to be one. I changed my mind." *Did Sergio sigh in relief, or did I imagine it?*

Abril was born on the first Sunday of August 1985 at seven in the evening. That day, Sergio spent hours at Palam airport to oversee the arrival of yet another new ambassador, Alonso Rivera, to replace the last one, who had died fourteen months earlier. He nearly missed the birth of his second child.

A smiling Dr. Khosla handed him his new baby. "It's a girl, Sergio. Congratulations."

"There go my chances of a son." Sergio cradled the baby. "Oh, and she's brown-skinned too."

"So?" I croaked. "It didn't hurt any less to give birth to her or carry her for nine months."

"Good God, Noor. Lighten up. You're so literal."

The following morning, I expected to fall in love with Abril as I had with Pia. But when Abril was ready to be fed, I didn't produce a drop of milk. Instead, I experienced a stifling indifference toward the tiny bundle who squirmed in my arms. Like with my bouts of rage during the pregnancy that I hadn't been able to control, I couldn't shake off my indifference.

But the worst shock was to realize *I didn't love Pia either* when the child arrived to visit with her new sister. My numbness suffocated me with the surety of a plastic bag over my head no one else could see.

In a week, I dreaded waking up at all. *Yet to whom can I confess this deadness inside me? As though my contact with my babies occurs from behind a glass pane? What would Sergio say if I revealed my true state to him? He's already disappointed in the birth of a brown baby girl. Is this what my mother underwent after I was born? Is that why she foisted her newborn on Didima without regret?*

No. My feelings for Pia and Abril were my own private business. *I grew the babies in my uterus, not Sergio. They were mine, not his. I would never fail them because I was not my mother.* My babies would have wonderful lives.

24

Abril came down with chicken pox at twelve days old. I found it difficult to breathe when the pediatrician diagnosed Abril with pneumonia on top of the chicken pox.

"But how can she have pneumonia while we melt in this August heat?"

"It's the frequent summer power outages," replied the pediatrician. "Babies become chilled after they sweat." He warned me how Pia could contract pneumonia as well. "Keep them hydrated, and don't leave them alone. Newborns are prone to choking."

Rani, our nanny, already worked from seven to seven. The poor soul needed sleep to be effective. That left me the nights to handle alone unless Sergio pitched in.

On the seventh night of Abril's wailing, Sergio threw his pillow to the floor. "From now on, I'll sleep in the study," he declared. "I've been so tired these last ten days, all I do at work is repeat-check what I write. This new ambassador isn't like the previous one. He just got promoted to the rank of ambassador, and he's very insecure. So each day, he's out to prove how stupid everyone else is, and I'm the favorite target in his daily line of fire." He picked up his two pillows.

"And what'll I do without you? How will I give Pia the bottle or change her diaper when Abril never stops crying and I can't lie her down? What if she chokes?"

"I don't know, Noor. All I know is I have to sleep. Otherwise, I'll lose my job and be sent back to Lima in disgrace. If this new ambassador gets a whiff of my poor mental state, he won't hesitate to strip my job from me like old wallpaper." Sergio marched out of the bedroom as if his explanation fixed everything.

"Right!" I shouted to his back. "I bet you wouldn't leave if Abril were light-skinned and a boy, though."

Sergio didn't answer me.

During the coming days, I seethed in anger as I drifted in and out of diplomatic engagements, too tired to register the nuances of the conversations I engaged in. Every evening, I rode with Sergio in the car in pin-drop silence until we walked into a gathering. Then he hissed, "Smile. People are watching."

And that became my cue for showtime, as it had been at our Catholic wedding ceremony in Lima. Standing in a church deluged with people, I had sweltered in my wedding finery, striving to approximate a solemn Indian bride until Sergio pinched my wrist and said those exact words. As if he had pressed a button, I had smiled on command but fumed underneath. *Why didn't he warn me? How was I supposed to know Western brides had to grin like Cheshire cats?* In India, that behavior would be unacceptable.

On the eve of my twenty-fourth birthday, Abril had been sick for nine days and Pia for six. I hadn't slept in ninety-five hours as I reclined in bed, balancing the children on my lap. *Surely, Sergio will take pity on me and let me sleep tonight, since today is a Friday and he doesn't work Saturdays? One night of sleep is the best birthday present he could give me right now.*

But Sergio came home after a dinner party at the Austrian embassy and changed out of his three-piece suit. "You know, I'm always amazed at how many people are impressed with what you have to say, even though you're just a green college kid. I spent half the evening explaining your absence. People will call you tomorrow."

As he moved around, I followed him with my eyes, wanting to scream, *Do you think I care? I don't care if I never see another diplomat again in my entire life. Look at me! Can't you see how red my eyes are from lack of sleep? Tell me you'll let me sleep tonight. I want you to understand I can't deal with the children being sick anymore. Please, please stop chattering. Please.*

But Sergio continued to talk.

Will he pretend he can't hear the mind-numbing volume of the children crying at different pitches on my lap?

He approached the bed.

Now. He'll tell me now he will watch the kids tonight.

Instead, Sergio ruffled the unhappy children's hair, readying to head for the study.

I swallowed my pride and cleared my throat. "Could you watch them for me tonight? I haven't slept in three days."

"You're joking, right?"

"Why would I be joking? Can't you see how red my eyes are? I'm beyond exhausted."

"Noor, I worked all day, attended a national day cocktail, then this dinner. All you've done is stay home for a week. And here I am being pleasant enough to tell you what wonderful things people said about you… but all you think of is yourself. You want to know what I *really* thought when all those people complimented you? That you weren't present like you are supposed to be. As a diplomat's wife, you're a dead loss. Other men have wives who are a help. You are a liability."

I watched my tears fall on Pia's plump little thigh as I lowered my head, and he walked out of the room.

At midnight, when my birthday ticktocked into existence, I rocked in a rocking chair, two crying and coughing infants reclined on my chest, my eyes closed, head thrown back on the backrest. It would end if I was patient. But it was hard to be patient when every strand of hair on my head hurt as much as my body did. I opened my eyes. Abril had fallen silent—her soft dark thatch of hair collapsed on my left breast so I couldn't see my baby's tiny face.

My chest heaved in alarm. *Jesus Christ. Is she unconscious? What if she's dead?* I let forth a sob, unable to lift the child's head with my right arm wrapped around Pia, who stared at me with blue eyes swimming in a lake of tears because she had absorbed my alarm.

"Ma-mamma-ma-ma," she stuttered from her four-word vocabulary.

Panicked, I smothered Pia to the middle of my chest and tried to straighten Abril's sunken chin with my right hand. "Amor," I said, "*Amor!*" Tears spilled on my baby's nose and lips. *No. Jesus, no. She can't be dead at nineteen days old!* "Abril!" I shook the baby, wiggling my own left arm as hard as possible. But Abril's eyes remained unresponsive. *Oh my God, no!*

I repositioned Pia, red-faced from howling in fright at my panic, back into the crook of my right arm. My heart boomeranged as I struggled to stand up with the uneven weight of an eighteen-month-old squashed to my right breast and Abril's featherweight pressed to the left. *I'll wake up Sergio. He has to call the pediatrician. I can't face this alone.* Right then, Abril emitted a tiny grunt, and I almost dropped her.

"God, don't you *ever* do that to me again," I heaved, kissing the top of my baby's head.

On weak legs, I maneuvered all three of us back into the rocking chair. "Shhh-shhh," I crooned and kissed Pia's wet face.

Why did my ribcage hurt as if my chest would rip open and spill my heart out if anything ever happened to Abril or Pia? In that split second, I knew what the pain was—love. Christ, I loved my children. Beyond the inexplicable numbness, beyond the flatline running through me, I loved my children. Tears coursed down my face. *I am not the monster my mother was.* I would never, *never* give up my children. Abril's eyes fluttered. The child coughed and cried, and I smiled, pressing her to my aching chest, knowing my children were alive.

At seven a.m., I handed the children over to Rani, made myself a coffee, and went to huddle on the antique colonial sofa in our drawing room, glazed eyes staring at the pink Belgian glass lamp hanging above our marble dining table.

I heard a door open, and Sergio emerged from the study, tying the broad sash of his blue-and-white striped kimono, bright-eyed from a restful night's sleep. "Hey, happy birthday, darling."

I ignored him and sipped my coffee. I had forgotten it was my birthday.

Without comment, Sergio disappeared through the swinging pantry door. In a while, he swung back out with a dirty wooden ladle cocked in one hand. "I'm baking you your favorite molasses cake with dried fruits and nuts. See?"

Those words snapped the last thread of sanity inside my hazy brain. I jumped up and threw the coffee mug at Sergio. "I'm fifteen kilos overweight. Your kids are dying, and you're baking me a *cake*? I hate you. Don't ever speak to me again."

Sergio ducked, dropping the wooden ladle, watching the coffee mug shattered on the floor. As if unable to believe his eyes, he looked down at the jagged porcelain shards, the spilled coffee, and the lumps of cake batter. Slowly, he raised his head. His eyes smoldered. "I'll never bake you another cake as long as I live."

"Of course you won't! Because our whole marriage is about you, never me." I buried my head in my lap and began sobbing.

By the end of October, Sergio and I didn't exchange one extra word in the privacy of our home. I ran each morning, attended my and my children's social obligations, and vomited whenever the anxiety of being fat like my mother defeated me.

In that suspended environment, Sergio declared, "I'm sleeping in the bedroom tonight."

"Don't bother." My jaw clenched. "I don't want you back."

"That's for me to decide."

"Then I want a divorce!" I exploded, my temper always my worst enemy.

"Fine," Sergio said calmly. "I'll be happy to give you one. But since it isn't my idea, I'll keep the children. When I go home to Lima next year, stay in India. Pia and Abril will come with me."

"No, they won't! I bore them. They're mine."

"Is that right?" Sergio's smile was not a smile.

That night, I lay awake and listened to Sergio snore so near my body I could touch his back. *What if he takes the children away from me? He could, given his diplomatic immunity. I don't even have the money to buy a plane ticket to Peru, let alone file a court case against him. Meanwhile, my children would be long gone to Peru before I could do anything to help myself. Now that he has finished using me to have his children, he can ditch me anytime… and I would have to return home to my parents with my tail between my legs.*

In the morning, unbeknownst to Sergio, I drove to my old college faculty in the Jawahar Lal Nehru University once Sergio left for the embassy and I had the car to do grocery shopping. At JNU, the *sambar* lentil smell outside the cafeteria and walking the familiar paths felt like a sharp punch in the face.

Has it been more than two years already since I was a regular figure around these parts? How simple life had been then, compared to now, yet how much I had hated it. Yet who can I blame for it all except me? I was the author of my own misery. I had chosen to marry Sergio. I had listened to him and dropped out of college. It was hard to face that my stepfather, of all people, had been right. I should have finished the BA part of my five-year, double-degree Spanish program. But I would fix that.

I picked up my pace. Thank goodness my classmates were in class right then, all seniors about to graduate. Therefore, no one recognized me or asked any difficult questions I didn't want to answer. How naïve I had been to think that marrying Sergio was the answer to all my problems. I knew if I wanted to divorce Sergio, the one crucial asset I needed was my college degree. Without it, I would never get a decent-enough job to support the children and me.

Up on the fifth floor, I addressed the Spanish faculty department head. "Sir, is there any way I can repeat my last semester to complete at least the BA part of my degree? You know what a serious student I was when I was here." I was more than conscious that I neither could nor would get my master's degree since that would require two more years of college and Sergio was due back to Peru for a home posting in less than a year, *if* he took me with him to Lima, but that worry could wait. Right then, I had to resolve what was within my reach.

"Let me research it and call you back." Dr. Dey smiled. "So, how is diplomatic life on the inside?"

"The same as any other life, I suppose," I said, scared to reveal too much. "Full of responsibilities and very busy all the time." I heaved a sigh of relief when he didn't pursue the subject.

The next day, I was on tenterhooks, but the phone remained silent. *If I could go back to school for six months, would Sergio even let me?* I hadn't dared ask him the question yet.

Dr. Dey called back the following afternoon. If the black telephone receiver had been made of glass, my grip would have shattered it. My heart converted to a boomerang waiting for good news.

"Noor?" said Dr. Dey. "You're two months too *late* to finish your degree. The grace period to be away is twenty-two months. Today, you are two days shy of *twenty-four* months. I'm sorry."

"But, sir," I argued. "Couldn't they reconsider? I was such a good student."

"Noor, Indian bureaucracy is based on English bureaucracy. Even if I filed a case on your behalf, the case alone would take months or years to review and decide. Won't your husband be posted out of the country by then?"

I hung up the phone and cried like a child. My education was a star-crossed unicorn in my life. Neither real nor ever functional. All I had wanted was to study English—yet that simple, simple desire had been denied me. Instead, I had had Spanish rammed down my throat—but there I was, unable to finish studying even that hated career. I would never receive that degree nor acquire a job to support myself and my children. *Is this what Sergio had intended all along when he insisted I quit school? My total and utter dependency on him so I could never escape? For as long as I live, I will never stand by to watch another dragonfly's tail being tied to "fly" it. Why had Baba never seen the cruelty of his little game? But this world is full of cruelty. Otherwise, why would people enjoy bullfighting or cockfighting?* One species's weakness was another species's power.

In an hour, I wiped my eyes, determined to remain positive. Right then, I was overwhelmed. But, after a night of sleep I wouldn't be so tired or stressed. The solution to reverse my setback was inside me, but I needed a calm head to find it without giving in to panic.

25

THE NEXT NIGHT, IN BED, I felt as if I had a fishbone stuck in my throat when I forced myself to say, "Serg, I'm sorry for what I said yesterday when we fought. I don't want a divorce." What I most needed was time to determine what to do next. If Sergio initiated divorce proceedings, I wouldn't have that time.

"Well, I do." Sergio didn't bother to meet my eyes. "Now *I* don't want a relationship with *you*."

Of course you don't, you bastard. You just used me to give you a couple of children... and now I'm expendable. But neither you nor anyone else will take my precious children away from me. I cleared my throat. "Maybe." I stared at Sergio to buy time and get a grip on my temper. Then, I added, "But you won't separate me from my children. If they go to Lima, I go to Lima." *Will Sergio notice how my hands are joined in frightened prayer?*

"Whatever." Sergio rolled over to sleep.

During the following few days, I was ready for our evenings out *before* Sergio even came home to change. He, however, didn't acknowledge the difference. Nor did he touch upon the possibility of making love to me or initiate any discussion of a divorce. And the less he spoke to me, the more driven I became to remain with my children.

A week after the night of our fight, I swallowed my pride. "Serg, would you make love to me if I asked you to?"

In answer, Sergio faced away from me, frightening me into a sleepless night altogether.

Two whole months passed. On a Sunday morning in November, I approached Sergio at the breakfast table while Pia sat in her high chair beside him and Abril burbled in a crib nearby, gnawing on a large piece of apple she couldn't choke on.

I cleared my throat and pulled back a dining chair. "Serg, can we please talk? It'll take a minute."

He lowered his newspaper, his green-brown eyes resembling flint.

"Look." I clutched and unclutched a fork on a place setting next to a butter knife. "Can I go back to college once we're in Peru?"

"Who says you'll go to Peru?"

My heart paused. "Well, won't I?" I gripped the edge of the dining table.

"I guess." Sergio's voice underlined reluctance. "Because the children still need you."

"Well, can I go to college there? You promised me I could when I quit JNU."

"What for?"

"*What for?* Because otherwise, I'll be a financial burden to you despite a divorce. Don't you see that? If I finish my college degree, I can acquire a decent job and not depend on you for money."

In India, for example, class segregation prevented an employer from hiring me to do the job of a store clerk. Conversely, even to do a receptionist's job, I needed a diploma I didn't have. I imagined Peru was similar.

Sergio bit into his peanut-buttered toast and took a sip of coffee. He raised his newspaper to block out my presence.

"Serg."

The newspaper rustled but didn't lower.

"Serg, I'm not finished." I picked up a breakfast knife then put it down.

The newspaper flew to the floor. "Can you give me peace on a Sunday, for Christ's sake? What do you want? What more can I do for you other than provide you with a life of no work and relative luxury?" Sergio's lips narrowed to a straight line.

"Talk to Nila." I tried to steel the tremble in my voice. "Ask her if Eduardo can enroll me into La Universidad Católica in Lima. He's faculty there, so he must have clout."

"You're serious!" Sergio laughed. "You want me to burden my sister and her husband with your new whim."

I wanted to ask how much burden one phone call was in their lives, but I controlled my rising temper. "Yes. If you could please. I need three more months of classes. I'll go to any university in Lima where Nila or Eduardo can enroll me."

"If I say yes, will you please leave me alone for the rest of the day? I have as much right to enjoy this apartment as you do."

I scraped back my chair and stood. "If I had known this would be your attitude, I never would have quit college on your command."

Sergio picked up the newspaper off the floor but didn't look at me. "Let me think about it."

26

By early December 1985, the Christmas parties in the diplomatic world of New Delhi were in full swing, since many diplomats visited families in home countries during the actual holidays. Two whole weeks had passed since I had brought up the back-to-university-in-Peru question, and Sergio had not said a word about it in the little he said to me. But it was a Thursday, and I would bring it up that night. I couldn't spend another weekend ignorant of my fate.

Right after Sergio left for work, I buckled down on a drawing room sofa to redo my nails for a ladies' luncheon that afternoon. The phone blared by the pantry door. *Who would call this early?*

"Hello?" I blew on the wet red nail-polished nails on my right hand.

"Is this Noor?" The voice was male.

"Yes, who is this?"

"Don't you recognize me?"

"No."

"It's Chirag."

I couldn't have been more shocked if a spaceship had burst through my drawing room wall.

"Noor? Are you there?"

"Yes. Yes, I'm here." My voice came out barely audible.

"Can I come see you?"

"No! Not at my house." As desperate as I was to see him, I couldn't jeopardize my marriage. "It's complicated. My servants and the nanny would tell my husband an unknown man came to see me. Can you meet me at Nehru Park in a half hour? The main entrance? I run there each morning."

My heart drummed as I charged into the children's room. "Rani? Can you bathe the children? I have to go out. It's urgent."

I was already out of the room as Rani replied, "Of course, *Didi*," in Bengali. "Are you alright?"

"Yes!" I shouted from my bedroom. "But I have to leave right away. If I'm not back within an hour, put the children down for their nap." I flurried back into the nursery and plucked Pia from her crib to hug and kiss her. "You two be good for Nana. You hear me?" I tickled Abril cradled in Rani's arms, placed Pia back in her crib, and wrapped the child's tiny fingers around her favorite stuffed duck. Then I ran out of the apartment.

At Nehru Park's main entrance, the silk cotton trees looked skeletal. Their star-shaped leaves blew around on the pavement in a fair winter breeze and crackled under my running shoes as I stepped out of my car in the carpark, deserted at that hour. *Did I mention the main entrance to him?* I couldn't remember. My heart thumped. Leaves crunched behind me, and I whirled, hand on chest, but it was a jogger.

"Noor?"

My head jerked halfway around. *Thank you, God.* He exited the park gate, older and more solemn than at eighteen, his long hair replaced by a sensible haircut, his lean body filled out.

"Hi." He approached. "I got here way early, so I decided to walk." He stared at me with those penetrating eyes etched on my heart.

I wanted to throw my arms around him, but I stood still.

"So, what happened, Noor? One day you stopped writing to me, and that was that."

"Oh, Chirag. Let's go sit and talk in the chrysanthemum garden south of here."

"You owe me an explanation, don't you think?" Chirag kicked a stone off the graveled pathway, those expressive eyes as hurt as his voice.

I gave him an anguished look, oblivious for once to the tattered phlox blooms lining the pathway. "Did you receive my letter telling you how I ran away from home after my doctor fiancé beat me up?"

"Of course I did." Chirag sniffed the smoky air. "I was so upset, I badgered my father to buy me a ticket to come back to India that very day. He said he would, but he convinced me I needed to graduate first, since school closed for the summer in twelve more days."

"Well, the day after I wrote you my last letter, my grandma died. The next morning, *the police* came to the working girls' hostel and arrested me for associating with your family. The policeman claimed your father was a smuggler of prostitutes. I had no way of knowing it was all a hoax my mother had invented."

Chirag stopped dead. "And you *believed* him?" He grasped my forearm like a tong. "Noor, you believed that about my family?"

"Of course not, but what could I do? He put me in handcuffs and drove me to my parents' house. There, he thrashed me and inspected my body for drug use." I rubbed my arm where Chirag had gripped it.

"Without a lawyer?" exclaimed Chirag. "That's illegal. And you let him?"

"Chirag, this is India. I was seventeen years old and scared out of my mind." I covered my eyes. "Did I tell you that police guy *stripped* me to beat me?"

"Stripped you? Why? Let me guess. Because this is fucking India and men can do whatever they want."

"He inspected every inch of my body. Two weeks after, I attempted suicide, but the memory of you stopped me from following through. I figured if I died, I would never see you again. Once a year passed then another and another, I stopped believing I ever would. In the end, I survived to escape my parents."

"Oh, Noor—why didn't you run away again?" Chirag stopped dead and pinned me with those wide, talking eyes.

"Run away how? And to where? All the money I ever had was for bus fare. Besides, I was petrified of the 'surveillance' watching me."

Chirag glanced at the sky. "I swear such shit only happens in India. Is this the chrysanthemum garden?" He pointed to a higgledy-piggledy jumble of chrysanthemums of varying heights and colors blooming in a ragged circle where the path widened into a quadrangle.

"Yes." I smiled. "They looked a lot better a week ago." I sat on a cold cement bench, pushing back the many heads of scarlet chrysanthemums poking through the wooden slats of its backrest. "Come sit?" I patted the bench.

"I can't believe this." Chirag shook his head.

"What?" *Did he sit a foot away from me on purpose?*

"That we're back on a winter park bench, stuck in our own recycled nightmare. As though our relationship is incapable of progressing beyond a park bench."

"How did you locate me?" My icy fingertips brushed the heads of a myriad bronze chrysanthemums bowing at my feet.

"I called the Peruvian embassy."

"How did you know to contact the Peruvian embassy?"

"I was in India the day before you got married," Chirag said. "I actually *saw* your wedding announcement posted on the Taj Hotel bulletin board. I couldn't believe you were marrying someone other than me."

My hand crushed several flowerheads, releasing their spicy, pungent aroma into the crisp winter air. "Then why didn't you come see me?" My voice sounded strangled. "I wasn't married yet."

"See you? Where? The Taj Hotel staff wouldn't have divulged your address. Or should I have come back the next day to watch you marry another guy? I was so angry, I called my mom in America from the hotel and said I'd marry the next girl she chose for me. You see, my mom was convinced I was her wild child, so she was always pushing marriage proposals on me. For three years, I rebuffed her, hoping to find you, but once I saw the Taj Hotel bulletin board, I lost it."

"Well, I've been married for three years. If all you had to do was call the embassy, why didn't you find me earlier?"

"I tried. Whenever I came to India, I called the embassy, but they wouldn't give me your home number. I don't know why they did this time."

"You're wearing a wedding ring too. When did you marry?" I touched his left hand, wanting to grip it, hold it, but I didn't in case he withdrew it, which would hurt worse than a snub.

"A month after you did. Once I said yes, my mom didn't lose any time since she didn't trust me not to change my mind."

"Do you have kids too?"

"No." Chirag's eyes shifted then met mine. "Run away with me?"

"Are you serious?" My eyes widened.

"Right here, right now. Let's run away." That was the Chirag I had always known as a child, totally reckless.

"Oh, love, I can't. I have two children."

"Bring the children."

"I can't." I felt the older of the two of us, even though I was a year younger than Chirag. "As a diplomat, Sergio has a lot of power. He'd catch us and confiscate my children. He's already threatened to leave me behind in India next year and take the children with him to Peru when he's posted back there," I confessed.

"Jesus, and you fell in *love* with this guy?"

"Chirag, we don't live in a vacuum, do we? That's why, as circumstances unfold, we fall victims to them. So, my answer is no. I didn't love Sergio the way I loved you—I liked him. But when I met him, I already hadn't seen you in three years… and I believed I never would. I married Sergio because my parents would have married me off to another stranger anyway, and he seemed the lesser evil. For me, he was there, and you weren't. You became this beacon I saw in my head, but however hard I tried, I could never reach you."

Chirag grabbed my hand. "You know, though we're not married to each other, it's not because I didn't want it."

I squeezed his cold hand. "I have to go. I have a lunch date. If I don't attend it, I'll be in real trouble with Sergio. Can you come here tomorrow?"

"Sure."

"Will you do me a favor?" I reached out and touched his cheek.

"What?"

"Hug me. Hug me as if none of this mess is true."

Chirag pulled me into his arms and smelled my hair. "I love your hair so much," he whispered, kissing my neck.

"If I close my eyes," I murmured, "we'll be back in that smelly South Extension alley." I touched my forehead to his, and we kissed, tongues dancing, breaths merging until the salt of our tears diluted the taste of the kiss.

I spent the rest of the day lost in the memory of Chirag's kiss and the childhood we had shared while I laughed, talked, and played the part of Sergio's wife. *How could Chirag's mere presence make me feel more alive than I have in the last three years, married to Sergio?* I imagined telling my mother, "Ma, I didn't just see Chirag. I kissed him. Even after all these years, I would run away with him if I didn't have Pia and Abril."

That night, I said to Sergio, "Serg, did you ever ask Nila about my university request?" *If I could go to Peru and finish college and become independent, maybe I could contact Chirag. If he didn't have kids, maybe we could get together. It's a wild dream, but when are dreams ever tame?*

"Yes." Sergio's glance was inscrutable. "The only university willing to consider your case of no-degree status is the UNIFE. *Universidad Femenina del Sagrado Corazon.* It's a girl's Catholic university. Nila's booked you an interview with the principal. You'll have to work out the rest and see what they say."

That was *not* what I had wanted to hear. I had wanted the certainty of a college enrollment. But at least it implied Sergio was taking me to Peru and I could remain with the children. It didn't pay to look a gift horse in the mouth.

The next morning, I walked on eggshells until Sergio left for work. I was rifling through my wardrobe when the phone rang, and I barreled out of the bedroom to snatch up the receiver.

A pause. "Hi. I'm not coming to the park."

"Why?" The bottom dropped out from under my feet.

"Because it hurts to see you."

"Are you drunk? You're slurring your words."

"Probably."

"Where's your wife? How do you explain drinking at nine thirty in the morning to her?"

"She left last night to see her parents in Bangalore."

"Then please see me. Please."

"Run away with me."

"I can't, Chirag. My kids need me. I see it in their little faces. I could never live with myself if I abandoned them as my mother abandoned me. I have never forgiven her, and my children would never forgive me either."

"Goodbye, Noor."

"Goodbye." I sagged to the floor. *Should I have run away with him?* I dropped the phone receiver, remembering how much I had associated my love affair with Chirag to the novel *Love Story*. Back then, I had assumed nothing could be worse than the heroine, Jennifer Cavilleri, dying. I was discovering how much worse it would have been if Jennifer had lived and married someone other than her Oliver. That was the twisted ending to my love story, the story of living the rest of my life without Chirag.

With tear-smudged fingertips, I touched the windowpane next to the black box of the telephone. Staring at the blue winter sky, I whispered, "What is it you want from me, Jesus? Why are my tests so hard?" *Will I ever see Chirag again? And if so, for what?* I sat there on the floor and cried my heart out—cried for the loss of Chirag, the loss of Didima, and the loss of my innocence.

Fifteen minutes later, I got up to make a mug of coffee. The caffeine and sugar with cream took the edge off my pain as I collapsed on our antique Peruvian colonial sofa. What I had to do was remember that Chirag had always been an unattainable teenage dream, and I was no longer a teenager. I was the mother of two darling children. My future lay in completing a college degree from Lima. There, I would embark on a new life with Pia and Abril, far, far away from India and Indian judgment.

OLIVE GROVE

27

Lima, May 1986

SERGIO, THE CHILDREN, AND I landed at Jorge Chavez Airport of Lima on the last day of April 1986. By the time we reached his mother's house, I was running a fever of 106 degrees Fahrenheit after flying for twenty-three hours on three international airlines. But fever or no fever, at least I was with my children. I had to remember that and be grateful. Furthermore, the next day was my interview at the UNIFE. Pray God, I could finish my degree and move on. Meanwhile, Sergio had to report to the Peruvian foreign office the next day as well, so it was unclear as to who would take me to the university, but I didn't want to ask that question quite yet.

In Lima, we would live with Sergio's seventy-three-year-old mother, Señora Xenobia Santander, since Sergio had always paid the old lady's rent. It was the least she could do for him until the construction of our own house was completed. Heavy-breasted and dressed to impress, Señora Santander served us lunch, restricting her conversation to Sergio, as if I didn't count because no one was good enough for her eldest son.

During the meal, she said, "My son, I don't want you hurt when you go out. Since last year, the Shining Path terrorists have relegated the provinces to focus on Lima. Their latest show of force is to bomb electric towers to leave as much of the city in darkness as possible. When they aren't doing that, they kill innocent people by planting car bombs in front of targeted buildings. You're not safe in the foreign office because their crowning aim is to overthrow the government and take over."

The following morning, I steeled my aching body and sore throat and located Sergio in the old apartment's one bathroom. "Serg, you *will* take me to my college interview, won't you?"

"I can't." Sergio continued to shave. "I'm due at work by nine. Nila will drop you. You'll have to make your own way home."

Ten months younger than him, Nila would always be Sergio's favorite.

I rubbed my aching throat and swallowed. "What if I get lost or get caught in a car bombing?"

"Then, don't get lost." Sergio splashed water on his face. "And as for the threat of a car bomb… attending university in Lima was your own bright idea, so you'll have to deal with the Limeñian reality, like I and every other person in the city. Neither Nila nor I intend to play your chauffeur. Learn to take buses here, like you did back in India before I married you."

It was at the tip of my tongue to ask, *Why not? Nila doesn't work. Her husband supports her. Her two kids are in school all day, and she lives five minutes from here.* But I converted my retort into a sneeze. Antagonizing Sergio within hours of landing in Peru wasn't the smartest idea. I would do well to keep in mind how alone I was and how quickly Sergio might refuse to pay my college tuition.

Grateful my mother-in-law had volunteered to watch the children for the morning, I meant to show the mother superior of the *Universidad Femenina del Sagrado Corazon,* or the UNIFE, my perfect grades from JNU. Fleetingly, I remembered my dream of studying English. Now, I would be lucky if I could finish studying Spanish and find a job. My grades would ensure my entry into the sixth semester of the Spanish honors career, and I could finish my interrupted degree. After that, Sergio and I could get a divorce, and at last, I could be independent—free of Sergio's dominance and free of my parents—to commence a new life with my children. Yes, Lima wasn't America, but at least it wasn't India. That was blessing enough.

"Excuse me, what did you say you studied in India?" The middle-aged mother superior of the UNIFE, Madre Buzio, frowned and drummed her fingers on her desk.

"Spanish honors. My grades will show I was a top student."

"Yes, but what do you wish to study in Lima?" Madre Buzio appeared puzzled.

Is the nun daft? "Spanish honors. I want to finish my degree here."

"Well, you can't." The green-eyed nun waved her hands in dismissal. "No such college major as Spanish honors exists in any Limeñian university," she explained patiently. "Join our four-year translation and interpretation program. It's the closest you'll find to your Spanish honors career. We're the only university in Lima to offer it."

"Do you have an English honors career?" I suspected her answer ahead of time, body tense, but I couldn't help asking anyway.

"Where are you unearthing all these outlandish career names from?" exclaimed Madre Buzio. "They don't exist here."

Defeat felt like an actual taste in my mouth. "In what year would I join your translation and interpretation program?"

"In freshman year. Where else? I doubt any of your college credits will transfer. But you'd better hurry up and decide. Our school year began on March 10. Today is May 1."

I left the mother superior's office with the world caved in on my shoulders. In silence, I trudged to the back courtyard of the UNIFE, besieged at the moment by a sea of students enjoying their lunch break.

Would Sergio pay for my schooling for four long years? What if he refuses? He won't. He wants a divorce now more than I do.

The students surrounding me in that courtyard appeared carefree and young, bringing home how I had never felt young nor carefree even when I *was* young, six years ago. The girls ate and chattered under the weak midday sunshine of an approaching southern-hemisphere winter. The smell of their lunches reminded me of how I had skipped breakfast, too ill and too nervous to eat while I waited for Nila to give me a ride.

But that morning, sickness notwithstanding, I had still had hope. Now, life loomed in front of me, an insurmountable mountain. *One step. I need to take one step at a time. Every mountain climbed begins with the first step.* I clutched my hurting throat and raised my voice. "Are any of you translation and interpretation freshmen?"

"I am." A slim girl with silky brown hair raised her hand.

"Hola." I summoned a smile to explain my dilemma.

The girl introduced herself as Carla Bustos. "Where are you from? You have a Spanish accent."

"India. I flew in yesterday." I controlled the urge to say South Americans had the wrong accent. I spoke Spanish the *right* way.

"Don't worry. You'll be fine here. I'm new too. I came from the province of Chiclayo. My father brought my sisters and me to the capital so we could attend college here. Come, meet my gang."

By the middle of lunch, Carla and company had photocopied—on their dime—five weeks' worth of the class notes I had missed since classes commenced in March. I panicked when I saw the copies.

"Christ," I said. "I don't know that I can read these."

"Why?" a girl named Veronica asked. "What can't you read? We lent you Ursula's notes because she has the best handwriting."

"The writing's fine. My confusion is all the symbols and shorthand—I mean, I know I *speak* Spanish, but it's still a foreign language to me."

"Hush," comforted Ursula. "Just do your best. Mark what you don't understand, and I'll explain it, okay?"

"Guys," interrupted another girl, "shouldn't she buy a psychology textbook today? We have that test tomorrow."

"But I don't have money!" I wailed. "Can't I borrow the book from the college library?"

"You mean like physically *borrow* the book?" Veronica raised her eyebrows.

"Yes. For the week."

"Are you joking? Libraries in Peru stopped lending books ten years ago."

"How? That's what they're for."

Veronica shook her head. "I know, but they don't lend them here because of terrorism."

I sank onto the steps of the photocopy shop, grasping my head with both hands. "Please explain to me what terrorism has to do with library books."

"Everything," insisted Veronica, "because the guy who initiated the Shining Path movement is a college professor. He got his followers, who were his own students, to borrow these socialist and Maoist theory books, read them, and twist the theories to rationalize the atrocities they committed. Once the government caught on, it banned libraries from lending books. Since I started second grade, to borrow a book, you have to write your name in a register, which allows you to search for your book inside an alphabetical filing cabinet. The librarian writes the book's name beside your name and goes to a no-public-access zone to hunt for the book. After all that, you borrow the damn book for fifteen minutes to photocopy whatever pages you need. Once you return it, the librarian double-checks your photocopies against the pages inside the book to ensure you didn't tear them out."

I unclutched my head. "That's so crazy. Why don't they just ban those books and stop people from borrowing them?"

Carla laughed. "Because we're supposed to be a *democracy*."

I blinked then rubbed my eyes. "I guess this is my welcome-to-Peru story." I clutched my throat again, wishing I'd worn a woolen scarf. "It sounds like a Russian Gulag."

"It is. It's the Peruvian Gulag." Carla pulled me to my feet. "Come on. We'll pool the money to buy you your textbook. You will bring us the money back tomorrow, right?"

"Of course. I promise."

At the end of lunch, my new friends shepherded me to their afternoon class. Jetlagged, feverish, and light-headed from hunger, I caved into a chair. Eyes closed, I placed my burning forehead on a worn wooden desktop. A pair of high heels click-clacked into the classroom.

"Good afternoon, ladies. Ready for more algebra?"

My head shot up. "We're in a *math* class?" I nudged Carla.

"Yes… shhh."

"Why do I have to study math for translation and interpretation?"

"Shhh. Because freshmen year is for general studies."

"Is there a problem, Señorita Bustos?" The blond math teacher infused such sarcasm into the word, Carla cringed.

"N-n-n-o, *P-Profesora*."

I jumped to my feet, cheeks, eyes, and forehead on fire as I introduced myself. "Good afternoon, Profesora." I choked on the word profesora. I sniffled and wiped my eyes. "I haven't seen a math problem since I left school eight years ago, and I was bad at it then. If I promise to study hard, will you cut me slack? You see, I have two children, and I need this degree because I'll have to support them once I'm divorced!"

Too late, I registered the silence that followed my outburst. I burned like a gaslight illuminating the astounded expressions of fifty teenage classmates.

Probably as astonished as my classmates, the young math teacher approached me with a tissue box. "Come to my office at the end of class, okay?" Her voice had softened. She handed me a tissue. "I'll lend you a basic arithmetic textbook to practice decimals, fractions, and equations."

My eyes thanked the professor more than any words could. I controlled the urge to hug the young woman who couldn't be much older than me. *I will get my degree. I have to believe that and keep going.*

28

THAT EVENING, SOMEHOW, I CAME home to the posh neighborhood of San Isidro without getting lost. *Mami*, as I had to address Señora Santander, lived there in a two-family, two-story home. The landlady lived downstairs, and my mother-in-law lived upstairs. Mami's household consisted of her godson, Horacio, and a live-in teenage housemaid. Horacio was not a relative. He had been born to a Santander family maid twenty-two years prior, but when his mother had moved on to have several other children with as many partners, Señora Santander had let the maid go. But as she was little Horacio's godmother, she asked Sergio to become his godfather, and Horacio had lived with Xenobia Santander ever since.

With the arrival of Sergio and family, that meant six bodies had to fit in a two-and-a-half-bedroom apartment. The maid slept in a rooftop room, Horacio in the half bedroom, and Señora Santander in the back bedroom. She had vacated the master bedroom for Sergio and me to share with Pia and Abril.

That night, I avoided telling Sergio he would have to pay for four years of university instead of one semester. I had no way out of it, however, when he asked me over dinner what had happened that morning.

"Four years?" He looked shocked. "You're expecting me to pay for four years of college for you?"

Conscious of my mother-in-law listening, I asked, "Can we please have this conversation later?"

In the privacy of our bedroom at bedtime, I asked, "Serg, would you prefer me to be a leech whom you will always have to maintain if I can't support myself?"

"If we get a divorce, I don't have to support you always. I only have to support you until the kids turn eighteen."

"So what are you saying?" I forced myself not to clench my hands.

"I'm saying it's up to you. I can't pay for your education and complete the construction of the house anytime soon."

"I don't care. I want an education more than I want a house."

I didn't know what Sergio told his mother during the next few days, especially when he chatted with her in her back bedroom for over two hours at a time, out of my earshot. What I did gather was that he never contradicted his mother when anyone else was around. Either way, any doubts I might have had regarding Mami's opinion about my college career became amply clear during our first Sunday breakfast.

She glanced at me then at Sergio. "My son, the housemaid has already complained about the extra work. Perhaps you don't know this, but reliable maids are hard to secure in these terrorist-ridden times. From now on, your wife will have to cook for you and your children and wash your clothes. As you well know, this apartment isn't wired for a washing machine. I will not lose my washer woman over laundry your wife should do."

"Does this mean I have to wash all our clothes by hand?" I asked Sergio later, when we were alone.

That would convert to the nightmare of my teenage years with Didima, when Didima had let go of the dhobi laundry man because she couldn't afford his services anymore. From then on, our laundry had been my responsibility. Each weekend morning, surrounded by a sea of buckets, brushes, and bar after bar of dull-yellow Sunlight soap, I had tackled our weekly washing, since Didima was too sick to do any kind of housework and I had no choice but to do it all.

"Yes," Sergio said. "I don't have money to hire a washer woman, pay for the construction of our house, and pay for your school as well."

"So I get to attend school and watch the kids and cook and do the laundry too?"

"Noor, I didn't ask you to join college or have a second kid this fast. I distinctly suggested we wait."

Within two weeks of my new routine, I grasped that if I intended to survive school in Peru, I would have to search for a place other than "home" in which to do my homework. I could be grateful I attended school at all, thanks to Xenobia Santander, who had reluctantly consented to watch the children while I went to college. But at the end of each class day, my mother-in-law threw Pia and Abril at me right when I came up the front stairs. If I wanted to address homework, it would have to be *before* coming home while my mother-in-law still watched the children. That place became the beautiful Parque del Olivar of San Isidro, an ancient colonial olive grove, which defined the well-established suburb. Every afternoon, the park cheered me up, with its gnarled old trees planted in the soothing symmetry of long rows, their twisted branches and thin, pointy leaves my special pleasure to look at, since Indians loved studying in parks and gardens.

By my third week of sitting on the grass, however, I wasn't so sure of my homework spot anymore. Being the end of May, officially winter in South America, an unrelenting winter drizzle soaked through my clothes and left me shivering. In a week more, the drizzle became so draining, I had to sit on a plastic bag to do homework in the park.

In class the next day, I asked my peers at school about buying a raincoat.

"A raincoat?" Veronica asked. Her brown hair and green eyes swung around from the next desk up. "But it doesn't rain in Lima."

"Are you crazy? It's raining right *now*, or am I dreaming?"

"No, it isn't. That's the *garua*—drizzle. Look." Veronica pointed to the paved path parallel to the garden outside our classroom. "The ground isn't wet, so it isn't raining."

I resisted the urge to hit Veronica.

In the evening, Sergio explained, "Lima is located in the rain shadow of the Andes Mountains—"

"What the hell is a rain shadow?"

"It's a mountain wall the rain clouds bump into where they shed their rainfall, before they cross over with little or no moisture left in them. Out here, that mountain wall is the western rampart of the Andes. The rain clouds come from the east, bump into it, shed their rainfall on the Amazon jungles, and we suffer this gray sky for eight months a year. We in Lima don't even see the garua drizzle anymore, but it sure is there."

That it "was there" became clear to me as the ceaseless garua collected on the pointy leaves of the two-hundred-year-old olive trees, and it "rained" unevenly under the trees where I studied. Thus, forced to choose the sky for cover, I discovered Lima didn't sell umbrellas, either, any more than it did raincoats because *it didn't rain in Lima*—so much so that the city streets didn't even have drainage sewers.

On each weekday, chilled to the bone and ravenous to boot, I didn't have one extra penny to relieve my hunger since Sergio's allotted five *nuevos soles* only covered my bus fares. Sure, I could pack a lunch, but cooking was a travail I faced every evening, exhausted. The meal I cooked lasted for Sergio, myself, and the children if I didn't touch it outside dinner.

My relief came on the days Sergio arrived home with some Peruvian sweetmeat I had yet to taste. On those days, I skipped dinner and ate whatever he bought me. My favorite was a crumbly pastry soaked in fruit syrup called *turron de Doña Pepa*. Sergio indulged me at least twice a week with a two-pound box of the pastry, and if it wasn't available, he bought me Peruvian chocolate-coated cookies. I gobbled the treats because life in Peru had rendered me bone thin. Furthermore, if I skipped dinner, the food I cooked stretched further, giving me permission to go to bed earlier.

That was my dinner plan, but hunger killed me at lunchtime until I came up with the brilliant idea to hop in and out of buses to avoid bus fares while traveling to and from school. I could do so in Lima because the bus conductor roamed all over the bus. If I got in and out fast enough, I escaped without paying at all. In that way, five nuevos soles bought me two chocolate bars and two packets of salty soda biscuits. Those treats comforted me as only junk food had since I could remember. Eating junk always took the edge off my emotions and made me feel better fast. And when comforted, my mind strayed to Chirag and the last desperate kiss we stole. After learning I had children, Chirag would rush to have his own. He had always been impetuous. Always. Then his life would swallow him up, as much as mine had. And never again would anyone light up my world from the inside like he had.

June was underway when, one evening, I came home from studying to see Sergio at the bottom of Señora Santander's stairwell bidding a gentleman goodbye. "Oh, here you are. Come meet my mentor, Jaime León. Remember I told you once how he influenced me to study diplomacy?"

"Yes." I dropped my schoolbag to the pavement and offered my cheek to a thin, brown-complexioned man of medium height.

With his wavy salt-and-pepper hair, angular nose, and prominent eyes, he was visibly older than Sergio. "The two of you must come to my place for tea soon," he said. "My mother hasn't seen Sergio yet, and she is demanding to know why, because she loves him like a son."

"Of course." I searched Jaime's face to gauge his connection to Sergio but couldn't decide whether it was fatherly or brotherly.

"Did you know your husband's nickname at the foreign office is *Espasa-Calpe*?"

"You mean, as in the Hispanic encyclopedia?"

"Yes. I nicknamed him that because he was the brightest young diplomat who ever worked under me." Jaime placed a hand on Sergio's back.

I smiled. "That doesn't surprise me. Sergio is one of the smartest people I know."

Upstairs, I said, "I remember you telling me in India you were really close to Jaime. If you're that close, why haven't I seen him before this?"

"Because I see him at work every day."

"So is he like a father or a brother? He didn't give me either feeling."

"A father, I think. He's twenty years older than I am."

29

WE WENT TO TEA AT Jaime's mother's place on a Sunday afternoon, *without* the children, which I found very odd.

But Sergio brushed it off. "If the children come with us, all we will focus on is them, and the grownups won't be able to talk. We'll take the children next time."

As Sergio drove us to the seaside district of Chorillos, I fell in love with the colonial architecture of the houses, all single storied in that district, paint-washed in bright ochers, brick reds, and dusky pinks. Most had long cast-iron-grilled exteriors with doors that led into roofed verandas with back walls. The living quarters were secluded behind each wall.

Jaime's house had three armed guards sitting in the veranda area, and I didn't have the privacy to ask Sergio why Jaime and his mother needed guards, because the latter would have overheard me.

As a first experience, what greeted me behind their back wall was an enchanting garden of fig and loquat trees and blooming frangipani in the middle of a tiled courtyard. The remarkable detail was that the tiles appeared Sevillian with their intricate leaf, flower, and animal motifs in yellow, royal blue, and green on a white background, where each motif was outlined in black.

"Yes," whispered Sergio, seeing my questioning look. "They are Sevillian."

We crossed the courtyard to a spacious inner veranda with beautiful cane furniture. As Jaime rose to greet us, I saw the tiniest lady seated on the cushion of an armchair. She was so small, her ballerina shoes hung inches above the floor.

"Sergio!" she exclaimed in a high, trembly voice. "It's about time you came to see me."

"Ernestita!" Sergio bent to kiss her on one cheek. "Forgive me. It's been hectic since I got back. How are you? You look splendid, as always."

Indeed, Ernestita looked like an expensive doll dressed in a sky-blue cashmere wool suit bejeweled with a lime-sized sapphire-and-diamond brooch, matching earrings, and her dyed brown hair coiffed into a chignon. So far, she had ignored I was even alive. Were it not for Sergio, who pulled me by the forearm to introduce me, she didn't seem to care whether I was there or not.

"Nonsense!" But her dark, bulbous eyes lit up with pleasure hearing Sergio's complimentary tone. "I grow older and more wrinkled each year while Jaime grows handsomer. Look at him! I couldn't ask for a better son. When I am too tired to walk, he carries me to my bedroom."

"Oh, Mamá." Jaime got up and kissed her on a withered cheek. "You are my blessing. What would you like? Tea or coffee?"

A service person brought out a tray with a silver tea set on it.

As if following an established pattern, Sergio hastened to pour out the coffee Ernestita asked for. He knew how much cream and sugar she used, the number of cookies to serve her. Meanwhile, I sat there, watching the strange pageant.

"Jaime," Ernestita commanded. "Bring me my glasses. I want to see how many new wrinkles Sergio has on that white face of his."

"Ernestita, would you mind if I showed Noor your living room? She will never see anything more beautiful in Lima." Sergio stood.

"Take me off this chair so I can join you."

On her feet, Ernestita reached my shoulders, and I was only five feet, five inches tall. That close, she smelled of a cloying perfume that reminded me of death. She grasped Sergio's forearm with knobbly fingers topped off by nails painted a dainty pink.

When Sergio switched on the living room lights, four chandeliers lit up a long room full of glass cases. Cases stuffed with Capo di Monte porcelain, antique dolls, and silver objet d'art to interrupt four seating arrangements. I was fascinated yet repelled by Ernestita as we admired the contents of the inlayed wood cases with mirrored backs. Soon, Jaime joined us, handing his mother her glasses.

With her glasses in place, Ernestita grabbed Sergio's face with both hands. "You should have come to live with us. You would have had a better life."

"Mamá!" I could tell Jaime was embarrassed. "Leave Sergio alone. He has made his choices. Let him live them."

And throughout the visit, neither Jaime nor his mother asked me one personal question, nor did either of them inquire about Sergio's children. Mostly, Ernestita reminisced about how Sergio had visited them every week when he was a teenager. The board games they had played, the meals Sergio had cooked for them, his sleepovers at their home.

Back in the car an hour and a half later, I said, "Jesus, Serg! You might have warned me of how strange they were."

"I'm sorry." Sergio smiled ruefully. "I'm so used to them, I forget how strange they are. They don't mean badly."

"Right, but the last person needed at that tea party was me. I was the out-of-sync fifth wheel."

"I'm sorry. Jaime is just very dominated by his mother. He's a normal human being outside her purview."

"So, how did he persuade you to become a diplomat? I want to know the whole story."

"It isn't that fascinating a story—"

"I want to know it regardless."

"I was only sixteen, so all bright-eyed and eager to please everybody. One day, when I had already worked my stenographer job at the foreign office for three months, I saw a notice in the library for after-hours volunteers to sort out and catalog old documents. As a counselor, Jaime was overseeing that project. He noted how fast I did what he asked. At the end of the project a month later, he suggested I go to college for law so I could apply to the diplomatic academy when I graduated. That's when I began visiting his house to study on weekends. So Ernestita has known me since then, and she is an extremely possessive old lady."

"And has Jaime ever been married?"

"No."

"That's because he's married to that mother of his."

"I suppose it's true."

"How does she handle it when he is posted abroad?"

"He pays relatives to take her to visit with him."

I stared out at the Pacific Ocean through the car window, wanting to say, *Of course he does. Like your mother visited every place you traveled to. Until you didn't have her visit with you in India, and that's where you picked up a wife, had a couple of kids, and your life took on a different direction*, but I kept my thoughts to myself. The details of Sergio's childhood history were still a mystery to me. *But how much minutiae do I need to know to figure out that he must have had a hellish childhood, judging from those scars on his back?*

30

Weekends became my special time to relive the nightmare of my teenage years as I drowned in my weekly laundry for four people in Lima. To multitask, on a Saturday at the end of June, when I had a history test to study for, I filled the ancient apartment's one bathtub with soapy water and marched on top of the clothes while I studied. I jumped when my mother-in-law banged on the bathroom door over the drone of my studying out loud.

"Noor! Open the door right now."

I glanced at my naked body. "I'm not done yet."

"Yes, you are! Open the door."

Only then did I realize how the rest of the bathroom was flooding.

At the door, my mother-in-law asked, "Are you crazy? My landlady downstairs is having a fit because her bathroom ceiling is leaking."

Wrapped in a towel, I gawked at her with nothing to say.

"Out!" Mami pointed down the corridor. "Take all your washing to the washbasin on the roof. That's where you will do your washing from now on, like a human being."

The washbasin was a cool antique. "I didn't know it worked. Does it?"

"Yes, it does. That's where my washer woman does all my laundry." Behind her, Sergio stood with his arms hanging, not daring to cross his mother.

At last, he said, "Go change and take the laundry to the roof. I'll clean up the flood down here."

"No, you won't." Mami laughed a sarcastic laugh. "Noor did this. She'll clean it up. You need to drive to Chorillos and fetch my landlady's plumber. And you'd better pray he can fix this today, because no one downstairs or here can use the toilets until then."

My revolutionary laundering method had not only flooded the bathroom but also flooded the open-air corridor outside the bathroom. The water had seeped into my mother-in-law's back bedroom, making her catch the transgression. History test abandoned, I mopped five buckets of water on my hands and knees, thanking God the floor was cement and not hardwood like the rest of the apartment three steps up, which led to the living room, dining room, and master bedroom. That day, I washed clothes under the cold trickle of that antique washbasin until six p.m., foregoing lunch.

At dinnertime, neither Mami nor Sergio addressed me at the dining table. Fearing both, I had peed on the roof twice because I hadn't wanted to ask if the bathroom had been fixed. Only upon hearing Mami flush the toilet after dinner did I know that my crime had been addressed.

In our bedroom, Sergio said, "Your little stunt cost a hundred fifty dollars to fix. On Monday, go ask if the UNIFE provides financial aid. If they don't, you might have to stop studying."

I got into bed in silence, *because what could I say?* My entire life plan hinged on Sergio's kindness, and I had challenged it to beyond its furthest point.

My incentive to finish laundry on Saturdays was that on Sundays, Sergio would take the girls and me to lunch at a Chinese restaurant in the neighboring district of Lince. He did so to give his harassed mother a break from our presence, and the children and I loved our modest outing. But on that Sunday, Sergio left the house in the morning without saying goodbye and didn't come home until four in the afternoon. It was his way of punishing my actions. The blow felt worse because on Sundays, Sergio transmuted to a different person. After lunch, he would drive us far and wide, disregarding the dismal garua drizzle as he pointed out majestic bronze or copper statuary to me. "See that man on horseback? You've studied him. He's Francisco Pizarro, the conqueror." Or "Here's Simon Bolivar. His plaza is better planned than poor Pizarro's. Pizarro's is so cramped, all you see is the horse's balls if you stand in that plaza."

As he talked, I would stare at my husband behind the steering wheel, wanting to remark on how much he changed outside the shadow of his domineering mother. But if I made him conscious of it, he would withdraw into the stranger he had become to me. I didn't want that. I wanted him like it used to be between us when we were recently married, when we loved each other the best we could. Until he dissected my shortcomings. Until I didn't love him anymore.

Every Sunday, I requested, "Serg, let's go see a church. I love how beautiful and sumptuous they are."

One day, inside the Baroque interior of the Jesuit's church, San Pedro, right next to the foreign office where Sergio worked, I sighed. "This is so beautiful. I wish I lived here."

"You know why, right?"

"What do you mean?"

"You haven't studied these? It's because these churches were the epicenters of colonial politics."

"Weren't they just here spreading Catholicism?"

"Good God. What do they teach you in that girls' university of yours? In viceregal days, the highest bureaucratic post a colonial person could attain was to become a bishop within a Catholic religious order. The foremost colonial families vied to place their smartest sons into the religious orders to control the political arena with money and favors. These churches received untold wealth toward their construction."

Sergio and I would get so lost in our conversations, usually the children brought us back to the here and now.

"Papá, I'm hungry. Buy us dumplings," Pia would demand. Then the conversation between us, too, became more personal.

"Noor, you must try one bite of my bean paste dumpling today. Their weird sweet-and-salty taste takes me right back to my vacation in China, when I wasn't much older than you, stationed as a young third secretary in Tokyo, my first posting abroad. How quickly time passes."

"But it's not China I want to see. It's Japan. Promise me you'll take me there to see peonies and irises. Remember the iris bouquet you sent me when Pia was born? They were so beautiful I cried."

"One day," Sergio would say, queuing to buy us fresh dumplings in Chinatown while he hoisted Abril into his arms, laughing as she waved her little hands to dispel the haze of smoke that blended the human congestion with the strong smells of incense, soy sauce, and dried fish.

On Monday, at school, I skipped the first class to go to the administration department.

"Apply for financial aid," a lady employee said, "but I can't guarantee you'll get it."

"What does it depend on? In my country, it depends on your grades, and my grades are good."

"It's different here. Here, it depends on the breadwinner's income. Bring me your husband's last three pay stubs, and we'll take it from there."

Infinitely relieved that the answer wasn't an outright no, I begged to call Sergio at work. His secretary informed me he hadn't come in yet. I left her a detailed message about what I needed and why.

I came home that evening, praying Sergio would bring me his pay stubs. Instead, Mami informed me Sergio had had a car accident, running it into a cement post in the foreign office carpark. He was not hurt, but I couldn't see him because he was nursing a headache, resting in the back bedroom, away from me and the children.

That night, Sergio slept in his mother's bedroom. She slept in our bedroom, and I slept on the anteroom sofa. The following morning, Sergio had yet to show his face when I left the house to go to college.

That evening, however, Sergio handed me his original pay stubs and their photocopies to hand in at the UNIFE.

"Are you hurt? How bad was the car crash?"

Sergio shrugged uncomfortably. "The front of the car is pretty smashed. The doctor said I'll have to watch out for headaches for a few weeks."

The car crash ended our Sunday outings until further notice.

At school, I handed in his original pay stubs so the clerk could verify the authenticity of their photocopies, which she could keep, financial aid pending decision. And each day I attended classes, I feared my college career would end the following week.

When Sergio got the car back fourteen days later, that second weekend in July, after lunch, he drove Pia, Abril, and me to the seaport of Callao. "I want to show you where I lived," he told me, as if to apologize for his weeks of extra-distant treatment.

Callao reminded me of Chorillos, but it was subtly different because the houses here didn't have grilled verandas and were sometimes two stories tall.

"That's a perceptive observation!" But Sergio's smile twisted. "The houses you're pointing to are called 'alleyways of one single water tap' because they *have* only one bathroom to share between twenty families at the entrance of each alleyway. Can you imagine? I used to live in one with my aunt."

"For how long?"

"Eight years."

"Can you show me the exact one?" I recalled Didima's two cramped back rooms in South Extension, our home for ten years until I ran away from it and let Didima die all alone.

"No, that street was demolished years ago, but seeing any of these is hard for me because they also bring back how my mother abandoned me."

I widened my eyes, unable to believe how much Sergio was sharing.

He said, "I love and hate coming here because my childhood with my Tia Marilena was so damn traumatic."

"She gave you those scars on your back, didn't she?" I blurted, and Sergio's astonished look confirmed it. "I'm sorry." I could have hit myself for asking. "I didn't mean to probe." I had put him on guard, and he would stop sharing. Four whole years of seeing those scars, day in and day out, questioning myself as to who could have done that to a child, and I had ruined it right when he had opened his mouth.

But Sergio squeezed my hand. "Thanks for all these years of understanding. I'm sure I'll tell you all about that part of my life someday. It just won't be today."

"Serg, it doesn't have to be any day, okay? We all have scars to hide. Yours being so visible doesn't give me the right to ask. How old were you when your mother left for Panama?"

"Four."

"Oh, Serg. Did you hate her for it, like I hate my mom?"

"Who? My mother or my aunt?"

"Both, I guess."

"No. My mother I forgot once she wasn't in the picture, but I couldn't hate my aunt even as a young man in Japan, where I enjoyed the luxury of health insurance to see a psychiatrist. Each week, that psychiatrist told me to express my anger toward my Tia Marilena, but how could I be angry with her when she housed me, fed me, and paid for French lessons so I would learn a second language? She wasn't cruel. She belonged to a generation that believed beatings could cure any digression."

"But you were such a little boy. What did you do to provoke her to beat you that badly?"

Sergio's eyes took on a haunted look. "I—I began wetting my bed once my mother left. One night, I had to do more than pee... so I headed to that bathroom at the end of the alleyway... but I was five years old. I got so scared, thanks to a hooting owl, I pooped half into my pajamas and half on that long, dark alleyway before I ran back into the house and to my room. The next morning, first my aunt beat me, then she rubbed my face in the congealed feces."

I hoped my eyes didn't reveal my pity as I touched his hand. "She did a lot more than that, didn't she?"

Serg stared straight out of the windshield and nodded. "On my sixth birthday, she wanted to throw me a party because I had entered first grade in first position. That morning, she baked empanada meat patties that I loved. I woke up to the smell, so I crept into the kitchen and wolfed one down, adjusting the others to account for the loss. She found me out because the grease spots on the paper doily didn't match anymore. Anyway—she said I was a thief and tied me up to sit inside the bathtub. Then she filled it with ice-cold water all the way up to my neck. I sat in that bathtub, teeth chattering from the cold, too scared to even cry. All I remember is that I urinated and defecated in that water. I don't have any memory of when she untied me. There never was a party."

I placed my hand on his arm. "I'll never ask you about it again. Talking about it forces you to relive it, and some details are best left in the past."

31

I DIDN'T KNOW WHETHER TO LAUGH or cry when a letter in the mail informed me I was eligible for a twenty-five percent reduction in my tuition. I showed Sergio the letter that night.

He said, "This will help," as if he had never meant to stop me studying in the first place, but I didn't dig into his rationale for fear of making him aware of how scared I had been the past four weeks.

That first winter in Lima, after ten hours of studying plus doing homework each weekday, coming home to cook dinner was hard enough, but my nightmare commenced after dinner, when I ironed wet diapers in the laundry room until my upper back tore with pain. As I ironed, I prayed for the chill attacking my feet from the open-air corridor or the steamy, rotting odor rising from the ironing board to kill me. Then logic would prevail. With Pia and Abril in the picture, death was not allowed. Women with children who were cowards enough to die were on par with the likes of my mother, who abandoned her child in life.

In January of 1987, I had spent nine months in Lima when a marked change came over my attitude toward the children during my first summer vacation from college. One morning, I noticed how the bulletproof glass wall that had sprung up inside me after Abril's birth had become so brittle, I could punch holes through it—jagged, uneven, painful holes through which I could stick in my head and experience how much I loved my children on a regular day, not just when they were sick or in peril of dying. At unexpected moments, I smelled their warm baby bodies, touched their gelatinous bones under tender, baby flesh, and kissed their sweet soft hair until it hurt so much that unanticipated tears sprang into my eyes.

With this newfound sensitivity, at Olivar Park, I plucked two handfuls of the olives that I had watched ripen for months. I bit into a purple olive, redoubling to retch from its sheer and unexpected bitterness, spitting to remove the acrid, itchy taste from my mouth.

That evening, I accosted Sergio as he handed me my box of turron de Doña Pepa. "Serg, how can you tell when an olive is ripe? I ate one today, and I swear my mouth still itches."

Sergio dropped his briefcase and barked in laughter. "The ones you love are pickled in brine, silly."

Hearing that, I brought home a bagful and parked them in salt water on my mother-in-law's kitchen windowsill while Sergio spent his Sunday morning playing with Pia and Abril at the olive park, which was his favorite part of the weekend.

On Monday afternoon, I took the children to the park to play, and my olives were the first items my eyes hunted for on our return from there.

Seeing me searching, Mami smiled a disparaging smile. She said, "That was a stupid idea, so I threw them out," as if she had cooked the sentence all day long to say it to me with just the right degree of slur.

Unwilling to betray how much that hurt, I hustled the children into the anteroom to watch cartoons on television so I could cook dinner.

In the kitchen, my mother-in-law's maid snickered. "The señora calls you a savage animal when you aren't around."

"A *savage animal?*" my windpipe constricted. "Why?"

"Because when you cook cauliflower, you eat the stub too. She says you're an animal because animals eat that trash."

I wrenched open the refrigerator door and stooped so the horrid maid wouldn't see me close to crying. *Of course, the maid dared to say this to me because my mother-in-law gave her that license.* I withdrew a whole chicken from the bottom shelf and slapped it on the cutting board. *What does it matter what Xenobia Santander, with her fourth-grade education, says?* I skinned and quartered the bird, biting my bottom lip.

A fancy family name didn't convert my mother-in-law into a lady. That was the privilege of the kind of solid education Didima and her sisters had received. Xenobia, on the contrary, had lost her mother to childbirth and had been relegated by her father to be raised as a seamstress by two spinster aunts. That was why her varnish of pseudorefinement served so little to hide her gargantuan ignorance and the acid envy Xenobia projected on those more fortunate than her.

How would an uncultured beast like her know that in India, vegetables are consumed seasonally? That carrots, cauliflowers, and turnips are winter fare while melons and mangoes are summer delights? Or that lychees from the foothills of the Himalayas are only available for three weeks toward the end of April? Yet however much I rationalized my mother-in-law's judgment of me, I couldn't swallow the lump in my throat at being labeled a savage only because people in my country ate every last bit of a fruit or vegetable that was edible. *Yes, that labeled me an Indian, but surely not a savage animal?*

Against my better judgment, I went to the living room. "Is it true you call me a savage animal behind my back?"

My mother-in-law smiled. "I can call you that to your face if you want. I have never met anyone as crazy as you."

She couldn't have silenced me faster if she had slapped me. I ran into the master bedroom, howling like a child. *How did I complicate my life this much just to escape my mother and a country that didn't want me? Why didn't Sergio remain the kind and funny fellow who used to do my homework assignments and propose to me once a week? And Chirag—he was so unreachable, he might as well never have existed for all the access I had to him.* A degree was the answer to the mess of my existence. With it and a job, I could build a life with Pia and Abril. I had to be patient.

When school reopened in March 1987, for my third semester, I had one window of salvation in the schedule. On Thursdays, the timetable read *8:00–9:30 a.m.* and *4:00–8:00 p.m.* That meant I could attend the morning class, race home to do chores, dedicate a part of the afternoon to the children once they came home from kindergarten, then race back to school.

On one particular Thursday in May, I meant to catch up on laundry and study for my four-p.m. philosophy test. The minute I unlocked the front door, I knew my mother-in-law was in the kitchen because the whole apartment smelled of her delicious pot roast.

I paused at the kitchen doorway. "Mami, I have a test this afternoon that I can't miss because the grades will affect my finals. Could you or Horacio please put the children down for their nap at one thirty? It'll be best if they don't know I'm around, since they won't find me if I'm up on the roof doing laundry anyway."

Señora Santander nodded but didn't bother to turn around. At the kitchen sink, the housemaid giggled, but I balled my hands and ignored the sound.

Ten minutes later, dressed in an old T-shirt, I hauled two buckets of hot water from the bathroom tap up the rickety wooden stepladder to the roof. I plunged my hands into the soapy water, the cracks on my reddening skin from the last load of laundry stinging as if I had rubbed chili pepper on them. Ignoring the pain, I scrubbed feverishly, rinsing each garment under the cold water dribbling out of the cast-iron tap over the turn-of-the-century iron sink. The slower it went, the less time I would have to study philosophy.

Hours later, I straightened up, wincing. The approaching winter haze in a sunless sky didn't let me guess the time as I hung the clothes on the clothesline. T-shirt front wet and fingers rubbery, I grasped the rickety wooden handrail of the narrow and weatherworn stepladder to rush downstairs.

In the open-air corridor outside the señora's back bedroom, I tackled two tight turns and ran up its three steps. One hand opened the patterned glass door of our bedroom, as cautious as a mouse, knowing the children would each be napping in their respective hand-me-down cribs.

My heart thudded as I inched into the room and glanced at Xenobia Santander's wall clock. It was past three o'clock. Thank God the children were asleep. My exam began at four. So much for studying any philosophy. With stealthy fingers, I opened my mother-in-law's wooden armoire, trying to stop it from creaking as I grabbed a dry T-shirt. I backed out of the room, sprinting to knock on my mother-in-law's door.

No answer.

I knocked again. Harder that time.

No answer.

I leapt backward and knocked on Horacio's half-bedroom door.

Silence.

Both she and Horatio were gone. The rage inside me felt hot compared to the cold skin of my cheeks. My mother-in-law had done it on purpose. To see what I would do or else miss my test. I galloped back to my bedroom to hoist the children awake. *Oh, you'll see what I will do, all right, you old cat! No one. No one in this universe, least of all you, will prevent me from getting a degree.*

Abril cried in sleepy confusion as I peeled off the child's dirty diaper and changed her. More time got wasted in struggling the children into warm clothes. Scooping two-year-old Abril up in the crook of one arm, I hooked my schoolbag on my free shoulder. I dragged three-year-old Pia down the apartment stairs.

Crying openly for different reasons, all three of us staggered at a snail's pace to the bus stop a mile down the road.

Inside a jam-packed bus, I felt as if my left rotator cuff would fall out from the weight of Abril, while Pia hugged my thighs like a tree trunk in the dense forest of bus passengers. *Can I afford to fail this philosophy test?* Not with my math skills. I got straight Cs and Ds in math. Those were already enough of a liability to bring my grades down. I bit my lips in pain. *I won't fail. I'm good at philosophical theory. I won't fail. Two failed subjects would mean failing the year, and that's not an option.*

When I faltered into the classroom with my children, all fifty heads of my peers looked up from the philosophy exam they had been pondering over for the last thirty-five minutes. Bettina Benoit, the philosophy professor, raised her elderly eyebrows.

My eyes got watery. "Profesora Benoit, I know this is unconventional. I can explain later, but could you hold Abril on your lap while I take the test?"

Profesora Benoit crossed her stockinged legs, patted her coiffed blond head, and laughed nervously. "What if she wets my lap? I don't have any experience with children."

"She won't. She's wearing a diaper."

"I saved a seat for you." From the back of the class, Carla pointed to the vacant chair beside her. "I'll help you with Pia," she said, as if to encourage the profesora to help me too.

When I sat next to Carla, my friend covered her face with slender hands and muttered, "*Amiga*, no one should have to work this hard for a college degree, not in the twentieth century."

With the extra time Profesora Benoit granted me, I knew I would do well on the test.

When I staggered back home at seven in the evening with the children, my mother-in-law didn't say a word as she avoided my eyes. And I couldn't say a word to her, either, because she could stop watching my kids altogether anytime she wanted.

The coming weekend, with no clothes to wash on Saturday and a math exam to prepare for, I requested, "Serg, can you drop me off at Carla's this afternoon? She'll coach me for math. No need to worry about the children. I can take them with me."

Sergio stopped chewing on his toast at the dining table. "Sorry, I'm busy all day. I can drop you now, if you wish."

"I can't. Carla is busy this morning. Can't Nila drop me later? Please?"

"You don't get it, do you?" Sergio's eyes narrowed, and he shook his head. "My siblings are *not* your chauffeur. Thank God Carlos and Frida don't live nearby, or you'd ask me to badger them for transport too. Tell Carla to come teach you here."

Frida was the wife of Carlos, Sergio's youngest sibling. Older than me by a year, Frida always kept her distance when I was around, as if my proximity would give her a contagious disease.

I knew better than to argue, but I couldn't help saying, "I'm sure Nila would help if Frida asked. It's me. I'm the pariah."

"No. Frida would have better manners than you. That's all."

"Right. Like she has the manners to openly ignore me at all family gatherings. You think I don't realize how much she dislikes me, though she doesn't even know me?"

"Well, I can't ask her to love you on command."

Out of solutions, I called Carla. "Car, if you don't come teach me, I'll fail the exam, and I can't afford to fail it. I can't walk to your place with the kids."

"I know. It sucks San Isidro and Magdalena are so close by, yet no direct bus goes from here to there."

"Well, 'close' is relative, isn't it?" I laughed bitterly. "I wouldn't call thirty blocks close."

"Don't worry. I'll walk over. No harm in adding exercise to teaching you."

My throat was thick as I hung up the phone. Without the help of my college friends in general, and Carla in particular, I wouldn't pass college in Peru, let alone with good grades. *Maybe the help I receive is a sign from God to keep persevering? Four semesters to go after this one. Four more semesters, and I'll have a college degree.* That goal was worth any amount of suffering. I had to take it one day, one exam at a time.

32

IT WAS CHRISTMAS SEASON AGAIN as my final semester of general studies at the UNIFE neared its end. In March 1988, I would embark on my specialty, Spanish-English translation and interpretation. Two more weeks, and I would never have to touch another math problem, ever. But right then, I had finals to pass.

At Olivar Park, I pulled out my statistics course book. Didima's wristwatch reported two p.m. Three hours. I could practice statistics problems for three hours. Thank goodness I understood statistics more than I did math. Cooking dinner and putting the children to bed would take three more hours. I could study for world history from eight thirty to midnight.

I yawned and rubbed my eyes. *God, I'm so tired already. What if I go to bed with the children and wake up at two a.m. instead? My mind would be fresher for the sleep.* I was good at world history, but I needed an A-plus to balance the C and D grades in math and statistics. I couldn't—didn't have time for laundry that weekend. Too much to study. *Will Sergio agree to take the girls out by himself on Sunday so I can study? Unlikely.* I dug my fingernails into my thighs until both hurt.

At five thirty sharp, I charged up the stairs to my mother-in-law's apartment, hungrier than ever. I dredged a smile at Horacio, seated in the living room with Abril on his lap, saying, "Who's your mommy? I'm your mommy, riiiight?" in his falsetto voice, higher pitched than a girl's.

I wanted to slap Horacio's smug face, but I controlled the urge, hearing my mother-in-law's footsteps coming up the corridor. If I objected to Horacio's misleading words, Mami dearest would do a tiger-pounce on me to indicate *I* was the children's mother, not Horacio, but I was never around. Then Horacio would emerge as the hero, whereas I would be labeled the irresponsible mother who always shirked her duties. It was best to keep mum if I wanted to receive their free babysitting services.

"Hi, *Naña* Noor." Horacio faked a smile. At twenty-four, Horacio's one duty was to keep Xenobia Santander happy. Lacking a formal job, he collected the children from their nearby kindergarten because I was in college at that hour.

I hugged Pia, who bounced out of my mother-in-law's temporary back bedroom.

With great show, Horacio extracted a creased typed sheet from Pia's lunch pail. "I forgot to show you this the other day," he said, eyes large, expression innocent, "but the kids require costumes for their pageant tomorrow."

"What pageant?" I retraced my steps.

"Their Christmas pageant at the kindergarten."

My heart sank. I would never study for world history. "Where do we go to buy them?"

"To Miraflores, but costumes are expensive to buy or rent. You do have the money, riiiight?"

I wanted to shake Horacio by the shoulders to ask why he hadn't told me about the sheet when he first saw it. He knew I never had money. But Sergio's mother was right there to indicate it was my duty, not Horacio's, to deal with Pia's and Abril's homework assignments. Besides, Horacio knew full well how Sergio controlled all money matters in our marriage. The young man wanted to needle me. That was all.

I scanned the page of instructions with a feverish eye. The Christmas pageant theme was the barnyard. The kindergarten students would parade on stage in costumes provided by their families. So much for studying for world history. I would have to wake up at two a.m.

"Mamá, let me be Cheetara from the Thundercats!" Pia jumped around the living room.

"Me toooo," imitated Abril.

"I can't, baby." I caressed Pia's face. "Barnyard means cows and goats and chickens. Your costumes will consist of those."

"So, what will I be?" Pia asked.

"And me." Abril skipped in place.

"Shhh. It's a secret." I smiled. *If I only had any idea.*

I begged a loan of twenty nuevos soles from Xenobia Santander and charged out of the house to the stationery shop two blocks down our street. My choice for barnyard animals would depend on the colors of crepe paper I could afford.

Half an hour later, world history gnawed on my brain like a rat on cheese while I improvised with craft paper, lots of glue, and a stapler. The children retired to bed with no idea about what I was doing.

I finished a fluffy white hen's head and body for Pia and a simpler yellow chicken costume for Abril at well past two a.m. In bed, I fell asleep as soon as my head touched the pillow.

Too soon, Pia woke me up. "Where's my costume?" she asked instead of saying good morning.

Abril ran out of the bedroom to investigate. She hopped back in and shouted with her pronounced lisp, "Pfia, Pfia! Dining loom. Come."

I fitted the now-dry costumes around the excited children's bodies as the señora teetered into our bedroom on wedge-heeled bedroom slippers. "The kindergarten is on the phone." She smiled her long-suffering smile.

"Please tell them I'll call back," I mumbled, a threaded needle clenched between my teeth.

"I'll try." Xenobia shrugged. "But they said it's important."

"Okay, okay, I'll answer it. Can you hold Pia's costume together? I have to tack it into place."

A female informed me that Sergio and I were required to attend a meeting at the kindergarten at noon.

"Can you postpone this meeting?" *How will I review world history with this new complication?*

"Señora," the woman reproved. "Five school administrators have called this meeting, so it must be important. Don't be late."

I raced to the meeting dressed in a summer T-shirt, a pair of jeans, and flip-flops, book bag slung over one shoulder. It was typical of Sergio not to attend, because how important could a kindergarten meeting be?

Will I reach my statistics final on time?

As a secretary ushered me into the headmistress's office, I brushed soda cracker crumbs from my lips, taken aback to see a five-panel jury fanned behind a table. Across from them waited two chairs. I unslung my book bag onto the polished wooden floor and collapsed into a chair.

"Where is Señor Santander?" the headmistress asked.

"He works downtown. He couldn't make it. I'm sorry."

The headmistress grimaced. Then the kindergarten psychiatrist, the school counselor, and both Pia's and Abril's class teachers spread a battery of my children's "final exams" between us for me to view.

The exams demonstrated—through repeated and tape-recorded interviews, stick-figure drawings, and illustration identifications of the primary family unit—that neither Pia, four, nor Abril, three, knew who their mother was. Pia, the quieter and more prudent of the two, had remained silent, but Abril, the babbling brook of the family, had assured her teacher, the kindergarten psychiatrist, *and* the counselor that Horacio Diaz was her mother.

Only once did she falter and second-guess herself to the psychiatrist and say maybe *Mimi*—Xenobia Santander—was her mother, but then Abril changed her mind and stuck to her guns. "*Olacho*"—Horacio—"*Olacho es mi mamá.*"

To my humiliation, the panel repeated, "Why?" *Why did my children have such outlandish ideations?* Their combined expressions of contempt and pity seared my skin.

Too late, I understood why. Added to Horacio's repetition to Abril about being her mother in his high-pitched, girly voice, I recalled an afternoon when I had overheard Xenobia Santander. She had assumed I wasn't around, but I had been hiding in the anteroom to snatch an hour to lie around and just read for pleasure.

My mother-in-law had been feeding Abril lunch, when she said, "Who am I?" to Abril.

"Mimi," Abril had replied.

"No," Xenobia Santander had scolded. "I'm your *mami, ya*? Now tell me again. Who am I?"

"Mami," Abril said.

That day, I had wanted to burst out of the anteroom to scream that it wasn't true. *I* was Mami, not the señora, but I had desisted, knowing that if I showed face, I wouldn't be able to go to school after. Selfishly, I had rationalized the facts to my own advantage, deliberately ignoring my children's needs, reassuring myself that they knew who their mother was. *Don't I bathe and dress them each morning and sing to them and teach them the prayer of "Our Lord" in English at bedtime? Who else could be their mother but me?* I was reaping the results of my omissions. *Yet what can I say in my own defense to this panel of kindergarten professionals?* They had already judged and condemned me. Besides, it wasn't their forgiveness I needed. It was Pia's and Abril's.

The headmistress concluded, "You would do well to reevaluate your participation in your children's lives, señora." She stood to indicate the meeting was over. "Your girls are bright children, but as a twenty-year preschool professional, I can guarantee you Pia and Abril are also two very disturbed children." She shook her head in pity or resignation or both.

"It's their foundation." The school psychiatrist scraped his chair back. "It's being laid down wrong. We can't plant a sapling at a forty-five-degree angle then complain in fifteen years that the tree grew at a slant."

I left the kindergarten headmistress's office ten years older. The Christmas pageant was already in progress at the Parque del Olivar, right next to the kindergarten school. The olive trees were festooned with colored streamers behind a podium glinting silver, green, and red under a smiling sun streaming down from a storybook-blue summer sky. As I walked toward the park, I spotted the kindergarten children, already on stage in their garish costumes, swaying to the music of Christmas carols in Spanish, which blared through hidden loudspeakers. Most appeared bewildered, but the parents, eager and proud picture-takers perched on wooden bleachers, loved the show. Nearby, a cotton candy vendor spun fresh clouds of pink sugar, which he stuck one by one onto a wooden stand behind his glass-paned workspace. Their caramel smell turned parents' heads and made me hungry as I climbed to the top tier of a bleacher.

I clapped on cue while my heart suffocated little by little. My mind flitted to the misfit diplomatic children-turned-adults whom I had met in my five years of marriage. And if I wanted specific examples, I didn't have to search far. Isabel was a hippie who had barely graduated school. Her brother, Tikku, did have a college degree, but he, too, was dependent on his parents. As much as I loved Angela and José Santanilla, I couldn't deny their slipshod parenting, too busy all their lives pursuing their own social goals to pay attention to their children's emotional needs. *Is that what I want for Pia and Abril?*

My statistics final was already forty-five minutes underway when I skidded into class.

When that exam ended and I had an hour to study for my history exam, Pia's and Abril's faces kept surfacing on my study guide instead of historical facts. I shivered. Pia and Abril would trust *a tree* was their mother if told that for long enough.

In the heart of India, girls too young to know better were wedded to trees—yes, *trees*—by their own parents to avoid paying a dowry and be able to claim their daughters were married, because in Indian society, an unmarried girl was unacceptable. Families backward enough burned brides on the tree husband's funeral pyre if the tree happened to "die."

Besides, am I not an example of what children are capable of believing? I had been six years old—much, much older than either Pia or Abril—when I had assumed I was meeting my mother for the first time. In my memory of that day, many things were new—the train travel from Calcutta to New Delhi, the horror of an Indian railway station, my first awareness of the existence of poor people—but the newest discovery of all had been the person whom I had to call Ma. And that day was stamped on my brain in technicolor.

***

In 1967, my first glimpse of New Delhi swung into view when I spotted the squat red towers of the New Delhi Railway Station from the train compartment window. I clapped my hands over my ears, swiveling my whole body to meet Didima's eyes, as a shrill whistle blast announced our arrival.

"Didima, are we there yet?" I asked for the eighth time since we had left Calcutta the day before.

"Yes, shona. This time, we are." Didima pinched my cheek and smiled a tired smile. "Come. Look out of the window, and tell me if you spot Uncle Jiten. He had a work meeting to attend, so he may run late."

As the train slowed, hundreds of faces crowded my vision on the station platform—lips smiled, heads bobbed, eyes peered, hands waved. Laborers in red shirts and white dhoti pants fought each other to carry colorful holdalls. Passengers lugged vegetable baskets. Two live roosters hung upside down from a fat man's shoulder. Mangy dogs sniffed at soiled newspaper balls on the cement platform already littered with *mumphali* peanut hulls and a myriad of discarded train tickets glinting red, blue, and yellow amidst trampling feet.

But most overwhelming of all was the noise, so different from the circumspect airport scenes I was used to. A million strangers cursed as they stumbled over the bodies of filthy people sleeping on the station floor.

"Ma, *Ma*!" shouted a fat lady in a pale-pink sari standing on tiptoes, waving a glossy magazine rolled up in her hand until she disappeared from view too.

I clutched Didima's hand. "Uncle Jiten! Did you see Uncle Jiten? I know it was him because he's so tall." No one was as tall or as thin as Didima's baby brother. I loved him because whenever he came to visit in Calcutta, he drew caricatures of all our family members, making me laugh.

"That's right, shona. That was Jiten. I hope he finds us once the train stops."

When we got off the train, in the heat of July, the platform reeked of fried food, cardamom tea, and bygone urine as Didima tried to avoid the sleeping homeless in the pandemonium of passengers hurrying to leave the station. My eyes fell upon a little girl, face black from grime, who begged for food with her palms outstretched. Frightened by the girl's misery, I hid my face in the folds of Didima's widow's-white sari and inhaled the comforting scents of sandalwood and dried rose petals. On the day he died, she took off all her jewelry piece by piece and cried as she wiped the red teep dot off her forehead. Since then, all she wore were her wedding band and a pearl ring—Dadu's last gift to her.

Finally, I heard Didima say, "Oh, Jiten, thank God you're here. I was scared you'd never find us!"

"I'm just glad you got here in one piece," Uncle Jiten said. "I should go hunt down Agya, or else he'll get lost in this craziness." Our servant, Agya, who had accompanied us from Calcutta—had traveled in the third-class compartment of the train with all our luggage.

"Hello, shona," a female said, fingering my two thick braids.

Reburrowing my face in the folds of Didima's sari front, I resented the unfamiliar touch. I sneaked a peek to see a glimpse of pale pink then wriggled away from the person and scuttled around to Didima's back. "Who is she?" I hid my face with Didima's white sari pallu.

Didima's voice sounded high and strained. "She's your mother, Jhummur, you silly girl."

"Ma shona, don't you remember me?"

That time, the fat lady tried to take my hand, but I shook her off. My bare toes in sandals curled in resistance.

"Noor Shona," Didima rebuked. "Come on. Be a good girl, and come around and say hello to your ma."

Reassured by Didima's tone, I peered from behind Didima's back. In that instant, I remembered the person called Ma coming through the dining room entrance of our Calcutta drawing room. Ma had stopped right by the black wicker armchair, where its backrest had scratched a long horizontal line on the whitewashed wall. I remembered the fat lady's bare foot peeking from under her striped orange sari and worrying the leg of that armchair with her big toe.

A little distance beyond had stood Baba beside two overflowing suitcases on the terrazzo floor. He'd shaken in sobs in Didima's arms because he was leaving India to go home to East Pakistan.

What had struck me was how dry the person called Ma's eyes had been compared to the snotty, dripping noses of Agya and Didima's middle sister, Auntie Shukhi, whose hankie was sopping wet, pressed against her mouth as she removed her eyeglasses to wipe the moisture from her scrunched pink eyes.

Remembering all those details, I retreated to the safety of Didima's back again. There, I draped Didima's long white sari pallu around myself from head to waist because it allowed me to pretend I was invisible. I pressed my face against the small of Didima's back, eyes closed. The musky aroma of Tuhina cold cream on Didima's skin eased the internal band constricting my chest about Baba leaving me behind for the first time in my life.

***

Since meeting my mother that day at the Delhi Railway Station—for me, the first instant that I could even recall having a mother—seventy-five percent of my interactions with her had ended in challenge. What little good I could salvage, I had rationalized only as an adult. That was my mother's legacy to me. In my efforts to become independent to support my own children, I was close to repeating that history. With supreme effort, I refocused on the world history study guide in front of me, which suddenly held little meaning in the grand scheme of my life. *Is my legacy to Pia and Abril going to be my absence, my neglect, my nonexistence? The controversial question of who I am in their lives?* That outcome would destroy everything I was fighting so hard to achieve. *So what will I do?*

33

FIVE DAYS LATER, AFTER TAKING my last final exam, my heart sat like a rock inside my chest as I approached the UNIFE mother superior's office.

"*You're* dropping out?" Madre Buzio's eyebrows shot up. "Why? You're doing so well."

On my lap, my hands clenched until my nails dug welts into my palms. "It's a long story. I'm not quitting. I just have to wait until my children reach school-going age. Right now, I'm doing well, but they aren't. I neglect them too much."

"How long will that be? It'll postpone your degree."

"At least two years. I don't have a choice. I didn't bring children into the world to shape them into delinquents. What grace period do I have to stay away and still return to finish my degree?" My face grew ridged at the memory of what had happened to me at JNU.

"Nothing specific," Madre Buzio said. "As long as you keep your transcripts safe—come back at the beginning of any semester. However, if the course work changes in your absence, you would have to do the new course. What does your husband say about this decision?" The nun looked curious.

I swallowed the bitterness in my throat. "He doesn't even know it yet, but I'm sure he and his mother will be thrilled. They never wanted me to attend college in the first place."

At lunch break, I told Carla my decision.

"You're kidding!"

"No." I recounted what had happened at the kindergarten meeting.

"Oh, amiga." Carla took my hand and squeezed it. "Then you're not quitting, are you? I know you. You'll get back to it."

The following morning, I stared out of the anteroom window in my mother-in-law's apartment at the busy street below. *Was Carla right, or am I cursed to never finish college in any country?* At that point, it really didn't matter. Nothing mattered but my children.

Finally, on Friday evening, Sergio said, "My mother tells me you've been home for three days. Did your summer vacation begin already?" He dropped a paper bag of chocolate cookies on my lap.

"No. I quit school." I focused on my toenails.

"What? Why?" Sergio's face showed genuine surprise.

"Isn't your mother happy I'm home to mind the kids?" Actually, my mother-in-law was *not* happy at all I was home. *But that's what she said she wanted, isn't it? Be careful what you wish for.*

"You're sidestepping my question."

Well, I won't confess my humiliation at the kindergarten to you, Sergio dear, since you never did ask me what happened at that meeting. "I'll wait for Abril to enter the first grade. I'll go back to school then."

"I may have a surprise for you too." Sergio kicked off his wine-colored Italian leather moccasins.

"What surprise?"

"You'll have to wait and see."

The following week, I reread the same page in a P. G. Wodehouse farce over the annoying babble of a television sitcom the children were watching. I would never be happy, much less independent. It was not written in my destiny. The lump in my throat felt so big I could never swallow it. Yes, logic intimated I could go back to university when Abril entered the first grade, but so far, logic had failed me far too often. *Why would it serve me this time around?*

In the evening, I didn't look up as Sergio strode in. "Are you ready for the surprise?" He snatched the book from my hands. "We move to Valle Hermoso next Saturday." Valle Hermoso was the neighborhood of our newly built house. "I can't wait."

"So, the house is finished?" I tried to register happy but couldn't pull it off.

"Nearly, but all we need is one bathroom and two bedrooms, and those are complete. It's enough for us to leave my mother's apartment."

"And the children's kindergarten? It'll be so far away."

"They can go to a local kindergarten near there."

Our brand-new home promised a spacious living room and study, a bathroom, and the kitchen, with a small courtyard, across which was a maid's room, her bathroom, a laundry room, and a storage room. A garden to be landscaped bordered half the house in an L shape, ending on a flagstone patio, where we could park a couple of cars. But right then, only two of the three bedrooms upstairs were finished, along with one bathroom.

On the day of the move, Sergio and I stood outside our house, staring at the bare brown hill whose right half belonged to a famous Jesuit school diagonally across from us. Soon, the transpacific container full of our belongings from India lumbered up the school road.

I remarked, "What will the traffic be like once the school reopens after the summer?"

"I've been wondering about that too." Sergio waved to the truck driver to indicate the right place to stop.

As the eighteen-wheeler parked, I smiled at Sergio. "You know, I *am* excited." *More excited than I thought possible after having to quit school.*

"Don't get too excited. This container sat in a warehouse in Callao for the last two years. All our belongings may have rotted from seaside dampness."

But refusing to share his gloom, I closed my eyes. Maybe it could be our fresh start. Together. Without my mother-in-law to dictate Sergio's every word and move. If Serg and I could patch up our differences and stay together, maybe getting a degree wouldn't be so crucial. It was such a positive possibility to hope for. After all, I was a lot more grown-up than I had been when I married Sergio.

Two hours later, as Sergio and I oversaw the unpacking of the larger cardboard boxes, my eyes watered while old memories and evocative aromas such as the sweetness of sandalwood incense, the bitter smell of dried neem leaves, and the minty fragrance of walnut bark emerged, layer after layer. The latter two had been my idea as tried-and-true Indian preservatives against potential mouse damage, since to even get all the way to Peru from India, the cargo had traveled for three months, first on ground then by sea. Both Sergio and I cried, coughed, sneezed, and laughed over our crazy discoveries, like how two-year-old condensed milk didn't rot—it converted to toffee inside its sealed tin.

In the coming days, I disobeyed Sergio's warnings against tin poisoning and gorged on the toffee until Sergio objected, "Hey. Share the toffee with us."

"No. What if the next tin is poisoned?"

Contrarily, all our Indian spices packed in plastic boxes had rotted to a uniform heather green. Dismayed, I scattered the lot over our yet-to-be-landscaped garden to serve as compost at least. In three weeks, the entire garden turned to a bright pistachio green, and Sergio laughed until he cried.

The surprises kept me from missing school or dwelling on where my life was headed. Instead, I was thrilled about how well Sergio and I were doing without his mother policing us. The children, too, had adjusted to their new kindergarten, and at last, I had a new friend, Ann Marie Lanata, the British owner of the kindergarten, located three blocks down the road from our house.

In that fashion, four months went by. Then, on one evening, I served Sergio a dinner of curried black chana beans from our garden, cooked to perfection with potatoes.

Seeing my inadvertent success with the chana beans, Sergio sowed red geranium cuttings outside the bay window of his study, knowing I loved geraniums. Red geraniums held a very special meaning for me because, one day in New Delhi, when I couldn't have been older than seven, Didima had come home from food shopping carrying a strange plant in a wire basket filled with peat moss. It had a flowerhead readying to bloom.

"What plant is this, Didima?"

"It's a red geranium, shona," she explained. "A Garhwali hill man was selling them by the vegetable store, and I couldn't resist the temptation to buy it, even though it was expensive and I know it won't survive the New Delhi heat." After that, Didima pulled out an old album and showed me a black-and-white picture of her as a child, holding a bouquet of geraniums outside their vacation home in Simla, before her father's death had plunged the family into misery.

During the following week, each morning, Didima cupped that flowerhead, closed her eyes, and breathed in its pungent fragrance. In those moments, I had seen Didima past her sunken cheeks and wrinkled face to capture the expression of a little girl smelling her favorite flower. It was my one memory of seeing a geranium until I came to Lima, where it was among the first flowers I recognized on our way home from the airport.

***

One day, Sergio returned home to declare, "Guess what? We can build the rest of this house a lot sooner than I had anticipated."

"Why? Did you win the lottery?"

"No, but I got promoted. Between my government salary and the Diplomatic Association stipend, I'll earn one thousand extra dollars a month. My new rank as a minister-counselor also entitles me to a car and chauffeur. We'll renew your driver's license for you to use our car."

"For what? I have nowhere to go." *I quit college, remember?*

"Are you kidding me? To drop and fetch the kids from kindergarten and go grocery shopping. It will be two fewer chores for me to do."

Of course. Those are the extent of the intellectual stimulations I am entitled to, aren't they? Studying had been an outrageous luxury that Sergio certainly didn't miss. But in truth, I, too, was relieved to be more present in my children's lives.

As such, furnishing our new home on weekends became an activity Sergio and I lived for. Aware of how I loved nature, he indulged my every whim to buy the plants and bushes I wanted for our garden, amazed when I asked to buy tobacco dust to eliminate slugs, chicken manure to fertilize the roses, and five different-colored bougainvillea that would grow and hide the iron spikes on top of our perimeter wall. High walls and iron spikes had become a part of Limeñian architecture ever since terrorism had overtaken Peru at the end of the seventies, but I was determined not to live in a mini jail.

"So, why bougainvillea?" asked Sergio, who didn't know much about gardening.

"Because bougainvillea creepers have enormous thorns," I explained. "Having bougainvillea covering the iron spikes will add to our defense if thieves or terrorists ever try to scale our walls."

While Sergio worked, I sewed nonstop. Each Saturday, I amazed my husband with the curtains, dishcloths, or bedspreads I manufactured with the fabrics we had purchased together in New Delhi.

On a Sunday, I was hanging up the curtains I had sewn for the children's bedroom when Sergio came in and flopped on Pia's bed.

"What's up?" I smiled. "Taking a break?"

Sergio's project that weekend was to hang up pictures and paintings.

"No." He smiled ruefully. "I'm just frustrated that I have the world's best home improvement toolbox, but I'm the problem. I can't even drill a hole straight into a wall."

"Hey, no one is perfect. I would give my eyeteeth to cook like you—but you do it better than me, and that's that. Why don't you go cook us dinner? I'm hungry."

"I already did."

"Are you serious? What did you cook?"

"I cooked *bacalao* cod."

"You mean Easter bacalao? I love that, but it isn't Easter!"

"So what? I'd love to cook turkey meals outside of Christmastime, too, only they don't sell turkey here unless it's December."

I finished hanging one curtain and got off the ladder. "What hole were you trying to drill?"

"I wanted to hang that silver-sequin Thai embroidery wall hanging in the living room, but it's heavy, so I need to screw screws into the wall—"

"And why didn't you just hammer in a nail?"

"Because this thing is heavy. So first, I need to drill a hole to wedge in a wooden peg, then hand-screw a screw into the wood."

"Come on." I pulled on his arm. "Forget the wall hanging. I'll lay the table for dinner. You serve."

"We need a housemaid."

"Yes, but we need one recommended by acquaintances. These are not the times to hire strangers."

I waited all the way until the end of February 1988 to broach the subject of maybe patching up our relationship. Yes, Sergio and I shared a king-sized bed, but we hadn't been intimate in over two years, since our fight over the children being sick in New Delhi. We had gotten along so well since our move into the new house. *Surely, Sergio had noticed?*

One night, in our bedroom, I asked, "Serg, would you consider making love to me? I mean, we've been so relaxed. Couldn't we at least try?"

Sergio smiled but shook his head. "Noor, you don't love me. Not as a husband. You made that clear after Abril was born. I often wonder if you ever did."

Instant tears sprang to my eyes. "That's so unfair. I did love you when we got married." My understanding of love was so much more complex than it had been when I was twenty-one.

"Yes, but you're not in love with me now, and neither am I with you. All we have in common are Pia and Abril. It's not reason enough to complicate our relationship."

"But can't you try for their sake? They're so dependent on us still."

Sergio didn't respond to that, but he also didn't say an outright no.

In the darkness, once we switched off the lights, Sergio pulled me to him, and we engaged in self-conscious sex. However, I couldn't pretend Sergio excited me, nor was he particularly passionate, and after a few nights, I asked myself if it had been the smartest move. Our intimacy was doing more to mark our differences than to unite us, so it was the opposite outcome of what I had hoped for.

Ten days later, on a Sunday morning, I was brushing my teeth when Sergio came up behind me and took my shoulders.

He stared at me through the bathroom mirror. "I can't do this."

"Do what?" I mumbled through a mouthful of spearmint-flavored toothpaste dribbling down my chin.

"I can't have sex to pretend we're okay."

I nodded and didn't insist.

When I came out of the bathroom, Sergio was on the phone, but his monosyllabic answers caught my attention.

When he hung up, I asked, "Who was that?"

"Oh, my mother. I'm going to see her later today."

I didn't know why his answer rang false. Therefore, as soon as he left the bedroom to head downstairs, I hit the redial number on the phone. The person who picked up said, "Jaime León residence. Who's speaking?"

I hung up, hoping Sergio wouldn't discover I had checked up on him. But his lie raised a tiny red flag in my head.

On Monday evening, Sergio asked, "Did you call Jaime's house yesterday?"

My heart thumped. "No, I must have hit redial by mistake when I picked up my hairbrush. I didn't call anybody."

I didn't point out that Sergio had said he had been calling his mother, and Sergio didn't catch the discrepancy.

34

In early March 1988, it was nearing Sergio's birthday, but we hadn't discussed how we would celebrate it in the new house.

"What of Carla from the UNIFE?" Sergio asked over dinner one night. "I never hear you mention her. Aren't you friends anymore? You two haven't seen each other in ages."

Why did Sergio bring up Carla? He wasn't friends with my friends, given the age difference. "Of course we are, but it's hard to keep in touch when I'm not a part of her college life anymore. She has a schedule to keep, and I don't."

"Go see her this Saturday. I won't need the car, because Nila wants to come with her kids and spend the day here with me."

"Will Eduardo come too?"

"No. He has a college seminar this weekend. It'll provide you alone time with your friend for a change."

Eduardo, Nila's husband, was a renowned philosophy professor from Uruguay, so he often participated in extracurricular interuniversity activities.

We had only hired a live-in maid, Dulci, the previous Monday, so I asked, "Can you make sure Dulci is ready for the children's bath in the evening? I'll come home before then."

Dulci was a cousin of our gardener and odd-job man, Mauricio. And Mauricio had worked for a long time for a fellow diplomat colleague of Sergio's, so we could trust him.

For Dulci's parents, who lived on a remote mountain farm, sending their eldest daughter to the city had a twofold purpose. For one, she would send her entire paycheck home to support the rest of her siblings, and the more important reason—living and working for us, Dulci would attend school once a week at our expense to finish her high school diploma.

"Don't worry so much." Sergio smiled. "If you're late, Dulci can talk them through their bath. Enjoy your outing."

Driving to Carla's, I reflected on how little we touched each other's lives once I dropped out of college. *Maybe I will feel less alone, less displaced, talking to Carla?*

The Bustos clan lived in a townhouse in the not-so-affluent seaside district of Magdalena. To visit with them, I dressed down to underplay the disparity in our circumstances, aware that Carla's father supported eight family members on his bank employee's salary.

After greeting the family, I asked, "Car, can we go for a walk to the beach? It's hard to believe I live in a city that is on the coast. I never seem to see the ocean."

Seaweed that resembled knots of disgusting dead snakes littered the beach near Carla's house, but I removed my flip-flops anyway. "God, this sand feels good on my soles." I turned my face to the bright summer sun.

"What's wrong, amiga?" Carla knew me too well.

"Why do you ask?" I stared out to sea, my heart heavy.

"Quit stalling. Fess up—what's bugging you?"

My eyes grew watery. "I asked Sergio to reconsider us getting a divorce. He refused."

"Noor, from what you've told me, the two of you don't even sleep together… so how could you expect him to say yes?"

"Actually, I *did* sleep with him, every night for ten nights until a week ago. Then, last weekend, he said he didn't love me and he couldn't pretend what he didn't feel."

"And do you love him?" Carla's bluntness pierced me like a thorn.

"I don't know, Car. I don't know." I pointed to a rocky coastal island a few miles offshore gleaming white under the sunlight. "Sometimes, he's the father I lost—at other times, he is an elder brother. But he is always my rock to cling to. Yet he can also be a dick, though lately, I haven't seen even a hint of his nasty side. It's like Serg is two people, the good Sergio and the bad Sergio, the Dr. Jekyll and the Mr. Hyde, and I never know whom I'm dealing with or what he wakes up as on any given day. I guess my worst problem is I don't love him like a man, like I loved Chirag. My love for Serg is different… because I know that both his good personality and bad personality are not anything he invents. So

I love him and hate him, and he loves me and hates me, too, only he flip-flops way more than I do."

"So can't you pretend to love him like you loved Chirag?"

"Easy for you to say. You've never *been* to bed with a guy. I find it impossible to fake feelings in bed. My body recoils."

"So what will you do now?"

"I don't know. Other than in bed, we're doing great without his harpy mother in the picture, and he hasn't mentioned a divorce in forever. He'll be in Lima for another year. A lot can change by then."

"Come back and finish school with us. Having a degree will help you feel so much more secure." Carla picked up a broken seashell and dusted the sand off its pearly-gray insides.

"That's so beautiful." I swiped the seashell from Carla's fingers and glinted it in the sun. "If I go back to school now, the kids will have the same issues of neglect they had when we lived at my mother-in-law's. I have to wait until Abril enters the first grade."

"Hang in there, and take it one day at a time. You'll be back in school before you know it."

That evening, I headed home from Carla's well in time for the children's bath. Outside our house, my eyebrows furrowed at the large number of unfamiliar cars parked along our curb. *Is there a school function at the Jesuit school?* Thank goodness the cars hadn't blocked our driveway. I honked for our new maid to open the garage door for me.

I overheard music playing inside the house as I parked the car. "Dulci, what's going on?"

"Señor Sergio said it was a party for his upcoming birthday."

So *that* was why he had sent me to Carla's house without Pia and Abril. He wanted them present but not me. I glanced down at my faded summer dress and slippers, and the back of my neck grew hot. And to think I had told Carla how nice Sergio had been to me lately. As if I had jinxed myself, there was Sergio doing his best Mr. Hyde performance, playing to a large audience. An audience I couldn't even avoid because our house didn't have a back door like many older homes did. *How can I not hate Sergio when he acts this mean?*

I squared my shoulders and walked into a living room full of Sergio's extended family, fashionable clothes, perfume, and the warm whiff of hor d'oeuvres, which Dulci's cousin, Mauricio, who played waiter, was offering around. I hunted for Sergio with my eyes, avoiding my mother-in-law's triumphant expression as she talked to a relative whose name I couldn't recall. Sergio walked in through the dining room French doors as my mother-in-law pointed to me and giggled.

"Hi," he addressed me as if I were a guest. "Would you care for a drink?"

Blood rushed to my face. "If you didn't want me here, why didn't you just say so?" I whispered. "But you wanted me to come back, didn't you? I can see how your mother is enjoying my humiliation." *Had this rejection been her idea?*

Sergio walked away, not letting me continue. Short of following him and making a scene that would embarrass me more than him, I had no place there. Regardless, beside myself, I chased after him against my better judgment, yanking his arm from behind. "Congrats, Serg!" I hissed. "If you intended to show me how much you don't love me, you succeeded. Enjoy the night."

But Sergio refused to react, giving me a polite smile that sent me dashing up the stairs, hugging my old cloth purse, tears of anger and shame blurring the marble treads.

HIBISCUS

35

AFTER THE BIRTHDAY PARTY, I stopped talking to Sergio altogether. It was my one defense when he was a bastard. The last thing I said to him was "From now on, I'm addressing your mother as señora, like Eduardo does. I'm done with the hypocrisy of calling her Mami. She hates me as much as I hate her, so I'm dispensing with the farce."

"As you please. I don't care."

But of course, he still brought me chocolate cookies to confuse me more. No one in my life reduced me to worse childish behavior than Sergio. Therefore, rather than act like the twenty-seven-year-old mother I was, I would snatch the chocolate cookies out of his hands, omitting to thank him. Instead, I would devour my chocolate cookies, rationalizing, *Why should I thank him?* He had humiliated me publicly because he had no use for me anymore. And when I remembered that, my mind would hark back to our bitterest argument yet, after the children had pneumonia in New Delhi. *Was it five years ago already?* Sergio had said, *"Fine. You want a divorce? I'll be happy to give you one, but since it isn't my idea, I'll keep the children. When I return home to Lima next year, stay in India. Pia and Abril will come with me."* Then my eyes would cloud, and my hands would curl into fists. *He would not get the children. Not now, not ever. They're my children, and I will keep them. End of story.*

Each night, I wanted to leave our king-sized bed and sleep in the study. *But if I do that, what will I tell the children?* With no one to talk to, I complained to Dulci about Sergio and how he had threatened to take the children away from me.

"Men are strange, señora," Dulci said.

"How would you know? Do you have a boyfriend?" Dulci didn't come across as having one.

"No, but I have a father who raped my mother's eldest daughter from a previous relationship. My mother hasn't been the same since my poor sister had that child, and my mother had to raise it as my fourth brother."

"Christ. And what happened to your sister?"

"She lives in and out of mental hospitals."

"And how do *you* feel about it all?"

"It was never about how I felt. I had to support my mother as the eldest daughter from this marriage. But I love my father, and I can never tell my mother that, because she gets furious."

"Oh, Duls. You have me to talk to now, like I have you." I hugged her, aware that no one in Lima or India touched their maids.

Two weeks later, I didn't answer when Sergio knocked on the study door. He barged into my space anyway, blatantly disregarding my refusal to talk to him. Here he loosened the Windsor knot in his foulard tie, extending a sheaf of papers.

My jaw clenched. "What is this?"

"Divorce papers," Sergio said as if mentioning the grocery list.

My heart jolted. *So soon?* Sergio pulled the tie out of his collar and unbuttoned the top two buttons of his pale-blue dress shirt.

To hide my shock, I realigned a pile of books on the floor next to the sofa where I sat. Then I straightened. "I won't sign them if it means you'll take the kids away from me."

"No. I've decided that's a bad idea. They can stay in Lima with you and join me during vacations after I leave for a posting abroad."

How should I interpret that? "Fine." I lowered my eyes so Sergio wouldn't see my confusion. But I mustered the courage to say, "When they start school, can I go back to college?" Finding strength in those words, I met his gaze. "It's in your best interest to pay for my schooling, Serg. Or else I'll sponge off you for the rest of your life."

"Fine, just don't neglect the children when you do go back to school."

In bed that night, the stark reality of our divorce hung over me in a pressure cloud that wouldn't let me sleep. Instead of four or five bathroom visits, a routine ingrained by Didima's diabetic needs throughout my childhood, I got up each hour.

Within three weeks, on Mother's Day, I realized Sergio appeared much thinner than he had in a while. *Hmmm. Is he preparing for the dating market?* The possibility bothered me a lot more than it should have, considering I had never loved Sergio as a man.

Two more weeks went by, and Sergio lost another few pounds, making me intensely curious. Reared in the shadow of my mother's fatness, I lived to control my weight and resorted to my Roman remedy of vomiting after meals if my weight climbed a gram over fifty kilos. After eight years of practice, I could vomit half a meal without a sound.

At bedtime, I said, "What diet are you on? Let me do it too."

"I'm not on a diet."

"Then how come you've lost weight?"

"I have a stomach flu—I've had off-and-on diarrhea for four or five weeks."

"Oh." I wanted to insist he see a doctor but didn't because I would only irritate him.

By mid-June 1988, Sergio hadn't mentioned the divorce papers once in a month and a half, and I never brought it up because I didn't want to face it. However, as he headed out of the house one morning, I noticed how gaunt he looked right as I was driving off to take the kids to kindergarten. I pressed on the brake pedal. "Shouldn't you see a doctor for your stomach flu?"

"No. I'm thrilled to wear suits I haven't fit into since Japan. Plus, I'm not sick. I just have a diarrhea that comes and goes."

"What harm will it do to see a doctor?" I worried about him falling sick in the same way he would worry if I fell sick, because we both had a connection we couldn't let go of despite how we acted towards each other.

"I don't have a primary since my last one retired eight months ago."

For once, I didn't wait for Sergio's permission to call Carla's mother for her doctor's information.

On her callback, Carla's mother said, "My doctor recommended your husband see Dr. Alberto Ritter, an oncologist with an additional degree in immunology. He thinks your husband might have an immunity-related issue. Rapid and unexplained weight loss is never good."

"It's not unexplained," I argued. "He has a stomach flu with diarrhea."

"Call this doctor. What's there to lose?"

I called Dr. Ritter that afternoon and described Sergio's symptoms.

"Bring him in to see me, señora."

At night, when I suggested it to Sergio, he blew me off. "I don't have the time for a doctor's visit."

The next day, I called Dr. Ritter again.

"Señora, he needs to see a doctor, but I can't see him unless he wants to see me."

"So he's okay?"

"I didn't say that. I said he has to want to see me, and he clearly doesn't. Why don't you wait a few days and suggest it again? His symptoms might progress a lot faster than he thinks. Bring him to see me then."

In five more days, Sergio's diarrhea emerged laced with blood. He felt so weak, he missed two days of work. By then, he was relieved I had sought help, though the earliest doctor's appointment was three days away.

On that Monday afternoon, the hundred-yard walk from a street-side parking spot in the Chacarilla market square and the elevator ride to Dr. Ritter's fourth-floor consultation office left Sergio breathless.

There, he pinched his nose. "I'm sorry, Doctor. The smell of your floor disinfectant makes me nauseous."

Dr. Ritter looked more or less Sergio's age, but he had gray hair, unlike Sergio's reddish-brown mop. He examined Sergio from head to toe with sharp hazel eyes, double-checking the excessive growth of his new patient's hemorrhoids. "Let's do a comprehensive blood test." The doctor clasped his hands. "Señor Santander, you might want to consider hospitalization because you appear severely dehydrated."

Sergio's face grew as white as the doctor's office walls as he nodded. Dr. Ritter explained he was the Clínica Internacional's main oncology consultant. As such, he could use his influence to have Sergio admitted the next day.

Outside the doctor's office, I had already pressed the elevator button when I heard Sergio say, "Doctor, did you include a test for AIDS?"

My lips curled in scorn. Sergio was showing off his knowledge of current events to the new doctor. I controlled the urge to run back in and say, "Serg, no one here knows of that disease, and neither would you, if you hadn't read up on it in *Time* magazine, the same as me."

From inside his office, Dr. Ritter replied, "No, it's a test only one laboratory in Lima offers. The Colichon y Cantela, in Miraflores. They import the kit from the US, and it's expensive. Do you still wish to include it?"

"Sure," Sergio said it as if money was of no constraint.

"Then don't go in for a blood test today. Stop by the Colichon y Cantela on your way to the hospital tomorrow."

On the way home, I asked, "Why would you want to waste forty dollars on a test you don't need?"

"Because it'll relieve me to know I don't have it."

At the Clínica Internacional in downtown Lima, Sergio received the hydration treatment he urgently required for a full seventy-two hours to stabilize his blood levels.

On Saturday morning, Señora Santander stunned me outside Sergio's hospital room with, "What doctor have you chosen for my son? Which doctor throws a patient's *mother* out of the hospital room? Besides, my son looks worse each day, not better."

The entire weekend, I searched for an opportunity to ask Sergio for an explanation on why he didn't want his mother to know what he might have, but in between visits from his family, colleagues, and subordinates who held him in high regard, I didn't find one.

Early on Monday, I dropped the children off at kindergarten and raced to the hospital. I caught Dr. Ritter near the Clínica Internacional's reception desk and confronted him point-blank. "Doctor, tell me right now what's wrong with Sergio." My heart beat so loudly I felt the vibrations. "His mother is crucifying me for how you throw everyone out of Sergio's hospital room. She's saying you're a lousy doctor. But Sergio is my husband, so I need to know what's going on. Anything that affects him will directly impact me and our children, so please tell me the truth."

Alberto Ritter stared at me for what seemed an eternity—then he glanced at the nurse behind the reception desk and walked me out of earshot. "Indeed, you do have the right to know, Noor. But Sergio wishes me to remain silent. Please allow him to tell you his own truth when he is ready."

"Is it cancer?" I clutched my throat. "Tell me if he has cancer."

Alberto Ritter grimaced. "No, Noor. Remember the AIDS test he asked for? The result was positive. I am so sorry." He raised his hands.

Something inside my body rushed to my feet.

A spray of cold water droplets on my face channeled me to hear Alberto Ritter's voice, but he sounded far away. "Noor? Noor, are you okay? You fainted and fell to the floor. Can you see me?"

My eyelids fluttered. I blinked to dispel the darkness, embarrassed by the stares of several strangers who had paused to enjoy the developing drama.

But Alberto Ritter ignored them as he held my hand. "Listen to me. I'll sit you up. If you become dizzy, let me know."

"I'm fine." I struggled to my feet. "But what will happen to Sergio?"

Again, Dr. Ritter led me out of earshot, that time of the people around us. "He wants to go to Miami for a second opinion. I'll arrange it because the director of the Mount Sinai Medical Center is a Peruvian friend of mine from medical school."

"What are the chances they made a mistake?" I pressed both my hands to my throat.

"None. This test is called the Western Blot, and it's a self-contained kit the Colichon y Cantela owners import from the US. In Miami, Sergio will undergo the exact same test. You should get tested too."

"Then, what's the point of going to the US?"

"Sergio needs time and distance to assimilate the enormity of his diagnosis. Right now, he's in complete denial. The Miami trip will let him come to terms with the frightening reality."

I was so frightened myself, I didn't trust my wits to visit with Sergio much less run into his family. Instead, on the highway home, I swerved so hard it galvanized every other driver into a honking fit. *What if I contracted Sergio's disease from the sex we had had back in January, when I had the brilliant idea to patch up our marriage? Did Sergio already have AIDS then? Who could have infected him? Has he be been having an affair? Is that why he didn't want to give our relationship a chance?*

In the afternoon, I told the children I wasn't well. We wouldn't go to the hospital to visit their papá that day. By evening, I developed diarrhea. The next morning, my used toilet paper ran traces of red, like Sergio's had a week ago. *Do I need any other proof I have AIDS?* I spent half the day huddled in bed, crying because Sergio and I would both die. *What will become of my children? Where will they go?*

During their ride to kindergarten the next morning, I kept glancing at Pia and Abril through the rearview mirror. *How will they cope to know both their parents are dying?* I fumbled to retrieve sunglasses from my purse and jammed them on my nose. If the children saw my red eyes, they would ask why, and right then, I didn't have answers.

36

That afternoon, I called Dr. Ritter with my symptoms.

"Your best bet is to get tested in Miami when Sergio is tested. Otherwise, he won't believe the results."

That entire week, I looked at Sergio with dumb pity. I wanted to hug him and tell him how sorry I was we were both dying, but I respected Dr. Ritter's request for confidentiality and waited for Sergio to share his diagnosis, which he never did.

On July 3, seated next to my husband in an American Airlines Boeing 747, I couldn't hold out any longer. I took Sergio's frigid hand in mine and shook with tears. "I know what you have, and I have it too," I whispered, thinking again of the children, housed with Sergio's mother for the duration of our trip.

"How do you know?"

"Because I bleed every time I poop, like you."

"Well, I won't settle until I have a real, thorough checkup in Miami."

"Aren't you scared I might have it too?"

"Not if I don't have it. Right?"

I nodded, but I couldn't remove the image of Alberto Ritter implying how, in Miami, Sergio would receive the same results.

We flew out of Lima on that winter's night to arrive in the cloying humidity of a Miami summer morning.

At the Mount Sinai Medical Center, a penthouse hospital room overlooking the bay was already reserved for Sergio's arrival.

On July 4, Director Luis Benavides, Dr. Ritter's Peruvian friend, paid Sergio a visit. "Señor Santander," the olive-skinned doctor said, "I'm sorry you have to wait until Monday for your tests and consultation with the infectious diseases experts. In this country, this weekend is such an important holiday, our hospital operates on a skeleton staff."

Later, while Sergio dozed, I spent the afternoon staring out of the hospital room's wall of windows, seeing but not seeing toy-sized boats, winking, sunny water, matchbox skyscrapers, and palm trees the size of tiny spiky flowers in a concrete field. However I had imagined coming to America someday, it wasn't under those circumstances. Over the blue of the water hung the blue of the sky, and in between the two, little question bubbles rotated inside my head. *Would I have done differently had I known my life would end at age twenty-eight?* I wiped my eyes.

I wouldn't be dying right then if I had run away with Chirag. *But how could I have, with him as married as I was and me having my two children? Where will my children go once Sergio and I die? To live with a Santander family member? Better them than with my mother and stepfather with his groping hands.* My fingers tightened spasmodically.

The day after Sergio's and my arrival in Miami, Nila flew in from Lima to accompany her brother. Nila was a retired airline stewardess, so she could fly for almost free anytime she wanted. I was glad she had come to Miami because she was Sergio's sister and his favorite, but I didn't know if Serg had told her the truth about his disease. She and I would stay with their cousin, Jorgina, who lived in Palm Beach with her husband and three daughters.

On the Sunday afternoon of July 5, Nila, Jorgina, and her daughters chattered around Sergio's hospital bed while his dinner was served. The disease, I would find, left him too bloated to eat the overcooked American fare, and Sergio pushed his food tray away.

"I just want to sleep," he said tiredly. "I don't have any appetite."

On our way to Jorgina's, Nila suggested we shop, since she had a list of utilitarian items to buy for her two daughters. "Let's do this now so tomorrow, I can accompany Sergio. He'll need me for moral support once the testing starts."

Will Sergio tell Nila he's testing for AIDS? I stared out of the van window. *Nila couldn't fathom how trapped I feel. But even in the worst-case scenario, Nila's life won't be affected. It's Sergio and I who will die.* I was so overwhelmed, I couldn't even cry.

In the huge floodlit arena of a Walmart, the family members scattered in their intended directions, and I, who didn't have money, cruised the clothing aisles. For no particular reason that I could indicate afterward, I grabbed a pair of beach shorts and shoved them into my large Lancôme purse. I pretended interest in other clothes, but my mind fixated on the colors, the design, the texture, and the shape of those shorts inside my purse.

I walked toward the cash registers to wait for Nila. Jorgina paid for three pairs of pantyhose. Seeing I hadn't shopped, Nila said, "Are you sure you don't want anything? Don't worry about the money. I'll settle it with Sergio."

"No. But thanks for the offer."

We headed out of the store in an uneven group. I was already outside when a young African American man approached me. "Excuse me, ma'am. May I check your handbag, please?"

"Hey, what's the problem?" interjected Nila.

The thickset young man pulled out a police badge. In one smooth motion, he removed my purse from my shoulder and extracted the beach shorts. "May I please see a receipt for this item?"

Nila looked at me blankly. She called out to Jorgina and her girls, who had gone on ahead.

"Please come with me, ma'am." The detective motioned me to follow him. "I have to process this."

"I-I'll pay for it." I ran to tap the fat officer's shoulder. "Please, I'll pay for it," I begged.

"Stop talking, you fool. You're going to jail," Nila hissed, her eyes two bits of gray rock. "Come on. Hurry up." She, too, motioned me forward.

We followed the detective into a cramped concrete surveillance office at the back of the Walmart building, full of what appeared to me to be a series of tiny televisions. I began to tear up as the detective took his seat behind a cheap metal desk and filled out a thick form. As I begged for mercy, he looked up.

"Ma'am, explain your story to the judge when you receive a summons. Right now, show me an identity document and sign this form, right here." He positioned the paperwork in front of me and placed a fleshy finger on a dotted line.

"Excuse me, Officer," interrupted Nila. "She can't wait for a summons." She outlined the circumstances of our visit to the US. "We leave Miami in two days."

The detective's nostrils flared. "You should have told me that ahead of time, ma'am. Now I'll have to fill out different paperwork."

I felt like we had been in that cramped office for hours when the officer had me sign what seemed my death warrant. He tore off the Xerox duplicate and handed me the copy.

In the van, Jorgina drove while no one glanced my way or spoke to me. Staring out the van window, all I could hear was that Xerox copy crackle in my handbag to my slightest movement. I was mystified as to what had possessed me to steal those shorts in the first place.

At Jorgina's house, everyone spread out in different directions, as if they couldn't bear to be near me.

Only Jorgina opened the refrigerator door. "Noor, are you hungry? I'll heat you leftovers."

Her words filled me with gratitude, but I refused. The sooner I went upstairs, the sooner I could bury my head in a pillow and cry.

The next morning, Nila's profile resembled a Roman statuette as we got to Sergio's bedside. "Why don't you tell Sergio all about your little adventure last night? My head is killing me, so I'll go find a cup of coffee."

Crying, I recounted my tale of woe to Sergio. "Serg, I'm so, *so* sorry. Don't ask why I did it. I don't know."

Sergio opened his arms for me to place my head on his chest. He stroked my hair. "It's okay, darling. Don't cry. People do strange things under stress. Give me the paperwork you received so I can read it."

On the safety of Sergio's chest, I closed my eyes and breathed fully for the first time in eighteen hours. My husband would always be an enigma to me. *Why is he so kind on one occasion and so mean on another? As if he's never sure of who he is?*

His hand sought mine. "Go to the nurse's station and ask to speak to the hospital's social worker. He, or she, will tell you how to reach the Miami Dade County Courthouse. Go resolve this charge right now. We have to sort it out before we leave the country."

"And what would happen if we didn't resolve it?"

"Probably not much. I have diplomatic immunity, but I'm sure the US Immigration authorities would red-flag my name because my shabby conduct wouldn't go unnoticed. Either way, for me, it's a policy of national pride *never* to disrespect the rules and laws of any country, so go sort it out. Hopefully, they'll have you pay for it in the form of a fine."

"How?" I sniffled, lifting my head.

"With the blank check I'll give you. We can't have this mishap leaked to the authorities."

"How can I pay anything with a blank check?"

"You write in the amount, silly." Sergio squeezed my fingers. "But stay here until the laboratory staff comes at ten to draw blood. You should be tested too."

I lay my head back down on the haven of Sergio's chest, fingers crumpling a portion of his blue-and-white diamond-patterned hospital gown. *Who is Sergio to me today? My father? A brother? Whoever he is, he's always my only safety net in a swimming world.* "What will I do if you die before me?" I whispered huskily.

"I won't." Sergio caressed my hair. "I'll bet you that test in Lima was a mistake. Don't be so pessimistic."

I hugged him and buried my face in his chest. *What if Sergio's right and Dr. Ritter was wrong?*

37

INSIDE THE UGLY MODERN BUILDING of the Miami Dade County Courthouse, a US marshal directed me to get in line with men who reeked of stale sweat, yesterday's alcohol, and other odors I couldn't identify. As usual, Sergio had been right. The hospital social worker, a middle-aged lady of Cuban descent, had been kind to me and supportive to a fault, unlike Nila's silent accusation and derision. She explained that if I didn't mind a long trek, I could walk to the courthouse. My best bet was to go there as soon as possible and ask for further help and clarification in the court clerk's office.

Standing in the line, I crossed my arms, starkly aware of the different glances I was securing, praying for my turn at the clerk's window to come sooner, but one man whose brow was so low it mimicked a rain catch was undeterred. He looked me up and down and emitted a catcall so loud my gaze dropped.

At the clerk's window, the lady clerk said, "The docket is already full. The soonest you can try again is tomorrow morning, but come early."

"I can't." I swallowed a growing knot of tension. "I fly out tomorrow at three p.m. My husband only came here for a hospital stay."

The clerk shrugged. "I have no way to help you. Come tomorrow at eight a.m., and I'll do my best."

Back at the hospital, Nila was with Sergio, forcing me to explain my court interaction to him in front of her.

"You can't go back to court tomorrow. We're flying out, remember?" Nila's gray eyes resembled two bits of cold, wet limestone.

Sergio said, "She has to. I can't leave the country with this court action pending."

Once Nila left the room, I begged, "Serg, please, *please* let me stay here with you tonight. I can't deal with Nila and her nasty looks—not with an AIDS diagnosis hanging in the balance."

"But you'll be so uncomfortable. There's no extra bed in here."

"I don't care. I'm used to it from a childhood with my grandma always in and out of hospitals. I can't bear Nila and your cousin's daughters treating me like an untouchable from India."

At six the next morning, after a sleepless night on the armchair in Sergio's hospital room, I went to the hospital cafeteria to prop myself up with a stiff shot of espresso.

Coffee in hand, I ran in on the tail end of Director Luis Benavides's visit to Sergio, catching the words "I'm so sorry, Señor Santander."

"Sorry for what?" My heart jangled as it used to when I stood too close to the electric bell in the inner patio of the Loreto Convent School and the bell rang without notice.

"My AIDS diagnosis." Sergio appeared three shades paler.

"And me? Do I have it too?" Something in my throat felt like a stone lodged there as I stared at the doctor.

"They wouldn't deliver your results here, señora. You're not an inpatient," Dr. Benavides said. "Go ask at the reception desk."

I charged out of the room.

The next three minutes trickled by like they were thirty as the duty nurse called multiple phone extensions while my ears pounded.

"Run to the second-floor laboratory," she said at last. "Your results are down there."

In the huge maze of the second floor, I got lost twice until reaching the right office. A female laboratory technician handed me an incomprehensible computer-generated sheet full of words and numbers.

I scanned it in dismay. "Can't you tell me what my results are? Please? I don't understand this."

The lab tech shook her head. "I'm sorry. You have to discuss that with your doctor. If I tell you anything, I could get fired."

"L-listen." My voice came out jerky. "Please—tell me what it says. I n-n-need to know if I have AIDS! My kids are little, and my husband has it… if I'm dying… I need—"

"Shhh." The lab tech got off her stool and pulled a crying me into her arms. She took the document from my hand and smoothed it on her desk. Her index finger traced down vertically. "See this, where it says 'neg'? It means you don't have AIDS. Please don't tell anyone I told you."

I hugged the lab tech. On the way to the elevator, I screamed, "I don't have AIDS!" to every passerby.

I entered Serg's room again, faltering to a stop at the sight of *two* white-coated doctors standing beside his bed, along with Nila, who had shown up as well.

"What do your results say?" Sergio asked.

"Oh, Serg! I tested negative for AIDS." I waved the document.

Nila immediately withered me with a glance while Sergio said, "At least *some* good news."

I wanted to hug him for being supportive to me even though he was under so much stress.

"Good afternoon, señora. I'm Dr. Bernstein." The younger doctor shook my hand. "I'm the gastroenterologist on our infectious diseases team."

"*Felicitaciones*, señora." Dr. Benavides looked grave. "I am so happy for you. But that's the good news. The bad news is you need to be tested again in six months. You'll be under the cloud until then. For safety's sake, have your children tested too."

Dr. Bernstein nodded. "In the early stages of incubation, señora, the viral load is so infinitesimal, it fools the test," he explained. "Don't neglect your own safety by not testing."

I ingested this piece of medical advice. "So maybe I have it, too, but we don't know it yet?"

"You may. You may not," Dr. Bernstein said. "It's the biggest medical mystery right now, ma'am. The current medical journals are full of varying case histories that report infection from one sexual contact on a Brazilian beach to the many cases of women with bisexual husbands who continue infection-free. Why? I don't know. The existing research data is too limited yet to write any declarations on stone."

Is that pity in the young doctor's eyes? "I need to get retested." I frowned. "My lab result may be wrong because I have diarrhea and anal bleeding, too, since the last eight days, just like Sergio."

"Do you normally suffer from anal bleeding?"

"No, never. Not until I heard of my husband's diagnosis."

"The symptom may disappear. Let me know if it doesn't."

"But why would I show the symptom if I don't have the disease?"

"From sheer stress, señora," Dr. Bernstein said. "In medical school, we studied the case of a barren woman in the nineteen hundreds who gave birth to a nine-month-old benign tumor, so great was her desire to bear children. Mimic symptoms are common in patients with high levels of stress. Let me know if your bleeding persists."

I wanted to say, *I won't be here to tell you anything. We are leaving today*, but I let it go. Right then, no one could reassure me I didn't have AIDS, and that was my cross to carry.

The doctors faced Sergio again.

Dr. Benavides said, "As a urology specialist, I rarely see AIDS cases. By contrast, Dr. Bernstein here sees cases all the time because he's a gastroenterologist, and the commonest symptom of AIDS is an off-and-on diarrhea. It fools patients every time."

Dr. Bernstein said, "Señor Santander, your best option right now is a drug called AZT. AZT isn't a new drug or even a drug for AIDS per se—it's a drug that was invented in the sixties to manage cancer, which didn't work out for cancer patients at all."

"So what does it do for AIDS?" Nila asked.

How did Nila react to her favorite brother having AIDS? I hadn't been around to see the reaction, but the expression in Nila's eyes was haunted, her face pale under makeup.

"I'm coming to that," Dr. Bernstein said. "Sadly, AZT doesn't kill the virus, but right now, it's the one drug that delays the virus's lightning speed of reproduction in a medium as pleasing to it as human blood."

"So, will I be able to go back to work?" Sergio crossed his hands over his stomach, his fingers relaxed, but a pulse in his neck double-timed the seconds ticking inside an electronic digital clock on his nightstand. "How long do I have to live?" His question heightened the chill of the air-conditioning, and I shivered.

Dr. Bernstein placed a hand over Sergio's crossed hands and squeezed them. "That's a personal response, señor. This drug is so potent that after three or four months of consumption, patients develop symptoms of severe nausea and migraines. Then the dose has to be lowered, and the AIDS virus multiplies again. Taking AZT is a dance. First you work up to a higher dose, then decrease it and increase it as the individual patient's tolerance dictates."

"So how long do I have?" repeated Sergio, eyes hollow.

"A patient of mine is still alive after three years. It's my longest association with an AIDS patient."

The doctor's visit to Sergio placed me in the Miami Dade County Courthouse at eleven a.m. "What happened?" the court clerk asked. "I told you to come back at eight a.m."

"I'm sorry." I explained my predicament.

"The docket is full again."

"No! You have to help me. I can't leave the country without resolving this."

"Go wait out in the hallway. I'll speak to the judge during the lunch recess at one p.m."

I felt the blood drain from my face. "That means I'll miss my flight. Can I go back and let my husband know?"

"If I can persuade the judge to see you, you'd better be here."

I ran all the way back to the hospital, my heart on fire from the heat and humidity of Miami in July. To my utter relief, Sergio was alone.

"Oh, good, you're back. You resolved it?" He took my hand.

"No." I panted out my explanation.

"You should have stayed there. Or called."

"I didn't have any money to use a public telephone."

Back in the courthouse, at two minutes to one, the clerk's window was closed. Desperate, I ran out into the hallway. The first person I saw was a bulky US marshal. "You have to help me," I begged.

"What do you need?" He had a heavy Italian accent.

Again, I explained my problem, handing him my paperwork. "You shoplifted an item worth six fifty in *Walmart*?" he asked.

I nodded, lips compressed.

"Why? Yves St. Laurent or Gucci, I would understand, but why Walmart?"

"I-I-I don't know. I've never stolen anything in my life."

"Come with me."

"W-where will you take me?"

"Into the courtroom to see if we can resolve this."

I walked behind him, praying we could still catch the flight back to Peru if I got lucky. The huge courtroom, almost empty right then, smelled of humid wood. It reminded me of the only courtroom I had ever seen as a five-year-old in Calcutta. That day, Didima had taken me to a high court, telling me that we were there so she could adopt me formally. Many years later, when I had asked her why, Didima had explained that she had done that so my baba, who was being forced out of India by the Indian immigration authorities after my parents' divorce, wouldn't change his mind and whisk me off to East Pakistan with him.

In the current courtroom, at the far end, elevated above ground level, sat a bald judge reading behind the bench. Seeing us, he glanced over the bridge of his tortoiseshell bifocals. "What's up, Vince? Aren't we in recess? Is it over already?"

"No, Your Honor." The marshal stopped me midstride. "You wait here." He approached the judge with my paperwork.

After two minutes, the judge beckoned me. "What happened last night?" He removed his glasses.

Again, I faltered through what I had done the previous evening. In the end, I added, "People in Lima think my husband has cancer, but his real diagnosis is AIDS, and I might have it too."

"People make poor choices in times of crisis, Mrs. Santander. I've seen this pattern in first-time shoplifters who had no reason to steal. For the longest time, it didn't make sense to me until I realized it wasn't about the money. It was to regain control."

I stared at the judge, too astonished to speak. "Thank you." I found my voice at last. "For making me understand why I did it. I didn't *need* those shorts. I didn't even want them. And since the minute I got caught, I've racked my brain to figure out why I behaved so out of character for me but couldn't come up with an answer."

"Well, I suggest you seek better ways to cope with your reality." The judge picked his glasses back up.

"So, what will happen now? Am I going to jail?"

"No. Fortunately for you, I can resolve this with a fine."

I immediately dug into my handbag to retrieve the blank check Sergio had given me.

"I will issue you the lightest penalty I can. It's for two hundred dollars. How will you pay it?"

I held up my blank check. "My husband said you would know what to do with this."

Seeing the check, a thin, oldish brunette I hadn't noticed at all got up from behind a desk positioned next to the far left of the judge's bench. She came down three steps and approached me. "Listen," she said. "Since you're a first-time offender, if you pay an additional amount of fifty dollars and don't repeat this conduct, in ten years, the court will automatically destroy this record. Would you like that option?"

"Who are you?"

"I'm the court recorder."

The judge nodded. "She's right."

I held out my blank check to her. "C-can you please write the check for me? I've never written a check, and this is the only one I've got."

"You're serious, aren't you?" The court recorder eyed me in disbelief.

"Yes. I've never written a check."

We completed the check operation, and I signed all the papers I was told to sign.

The judge smiled when I said, "Thank you for resolving this for me, Your Honor. And thank you so much for your help, too, ma'am." I bobbed my head at the court recorder.

"Thank Vince." The judge glanced at my US marshal. "He's your real savior. Show her out, Vince, won't you?"

I ran back to the hospital despite knowing that we had surely missed our flight. At the hospital entrance, I was dashing in when Nila stopped me dead, yanking on my arm.

"Why aren't *you* dying instead of my brother?" she spat. "I will never forgive you for making this trip all about you, when it was Sergio who needed the help. The flight cancellation cost Sergio over five hundred dollars. I wish I could shoot you. And don't you dare tell my brother I said this." She stalked off without a backward glance, and I faltered into the hospital after her, petrified I had acquired an enemy for life.

38

Back in Lima, under his new AZT regimen, Sergio blossomed like a revived flower. By that time, more habituated to the enormity of his diagnosis, I wanted to ask Sergio how he might have gotten AIDS, but I never pulled the trigger on it. *What will I gain from cross-examining Sergio? He's as much a survivor of his childhood as I am of mine. How would I feel if I were in his place and he hurt me or needled me or embarrassed me? Besides, could I blame him for cheating on me? We hadn't been a couple since Abril's birth.* So I pretended to believe his story that he had gotten infected by the AIDS virus during his posting in Japan, which was ridiculous. He couldn't have had two years of sex with me and not given it to me, too, let alone fathered two healthy children.

When Sergio telephoned my mother once a month in India and fostered the fiction of cancer, I let that slide too. *Why does my mother need to know he has AIDS?* She couldn't help him. At times, I had the wildest urge to dig up Isabel's address and write to her, or Angela, but each time I thought it through, I didn't do it. They were connected to the Peruvian foreign office, and if the powers that be found Sergio out, no one could predict what consequences that would bring. Indeed, Peru was as homophobic as Isabel had described it to be… *was it only six years ago?* In Lima, most homosexual males were relegated to be hairdressers from the lower dregs of society, ridiculed by all. Homosexuals in Lima's high class were condemned to secrecy.

Instead, I thanked God each day for how lucky I was the children had tested negative too. We crossed another milestone when both Pia and Abril joined the Villa Maria Catholic Girls' School despite their late applications due to the upheaval of Sergio's illness.

On one random school day, however, I decided to leave the house early for the school car pool to drive by the cliffs in Miraflores before I picked up the children. Maybe the sight and sound of the ocean would calm me.

But rather than calm me, the sea air sharpened my focus. On the horizon, where the ocean met the sky, the writing read I would never go back to college unless a cure for AIDS was found. Right then, I needed to think of my children's upbringing, not paying for a college career.

I got out of the car and stood at the cliff edge, eyes plugged to the roiling sea crashing against the cliff bottom far below. *What if I sink to the floor of the ocean, hair afloat above my head in the Pacific current? All I have to do is jump, and my problems will be over. I don't know how to swim—I would never survive the deep sea unless help arrived.* One foot snuck over the cliff edge, and my arms shot up to hug my body. I shivered and blinked as the images of Pia's and Abril's faces washed over me like a dousing of the cold seawater so near me. *What am I doing here? What time is it? Am I late for the carpool?* I had forgotten to wear Didima's wristwatch.

I jumped back into the car, hit reverse, and neglected every speed limit to reach the Villa Maria School.

"Señora? Where have you been?" the school guard accused me. "They telephoned your home, and the housemaid said you had left hours ago. You better go in and speak to the mother superior. She's waiting to hear from you."

"The children? Where are the children?" My voice was ragged.

"They're gone. Señor Kozinski from your afternoon carpool group left work to come fetch them. He did the carpool for you. Where were you?"

I knew the old guard wasn't being cheeky. He had worked for the Villa Maria for thirty-five years. His duty as gate guard was well-earned, given the school administration's paramount fear of terrorism-related kidnappings. All any private school needed was *one* kidnapping incident, and it would ruin their institution. That was why the hierarchy mandated each parent enter the school premises and fetch their child. At home time, the whole parking area around the school was patrolled by armed guards the school hired on its own dime. The Villa Maria took parents' participation in the carpool system with utmost seriousness because carpooling was their answer to school transport, since terrorism had eradicated school buses.

On my way to the mother superior's office, shame pricked my body like a hair shirt. *Should I tell the nun the truth about Sergio's diagnosis and my urge for suicide today?* It would garner me the sympathy I craved. But Lima's high class was painfully small-minded and provincial. If the mother superior shared my little confession, the news would reach Sergio's workplace in no time.

"Madre Alvarez-Calderón, let me tell you why I was late," I heaved before the mother superior could open her mouth. I wavered through my explanation, substituting cancer in place of AIDS. "I promise it won't happen again. I'm not known for irresponsibility."

"Don't apologize to me, Señora Santander. Apologize to Paul Kozinski, who came to your rescue, and hope that your carpool members don't expel you."

On the drive home, I was incredibly relieved that it was Pauly Kozinski who had come to my aid and not the mothers in our group. Women tended to be rancorous, whereas Pauly was all heart. He knew that Serg was sick, though of course he didn't know Serg's true ailment.

In the house, I hugged the worried children. "I'm fine, see?" I held my palms outward. "I had a flat tire that took too long to fix. Now, get back to lunch so you're not late for homework."

But I told Sergio the truth and how Pauly had saved the day.

"Call Dr. Ritter," Serg said. "You're depressed. Do you want me to call him? I can talk to him. Then bake a cake for your friend Pauly. Bake him your banana bread. He'll like that."

Before calling Dr. Ritter, I dialed Pauly's number. "Pauly, I'm really sorry I messed up. I'll make it up to you."

"Noor, forget about me. I'm not your problem. Call Vera Gamarra. She's convincing everyone to expel you from the carpool."

"No! I can't let that happen. If I lose Pia's carpool, poor Abril will have to come to school early with me and wait for an hour at each end of the day, since kindergarten starts later and ends earlier than Pia's first-grade schedule."

"Call Vera. She's the enemy."

My hand trembled as I dialed Vera Gamarra's number. "Vera, I know I messed up today, but give me another chance. As penance, I will do the next week of carpool all by myself. Please don't expel me."

"I'll call you tonight," was all Vera said.

Fortunately, Dr. Ritter was kinder. "Come see me right away. I'll talk to you before my consults begin. Don't worry. I won't charge you for this visit."

In the doctor's office, I said, "Oh, Doctor, I don't know what is wrong with me. *I should be happy* I don't have AIDS, at least until I get retested in six months. Instead, I wish I were dead."

"You need antianxiety medication. Now."

"But I'm not anxious."

"Yes, you are, and you don't realize it. You're anxious and depressed, and you'll have a nervous breakdown if you don't watch it. Take the meds. I have samples. Buy the rest. They're really cheap. Your family doesn't need you to break down at this juncture."

"How will I pay for the children's school if Sergio really dies on me?"

In Lima, the same as in India, public school education was only an option for the poor. Its shabby quality drove the upper class to seek private education, and the Colegio Villa Maria, at two hundred and fifty dollars per month, per child, was a good, solid Catholic school that Dr. Ritter himself had recommended.

"Won't you get a pension?" Dr. Ritter asked.

"His government worker's salary in Lima is three hundred and sixty dollars in Peruvian money. My pension will be that amount."

"It doesn't matter because, when he dies, you won't *have* to pay tuition if the children are already enrolled in the school."

"Why not?"

"Because a law here exempts tuition for children who lose their wage-earning parent. But please don't worry about that right now."

"Doctor, before Sergio's diagnosis, he served me divorce papers. What if I divorce him? Maybe that will help me feel less anxious. Why should I risk getting his disease when he was about to divorce me anyway?"

Dr. Ritter's expression became intense as he placed both hands on his desk and leaned forward. "No! Do you hear me? A divorce in this country takes at least three years to finalize. Sergio will be dead by then. But if you divorce him, your children will never forgive you for leaving their sick father. Sergio isn't your flesh and blood, Noor, but he is certainly theirs. Don't even go there. Just take these meds, and stop overthinking everything. I guarantee you'll feel better."

At home, I took the meds, noting no difference three hours later. By seven p.m., I was so anxious about the carpool, I called Pauly again.

"No," he said, "I haven't heard from Vera."

"Then find an excuse to call her. I have to know who will take Pia to school tomorrow, Pauly, or else I have to plan for it around Abril's kindergarten drop-off."

Pauly called back. "You're all set. But I had to tell her your husband has cancer. I could tell she wouldn't relent otherwise."

"What a bitch. Whatever. Thanks, Pauly. I'm baking you banana walnut bread even as we speak."

"You're the best." I heard the smile in Pauly's voice.

Two weeks passed, and one day, I just noticed how invisible sandbags had lifted right off my shoulders. I laughed more at Pia's and Abril's chatter during their bath and bedtime routine. Maybe I was dying, but at least while I was alive, I could make positive memories for my babies.

The following Friday, I was happy for Sergio when he told me Jaime León would visit him one afternoon in early July.

When Jaime came, however, Sergio said, "Noor, why don't you go upstairs? Jaime and I have to talk about work stuff. It'll bore you."

His obvious dismissal made me think of that stray phone call to Jaime he had lied to me about months ago, but I went upstairs as instructed. Sprawled on my bed, I reflected on how all Sergio's visitors, who were mostly Nila, my mother-in-law, and Jaime, had no use for my presence. But Sergio didn't face that discomfort, because no one I knew ever visited our house.

By August, Sergio gained back seventeen pounds and returned to work with his "cancer." But his recovery was skin-deep. Each evening, he came home from work dead tired. He spent the weekends in bed just to build up the strength he needed to face another workweek.

In November 1988, on the surface, we lived a normal life. Sergio worked. I did my school carpool duties and grocery shopped, and Sergio bought me chocolate cookies twice a week. He never mentioned the divorce papers again, so I never brought them up, either, but I worried about it in silence. Except for his tiredness, Sergio looked well. He was still my rock to lean on, and I couldn't imagine a life without him.

The New Year of 1989 came and went, but the world was no nearer to finding a cure for AIDS. We learned never to mention Sergio's disease, like we didn't mention sex or our possible divorce or Sergio's life expectancy. For me, as long as we could go from day to day, I didn't want to upset our balance. The balance included my not testing for AIDS again. I knew I needed to do it, but since I couldn't face knowing I might have it, too, I never brought it up.

During the last week of February, however, that balance was rocked by a phone call.

"Is this Mrs. Noor Santander?"

"Yes." *Who would address me in English in Lima?*

"Great. This is Dick McBee from the Roosevelt School. Assistant headmaster. Would you care to work with us for the rest of this school year?"

"Excuse me. What am I missing?"

"Sorry. Let me back up. Your friend, Ann Marie Lanata, from your children's kindergarten, gave us your number. This past weekend, our English teacher fractured her foot in three places. Ann Marie suggested we called you as a substitute. Could you come in for an interview perhaps?"

"Are you offering me a job?"

"Not quite yet. But yes, we would like to interview you."

"Thanks. Would you mind if I discussed this with my husband and got back to you? He was diagnosed with cancer three months ago." I hung up, my heart booming at the possibility of working for the first time. Nerves wet my armpits despite the winter chill of no central heating in our house. Yet a job would help me supplement Sergio's Lima income. *How hard could it be to teach a bunch of kids?*

That evening, when Sergio came home from work, I mentioned the job offer to him right as he came through the door. He parked his briefcase on the floor of the downstairs hallway. "If you get the job, do it. You'll need the work experience once I'm gone."

"Gone where?"

"Gone, as in dead. You heard what that doctor in Miami said. He's never seen an AIDS patient live past three years."

"Yes, but that might not happen. They might find a cure for AIDS," I argued, desperate to cling to the normal. "If you get cured, will you divorce me? You served me those papers, remember?" I said it as if divorce was the antidote to AIDS.

"Noor, they won't find a cure for this any more than they've found a cure for cancer or diabetes or Alzheimer's. What's the point of a divorce when I have a death sentence hanging over me?"

"Oh, Serg." I placed a hand on his arm, brutally sobered by his pragmatism.

He squeezed my hand, turning away, but not before I caught tears glistening his eyes as he picked up his briefcase to head into the study. His words made me realize just how unprepared I was for the truth to overtake our lives. And when it did, it wouldn't be in the form of a divorce.

39

On March 1, 1989, I arrived at Assistant Headmaster Dick McBee's office at 11:20 a.m., dressed in a gray tube skirt and a white blouse with my hair in an uncompromising chignon. The Roosevelt School, or the "American school in Lima" as it was referred to, had hired me to substitute teach sixth-grade Drama, tenth-grade Literature, and eleventh-grade College Reading until their school year ended in May. What sweet irony I would be *teaching* English, when it had been the one language I had always wanted to study. I approached Dick, who chatted with nine eleventh graders taller than me and, in the case of the girls, wearing more makeup than me.

After introductions, I led my new College Reading class toward the school library nestled in the foliage and yellow blooms of robust hibiscus bushes under each of its airy windows. As my students outdistanced me, I hurried to catch up, the injured teacher's coffee-stained student register hugged to my chest.

In the library, the students swarmed a worktable. A model-thin blonde took the lead. "Each week, we read a new book and hand in a book report on Friday. Otherwise, we sit and read." I kept my face deadpan, but I could have hugged the girl. If I didn't have to teach the class, I could do prep or explore the fabulous library.

"What happened to Miss Peg?" The tallest boy raised his eyebrows. "We loved her."

After I explained what little I knew, they scattered, leaving me to review the literature textbook I would teach to tenth graders the next day.

Four days into the new regime, on a Thursday, the same tallest boy approached me as I corrected a tenth-grade composition at a library table. "Miss, you won't receive a book report from me tomorrow," he announced respectfully.

My eyes narrowed. "Why not?"

"Because the school administration holds weekly meetings to decide whether to expel me now or fail me at the end of the school year. I can't confuse the authorities by doing assignments for College Reading."

I contemplated the loose-limbed teenager. "What is your name again?"

"Armand Schulz. I'm the last name on your student roster."

I opened the student roster and tracked his name with an index finger. I straightened my composition notebook, pen, and pencil and interlaced my fingers over them on the library table. At last, I gestured. "Please, sit. I, too, have a story to tell." I cleared my throat. "As it so happens, the school guidance counselor has asked me twice already to stay back for a group meeting on you, but I declined, thinking you're doing fine in my class. For God's sake, how was I to know you were lurking in the wings to prove me a liar? Besides, my husband's home sick with cancer, so I don't see why I should stay back to attend meetings on you when you've already decided you don't give a damn. So"—my eyes perforated his—"if you ever skip my class, I swear I'll skin you. Now go pretend to read."

Armand retired, chastened, probably as confused by me as I was by him. I saw him choose a book and open it. *But is he reading it?*

The following week, Armand didn't come to College Reading on Monday, Tuesday, or Wednesday. I huffed from desk to desk in the school administration office to ascertain he was absent from school altogether and hadn't just skipped my classes.

On Thursday, when he arrived in class, I asked, "Were you sick?"

The boy had the prettiest green eyes the color of young banana leaves behind steel-rimmed glasses.

"Nope." Armand sounded dead serious. "I decided to spend more time at my painting studio."

"And your parents? They let you miss school for that?"

"My only parent in Lima is my mother, and she doesn't know."

"Doesn't she have to sign your absentee slips?"

"I sign them for her."

To avoid an argument, I changed direction. "What's so great about your painting class?"

"My instructor, Miguel Gallo. He's a Spanish cartoonist and a World War II veteran who came to Lima years ago."

"And that makes him great?"

"No. He's great because he doesn't talk down to me as if I'm some stupid teenager, and I can relate to the way he speaks. I hate the way Peruvians distort Spanish with their local accents."

I resisted the instantaneous urge to sympathize with Armand's language alienation. Instead, I asked, "And are you Peruvian or Spanish? You do have a Spanish accent."

The Roosevelt's student population was international.

"I'm Peruvian, but I spent the last eight years in Spain, since I was ten. I hate Lima."

"Does your family live in Spain?"

"My dad does. My mom came back to Peru after they divorced."

What would my children tell people if Sergio ever divorced me? "Did you meet your teacher in Spain?" I was beginning to like the boy despite myself.

"No, I met him here, but I love Miguel because he respects how much I want to become a painter."

"I'm glad you're serious about something. I mean that. Where's his studio?"

"In San Isidro."

"Oh, my mother-in-law lives in San Isidro." I forgot to be severe. "I lived there for two years until we moved to Valle Hermoso."

"Where in San Isidro?"

"Right by the Parque del Olivar."

"I live next to the Golf Club."

"This studio, is it close to your house?"

"Yup. On Calle Roberto Dasso. On the days I miss school, I walk to Miguel's and have breakfast with him and his dog at a café. Once his morning students arrive, I mix vodka cocktails, and we smoke, drink, and practice drawing or painting."

"Christ. Doesn't Peru have a minimum drinking age law?"

"Nope. Neither does Europe. Therefore, on school days, I go home in the afternoon and greet my mother. That's when I officially head to the painting studio for the evening class with my friend Eva."

"How old is Eva?"

"Fifty-one. Younger than Miguel."

"And neither of these two characters care that you'll fail school?"

"They trust I'll become a painter."

"How did you get into painting?" I gave up pretending that we were having a normal student-teacher exchange. The boy, notwithstanding his academic defiance, wasn't stupid or deluded. He simply wanted to be an artist, and he knew it. Like I had always known I wanted to study English. *How can I penalize him for that?*

"By accident. My father's a huge art buff, so when we got to Madrid, he dragged my older brother, my sister, and me to the Prado Museum on our first weekend there. I was only ten, but I fell in love. I couldn't believe what those painters had achieved with the same paints I dabbled with in school. For me, the Prado became my instant Disneyland. Madrid wasn't unsafe like Lima, so I wandered around alone and spent all my pocket money on museum tickets. The more I visited the Prado, the more I knew I'd become a painter."

"So, you'll go to college for painting?"

"Why are you making painting sound like a bad word?"

I bit my lower lip and glanced away, embarrassed that he had read my mind so easily. "You're right. I *am* against art, because my mother and stepfather are both artists. Particularly my mother, who graduated college in first position and did nothing with her life, and it sticks in my craw."

Armand shook his head. "Well, I won't go to college for art, because with my school performance, I'll never get into one."

"And your parents will allow this?"

Armand shrugged. "Don't know, don't care."

A month later, I handed Sergio my seven-hundred-American-dollar paycheck.

"So, how do you feel?" Sergio asked.

"I can't believe I've earned seven hundred dollars without a degree from any university."

"That's double my Lima government salary! Ask them if they can hire you to teach full-time."

"Not yet. First, let me do the three months of substitute teaching they need me for. If they are happy with my performance, that will be the time to spring that question."

The very next day, Armand joined me at my library table, uninvited.

"What?" I was correcting tenth-grade literature essays on *Beloved* by Toni Morrison.

"I read *Crime and Punishment*. I can give you a book report on it if you let me tell it to you and not write it."

As always, Armand left me wordless since I could never stuff him into my idea of a student box. And my only "box" was my own student experience in an astringently disciplined Catholic convent school. Therefore, in truth, I didn't know what to do with Armand. "Fine. Tell it to me. At least that will justify some part of the grades I invent for you."

"Have you read the book? How will you know if my analysis is accurate?"

Stung, I said, "Yes, I have, if you must know. You're so impossible to deal with it's ridiculous! Now talk."

A week shy of graduation day, Armand strolled into College Reading class with an armful of pink roses.

"Are you sick?" I raised my eyes from the tenth-grade literature questions and answers I was correcting on the life and work of Albert Schweitzer.

"No. Why?"

"Because you're smiling. You never smile."

"I'm leaving." Armand handed me a rose. "I brought roses for my lady teachers."

"Whew." I placed my rose in the centerfold of my student register. "What an achievement, a whole seven days short of graduation. Out of vulgar curiosity, what *do* rich kids do once they're expelled?"

"I wasn't expelled. I didn't fail either. My mother withdrew me from the school."

"You won't receive a diploma."

"I'll take a general equivalency exam."

I watched Armand hurry out of the library with his armful of pink roses. If only my worries were half as simple as his.

I sprang the possible permanent-job question on Dick McBee at the graduation buffet.

"Oh, Noor, I wish," he said. "Giving you the job would totally resolve my headache of having to find a teacher as reliable as you."

"Meaning?"

"Meaning I can't do it. Our local staff is mandated to follow Peruvian teaching law requirements. So without a BA degree, I can't legally hire you."

His answer felt like a physical blow because I had banked so much on getting the teaching job. But the law was the law, and I had always known that without a degree, I would never get a reasonable job in a third-world country. Dick's answer only confirmed it.

40

BY THE END OF 1989, over a year and a half had passed since Sergio had been diagnosed. But I refused to face another AIDS test for myself. Meanwhile, nine months after my substitute teaching job ended, Sergio came home from work overjoyed on March 5, 1990. He hurried into our bedroom to announce, "I've been posted to Los Angeles! I couldn't be happier. The secretary-general called me into his office and gave me the news personally. In our foreign service, the secretary-general holds the highest post any career diplomat can hold. He hoped I would receive the best possible treatment for my cancer. What's the matter? Why do you look so glum?" He eyed me searchingly.

"I don't want to go to Los Angeles."

"You don't have to. I've already decided I'm going alone."

"Without even consulting me?" My eyebrows shot up.

"Hello? Didn't I hear you say you didn't want to go?"

"I know, but you could at least have asked me!" My cheeks grew warm.

Sergio sat down on his side of our king-sized bed and unlaced his shoes. "Okay. Let's start over. "Why don't you want to go to Los Angeles?"

"Logistics. Until they find a cure for AIDS, your health will only deteriorate. If I go with you, I'll have to come back to Lima with you in worse condition and the children out of school and face the task of settling down again. Where's the upside to it? It's just more prudent to have me stay here, keep the children in school, and have a functional home ready for you to come back to."

"That's actually great reasoning," Sergio said. "My reason is simpler."

"Like what? You don't love me?" I smiled bitterly. "I already know that."

"No. I was thinking of my job and treatment. It'll be a lot easier to focus on both if I don't have to worry about the children's school, transport, and the daily burden and stress of life with kids. I'll send you money to keep all this going."

Sergio waved his hand to encompass our lives. "You and the kids could come visit me on school vacations."

His answer relieved me because I knew how to take care of my children by then, and I could manage it. It was not the same as when they had been babies and their care had overwhelmed me.

One afternoon toward the end of March, with two weeks left until Sergio's departure, the phone rang as I headed out the door to do the carpool. I ran back in to snatch up the phone in case it was Sergio from work.

I frowned when the caller asked for Señora Noor. "Excuse me, who's speaking?"

"Tell her it's Armand."

"How did you find my number?"

"I questioned everyone I met if they knew a Peruvian diplomat with an Indian wife."

"You're such an ass." I had to smile. "How are you? Listen, let's talk another day. I—"

"I got into La Católica University's art program," interrupted Armand.

"Impossible. Besides, what happened to 'I'll never go to college'?"

"You were right. My dad didn't listen to that nonsense for one minute. Not attending college was not an option."

"How did you get in? Did your parents donate a wing or buy the whole university?"

"No. And no. First, my dad forced me to pass a GED exam. Then, I got lucky because the Católica entrance exam was mainly for drawing and painting, so very little writing. It saved my parents buying the university."

"Well, congratulations! And thanks for thinking of letting me know."

"I had to tell you. You were the only person who ever cared to ask me about college, considering my sad school performance."

"Hey, so did your dad, apparently."

"No. He *coerced* me into college. He didn't care about it. But you made me feel like you cared."

Armand called back in a week.

"You again?" I exclaimed. "Don't you have anyone else to call?"

"Can you come meet my friend, Eva? The one from the painting studio?"

"I'm too busy. My husband leaves for a posting in Los Angeles soon."

"So you're leaving and you didn't tell me? Doesn't your husband have cancer?"

"He does have cancer. In Los Angeles, he'll receive state-of-the-art treatment, but I'm staying back in Lima. Look, I have to go."

"Wait. When does he leave?"

"On April tenth. Bye."

Once Sergio left, I didn't know what to feel. *Did I miss him?* Yes, in a hundred ways. I hadn't slept alone in our bed in the last seven years. No one bought me chocolate cookies anymore, but more than anything, I missed his presence.

I constantly waited for the phone to ring. My opening was usually, "What did the doctor say? Are you okay? How are you feeling?"

And each week, it was a different story. One week, he had a little energy, then the next week, he missed two days of work. The worst ordeal came when one day, a month into living alone in LA, Sergio said, "I have *Pneumocystis carinii*. It's a pneumonia sheep used to get before AIDS came along to crush those barriers."

My heart felt like it jumped up into my mouth as I stopped myself from asking, *Will you die, then?* Instead, I asked, "What does your treating doctor say? Can they cure you or deal with it?"

"Yes. With an experimental procedure called a lung wash. I'll be under anesthesia, and they'll literally wash the pneumonia infection out of my lungs. That way, I won't have to take antibiotics, which will weaken my immune system more than it already is."

"Then do it. We don't need you getting worse or weaker."

"That's what I thought."

"So, when will you call me next? It'll suck to sit here and guess how you are. Maybe I should go there to be with you." With Sergio gone from my immediate vicinity, I worried about him nonstop.

"No. That'll end up being more work for me. I'll call in a week. I wish transatlantic calls weren't so expensive. Otherwise, I'd call you from the hospital."

Days after that phone call, my sister-in-law, Frida, knocked on my door. Frida and Carlos had moved next door to us six months before, but they hadn't bothered to invite us over like we had to welcome them. At that point, I didn't care all that much anymore, even though Frida was only a year older than me and we could have been friends.

She stood at my doorstep, diminutive in size, with a narrow, freckled face and silky, shoulder-length brown hair that framed warm brown eyes. Warm for everyone other than me, of course.

I looked at her thinly. "Yes? Can I help you?" I refused to invite her in.

"Hi, can we talk?"

"About what?" I sounded as hostile as she had always been to me.

"Let me come in, and I'll explain."

In my living room, Frida smiled an abrupt, nervous smile. "This will seem strange," she began, "but I want to apologize for being so distant all these years." I couldn't even react while she rushed on. "I know that if *my* husband was diagnosed with AIDS for cheating on me, I'd leave him on the spot. Instead, you stuck around and nursed Sergio. It says so much about you."

"So, why did you wait so long to tell me this?"

"I guess I wasn't comfortable saying that to you with Sergio listening? I've never felt at ease around him."

"Well, thanks." More moved than I cared to admit, I told Frida how Sergio had threatened to leave me in India and bring Pia and Abril to Peru.

"Why *didn't* you leave him?"

"The answer is complicated. I don't *have* anywhere to go. My parents in India are not an option for me."

"Can we be friends?" Frida asked simply.

I had to smile. "Our in-laws wouldn't approve of our friendship."

"Why do they need to know? I won't even tell Carlos, so he doesn't have to take sides."

"Fine by me." But deep inside, I was incredibly touched by Frida's gesture.

When the phone rang on Saturday afternoon, I grabbed the receiver. "Serg? Is that you? Are you okay?" I wanted to tell him of Frida's visit, but I knew I wouldn't. If Sergio blabbed it to Nila, she would inform the rest of the clan. Then Frida would know I was a blabbermouth.

"Err, who?"

"Who is this?"

"Armand."

"Oh, you. Hi."

"You sound disappointed."

"I am. I hoped it was my husband."

"I'm calling to see if you'll come meet my painting studio friends now that your husband is gone."

I rolled my eyes. *How can I escape this without sounding rude or hurting Armand's feelings?* I didn't want to be friends with him. He was a kid. "You artist types run late, and I wake up early to take my children to school. I go to bed by seven or eight." That sounded lame even to my own ears.

"Not on a Friday you don't. We'll get together at six. Can I pick you up next Friday?"

Forgetting to remain polite, I burst out, "Why do you want me to meet them so bad?"

"I don't know. I think they'd like you and you'd like them."

Out of excuses, I conceded, "I'll go if you promise to stop pestering me after that. But make it the following Friday. I've been deathly tired since yesterday. I may be coming down with something." I didn't mention that something might be AIDS.

"Noor." Dr. Ritter got mad when I called him. "You need to test for it."

"Doctor, don't push me. I can't handle another challenge, okay? Diagnose whatever I have and treat it. Why do I want to know if I have AIDS when no real treatment exists for it anyway?"

Sergio finally called on Wednesday. "I'm well. A little weak but well."

We both cried on the telephone.

"Now guess who has pneumonia?"

"Who?"

"Me. Dr. Ritter says I have walking pneumonia."

"What were your symptoms? Coughing?"

"No. Crazy, extreme exhaustion. I could barely pick up the children from school these last two days. Dr. Ritter said the coughing will come later. I'm on ten days of antibiotics."

How easy it was to have an amicable relationship with Sergio at a distance. As if all his past meanness to me had been deleted because he was ill. I would do well to remember that if he hadn't fallen sick, we would be divorced by then. *Will Serg ever tell me where he got AIDS?* But each time I wanted to confront him, I felt like a heel and didn't do it. Instead, my mind went around in circles about Sergio's friendship with Jaime León. But since I had no clue as to what exactly bugged me about it, I had nothing to voice.

Therefore, Sergio had all my pity, if not my love, because unless a cure for AIDS was found soon, he might die from it. And the possibility defeated me. I did not want Sergio to die. I did not want my children to lose their father like I had lost mine.

41

On the day before the outing with Armand, I phoned him triumphantly. "Listen, about tomorrow—I have to cancel because I've got walking pneumonia." *Now, that was a solid, credible excuse to escape doing what I didn't want to do anyway.*

"Since when?"

"I was diagnosed ten days ago."

"Yeah, right."

"You don't believe me? Come over and see for yourself. I'm as sick as a dog!" I exclaimed, too late to take it back. The last thing I wanted was visitors. *Ahhh.* I shook my fist in the air. Me and my unstoppable temper.

"What is your address?"

"You found my phone number. Find my address too." I hung up.

On said Friday, I hoped Armand hadn't found my address and wouldn't show, but he did.

When Dulci announced him, I came down from my bedroom swathed in my heaviest winter coat.

"Boy, you *are* sick. I'd be roasting in that coat." Armand wore jeans and a paint-stained dress shirt.

"I'm glad we cleared that up." I drowned in a coughing fit and collapsed on my Peruvian colonial sofa.

"Your living room is crazy cool. What's that smell? Can I please stop calling you Miss Noor?"

"Stock." After my cough attack, I touched the white-and-purple flower stalks in a silver vase. "I'm a flower freak. I would live in a garden if I could. And yes, call me Noor. Listen, you'll have to leave soon, okay? I'm really tired."

Armand glanced around, paying no attention to my declaration. "This is like my father's apartment in Madrid."

I smiled. "Why? Is he into Persian rugs and antiques too?"

"A hundred percent. Where are your children? Didn't you tell me once you had two kids?"

"I do. Pia and Abril."

"Can I meet them? I love talking to kids."

"Why?"

"Because it reminds me of when I was a kid, before my parents divorced and I had to grow up fast."

Armand's words caught me off guard because, even at twenty-eight, I had yet to outrun my checkered childhood. *What would my children's story be?*

"Maybe another day. They're watching the little TV they watch between homework and bath time. They won't appreciate the interruption. Their bedtime is a quarter to eight, as they wake up for school at six."

"They attend school on Saturday?"

"No, but they follow a routine. Neither my husband nor I want spoiled children. I don't want them getting out of hand now that he's gone."

"So, how come you didn't go to Los Angeles with him when he's sick?"

I jingled my bracelets to delay answering. *Should I tell him the truth about my marriage to Sergio? What do I have to hide?* "The truth is my husband and I aren't together. We aren't divorced, though, because our children are too young." What a big fat lie, but I could hardly confess Sergio's AIDS diagnosis to the boy, let alone that I was under the cloud too. That burden of secrecy weighed so heavy on my shoulders, I felt old and even more tired. "Hey, I don't mean to be rude, but I want you to leave. I am exhausted."

"Fine, but will you come out with us another day?"

Has this boy never heard of "quit while you're ahead"? "Let's talk it through when I'm well, okay?"

I asked Dulci to show Armand out.

Armand called again that Sunday. "Are you well now?"

"Not if you'll ask me to see your friends again."

"Can I come see you?"

"Christ! You were just here on Friday. Why do you want to see me again?" *Would this boy never stop bugging me?*

"Because I want to talk to you."

"And you can't do it over the phone?"

"Please?"

"When do you want to come?"

"Now."

"No way! Come at eight thirty. I want to put my children to bed before you distract me."

Armand wasn't yet inside the archway of my living room when he blurted, "I want to date you." He knew it was sudden, but he didn't have the patience for the farcical nonsense of a "conventional buildup."

And while he spoke, my face and hands twisted to register my varying emotions of disbelief, incredulity, and finally, though Armand would never know it, the possibility of how I would have reacted if it were Chirag, and not Armand, in front of me. I had refused Chirag the last time I had faced him. *Would I refuse him now?* No. More likely, I would jump up and hug him.

To dispel the regret of Chirag, I switched on a Japanese lamp on a side table, and the room glowed golden. More time passed. Armand stood there, without coming in any farther, without sitting down.

At last, I asked, "Did I ever give you the impression I was flirting with you?"

"Flirting? You? No! Why?"

"Because why else would you ask me such an outrageous question? I must be what—ten, twelve years older than you? What could have given you the idea to date me?"

"It isn't you. It's me. I liked you the minute I saw you because you were funny and quirky and you didn't take nonsense."

"Funny and quirky? I don't recall one funny conversation with you at the Roosevelt."

"Of course you're funny. Can I sit down?" He perched on the edge of a chair closest to the entrance, as if scared to trespass on my fragile emotions. "I've been a lousy, dyslexic, and useless student in four schools, and no teacher in the world has ever said, 'I don't care what you do since you don't care, but I'll skin you alive if you get me into trouble.' When I told Miguel and Eva about you, Miguel laughed so hard he nearly wet his pants. He wanted to meet you, but I couldn't come to class and say, 'Hey, Miss Noor, my friends think you're wild. They want to meet you.' It's too bad Miguel went back to Spain to be near his parents because they're old."

I laughed a short, nervous laugh. *What would Armand say if I told him of Sergio's real diagnosis, never mind my own possible AIDS diagnosis, if I ever took the test? Would he still want to go out with me?* "Listen, all I can offer you is friendship. I have too many problems without adding cheating to my list of sins."

"But if you aren't with your husband, how could you be cheating on him?"

He had a point. "Armand, when I want to date, it won't be someone half my age. So this isn't a debate, okay? Be my friend or else leave."

"I'm not half your age. You're only nine years older than me."

A nine-year gap was way less than the sixteen years that separated Sergio and me, but I said, "Guess what? That's nine years too many. Now leave because I want to get to bed. I'm an early-to-bed, early-to-rise type. Remember I told you that?"

I went to bed with my head spinning. Of course I would never date Armand, but it flattered me that he wanted to. And he was right about the cheating. Sergio and I hadn't been a couple in years. It was Sergio's bad luck he had gone and slept with someone infected—and there we all were, paying for it. But Sergio's life expectancy, and my own for that matter, and where he might have contracted AIDS was my daily battle, and it always ended in guilt and pity. Pity he had a wretched childhood like mine, guilt I had never been able to love him as a man, and in the final run, pity he would pay for his extramarital sex with his life. Armand didn't fit into the equation. Besides, all nineteen years of Armand would scare off into outer space if I told him of my pending AIDS diagnosis. On that discomforting note, I slept.

42

WHEN SERGIO CALLED SIX DAYS later, I was sitting in bed, having my morning coffee, watching through the bedroom French doors as the September sun struggled to assert the oncoming spring. I smiled at the thought of his reaction if I confessed that someone, certainly half *his* age, wanted to date me. But Sergio enjoyed the privilege of the sick, where people refrained from upsetting them for any reason. Therefore, we had our usual conversation focused on him and his health.

"You don't know how much I'm waiting for the children's summer vacation," he said. "I wish I could see you now, but I know that's impossible. Let's hope I don't fall sick with anything crazy when you're here."

"Of course. Buy the tickets now, so they'll cost less. And if you fall sick, at least I'll be around to take care of you. We can fly out on the night of December 12."

In the meantime, Armand didn't call once, which I noticed, and it didn't comfort me one bit. He called two weeks later, when I had given up on hearing from him.

"Hi," he said casually. "What would you say if I said my friend Eva invited you and your children to her beach house?"

Beach? What's the harm in an invitation if it includes Pia and Abril? But I didn't want to sound eager. *Why am I this happy he called back?* "Will anyone else be going?"

"Why? Are you scared I'll pounce on you around a lonely corner?"

"No, dumbass. But my kids are five and six. I know my eldest, Pia, wouldn't talk if I told her not to, but I don't trust my youngest. I don't need her to go to Los Angeles and prattle to Sergio about my 'one male friend,' Armand."

"So you'll come if more people come?" Armand's voice had a smile in it.

"I didn't say that. I asked a hypothetical question."

"My best friend at college and his girl are coming."

"Fine. Then I'll come. God knows I could use a few friends."

"What about your other college friends? Didn't you attend the UNIFE here?"

"Yes. But they're all busy. This is their final year."

My hand tightened around the phone receiver. It would have been my final year, too, if life had permitted it. But a college degree wasn't in my stars. What was in my stars was a possible death sentence by AIDS. *Stop.* The last thing I needed was to lose hope right then, hope for a better future with Pia and Abril. I would get there if I kept steady.

Armand arrived early the next morning with his best buddy, Salvador, an architecture student, and Karina, Salvador's girlfriend, who was with Armand in his painting major. Their very youth brought home how I was twenty-eight. *Do they think Armand is a weirdo to want me for a friend? At least I'm as thin as Karina, with her bob of loose brown curls.* She and Salvador, with his dark, wiry Italian good looks, made a cute couple.

Standing in the hallway of my house, Armand didn't remark on my pink bikini top with crinkly purple shoulder straps or the turquoise-and-purple silk scarf I had wrapped around like a skirt. Neither did I mention how he appeared older than nineteen in his baggy, geometric-patterned Ralph Lauren swim trunks.

In silence, I absorbed his tousled brown hair, the unshaven five-o'clock shadow accentuating the bony contours of his sharp jawline, and of course, those banana-leaf-green eyes behind the prescription glasses. He had to be half a head taller than Chirag. *What does Chirag look like now?* If I was twenty-eight, he was twenty-nine. My jaw clenched, and I shifted my gaze.

Karina fell in love with talkative Abril on sight. In the back seat of Armand's old Volvo station wagon, she sat Abril between herself and Salvador. But Pia, the quieter one, wanted to sit up front with me, so seat space was not an issue.

"What beach is Eva's house on?" I would have fun on that day and try to stop dwelling on Sergio or Chirag or my possible death sentence.

"Punta Hermosa." Armand focused his green eyes on Pia. "Pia, do you like to draw by any chance?" His hands on the steering wheel had all sorts of oil paint stains that hadn't washed off.

"Linseed oil!" I exclaimed. "That's what I smell, isn't it?"

Karina laughed from the back seat. "My mother says it's the only perfume she ever smells around me."

Pia nodded to Armand, pride making her voice perkier. "I got the school award for art last year in my category. I have a certificate that says so."

"I always tell my children that art is a good hobby," I said.

"Art isn't a hobby for me," replied Armand. "It's my whole life."

"Yes—that's exactly what I don't want for my children."

"Why?" Karina asked.

"Because my mother is an artist, and she did nothing with her life. Yet she graduated first position in her college class. I don't want my children to be artists." Bitterness sharpened my voice, and Armand heard it.

He shot me a glance. "Well, Noor dearest, you may yet discover that art is a force you can't stop. My father found that out with me. And you might have to accept it in your children."

I stared at the scenery racing by the passenger-side window, hoping Armand's words were not a portent.

Outside her beach house, Eva Nalvarte greeted me like an old friend. "At last, a face to the name!" She ran a hand through her short blond hair. "I can't tell you how much our friend and instructor, Miguel Gallo, would have loved to meet you. Armand literally talked—and still talks—of you nonstop."

My cheeks grew hot as I stole a glance at Armand, holding Pia and Abril by their hands as they all ran into the glass-and-cement-exterior beach house. I handed Eva a Tupperware of the chocolate chip cookies I had baked as a thank-you present for her hospitality. Salvador had brought her a box of orange-flavored croissants, a specialty item from his dad's bakery in San Isidro.

Inside Eva's living room, Pia and Abril were entranced by its all-glass ceiling when Armand reappeared from the back of the house, carrying a stack of crayon boxes, colored pencils, and watercolor palettes, which he dumped on the living room coir matting rug. Seeing the art materials, the children forgot the ceiling and crouched to check out the supplies.

"Windsor & Newton?" I put my hands to my cheeks. "That's the brand my stepfather uses for his graphic design work. They're so expensive. Why would you waste those on a couple of kids?"

"It's not a waste. Good coloring materials foster creativity. Crappy Crayola crayons kill it. Let me decide what art supplies I share with your kids. Okay?"

Eva looked at Karina and me. "The water is too cold for a swim anymore, but would you girls care to walk the beach with me?"

"Yes." Karina smiled. "Let's leave all the children behind to play." Karina was a year older than Salvador.

The word "beach" for me always brought to mind the description Didima used to give of the balmy beaches Didima and Dadu had frequented in Goa, complete with palm trees, nut trees, and pale-yellow sand. All the beaches in India were blessed with the warm Indian Ocean or the Arabian Sea waters. By contrast, the Pacific beaches of Peru were stark, indurate, and freezing cold with water that traveled up from the South Pole, which Sergio loved. I touched my chest. Sergio would never enjoy a swim in the sea again. His body was too weak.

Outside the house, Eva said, "I hear your husband has cancer," as if reading my mind. "I'm so sorry."

"Yes. I was thinking how much he used to love the beaches of Peru."

"Armand hates it. He lived by the Mediterranean for so long, Spain will always seem more like home to him than Peru."

"Why did his family move to Spain?"

"Oh, he hasn't told you? His father was quite the noise here fifteen years ago. He was also one of the richest industrialists, which went to his head. Let's just say Armand's life hasn't been easy."

"No, no, no." Karina shook her bob of windblown brown curls and wagged an index finger. "Don't say that and leave us hanging."

"Yes. Do tell. We won't tell Armand anything, right?" I met Karina's eyes.

Karina raised her right hand. "Promise."

Eva laughed. "You two are a persuasive pair." She picked up a handful of sand and threw it at a seagull chasing a fleeing crab. "But please do keep quiet, because Armand would be mortified if he knew I had divulged his past. He's extremely private."

I shivered. "Oof! This May breeze is cold, isn't it? The sun isn't doing its job. I should have brought a cardigan."

"You want me to run back in and grab you one?" Eva touched my bare shoulder.

"No. I'll warm up as we walk. I'm too curious to wait."

"Like I said, Armand's father became rich, and the fame that came with it went to his head. He wasn't yet forty when he owned countless businesses all over Peru, two hotels in Lima, a state bank, and even an airline company.

And yet he wanted more, so he bought a provincial newspaper to meddle in politics—"

"Meddle how?" I focused curious eyes on Eva.

"He forced his personal opinions through the newspaper he owned. In the end, I guess he managed to anger enough people in the government that they came down on his bank with a surprise audit. He wouldn't have survived it, so he ran."

"Was he corrupt?" Karina's green-brown eyes narrowed to counter the on-shore headwind.

"Only technically. Bank owners are not supposed to lend money to their own businesses. In reality, all bank owners do it, but they can't get caught at it. Therefore, whoever was behind Armand's father's downfall in Peru knew the right time to catch him red-handed. But he had friends in the military who flew him out of the country. He lives in Spain because he's considered a fugitive in Lima. Now you know why Armand is so insecure about who he is."

I looked at Eva with new eyes. "I can see now why Armand is so self-conscious. But his father's doings are not his burden to bear."

"That's such a fallacy, my dear." Eva sounded sad. "We all bear the burdens of who our parents are."

"You're right." I kicked the gray sand with bare toes. *Have I ever stopped bearing the burden of my Hindu mother marrying my Muslim father? How easy it is to dismiss the pain of others.*

"Perhaps," continued Eva, "they would be less his burden to bear if his father was the warm-and-fuzzy type to his children. Instead, he's an ogre, overbearing, commandeering, autocratic, and insensitive above all else."

"How?" I asked.

"Give us an example," echoed Karina.

"Oh, I have a good one. The audit happened on Armand's birthday. That's why Armand hates his birthday. But his father rubbed it in, telling a shy, dyslexic ten-year-old it was one way never to forget Armand's birthday! You don't say that to anybody, least of all a child. And his mother is a self-involved, self-centered airhead who followed all her husband's wishes until he dropped her for a younger woman and sent her home to Peru."

I stopped walking. "And how did Armand take that?"

"Badly. He doesn't fit in here. For all practical purposes, he is a European teen, not a Peruvian one. That's why, once he found the art studio, Armand clung to Miguel and me. We became his surrogate parents because we're freethinkers. The two of you will never understand how happy I am to meet you all. Armand desperately needed friends his own age."

"Well, that counts *me* out." I removed strands of hair from across my face that chose to obey the wind and not my fingers. "I'm nine years older. Did he tell you I was a teacher of his at the Roosevelt last year?" I asked Karina.

"Nope. He just told us you were a friend yesterday."

Eva shook her head. "Once you know Armand well, you'll see how he doesn't tell his left hand what his right hand is doing. Shall we head back?" She faced the wind again. "We could all use a hot drink."

I walked beside them, secretly relieved they didn't think my friendship with Armand was odd.

At Eva's beach house, Pia, Abril, Salvador, and Armand were finishing coloring a large sheet of craft paper, slurping Coca-Cola in tall plastic glasses.

"Hey, that's my Yorgi!" Eva stared at their artistic efforts. "But he isn't here. How did you draw him so well?"

"Is Yorgi a malamute?" I asked Eva.

"Yes. He's my baby. He's missing today because my son has him for the week."

I looked at the artwork on the floor again. The dog's eyes, seemingly of no particular color, jumped off the paper, as if saying to me, *See? So maybe Armand can't study, but now do you see that he can draw?*

"I brought a photograph." Armand smiled. "The drawing is a present for you." He hugged Eva. "Who wants to play beach ball? Raise your hands!" he shouted.

We all trooped back out to the beach, with Armand leading as he ran on ahead of Pia and Abril, defying them to catch him. How easy it was to judge people on face value. Armand was the opposite of the frivolous teenager I had assumed him to be at the Roosevelt, especially when he had dropped out of school. *Was it a coincidence that challenged people attracted other challenged people?*

We played volleyball, Armand, Salvador, Pia, and Abril on one team, and Eva, Karina, and I on the other. As the losers, Eva, Karina, and I cooked the fresh-fish lunch Eva had planned. We wolfed it down with steaming white rice prepared with the typical Peruvian fried-garlic seasoning and a salad.

Everyone was tired by the time we gathered on Eva's porch to watch the sun sink into the sea, orange, purple, gray, and indigo poised over the brilliant dark blue of the ocean. The only sound came from the seabirds that screeched and squawked in the distance. Watching them, we slurped hot teas and munched on the homemade cookies I had brought, together with the orange-flavored croissants from Salvador's dad's bakery.

We bid Eva goodbye at six p.m., leaving her with the happy task of deciding where to hang the portrait of her beloved malamute. On our ride home, I stole another glance at Armand. *When last have the children and I had such a marvelous day?* In their short lives, Pia and Abril had rarely experienced good times. All they knew were our cramped lives with my mother-in-law in San Isidro then a little more space and comfort in our new home. In my head, I was lamenting that when Armand pulled up outside my house.

I got out first while Armand hurried to help the children.

Outside my front door, I said, "Pia, Abril, say thank you to Armand for a lovely day. And thank Salvador and Karina, too, for playing with you nonstop."

The children obeyed shyly as Dulci opened the door to let us in.

Then Armand said, "Hey, wait a sec, will you? They left something in the trunk that's theirs." He smiled at Pia and Abril.

"You must be wrong." I swung my large gray Lancôme bag onto my shoulder. "All we brought was this beach bag." But Armand opened the hatchback to his old Volvo station wagon. He pulled out two brown paper bags and handed one to each child.

"What is it?" Abril was thrilled to receive a surprise.

Pia peered into her bag. "Oh!" she exclaimed. "Mamá, he's giving us the crayons and colors we used at the beach." She held out the bag for me to inspect.

"Armand!" I exclaimed. "These are too expensive. Don't give my kids these. It's ridiculous."

"No, it isn't. I wasn't much older than them when I stumbled upon the joy of painting. I want them to have that same joy. You're not my teacher anymore. You can't tell me what to do."

"Right. You seem determined to convert my children into artists, and I'm not sure I like that."

Armand smiled. "Noor, if your children choose art, you won't be able to stop it."

I closed my front door behind the teenagers. *What did I do to deserve such an incredible day?* Armand was indeed a revelation. *Thank you, God, that he wants to be my friend even if that friendship is based on half-truths.*

43

THE FOLLOWING FRIDAY, ARMAND CALLED with a question. "Salvador asked me to ask you if you've ever been to a peña bar. Have you?"

"Yes. Twice. Sergio's sister, Nila, is a huge fan."

"This Sunday, Salvador wants to take Karina, you, and me to one because *I've* never been to one. He lectured me over lunch today on how peñas remain the only intercultural manifestation of the African slave presence in Peru, blah, blah, blah."

"But you're *from* here. How can you never have seen one?"

"Because I was too young when I left for Madrid, and upon coming back, I had no friends except Miguel and Eva, and Miguel hated the pulsating Afrobeat music they play in peñas. With him, we frequented jazz bars. Are you into Afrobeat music?"

"No. It's too sexual and loud for me." I wanted to add, *Sergio said I couldn't appreciate it because I was frigid*, but I kept quiet. If I said that, Armand would assume it was a come-on. That wasn't what I needed from him. I needed a friend, nothing more.

"I wish you had met Miguel. You would have loved him."

On Sunday evening, seated opposite Karina and Salvador in the peña Salvador had chosen, I reconfirmed how little I enjoyed the drum and thrum and throb of the live Afrobeat music. Unlike me, Sergio was a fabulous dancer. He had danced to the African beat and rhythm with a lightness of foot and a hip swing that I, with my Indian cultural prudery, could never emulate, even with a hundred years of practice. I stared out at the dark sky. *Why, Serg? Why? Why did you morph our marriage into a Greek tragedy by getting AIDS? Why couldn't you divorce me, go your own merry way, and let me go mine?*

"Noor, did you know Armand will fail Introduction to Painting tomorrow?" Karina picked up an hors d'oeuvre of boiled and crispy fried yucca sticks and dipped it in cilantro sauce.

"What?" I blinked. "Why?"

"He forgot to do our term assignment."

I looked to Armand, who appeared unconcerned. "So, tell me, why are you sitting here and not finishing your work? How could you *forget* a term assignment?"

"It's because of the garua chill in our intro class," piped Karina. "Some vandal trashed our classroom, and Armand gets so tired and cold from standing for five straight hours by the broken windows that he walks out and sprawls on the corridor floor as soon as the teacher says, 'Okay, brushes down, folks.' He never stays to write down homework assignments. He didn't even know we had this assignment until two days ago."

"Two whole days?" I clutched my head. "So why didn't you just do it?"

Armand's head tilted to sluice the last of his second glass of red wine. "Because the assignment requires us to hand-paint ten sheets of craft paper, cut each one into two-inch squares, then stick one square at a time to compose a three-by-six-foot mural."

I caught Armand's forearm. "Come on. I'll help you. Let's go do it now."

"Now? It's near midnight. The assignment is due at nine a.m."

"So? I said I'd help you, didn't I? Don't you want to at least try?" I didn't add that it would constitute my payment for that wonderful day he had given my family at the beach.

"We'd have to detour all the way to my mom's in San Isidro for the supplies."

"Then let's stop wasting time and get to it!" I stood and pulled on his arm.

"But the main show hasn't begun yet," objected Salvador. "I paid for the whole evening."

"Salvador, do you want Armand to see a peña show or pass his course? If you say one more word, I'll haul the two of you to come do that assignment with us."

Near two a.m., I thrust an armload of old newspapers into Armand's hands. "Cover my Persian rugs while I change into my pajamas."

Like a lamb, Armand obeyed my commands, demurring only when I switched on a hair dryer to dry the sheets he was painting. "Hey, you'll wake up your kids." He pointed to the ceiling.

"Good thinking," I whispered, clicking the dryer off. "Let me set you up on the porch so you can dry the next few sheets outside."

In an hour, with thousands of two-inch-by-two-inch squares to cut for his project, we needed a handier tool than a pair of scissors because Armand had forgotten to retrieve a razor blade from the supplies at his mom's house.

"Never mind." I raced to the kitchen to bring out my kitchen cutting board and a steak knife. "Watch me do magic with these."

As we whispered and worked, too soon, the sky competed with the lighting in my living room. "Won't your mother wonder where you are? You've been out the whole night."

"She isn't here." Armand paused to wipe his damp forehead.

"Where is she?"

"She left for Europe midweek with her new boyfriend."

"And you didn't mention it?" I remembered Eva's judgment of Armand's mother.

"I guess, for me, her absence is such a habit, I don't think of it."

Of course you don't. For all practical purposes, you don't have a mother. "How long will she be gone?"

"I don't know. Six months?"

"No!" I exclaimed. "Then who will you live with?"

"I'll still live at home with my older brother. My mother leaves her aunt in charge of us, and the maid, of course."

"And this aunt won't worry about where you are?"

"Mamá Juana's eighty-seven." Armand laughed. "If my brother and I run into her, we pretend we saw her an hour ago, and she believes us."

At six a.m., the newspapers under our feet crackled as Armand stood and sank onto a sofa. "You know what? I'd rather fail."

"What?" I clamped my fingers around his sagging shoulders. "After all this work I just did?"

At our feet, his color-coherence mural to blend blues, yellows, and greens lay a third done.

"Look at it!" Armand kicked the mural. "We'll never finish. Besides, your kids will wake up soon, which means you'll head out to take them to school. Worse, my class is at nine, which requires me to leave here by seven anyway. I'm failing. Period."

"No! Hand in whatever part we finish. Don't you have any pride? Or self-respect? Or care what your professor might think of you?"

"No, I don't. I've never had a teacher who gave a damn about what I did, because I was dyslexic and slow."

"Armand, teachers care when you care, and you never have. I know from personal experience, remember?"

"No! You know how they care? When they're private tutors who receive lots of money from people like my parents."

"Then why are you such an awful student? Money can't buy it all."

"My parents say otherwise. I've had the best tutors since I was six years old."

"Right. And a fat lot of good it did you."

"That's my *point*. It doesn't matter what we do. I won't pass this stupid class, so why kill ourselves over this lousy assignment?"

"You'd prefer to fail without trying?"

"Yes."

"Why?" I insisted. "Because your parents are rich and they can pay for you to do the class over? This is your chance to become the painter you've wanted to become since you were ten years old, so why can't you be more proactive?"

"Proactive how? Yes, I know I should have done it two days ago, but I didn't."

Armand stared at the ceiling.

I sank onto the sofa beside him and took his cold hand in my own. "Listen, if you fail this class, you'll fail first semester of freshman year and never catch up. Then you'll become like me, a dropout without a degree. Come on. I'll stick the stupid squares too. At nine a.m., hand in whatever part we've done. Show your teacher you tried.

That evening, Armand knocked on my door at eight thirty p.m. without calling ahead. When I saw him, he smiled from ear to ear.

"What are you doing here?"

"I wanted to tell you the good news in person." Armand's smile widened.

"Why? Did the professor pass you?"

"No, but I told the professor the truth. He granted me a two-week extension to finish the assignment. I wanted to thank you in person. Are you proud of me or what?"

Without thinking it through, I hugged him. I couldn't stop myself. And he hugged me back as if he would never let me go.

Hours later, I went to bed happier than I had been in a long, long time, thrilled to have shaken Armand's stereotype of teachers. Perhaps he would be more mindful of teachers just being *people*—with feelings, opinions, and judgments—not the heartless harpies he presumed they were. Changing the world started with one person, and I had helped change Armand. It was my victory to cherish, even if I had no degree from any country.

44

Los Angeles, December 1990

By December, Armand and I had been friends for six months. Mostly, our outings included Pia and Abril, if not Salvador, Karina, and Eva also. But on December 3, we ended up alone with each other because Eva begged a bout of fever and we had tickets to a movie in the Catholic University theater.

Uncomfortable that the outing resembled a date, after the movie, I said, "Hey, you drove us here, so let me buy you ice cream."

At the Quatro-D Italian delicatessen on Angamos Avenue, I licked my double-chocolate ice cream cone. "I haven't told you this yet, but I leave town on the twelfth to take the kids to see Sergio in Los Angeles. That's when the kids finish school for the summer."

"Will you jump all over me if I say I'll miss you once you're gone?"

"Why would I jump all over you?"

"Because you'll think I'm hitting on you, and I'm not. I'll really miss you."

"I'll miss you too." I met Armand's green gaze. "I've never thought about it, but I will." *Especially if I might die in the near future. I will always remember how happy my kids and I have been with you during these past few months, giving you little in exchange.*

"So, will you call me from LA?"

"No. How can I? What would I tell Sergio—I have a friend who's a guy? He wouldn't like it."

"Why would he object to a friend? It's not like I'm your boyfriend."

"Because, I guess, marriage isn't that simple? Also, both Sergio and I have an image to protect while we stay married. Having a friend who's a boy doesn't fit into that image, and I'm realizing it more and more." *Yet these days, I can't imagine what I would do without you in my life. Strange, but that's the truth.*

"Please don't add you'll stop seeing me. It'll be too trite."

"I won't," I said too quickly. "I want to see you and stay friends with you as much as you want to see me. But I can't shout that out loud from any rooftops. I should have factored that in before I began spending time with you."

"Maybe I can call you?"

I shook my head. "He misses work without notice, so I couldn't tell you when he'll be home. If I find the window, I'll call you. Promise. It's the best I can do. Let's pray you're home if I call. And don't hold it against me if I don't, okay? I hope I get through this whole Los Angeles vacation in one piece. Living day-to-day with Sergio again will unleash all sorts of feelings I'm not ready for, and I'm so nervous. It's crazy how sickness cancels out all the nasty, mean things someone has done to you... and all that reigns is pity."

"I'm sorry you have to go through this. I wish I could be there for you." Armand spoke through a mouthful of crunchy sugar cone.

"You already are. I didn't know how colorless my life was until you came along to brighten it up for both me and my children. I can't thank you enough." I placed a hand on top of his on the table. "I hope we'll stay friends forever."

On the afternoon Pia, Abril, and I landed in Los Angeles, it was winter and raining because we had changed hemispheres. Pelting drops of moisture slanted down from the sky. Pia and Abril had never seen that kind of "real" rain. All they knew was the feathery garua drizzle from Lima that they could barely see. On the tarmac, Sergio waited for us, holding two giant golf umbrellas. He opened one for Pia as she hugged him.

"Papá, is this normal?" She peered at the gloomy sky.

"Yes," I said. "This is real, God-honest rain. It feels good to see rain after so many years! You never know how much you miss something until you see it again." I gazed at the sky even though the raindrops felt chilly on my face.

"Don't." Sergio shaded me with his umbrella. "You'll catch your death." Right then, Abril engulfed him in a bear hug at waist level, and Sergio handed me the umbrella, trying to lift her up, but he couldn't. He had lifted her seven months ago when he had said goodbye to us to come to Los Angeles. *Does he recognize he's weaker?* I rubbed the tight spot on my chest with the umbrella handle.

"Come on, all of you. I don't want to get wet or sick." Sergio grabbed Abril's hand.

At home, the children stared at the one-bedroom condo Sergio had rented in the neighborhood of San Vicente.

Pia sniffed the air. "It smells different, like a store."

"This place is a block away from Wilshire Boulevard, where the consulate is," Sergio said. "That way, when I'm too sick to drive, I walk, but that convenience costs me dearly." He sank onto the living room couch to take off his shoes. "Go to the first kitchen cabinet on the right. I have a surprise for you."

I hurried to do his bidding and found five kinds of instant coffees and a pile of different-flavored Cadbury chocolates. "Oh, Serg! They sell Cadburys here?"

"Yes. As soon as I saw them, I remembered how much you loved them back in India."

"And why did you buy five coffees?"

"So you could try them all and see which one you like. I'll buy you more of that one to take back to Lima."

I bounded over to hug him on the couch. "I smell food. Did you cook?" My eyes swept over an alcove beside the doorway into the apartment that I had missed. It had a queen-sized bed that fit right into a niche in the wall. "Is that where the children will sleep?"

"I don't cook. No energy. I have a contract with a food service that delivers two meals each evening. I only warm them. Today, it's lasagna for you all. Let me change into my pajamas." Sergio wiggled his toes. "More comfortable."

I touched Sergio's arm. "Cancel it for the next two months. It'll save money. I'll cook for us while we're here."

"We'll see about that. Remember the Miami doctor, Dr. Bernstein, who warned us that the AZT pill would go against me after a while? These days, all food smells make me queasy. My doctor here plans to prescribe me a lower dose in a week."

"How many do you take right now?"

"Eight pills a day. But the side effects are never-ending. I take seven other pills to counter bloating, nausea, heartburn, headaches, muscle deterioration, fatigue, appetite loss, and God knows what else."

"Oh, Serg!" I pulled him into a hug.

"Let me switch on the TV for the kids. I don't want them to hear all this," he whispered. "They'll be in heaven here. My cable TV contract includes sixty-eight channels."

But the children were glued to the back-porch door, staring at the rain coming down in sheets.

"*Niñas!*" Sergio clapped his hands. "Who wants to watch *Tom and Jerry*?"

"How is it happening, Papá?" Abril asked. "Who is pouring water out of the sky? It never stops." She gazed at Sergio then at the uniform gray sky.

"What's *Tom and Jerry*?" Pia asked.

"I'd forgotten how exhausting it gets to answer all their questions," muttered Sergio.

"You'll like it." I shepherded the children away from Sergio to provide him with the opportunity to disengage. "Tom is a cat, and Jerry is a mouse, but Jerry always fools Tom. Come on. Take off your shoes, and sit on this couch. I'll warm the food."

"And I'll go lie down for a bit." Sergio headed for the bedroom door.

As soon as he lay down, Pia ran in behind him and pulled out her year-end art-excellence certificate from one of our suitcases. "Papá, look at this!"

"Come on," I said. "Show it to him later. He has to take a nap right now."

But Sergio took the certificate from Pia's hand then glanced at me. "Apparently, we'll have a junior artist in the family, after your mother."

"Don't even say that in jest! I don't want my children to be anything like my mother."

Sergio smiled. "Art isn't a talent you can stop, Noor. But I know what you mean." And his words conjured a sharp image of Armand's face in my mind.

That night, after we put the children to bed, Sergio pulled out a large notebook to show me his doctor's appointments. "Mostly, I receive treatment at the Cedars Sinai, pretty close to here, but twice a month, I have to drive to the Kenneth Norris Cancer Hospital a bazillion miles away. Driving there, I always lose my way because when I get tired, too soon, all the highway signs and exits and more highways and more exits become utterly confusing. Maybe AIDS has affected my short-term memory. That hospital should be familiar to me by now, but I get lost each time I go there."

"Oh, Serg, how awful. How are you handling being alone?"

"After a workday, I'm too tired to think or care. At other times, I cry. I watch TV a lot."

Sergio had never been a TV watcher. "Would it have been better if we were here with you?" My voice came out anguished.

"I don't think so. Don't get me wrong. I miss the children, but I couldn't have handled the stress of them being children. Their boundless energy is too exhausting for me."

As usual, when Sergio took his clothes off, the crisscross scars on his back—even more visible since he had lost so much fat—impacted me, but when he faced me, my eyebrows rose as I saw a new bump under his left collarbone.

He touched it. "Are you wondering what this is?"

I nodded.

"It's a catheter that they call a port inserted permanently under the skin. It provides the nurses easy access to a large vein for intravenous treatments without causing me too much pain. Otherwise, the constant and multiple needles used to have me in tears."

Close to tears myself, I couldn't trust my voice to say anything, so I just nodded.

Long after Sergio snored heavily, courtesy of some medication, I lay awake beside him, hands crossed under my head, unable to fall asleep despite my own anxiety meds. Sergio's rosy glow of health from seven months ago had been replaced by weight loss and pallor. At dinner, he had pushed around a small portion of lasagna on his plate rather than actually eating any of it. *How long can he live like this?* The kitchenette counter had zero space left over after accommodating his plethora of pill bottles. Like I had said to Armand, watching Sergio live and suffer at such close quarters would be excruciating.

I felt I had slept for five minutes when the children bounced into our bedroom.

"It's stopped raining," Pia said.

"The sun is shining," Abril said. "Papá, I'm hungry. Can you make breakfast?"

Sergio's movements were slow as he swung his feet to the carpeted floor, slipped on his familiar black-suede Gucci bedroom slippers, and struggled into his blue-and-white-striped kimono dressing gown. That dressing gown had seen it all. He had worn it on the day he had opened the balcony door of the Peruvian residence in Delhi when I'd informed him I would marry him. If garments could talk, that dressing gown could recount every single tale of our union, our fights, and his slow decline from AIDS.

In stark contrast to Sergio, I sprang out of bed to manage the situation. "I'll serve you breakfast." I herded Abril out of the bedroom. "Don't bother Papá. How about fried eggs on toast?" Abril loved eggs.

"Noor, relax." Sergio caught up to us and hugged Abril. "I've got this. America runs on cereal. I have eight kinds for them to choose from. They'll love it."

"Then I'll heat the milk for it."

"No. That's your colonial English way. Here, they eat cereal with cold milk."

"Yuck." I shuddered.

"Come on, you two. From tomorrow onward, you'll serve me breakfast." Sergio urged the children toward the kitchenette.

"Should I fry you eggs?" I followed the family. "All I want is my coffee."

Sergio shook his head. "No. No eggs for me. I'll have cereal too. I don't want to deal with the smell of frying." Sergio had loved fried eggs for breakfast ever since I met him.

"Who wants to go to Disneyland?" He pulled an armful of cereal boxes from a kitchen cabinet.

"What's Disneyland?" Pia held out her arms to help Sergio.

"Don't you have to go to work? It's Monday."

"No. I took the week off. Oh, you'll love Disneyland. Wait till you see it." He handed Pia as many cereal boxes as she could carry.

"How far is Disneyland?" I asked after Sergio had driven for more than an hour. *Have the dark circles under his eyes gotten darker?*

"The map said two hours." Sergio's look was hollow.

"Oh, Serg. Why didn't you wait until I could drive here too? Now you're exhausted."

"I wanted to do something memorable with the kids. Now I'm asking myself how I'll live through the day."

"Oh, I'll see to it that you do," I said grimly, "even if it means I have to drive back. As soon as we're there, I'll speak to management to secure you a wheelchair. I don't know how big Disneyland is, but I know you're in no state to walk anywhere. I wish you had consulted me before deciding to do this." But of course, Sergio had rarely consulted me on anything in our marriage. *Why would he consult me now?*

In our lives, when Sergio had been well, he'd had a routine he followed, especially with the children. On weekend mornings, he had always shared an elaborate variety of typical Peruvian breakfast fare with them. Then, Sunday afternoons post lunch had been his time to dress up Pia and Abril and take them to have tea with his mother in San Isidro. He'd even combed their hair into crazy hairdos, which became a game in itself. Usually, his real mission had been to take them to Olivar Park and shoot endless footage of the children—running, playing, climbing the ancient olive trees.

Since I'd met him, Sergio's two passions were cooking and photography. But now he couldn't stand food smells and rarely touched his camera, and I never brought it up. *What is there to take pictures of? How sick he looks?* Yet that day, he clearly intended to take pictures because he had stowed his Nikon camera case in the trunk of the car.

I gazed at the passing landscape, tears filling my eyes at how those photos would torment me in the years to come. We had started having children within our first year of marriage because Sergio had wanted to be a father before age forty. *For how long will he live to enjoy his precious girls?* Each time I was pregnant, Sergio had hoped for a son because, like Indians, Latin Americans, too, craved sons more than daughters, but after our kids were born, no one doted on his daughters more than Sergio. *Why, Serg? Why did you get AIDS and destroy all our lives?*

When we entered through the gates of Disneyland, the children were dazzled by its fairy-tale glitter.

"This is where I want to live," Pia said. "Papá, why can't we live here?"

"Papá, why are you sitting in a wheelchair when other papas are standing in line?" Abril gazed at Sergio through the lenses of her pink heart-shaped sunglasses because she didn't remember ever seeing Sergio in a wheelchair.

"Because the other papas didn't drive this far to bring their children here." Thank God Sergio was better than me at quick rejoinders.

"Mamá, look, the wolf and Red Riding Hood! They're walking side by side. Will he eat her?" Abril covered her mouth with both hands.

"Not right now," I said. "Maybe later." I bent to speak to Sergio. "Do you want water? I have water in my beach bag."

"How did you sneak it in? They don't allow any food or drinks."

"I didn't. Maybe they didn't check me because of your diplomatic ID."

At three in the afternoon, Sergio said, "Let's do one last ride and wrap it up. I still have to drive us back."

"I want to do the teacups from Alice in Wonderland again," Abril said.

"Abril!" Pia pulled her sister's pigtail. "Did you forget how dizzy that made you? Let's go see the Dick Tracy movie again."

"We're not repeating any rides," Sergio said.

"Then let's head home." I placed my hands on his drooping shoulders. "We've done so much already. They don't need another ride." *Can he manage the drive back?*

"No. I'll break my rule and let Abril do the teacups again. I don't want the children to pay for my fatigue."

Sergio spent the next three days in bed to recover from the Disneyland trip. Meanwhile, I requested the condo manager's wife teach me how to drive Sergio's automatic, since I only knew how to drive stick-shift. It was easy to keep the children entertained after that. Their daily thrill, post-Disneyland, was the local supermarket because it was vast compared to anything they had ever seen in Lima. Soon, I had to ration the number of candies they could buy on each outing. While they watched TV and ate M&M's, pizza and Coca Cola in the living room, I watched old movies with Sergio, either on TNT or AMC, but Sergio couldn't eat junk food any more than he could handle real food. And his lack of appetite was so alarming, heartrending, and scary, I was shutting down just to get through each day—like I had gotten through the days of living with Didima, watching her die month by month, minute by minute, where the days were long and years were short, with nothing I could do to control any of it. But what I could control was eating too much pizza or corn chips or Cadbury chocolates and vomiting it all out after. So that was what I did every day until my stomach muscles simply couldn't hurl up again. Then I would go to the fridge, prepare myself a salad, and eat that.

The following Monday, Sergio went back to work. Without the distraction of him at home, I missed Armand at odd moments. I could have called him, but I didn't, and I didn't know why.

Will I go on seeing Armand when I go back to Lima? It was a good question, since Armand hadn't caused Sergio's illness, yet seeing him racked up my guilt since he brought joy into my life and the children's lives while Sergio struggled alone in Los Angeles. The correlation wasn't logical, but it bothered me nonetheless.

That evening, Sergio had a doctor's appointment at the Cedars Sinai. "Do you want to come with me or stay home with the children?" His face looked drawn and pale as he came into the living room.

"Don't you want to eat first?" *Oh, Serg, what have you done to yourself?*

"I don't have the time. I can't be late."

"We'll come with you." I pointed to the children. "They've been home all day except for a walk in a park near here. I'll keep them busy while you see the doctor. It'll be a change for them."

On the way back home, Sergio said, "From now on, I have to go to the hospital three times a week for a special nutrient IV injection. The doctor is not happy with my bloodwork."

I stared out of the car window because there was nothing for me to say.

I called Armand a week before the children's summer vacation was due to end, on the second-to-last day of February. I called because not calling him bothered me as much as calling him would. I hoped he wouldn't be home, but he was.

"Hi. I thought you'd never call," he greeted me. His voice transported me right back to Lima and how much I enjoyed his company—enjoyed it while Sergio was dying.

"I didn't find the opportunity," I lied. *Can I stop seeing him? No! He's the walking stick I need to lean on.*

"How is your husband? How do you feel? All I've done these past three months is worry about you. Are you okay?"

"I'm fine, but my husband isn't. He's sick most of the time from his chemotherapy." It was a truth of sorts.

"When are you coming back?"

"Next week."

"You sound dead."

"I am dead from watching him suffer in a thousand different ways all the time."

"Do you love him?"

"It's not about love or hate. It's about watching your children's father deteriorate moment by moment. It's about humanity."

"Oh, Noor. I'm sorry for both you and him."

I hung up the phone, undecided about whether I would call Armand upon my return.

Sergio came home from the consulate at lunchtime. "I have a surprise for you."

"What?" I had a towel wrapped around my wet hair.

"Get ready, and you'll see." Sergio smiled his gaunt smile, breaking my heart.

He drove us south, down Wilshire Boulevard, refusing to disclose his surprise until he parked the car.

"This is so far—don't you have to go back to work?"

"I took the afternoon off because I had a little energy."

I looked out the car window so he wouldn't see the pity in my eyes.

Sergio parked the car and addressed the children. "This is Rodeo Drive, the equivalent of Fifth Avenue in New York. We're getting Mamá a pair of new sunglasses at the Porsche Boutique. Then we'll go out to dinner."

"But, Serg, I don't *need* new sunglasses—least of all ones that will be as expensive as Porsche, and you don't eat any of your dinner anyway. Why are you wasting the money?"

"Come on. Indulge me, will you?" Sergio's eyes looked haunted. "I just want to feel like a normal human being for a little while."

When will I understand what makes my husband tick? Time was racing. I would have to hurry, or else it would be too late for me to ever understand him.

At the airport a week later, I knew that if I cried, the children would cry too. But it was Sergio who initiated the tears. "I'll miss you." He hugged the children, staring at me over their heads.

Tears rolled down my cheeks, too, as my throat choked. "I know. But we'll come back at the end of June. It's only three months. They'll go by in no time."

Before entering the plane, I waved. *How many more times will I wave like this?* I wiped my eyes and nudged the children forward.

VIOLETS

45

Lima, 1991

BACK IN LIMA, I BUSIED myself with the preparation of the children's school reopening. Abril would join first grade that year, which would have been my time to return to college, too, *if* Sergio had remained healthy.

If. It was such an innocuous word, yet it changed the course of entire stories. Troy would have remained independent indefinitely *if* the Trojans hadn't pulled the Trojan Horse into their city. Juliet would have lived life happily ever after *if* Romeo hadn't killed himself. Language defied logic because "if" should have been a word as long as *supercalifragilisticexpialidocious*, but it wasn't. Like a bomb appeared to be an unremarkable black box until it exploded. Like a volcano was an ordinary mountain until it erupted and destroyed everything for miles around. And language *never* conveyed the true length and breadth of the human experience. No words could capture the pain of pain or the joy of joy or the fear of fear or the sheer powerlessness of hope. In that regard, language resembled time—objective and dispassionate, just another tool to record a story. Like the story of Didima dying, and now the story of Sergio dying. Slow. Steady. Inexorable.

The first week of school raced by as I readjusted to a new carpool group that now included both Pia and Abril. New parents, new children, new home stops. I told myself I wasn't calling Armand because I was busy.

On Monday morning, I came home from the carpool and slammed my foot on the brake when I spotted Armand's metallic-brown station wagon parked outside my house with him in it.

"Hi." I switched off my car and didn't honk for Dulci to open the garage door. I got out and approached Armand's driver's-side window. "What are you doing here? Don't you have college to go to?"

"I took the day off to come ask when you will call me." Armand unwound his limbs from behind the driver's seat to stand in front of me.

How tall and handsome he was, more so than when I had met him at the Roosevelt a year and a half ago. I wanted to hug him, wanted to say, *I missed you, and now that I see you, I realize how much*, but I glanced away. "It's complicated." I sighed, closing my eyes. *This boy will never understand my guilt about him being healthy when Sergio is sick, my worry as to what would happen if I got an AIDS test and discovered I have it too.*

Armand misinterpreted my sigh. "Don't worry. You won't have to see me for long." He sounded bitter. "I'm off to Spain tonight. I came to say goodbye."

"Spain?" My eyes opened wide. "You had the whole summer to go to Spain. Why now, when school reopened?"

"Yours is not the only complicated family. These are my father's orders—and we jump when my father cracks the whip. It's how my family runs."

I remembered Eva's take on Armand's father. "Who's 'we'?"

"My brother, he flies from here with me. My sister, she'll come from Denmark. My father's girlfriend and her two kids. We'll meet him in Madrid and fly to Thailand for three days."

"*Thailand?* That's insane. Going to Thailand is like going to India. You'll lose more hours in transit than on the ground."

"I know. I hate it. But I can't change it."

"Any special reason for this journey? Birthday? Anniversary? Why would your dad make you miss school?"

"It's called my father's whim. And I've danced to my father's whim since I can remember, so I don't question it anymore."

"Will you see your mom? She's in Europe, too, right?"

"Yes, but I don't know where she is. This trip doesn't involve her."

"When will you be back?"

"In seven days."

"I guess I'll see you then." I lowered my head and kicked imaginary dust on the sidewalk.

"Yeah. Like you saw me now."

"Don't be sarcastic. It doesn't suit you."

"Bye." He drove off without looking my way.

I honked for Dulci to open the garage door. *Why hadn't I called Armand? I owed him that much for all the time and attention he had showered on Pia and Abril, if not myself. I should have had the courtesy to do that. What is it I don't want to face?*

Instead, each morning after carpooling, I sat on my porch for hours on end, staring at the robust croton bushes coloring the west end of my garden in yellows, reds, oranges, and maroons. Underneath the crotons were violets Armand had bought me to plant. They grew in shy clumps of pink, purple, mauve, and white, thriving in the damp shade.

Take the children to school. Bring them back. Worry about Sergio. Take the children to school. Bring them back. Worry about Sergio. That was my life. Armand didn't fit in it. *So then why do I think of him all the time?* I tucked that question in the farthest corner of my mind and went about my business.

By the fifth day of Armand's absence, I was exhausted from thinking in circles—Armand's looks, those green eyes, his unfailing attention, his sensitivity toward my children, his kind gestures, his vulnerability to seek my approval. And Sergio.

That night, I put Pia and Abril to bed and switched from rereading a P. G. Wodehouse farce to a book by Gerald Durrell, *Golden Bat and Pink Pigeons*. I was eager to accompany Durrell on his trip to Telfair to capture skinks and Gunther's geckos to avoid my own life.

Why is Armand so upset I didn't call him upon my return? Does he like me beyond friendship? The truth, when it hit me, hit me like a freight train. I loved Armand. I had fallen in love with a twenty-year-old. For a second, the page in front of me blurred. *That* was why I had been so reluctant to call him from Los Angeles—and hadn't called him after coming back. Because I didn't want the truth to confront me. *Does Armand feel anything similar? He's twenty, for God's sake. But didn't he want to date me six months ago? How does he feel now?*

Unable to focus on a single sentence anymore, I switched off my bed lamp.

How had I missed the danger? Armand was the only person to secure my attention since I lost Chirag. I had to stop seeing him before he found out what a fool I was.

The next morning, I woke up feverish with body aches from sleep deprivation. To do the school carpool, I jammed on dark glasses to hide my watering eyes.

Back at home, I broke down and had a good cry. *Frida. I'll talk to Frida. She'll have a solution for me.*

I ran out of my house to knock on Frida's door fifty yards further up the sidewalk.

"Hi. Are you okay?" Frida frowned. "You don't look so good."

"Are you free? I'm dying from worry."

"About Sergio?"

"No. This is different."

"Come on in." Frida swung an index finger.

"No. Come to my place."

In my living room, Frida frowned through my stuttering recital.

"You don't approve." I waved my hands. "I can see it in your eyes."

"You're wrong." Frida sounded serious. "What could be more natural than you falling for the person who offered you a bit of support and kindness? God knows it doesn't come from the Santanders, including my husband. I couldn't survive a week of doing what you've already done to look after Sergio—not without my family to back me up."

"Yes, but who else would say that?" I wrung my hands. "And now I've ruined it by falling in love with the one person who helps nonstop."

"How do you know he doesn't love you too?"

"Frids, if he loved me, he would have said so. Like he was super direct about wanting to date me."

"Come now. Don't beat yourself up for falling for him. How could you resist falling for Armand when you're so alone? With the way you tell me he runs around with you and your kids, not to mention he must be handsome, too, if he's got brown hair and freckles, like me."

My smile changed to a frown. "For Christ's sake, tell me what to do. I can't be the fool in love with a younger person who doesn't love me. It's too humiliating."

"When does he come back?"

"I don't know. Two, maybe three days?"

"We have to wait and see if he's fallen for you, too, or if, for him, this continues to be just a friendship."

"How?"

"Once he's back, either he'll call you right away, which will mean he doesn't love you, or else, he'll be as upset as you are and he won't call."

"Hang on." I shook my hands as though they were on flames. "If he loves me, he *won't* call?"

"Yes. Didn't you do that to *him* after returning from LA?"

"But I didn't know I was in love with him."

"You did. You didn't want to face it or deal with it. If he feels similarly, he won't want to deal with it either. We'll have to wait and see."

"I have one more problem."

"What?"

"What if the Santanders discover he exists and tell Sergio?"

"If they threaten you, attack them. My dad's best friend is a lawyer, and that's what he always says. That attack is the best form of defense. Attack them with the fact that Sergio didn't get AIDS from you—so you have the right to a lover. You'll see how they'll back off like wet cats. You're the one who takes care of Sergio. Trust me—*no one*, and least of all the Santanders, want to expose themselves to AIDS day after day like you do. Whatever they say to you, it won't go far." Frida's assessment didn't bolster my confidence, but if I wanted to continue at least my friendship with Armand, I had no other choice.

Four more days elapsed then ten, and I didn't hear from Armand.

"Mamá, where's Armand?" demanded Pia on a Friday afternoon. "I want to go to the beach tomorrow."

"Why hasn't he come to teach me how to draw?" complained Abril.

"Because he's gone to see his papá in Spain, amor." My throat hurt from controlled tears.

"When will he come back?" Pia placed her hands on her hips.

"I don't know, amor." And I wouldn't find out because I refused to call his house and come across as some trashy old lady chasing after him.

46

On day fourteen of no call from Armand, I called his friend, Eva Nalvarte.

But before I could tiptoe around the question of Armand, Eva said, "If you're not busy, join me in Miraflores for a coffee."

"Only if I can bring Abril. We need to go there to buy her school supplies. This will be the perfect opportunity to do both."

In the El Haiti Café, Eva kissed Abril. "Hi, sweetheart. Did you buy your school supplies already?"

Abril shook her head shyly. "Not yet." She hugged me around the waist and looked up.

"Well, honey, why don't you go to the pastry cart and choose six pastries for us? That nice man will serve us whatever you choose." With Abril out of earshot, Eva murmured, "Why didn't you join us last Friday?"

"Why? Is Armand back?"

Eva's face reddened. "N-no," she stuttered. "I meant with the rest of us."

"Eva, please." My cheeks burned. "Don't lie to me. Armand and I aren't dating. But I wasn't invited Friday."

That night, as soon as the children were in bed, I phoned Armand's house.

Armand answered. "Hi—"

"When did you get back?" I cut in.

"Last night. I slept until now."

"Stop lying," I whispered, scared my voice would wake the children. "I saw Eva, and she told me you came back last week." I punched the mattress because I couldn't raise my voice. "This is it. We're through."

"Hey, wait—"

I slammed the phone back on its cradle.

My satisfaction to have wrought justice was short-lived. I buried my despair in my pillow. If only Frida was available. But if I phoned her at that hour, Carlos would pepper Frida with questions. Blinking wet eyelashes, I inserted a VHS tape into the player next to my bedroom TV. I would watch *Roman Holiday* because Gregory Peck reminded me of my grandpa and made me feel less alone.

I had dozed off when the doorbell rang. I sprang out of bed and charged down the stairwell, afraid the noise would wake the children. Armand stood at the door, his hands full of a brown paper package. I tried to slam the door, but he put his foot in to prevent me from doing so.

"What d'you want?"

"To come in and talk maybe?"

"I don't want to be friends with a liar. Don't treat me like some twenty-year-old college girl."

"Then stop behaving like one. Here, I brought this for you from Spain." Armand thrust the package into my arms.

"Armand—I don't want a present." I threw the present on the patio floor. "I want to know why you lied to me for no reason."

"Because!" Armand yelled, "I love you, and I don't know what to do about it—I—"

"You love me?" My voice sounded stunned.

"Yes. But I'm scared. Plain scared to love a married woman with two children who doesn't even bother to call me. There—happy now? Now you know why I didn't call. So throw me out, because I know you don't want to date me."

"This is crazy—because I have the same problem. I can't tell you how depressed I've been since I figured out I've fallen for you too—"

Armand kicked the brown paper package and yanked me into his arms. Our kiss lit my body on fire as if we were melting against each other. *When's the last time I felt this alive?* But it was I who began struggling in his embrace.

"What? What is it?" Armand kissed my tousled hair, my neck, his hands baring my shoulders—

"Listen!" I pushed him away. "We have to talk—"

"We can talk later—"

"No. We have to talk now—let's sit in the living room and talk. Armand, listen to me. Stop kissing me!"

In the living room, Armand pulled me close on the Peruvian colonial sofa.

"So we don't wake up the children," he whispered, smoothing back my hair. "Tell me, what could be more important than kissing right now?"

I took Armand's hand in my own and closed my eyes. "It's bad. Real bad."

"Jesus, you're scaring me."

"You should be scared. My husband doesn't have cancer. He has AIDS."

"Oh, you mean that bug going around in Africa? How did he get it?"

"Armand. It isn't a 'bug going around in Africa.' It's everywhere. And once you get it, it's a matter of time until you die unless a cure is found."

"So what's the difference between that and him having cancer? Cancer would kill him too."

"Infection. AIDS is an STD. You get it from contact—and I may have it too. I'm sorry we kissed. All the doctors tell me it can be transmitted through any bodily fluid if someone has one open cut on their body."

"Why didn't you tell me?"

"Because AIDS is associated with homosexuality. That's why Sergio hides behind the cancer diagnosis. He doesn't need to be branded a homosexual in Lima. We don't even know what the reprisals would be if the foreign office found out. So, first I didn't tell you because I didn't trust you. Later, it seemed unnecessary… until now."

"So, what do you mean you *may* have it? Either you do or you don't. Which is it?"

I caught the urgency in Armand's tone and broke into muted sobs. "I had sex with him, not this past January but the January before. The worst joke is it was my idea. I wanted to patch up our marriage. The doctor in Miami said I'd be under the cloud for six months. I should have been tested at the latest this January, but I didn't do it because I was too scared."

"Wait a minute. So you didn't have it the first time you tested?" Armand gripped my arm, his voice full of hope.

"No. Thank God. And the kids don't have it. But don't sound so hopeful. I might test positive now. If I have AIDS, too, my children will become orphans. I couldn't face it… so I didn't test again."

Armand freed my arm and bear-hugged me. "You've got me now, okay? Where do you have to get this test? I'll take you there tomorrow."

"Aren't you mad I might have given it to you?" I placed a hand on his stubbled cheek, staring into those hypnotic green eyes. "All it takes is one cut. If the virus gets inside a cut—that's it."

"Well, if you've infected me, then that's that. But I don't have any cuts inside my mouth. Do you?"

I shook my head.

"Then I doubt I caught it."

"Would you date me even with the six-months-suspicion factor?"

"Do you have to ask? I've loved you a lot longer than you've loved me."

"But what if I test positive tomorrow?"

"Let's worry about that when we get to it, shall we? Let me sleep on your sofa tonight. I can't leave you alone after this."

"Thanks."

Armand got up.

"Where are you going?" I clutched his shirttail.

"To get you your present. You need the cheering up."

Receiving the package, I tore open the brown paper. "What is it? Chocolate? Godiva? I love Godiva! Please stop me from finishing the whole box tonight."

"Open the box."

On top of the chocolates lay an enormous Armani silk scarf patterned with foot-long squares in reds, blues, greens, and yellows, outlined by black. I pulled it out, unfurled it, and draped its softness around myself. "How did you know to bring me what I love?"

"It wasn't hard. You wear silk scarves all the time… even to the beach."

I went upstairs to bed at three a.m., unable to stop smiling. It was the first time in thirteen months I felt I might not have AIDS after all. The next day's test would tell for sure. *Thank you, God, for Armand's support.*

47

A BRIL WAS THE ONE WHO found Armand asleep on the sofa when she dashed down for breakfast ahead of Pia. She shook Armand awake. "Armand, Ar*mand*, wake up. Why are you here when I have to go to school? I want to paint with you. When did you come back? We missed you—"

"Hi." Armand rubbed his eyes, sat up, and stretched his arms. "We can paint tomorrow." He yawned. "Today, I have a surprise for you both."

"What surprise?" Pia sat down beside him.

"It wouldn't be a surprise if I told you what it was, would it?"

When the children went to the kitchen for breakfast, Armand said, "Let's do the pool in my car. Your car won't fit me and all the pool kids. We'll go to the lab straight after. Labs open early."

Without the crazy Lima traffic to drive through, I stressed nonstop. *What will I do if I have AIDS?* Each time I faced the possibility, I experienced a feeling of walking into space with no tether. Without meaning to, Armand had brought my day of reckoning to *that* day instead of someday. At least he wouldn't ditch me for a positive AIDS diagnosis. *Would Sergio send me AZT pills from Los Angeles? How would that work with our health insurance? But the health insurance is international—*

"Hey." Armand shook me by the shoulder. "We're here. Don't you have to walk the kids into school?"

At the Colichon y Cantela laboratory, my hands trembled as the receptionist handed me a form. "Don't worry, señora. It's anonymous. But everybody who takes this test has to fill out this form for an American medical census company since AIDS is such a new epidemic and the testing kit comes from America."

"Señora," Armand addressed the receptionist. "May I have a form too? I'll take the test as well."

"Why?" My pupils felt like question marks.

"I'll tell you later."

"Señora, we'll get the results tomorrow, right?" I pushed the form back over the counter surface so the tremor in my fingers would be less noticeable.

"Day after tomorrow, señora," the receptionist replied.

"Oh, God." I placed the back of one hand to my forehead. "Welcome to my world. The waiting is pure hell."

In the car I said, "Okay. Confession time. Why did you take the test too? Was it because we kissed last night?"

"Well, that and because my one sexual experience was in a Spanish brothel on my fifteenth birthday."

"What? Why would you go to a brothel, let alone when you were that young?"

"It was my father's birthday present to me before my mom and I returned to Lima after their divorce."

Again, I remembered Eva's assessment of Armand's father. "So, what? You had unprotected sex?" My eyes became round.

"No. They handed me a bunch of condoms when I got there."

"Hey, I'm glad you told me this, and I'm grateful you took the test too. How did you feel about visiting a brothel at fifteen?"

"I was so overwhelmed. I don't remember much. But later, in my memory, it felt like a roller-coaster ride. I don't like roller coasters."

At home, I asked, "Would you mind if I told Dulci about us? You know how much she loves you." Dulci adored Armand because they were the same age—both born in 1970, and he treated her as a social equal, whereas Sergio, born and raised in Lima, treated Dulci as a maid, or an inferior being, like the rest of upper and upper middle class Peru did.

"Does she know of the AIDS?" Armand sounded dead sober.

"No. I doubt she would understand, even if I explained it. AIDS hasn't hit mainstream television yet. I never let her touch Sergio under any circumstances. That is my burden to bear. I married him. I get to deal with the consequences." I laughed a harsh laugh. "You should hear my sister-in-law, Frida, on the subject. She would have left her husband on the spot if he'd confessed to having AIDS."

"You should have too. You're a kindhearted fool."

"Maybe. But I have nowhere to go, neither here nor in India. Living with my mother and stepfather would be worse than nursing Sergio. He doesn't have my love, but he will always have my gratitude for saving me from them—and India."

"And do your kids know?"

"No! They are six and seven. What would they understand of any disease, let alone AIDS? This is not their burden to carry—not yet, anyway."

"Dulci?" Armand yelled inside the house. "Where are you? Come here. We need to talk."

"Are you hungry?" Dulci popped her head around the kitchen doorway. "You didn't have breakfast. Would you like an omelet?"

"Thanks, Duls, later. Come sit with us in the living room for a minute."

Dulci perched on an antique colonial armchair, looking terribly self-conscious. No one in Lima society had their live-in maids, or any maid, sit with them in their living rooms.

"Duls, Armand and I want to be together." *That is, if my test comes out negative.* "I guess we fell in love." *At least that part is true.* My face flushed.

"You *just* figured that out?" Dulci laughed in twenty-year-old delight. Her entire knowledge of love came from following Venezuelan and Mexican soap operas on the kitchen TV, which she devoured while she did her chores. She believed every word she heard on daytime television. Growing up, Dulci had never met anyone except the members of her extended family, who lived on a remote mountain farm. "I knew from the minute I saw Armand," she continued, looking at me. "How could you not fall for him? He's so handsome!"

"Oh, Duls." Armand smiled bashfully.

"Duls, you'll have to help me keep this a secret from the children. Señor Sergio can't find out, either, even though we haven't been together in years."

"No, he doesn't need to know. He already has enough to deal with, with his cancer. Besides, I know you don't love him."

Boy, if you only knew the truth. "How do you know?"

"Because of the way you treat each other. It's like friends, not like a couple. He's more your father than your husband."

How perceptive of you, even though you have so little life experience.

With Dulci on our side, Armand and I went to lie upstairs on my bed together for the first time since we had met.

"I feel like we've done this forever." Armand patted the crook of his shoulder for me to place my head on.

"I can't tell you how much it means to me that you're hanging out with me while we wait for those awful results."

"Wouldn't you do the same for me?"

I reached up to kiss his thorny cheek. "I'm sorry you're missing school on my account."

"How about the fact that my dad made me miss eight days of school? Besides, today is Painting II. I wouldn't even *be* in that class if you hadn't helped—no, goaded—me to finish that assignment. Painting is easy for me. I'll talk to my teacher on Monday."

"You won't go to school tomorrow or the day after either?"

"Do you think I'll leave you alone to sit and brood over the possible AIDS diagnosis? You worry too much already. You're a worrywart. I'm sleeping here tonight. Again."

"And you're sure your grandaunt won't worry?"

"I'll go tomorrow morning and have tea with her. I'll tell her I woke up late. She can't tell one day from another. She's the perfect caretaker. My brother and I love her watching us."

"Doesn't your mom know this?"

"Hey, don't waste your time trying to understand my family. Okay? It is what it is. I'm used to it. She's been doing this since I was sixteen. That was hard. It isn't hard anymore."

I shook my head, thinking of Dulci's parents, my parents, Armand's parents.

"What? You're judging my mom, aren't you?"

"No. I'm thinking of how parents can be so hard to deal with."

"Believe me. I sometimes hate mine."

The children came home from school, overjoyed to find Armand sprawled on the living room floor, surrounded by art material and two huge sections of craft paper. At three in the afternoon, we were all in Armand's car, en route to the surprise he hadn't divulged even to me.

"The suspense is killing me," I complained when Armand drove into the basement parking lot of a building I didn't know in downtown Lima.

Armand took the girls by their hands as we rode in an old-fashioned brass elevator up to the main floor.

"Oh, Armand." I stared up at an oval stained-glass ceiling when the elevator opened to a lobby. "What a beautiful old building this is."

"Is this a part of Disneyland?" Abril asked.

Armand laughed. "No. This is the Hotel San Martin. When I was a little boy, my grandma, my father's mom, brought me and my brother and sister here each Saturday to have hot chocolate and cakes in the tearoom." He smiled down at Pia and Abril. "Today, I wanted to share that memory and experience with you two. Do you like cakes and pastries?"

The children did little skips of happiness, and something in my throat caught while I followed the trio. How typical of Armand to omit mentioning that the hotel belonged to his father. *When and how will I ever repay Armand for all his gestures? God, please don't let me have AIDS so I can be with him. I'm so sick of worrying about Sergio and the future.*

On Friday morning, outside the Colichon y Cantela laboratory, I clutched Armand's hand like a little girl, about to cry. While the receptionist searched for our results in a fat folder, I prayed, *God, please let them be negative. Please.*

Armand's mouth registered white around the corners despite the brave front he was projecting.

Unlike the lab assistant in the US, the Peruvian receptionist smiled when she found our lab slips. "Congratulations, you two. You both tested negative."

"Ohhhh!" I jumped up to hug Armand, and he lifted me right off my feet to kiss me. "Not here." I looked around, embarrassed, but no one looked familiar.

We walked out of that lab on air, grinning like a pair of schoolchildren who had escaped the headmaster's whip.

In my bedroom an hour later, we fell upon the bed in a confused heap, mouths, hands, arms, legs seeking company. I smiled. It was the first time the ghost of Chirag hadn't intruded upon an intimate encounter. *How odd, yet how releasing.* Together, we were shy, bold, eager and reticent all at once as we undressed each other in an awkward and unpracticed symphony of passion.

"Wait, let me put my glasses somewhere safe. I break them all the time." Armand placed his glasses on Sergio's night table.

"I have stretch marks on my stomach," I whispered in total mortification.

"I know them from the beach, dummy. And I love them. I wanted to kiss each one, one by one, when I first spotted them."

"I never would have guessed. You were so good at hiding your true feelings."

"You needed time and space—and if that meant never, that was okay, too, but my interest in you was never platonic."

"Please be gentle with me. I haven't made love like this, ever."

"What d'you mean?"

"I mean, I never felt this with Sergio. That was the problem."

"Like how? Like this?" Armand kissed my nipple.

"Ahhh... yes." My eyes dropped. "I've never come with a guy," I whispered.

"Wait. You have two kids, but you've never come with a guy?"

"What does having kids have to do with it?"

"That was stupid. Sorry. But I won't come until you do."

"But that's so much pressure..."

"Not true. The truth is you don't know what making love feels like."

"Neither do you. Your brothel visit doesn't count."

"We'll learn together... beginning right now."

"So, how will you make me come?"

"You'll come if you forget I'm here and concentrate on you." He stared at me with his banana-leaf-green eyes as he rolled me on top of him. "Today, I want to caress your whole body until you relax." He cupped my breasts ever so gently and let them go. His lips traced the hollow line of my midriff until he kissed my stretch marks.

"Go down on me," I whispered. *What Sergio wouldn't have done to see me behave with this abandon and say those words.* But I couldn't think of Sergio right then. I had given him my whole life. It was my body. I had the right to feel pleasure without guilt.

"Okay, but close your eyes, and imagine you're lying naked in a summer garden... with the sun on your skin..."

Why is life so unpredictable? Why couldn't I have this connection to Sergio? Is it because he's more attracted to men than women?

"You're tensing up. What are you thinking?" Armand kissed my fingers.

"Sorry. I was thinking of Sergio and our disaster of a physical relationship. This is beyond any heaven I ever imagined... come kiss me, and don't stop."

"Listen to me." Armand took my chin. "I want to make you happy. Did I ever tell you why you attracted my attention in the Roosevelt?"

"No."

"It was because you always appeared super sad under the perfect clothes and makeup."

"Did I? I didn't know that."

"Yes. All the time. Then, on the day you reamed me, you said your husband had cancer, and I figured, 'Okay, that's why she's always sad.' But, on the first day I came to your house, you told me you guys aren't even together, and I got really confused. Of course, after you told me about the AIDS, I got it all. But what I wanted to say is your sadness felt like a reflection of my own. And I itched to wipe the sadness off your face."

"And why were *you* sad?" I traced a finger down his cheek.

"Because my family sucks. That's why I mention them so little. I don't have a mother or father, and I hate it."

I pulled him into my arms. "You have me," I whispered. "You'll always have me, like I have you."

48

NEAR CHRISTMAS OF 1991, I had spent eight months of bliss when Armand said, "When are you leaving for LA?"

"As soon as Carla's family secures her passport from the passport office."

"And you think taking her to LA is a good idea?"

"It's the only way I can leave the children and go with Serg to his doctor's appointments. He was the one who suggested she come along."

"Is he getting worse?"

"I'm sure he isn't getting better. He had another lung wash recently." I explained Sergio's special pneumonia to Armand.

"How horrible. I want to be mad at him for exposing you to AIDS, but mostly, I'm sorry for him."

"Yeah. Me too. My feelings for him are so mixed up. I don't even try to understand them anymore."

"You're leaving, and my mom is coming back from Europe." He pulled me close behind the locked door of my bedroom at ten p.m., far past the children's bedtime, so they would never know he was around.

"Ouch. What will she say if you tell her you're dating a woman nine years older, married, and with two kids?"

"With you gone, I'll spend a lot of time at home, so she won't notice the difference." Armand flung back the covers of my bed and snuggled in. "I love your bed because it smells of you."

"That sounds terrible. How does it smell?" I climbed in too.

"Spicy. Like cloves… blended with honeysuckle. It's a fresh, sweet, spicy, heavenly smell. Whenever I sleep in my bed at home, I try to recapture this smell in my imagination, but I never succeed."

"That fragrance is First by Van Cleef and Arpels. It's my favorite perfume right now."

"Have I told you I love you lately?" He pulled me to him.

I let myself melt in his arms, reflecting on how different my life was with Armand in it. He was the drug that took the edge off my worries. I still worried about Sergio, obsessed over the future, cried through each variation in Sergio's health, but it didn't hurt as much.

In Los Angeles, Sergio was eager to introduce me to a new member of the consulate, Magda León. "She's Jaime's niece. You'll love her."

My ears pricked up at the mention of Jaime. *Will the niece be as weird as Jaime and his mother?* Sergio invited her to lunch the next afternoon, leaving me to decide what to cook.

My immediate reaction to Magda was "Hey, you don't look anything like your uncle Jaime!" Magda had large, dark eyes in her white delicate-featured face.

"No. My father doesn't resemble his brother. Thank you for cooking. I live so far away from the consulate that I don't cook on weekdays."

"I've prepared *lomo saltado*. Do you like that?" Lomo saltado was sautéed beef prepared Peruvian style.

"I love it!"

Throughout lunch, I was struck by how normal Magda was compared to the strange duo of Jaime and his mother. As she focused on my kids and described her two children, I liked Magda despite my reservations.

After lunch, Sergio told Carla to take the kids to a nearby park and gave her money to buy them all ice cream at a neighborhood creamery. Once they left, he said, "I've told Magda my real diagnosis."

"Why?" I couldn't control my shock.

"For our safety. Someone here needs to come to my aid and contact you in case of an emergency. I would rather that person be Magda and not another member of the consulate."

"Noor." Magda's voice was full of understanding. "I totally get your secrecy issue, but Sergio is right. Meet me for lunch tomorrow at a restaurant near here. My treat. We can go over some basic planning."

The next afternoon, Magda said, "Has he told you how he got AIDS? He never brings it up, and I don't ask, but I have my suspicions."

"No. He pretends he got it in the Far East before he met me. As if we could have sex for two years and have two kids without any of us getting it too."

"Did you know my Uncle Jaime is gay?"

"No! I know I don't like him, but I can never articulate why."

"I wouldn't be surprised if that's the source of Sergio's infection."

"Why, does Jaime have it?"

"I don't know. But have you ever been to my grandma's house, where he lives?"

I shuddered. "That was one skin crawling experience."

"Did you see any male help around?"

"They were all male. His security guards, the cook, the cook's helper."

"I haven't told Sergio this, but my father hates Jaime. He told me that Jaime has sex with all his staff. Jaime developed a taste for men after a posting in Algiers. Men and heroin—he does both. And maybe he liked men before too, but after that posting he began boasting about it. And Sergio met him awfully young."

"Oh, Magda. Why doesn't that surprise me? I find Jaime creepy as all hell, but Sergio loves him, so I don't get in the middle. He made Sergio study to become a diplomat."

"Either way, I've come to love Sergio because he's such a decent soul. I don't know what he sees in my uncle, but whatever." She took out a folded note sheet from her purse. "Here is all my information. Write to me or call me anytime you want. I will do the same. You have me here in LA to count on."

I left Magda with my head in a whirl over all she had revealed to me about Jaime León. I wished I could strangle Jaime if he was responsible for Sergio's AIDS. And alternately, I wanted to strangle Sergio for ruining our lives.

But that evening, when Sergio came home from work, all my anger melted at the sight of his hollow eyes, his gaunt face, his deathly complexion.

"Where are the children?" He put down his briefcase in the living room.

"Out with Carla. Do you want a drink? Or something to eat?"

"No. I need to lie down. I'm dead on my feet."

In the bedroom, I settled on the bed next to Sergio and folded my legs under me. "You got AIDS from Jaime, didn't you? You need to tell me the truth right now."

I didn't think Sergio could get any paler, but he did. "Did Magda tell you that?"

"No. But she told me she suspected it."

Sergio couldn't meet my eyes. "I probably caught this in 1986, after we got back from India."

"Serg, you better tell me the whole story right now. I married you even after Isabel told me you liked men *and* women, but this isn't what I bargained for, nor is it what I deserved. Don't you think you owe me an explanation?"

Sergio teared up. "If I tell you, all you'll do is judge me, and I can't take it."

I wiped his tears, my own eyes filling up. "I won't. I promise. Tell me what happened, already. Okay?"

"Remember that car accident I had after you burst the bathroom pipes in my mother's house?"

"Yes. I remember how your mom wouldn't let me see you. You were in her bedroom."

"The day after the pipe burst, I was so aggravated, I went to Jaime's to complain. And he said a line that sealed my fate. He said, 'Sergio, maturity is the difference between knowing what you can change and accepting what you can't. Come back tomorrow morning. I'll organize a cheer-up-Sergio party.' I pointed out that it was a Monday, and Jaime said, 'Exactly. No one needs to know you went to a party. Tell your secretary you'll come in to work in the afternoon.'"

"So is Jaime your lover?"

"No. But his house was the scene of my first gay experience."

Sergio's confession reminded me of Armand's dad sending him to a brothel, but I couldn't tell Sergio that. "Yes. Magda told me about Jaime's preference for young males."

"And who told Magda?"

"Her father. He hates Jaime."

"Yes. He also hates how their mother turns a blind eye on all Jaime does."

"Who told you that?"

"Jaime did, but he interpreted it as jealousy."

"So, what happened at the party? What did he do to you?"

"I remember going to his house that morning. I recall him offering me a cigarette out of an exquisite ivory box and laughing when I said I didn't smoke anymore. He lit the cigarette anyway and handed it to me. In his elegant living room, five young men loitered stark naked. I'm convinced that cigarette was laced with drugs because my last memory is of Jaime patting a white powder on the erection of one of the men. The next thing I remember is Jaime injecting me with something to wake me up. He said, 'Time to wrap it up, my boy.' All I recollect after that is ramming my car into a cement post in the foreign office parking lot."

"Oh, Serg." I squeezed his forearm.

"Please don't condemn me. I'm already pretty condemned."

I wiped my eyes, wanting to say a thousand things, but all I said was "When did you suspect something might be wrong with you? I know you suspected it, because otherwise you wouldn't have asked for that AIDS test when you did."

"I think a year and a half later. I would get these inexplicable bouts of fatigue. But I had nowhere to go to research what might be wrong with me, so I requested my primary to prescribe me an STD test, but of course, those tests were clean since they didn't test me for HIV. By the time we moved to the new house, I knew something was definitely wrong, but by then, I didn't want to know what because I was so scared. My sixth sense told me it wasn't cancer. Then the weight loss began, and I went into denial, focused on getting a divorce, contemplating starting over. You know the rest."

"Does Jaime know what you have?"

"Yes. Whatever he is, he is the one father figure I have."

"Oh, Serg, how can you like him when he is the cause of all this?" I wiped my eyes.

"Because he isn't. I made a choice, and I'm paying for it. I knew Jaime. I guessed his party would involve sex. But I didn't have the will to refuse since I hadn't had sex in such a long time."

I glanced away, my unshed tears blurring the view of someone else's backyard from our bedroom window. *Would Sergio have gotten AIDS if I hadn't fought with him after Abril's birth? If I had provided him with sex? It all boiled down to an "if," the most volatile word in the English language.*

I woke up the next day burning with hatred for Jaime León. My anger only escalated because I couldn't tell Carla a thing, so it brewed inside me like black tea on a slow boil. The more days passed, the more determined I became to confront Jaime when I arrived back in Lima. But I didn't burden Sergio with my anger since I knew it would upset him. Already, my confronting Sergio in the first place must have upset him more than enough, because when we visited his AIDS lung specialist the following Friday, he said Sergio's viral load was high.

"Has he been stressed lately?" Dr. Akil asked.

"Yes," I said, not letting Sergio reply.

I liked his doctor a lot because I could tell he really cared for Sergio and gave him extra time, always asking him about Peru and telling him about his own childhood spent in Jordan before his parents emigrated to America.

"Well, he needs to rest and increase his AZT intake again." Dr. Akil gave Sergio a stern look.

"I can't," Sergio said. "It gives me too much nausea and headaches."

"Increase it a quarter pill at a time." The doctor rummaged through his desk drawer. "Here is a pill cutter a med rep gave me."

On Monday, the doctor's recommendation was cruelly proved to us when Sergio left for work and came home an hour later.

"What happened? Are you okay?" I took his hand. "Come sit in the bedroom, and tell me what happened." The bedroom was our private place, since the children either watched TV in the living room or else, in the studio apartment Sergio had rented for Carla's use.

"I can't." Sergio's eyes pooled with tears. "I had a diarrhea attack I couldn't control. I have to take a shower and go back to work."

"Christ. I'll take care of your dirty clothes. Do you have anything to control the diarrhea?"

"Only AZT. I'll take two pills right now. From now on, it'll be safer if I wear adult diapers. I can't risk this happening to me when I am attending work meetings."

I nodded because I knew that if I opened my mouth, I would cry, and Sergio didn't need that. After he showered, I said, "Let's go to the supermarket right now and buy you those diapers. Wearing one will help you feel less vulnerable."

Yet despite all his health limitations, the following weekend, Sergio insisted on a trip to Disneyland to entertain the children for not participating more in their lives.

"Then I'll drive," I concluded. "And this is not a discussion. You can follow the map and direct me."

49

AT THE END OF THE second week of February 1992, my heart felt broken when Pia, Abril, Carla, and I boarded an airplane to fly back to Lima, leaving Sergio at the LAX Airport. To keep the children distracted during the long flight, Carla had packed several photo albums of our time in America, and she pulled one out. Grateful for her help, I closed my eyes. With effort, I controlled tears as I remembered Sergio's bird-frail form standing alone on the tarmac, waving us goodbye. I couldn't imagine his loneliness, driving home to an empty apartment. *Does he know his nose looks bonier than the last time we visited? Or his cheeks hollower? Or his calves more emaciated?* Even his shirt collars ran two sizes too loose for him, and it was heartrending to watch.

Next to me, Pia thrust a picture of Abril's dizzy spell in the giant teacups from *Alice in Wonderland* right into my face, making me open my eyes. She laughed because she never got dizzy. To counter her, Abril thrust a picture of Pia's face of fear in the elevator of the haunted house, which we had visited that time around.

She bragged, "I wasn't scared in the slightest, but Pia was."

"No, *ya*?" replied Pia. "I wasn't scared of the ghosts. I got upset because the elevator fell."

"Stop it!" I scolded. "We have to fly for hours and hours, and I'm not doing it with you two buzzing in my ears like a pair of angry bees."

"Look." Carla drew their attention. "Here's that wolf from *Red Riding Hood* kissing your mamá's hand." They all laughed at a photo of Carla frantically licking a dripping triple-scoop ice cream cone. But all that those photos did for me was remind me of what a fabulous photographer Sergio was. Even sick and exhausted, he still knew the exact moment in which to snap a shot that most reflected the mood.

I closed my eyes again, thinking back to my lunch with Magda. As she had walked me to the apartment, I had said, "Magda, is it my imagination, or are there a significant number of gay men in the Latin country foreign services?"

"No. You're not imagining it. But most marry to hide their true leanings because South America in particular, and Latins in general, are so homophobic. Becoming diplomats is their ticket to living in far-off countries where no one is watching or judging their extracurricular activities."

"And do you think that's why Sergio married me?"

Magda placed a hand on my forearm. "You know, it might have been the initial reason, but I think Sergio really loves you now. He talks of you all the time."

I laughed a bitter laugh. "Then his love must be new, because before his diagnosis, he served me divorce papers."

Magda had shaken her head. "Don't be so hard on him, Noor. Love is a very complicated emotion. I'm sure he has always loved you at some level. I see it in his eyes when he mentions you."

Thus trapped in my private labyrinth, I reflected on how everyone's stressors were unique to them alone. For example, my lifelong stressor of being a half-caste was the ultimate nonissue in Lima, where only the overeducated, such as Nila's professor husband, knew of the Hindu-Muslim conflict. The rest of Peruvian humanity couldn't locate India on a world map with two hands and a flashlight—not because they were stupid but because India, like Australia, was too far away to impact anyone in Peru. The same as South America, for me, as a child, had been a big green chunk on the world map in a children's book, dotted with little figures wearing cowboy boots and Mexican sombrero hats—until my mother had forced me into a Span-ish degree, and I'd found myself immersed head over heels in a culture I had eventually married into. That was how my secrets were too. On the sur-face, nobody cared about them because nobody knew what they were. Yet they existed inside me like geographical fault lines, cracks no one else saw but liable to erupt without notice.

Eleven hours later, at Jorge Chavez Airport, my mind was a yo-yo as I greeted the Bustos clan, dressed in their Sunday best to fetch Carla. We spent twenty minutes sorting out baggage, then I arranged for a taxi to take the Bustoses to their home with Pia and Abril. Carla knew how much I craved time alone with Armand, so she offered to keep the girls at her house for two days since her eight-year-old sister, Maria, was also out of school for the summer. Our excuse to the Bustos family would be that Dulci was gone on her annual vacation and wouldn't be back for a week yet. I needed time to clean the house, grocery shop, and attend to dirty laundry.

I said, "You two be good and don't fight with Maria, or else Carla's mom will tell me, and she won't invite you guys to play with her again."

After they left, I dared to scan the crowd for Armand. He stood in a far corner, a head above the rest as he leaned into his shadow on a wall, arms crossed. He waited until I saw him, ambled over, then embraced me off my feet.

"I missed you," I whispered into his neck, nose burrowed in the familiar smells of paint thinner, linseed oil, and turpentine on his striped cotton shirt. "I missed you each minute of every day."

He put me down. "Twice, I had nightmares that he was worse and you would never come back."

My eyes narrowed. "He *is* worse, and that isn't even the half of it. This time, he finally confessed where he got AIDS." And right there, in the middle of the airport, I told Armand of Jaime León. Emotion made me grip Armand's arm. "I can't wait to confront the slimy bastard. I hope he dies a miserable death."

Armand just picked up my suitcases without comment. On the drive home in his station wagon, he held my hand and pressed it to his chest. "You're wrong about confronting this Jaime guy. Don't do it."

"Why? I want to eat him alive."

"Because doing it won't change one single detail. It'll only complicate Sergio's relationship with him. I can't believe I am defending Sergio, but there it is. As sick as he is, he doesn't need another problem on his hands."

"I don't care. I'm doing it anyway."

"Hey, I've never known you to be illogical. Tell me one upside to confronting Jaime."

Armand's brutal objectivity hit me like a bucket of icy water, but still I resisted. "I'll think about it."

"Promise me you won't do it without telling me."

"Fine, fine. Now, can we please buy food on the way home? I'm so hungry."

"I already did that. It's at the house."

"How did you get in?"

"I called Frida when I figured your idiot brother-in-law wouldn't be home. She lent me the keys."

On my patio in Valle Hermoso, Armand leapt out of the car to block the front door. "Close your eyes. Don't look until I say so." He guided me into the house.

Inside, the scent of paradise hit my brain receptors like a starburst. What appeared to be a thousand roses in yellows, pinks, oranges, and reds were displayed in every receptacle imaginable, including cooking pots when Armand had run out of vases.

"Where did you buy so many roses? You must have spent a fortune."

"I didn't. They're from the Católica rose farms. They were so cheap, I bought you twelve dozen."

"Wait a minute. You bought me one hundred forty-four roses?"

"Yes." Armand dragged me into the kitchen. "Open the fridge."

I saw enormous wedges of Camembert, Brie, and Gorgonzola, my favorite cheeses, lining the top shelf. The rest of the fridge was stuffed with Italian prosciutto ham, Russian sausage, crabmeat, a duck to roast, and every fruit and vegetable I loved.

"I didn't buy bread because Salvador stocked us up from his dad's bakery in San Isidro." Armand fished out a carrot roll from a cellophane bag full of flavored petit rolls on the countertop, popping it into his mouth. "Open the freezer."

The freezer held my, Pia's, and Abril's favorite ice creams from the Italian delicatessen, Quatro D. "Oh, amor. No one has ever welcomed me like this in my life." I pulled his head down to kiss him.

In the bedroom upstairs, I smelled more roses. There, Armand had arranged three vases with the flowers.

"Can I place one vase on my nightstand?" I rested my head on his chest. "I want to smell them as I wake up."

"No." He steered me to sit on the bed. "Close your eyes."

I heard him push the latticed doors to my walk-in closet. He came back to unbutton my shirt and freed the ends tucked inside my jeans. I loved his calloused hands with pronounced knuckles, his cuticles stained with the paints used that week. They touched me, cool and dry in contrast to the rising heat in my body as he traced the concave line of my spine and unclasped my bra.

He cupped my breasts to bury his nose in the crevice. "How can I love you more than I already do?"

"Can I open my eyes?" I embraced his head and smelled the shampooed warmth of his hair.

"Not yet. I want you to lie back on the bed." He gave my body a gentle push.

I let myself fall, arms outstretched as the fresh coolness of cotton sheets billowed to cradle my weight. Soft things like feathers drifted down.

"Open your eyes."

I fingered white rose petals on my chest while he bent to the floor.

"Here. Here are the roses for your nightstand."

Nestled in Sergio's Japanese ceramic vase were eight of the brightest red roses I had ever seen.

"Oh my God. They're the cornelian red of the beaks of wild parrots from my Calcutta childhood."

Armand straddled my legs to reach the nightstand.

I kissed the hollow in his neck. "Don't move," I whispered. I unbuttoned his shirt and ran my fingers over his erection pushing on the zipper of his jeans.

"Lord. Take my pants off. I can't wait."

I obliged, and he pushed my head downward and put himself into my mouth. Then he withdrew, gripping my underarms to pull me further up on the bed.

In a dreamlike state, I directed his hardness with my hand as he paused to spread my legs then sank in with a cry.

"Do you know how much I missed you?" He nibbled my earlobes and dug down while I spasmed to accommodate him, body arching. The bells of the Jesuit school chimed six times to herald the evening. "How can I live without you?"

Armand pushed to meet my thrust, my breasts pressing against the film of perspiration on his chest. The smell of the rose petals snared in between us mixed with my musky, brandywine fragrance of Must de Cartier.

"I want you to come." He moved his hips in the way he had discovered to please me.

"I'm coming." I arched backward. "Come now!"

He pushed faster and deeper until my legs closed in around him, ending in a slow shudder. "God, I love you." He dropped to shield my body with his own.

We lay in each other's silence as I nestled in the crook of his shoulder, arm flung across his stomach. In the near distance, the outline of the Jesuit school dissolved into the dusk. A mauve moon peeked out from behind the bare brown hill in front of my house and stared at us through the French doors. Beyond the bedroom balcony, the leaves of the magenta bougainvillea drained their green to the silvery pallor of slumber.

It was dark when Armand said, "Oh! I have another present for you."

"Another present? You'll ruin me."

Armand switched on my nightstand lamp. "Close your eyes. I have to fetch it from your walk-in closet, so don't cheat, okay?" He bounded off the bed. "Okay, open your eyes."

Poised on the bed, an oil painting of my face stared back at me.

"It's incredible," I whispered. "You've even captured the sadness in my gaze."

"Naaah. You say that because you're a layman. We'll see what my painting teacher says once I hand it in. I painted it all summer for my portrait assignment."

"So, can I have it?"

"Of course, but at the end of the school year."

"You did it from memory?"

"Jeez, no. I swiped two of your photo albums before you left."

"Aren't you supposed to paint someone in person for a portrait?"

"Yes, but I wanted to paint you, and you were gone."

"You know, I begged my mother to paint my portrait, yet with all her talent, she never did. She painted Sergio, though. She loves everybody more than she loves me."

"Why do you say that?"

"Because my mother's emotions toward me are ridden with a guilt she won't admit for dumping me as a baby. So instead, she's forever emphasizing how I am wrong and she is right. Trying to prove what a fabulous human being she is… so she painted Sergio to underline that."

"My mother didn't ditch me, but she was also never there for me." Armand stared at the silhouette of the Jesuit school bell tower off in the distance, etched against the darkening sky. "I realized that the day you pulled that all-nighter for my art project. I had the best tutors money could buy, but I can't recall one homework assignment my mother sat through with me. Now her game has become to share all holidays and birthdays with us because she's gone for such long periods of time. The more she's gone, the more she insists we spend holidays together, as if we're one perfectly united family. As if the rest of the year doesn't count." Armand propped the portrait on the Indian dhurrie rug at the foot of my bed. Then he gave me a guilty look.

"What? What are you hiding?"

"Weeelll." Armand emitted a lengthy sigh.

I angled myself up on one elbow. "Come on. Out with it."

"It's not my fault I haven't done it." Armand was stalling, and I knew it.

"Amor, if you don't actually tell me what you need, I can't help you, now, can I?"

"I have to write an art history paper on mastabas, and I have two days left to do it." He did his best guilty little boy impersonation.

"What the hell is a mastaba?"

"It's what the Egyptians used to build before pyramids."

"And?"

"And I couldn't do it because the only book the Católica library has on mastabas is a fat archeology book in *English*. With my dyslexia, an English book is ten times harder for me to read."

"Well, thank God for small mercies. Do you have the book?"

"Yes. It's in my backpack."

"Go get it."

"Shit!" I exclaimed when he handed me the three-inch-thick book. "That's not a fat book. That's an obese book. And you need this paper for when?"

"I have to hand it in the day after tomorrow."

I sighed. "Then I'd better start it, shouldn't I?"

"No. Read it tomorrow when I'm gone to school. Right now, I want you to stop talking and kiss me."

I placed the book on my night table and sought the refuge of Armand's arms. How strange relationships and our reasons for having them were. I loved Armand because he protected and loved me, like Dadu had when he was alive, and when my baba lived with us in Calcutta until he left me, married again, and relegated me for a brand-new family. Armand loved me because I paid him the attention he had never received from his family members. And Sergio—he had loved the idea of me because I had represented the normalcy he craved to show to the world. But he loved men more. And it hadn't helped him to lose his father when he was so very young, nor endure the abuse he had at the hands of his paternal aunt. *With this history, how will I build healthy parameters in the heads of poor Pia and Abril if Sergio dies? If no cure for AIDS is found soon?*

50

Two weeks after returning from Los Angeles, Pia and Abril went back to school. That was my time to either confront Jaime León or let it go, like Armand wanted me to. I was in two minds about it when, on a Tuesday afternoon, heading out of the bedroom to do the afternoon carpool, the phone rang.

"Noor?" Sergio's voice crackled from Los Angeles. "Can you hear me?"

"Yes." Through the French doors, I watched a swallowtail butterfly land on a vibrant-pink bougainvillea bloom cascading off the perimeter wall.

"I'm coming home."

"To Lima? Why? We just left you a couple of weeks ago."

"Because I found out this morning I've lost my health insurance. I have to come back to Lima for good."

My legs buckled next to my nightstand.

"Noor. Noor? Did you hear me?"

"Do you think Magda told on you?"

"No, of course not. She would never do that. This isn't related to her. This has to do with the health insurance company renewing their contract. They doubled their premium because the seven terminally ill diplomats, including me, have drained their coffers. Therefore, I suspect this was the foreign office liaison worker's perfect opportunity to ask them exactly what ailed the seven sick diplomats. It's my luck I'm caught right in the middle of it."

"And no law will protect you?"

"Not in the Peruvian justice system."

"But how will we afford treatment for you in Peru on your 'at-home' salary? Wouldn't it be better if you stayed in LA and received the best treatment?" I shoved my hand under my body to avoid biting a raw hangnail, well aware that my concern was rooted in his welfare as well as my own.

"On my salary of nine thousand five hundred dollars a month? My last hospital stay cost twelve thousand dollars. Plus, Dr. Akil tells me that in the US, by law, I would be taken to the nearest emergency room if, for example, I fainted on the street. I would receive mandatory treatment, and afterward, as a foreign diplomat, I'd have to pay for it. Without health insurance, my doctor says the hospital would go after our house in Lima for payment, and if I default as a diplomat, it'll reach the newspapers."

"So what will happen now?" I struggled to my feet and fell flat on my back on the bed.

"From today on, I am responsible for the cost of each AZT pill I take. At ten dollars a pill, that's sixty dollars a day for two pills every eight hours. Multiplied by thirty, along with the seven other pills my doctors have ordered for a hundred other symptoms and conditions and side effects I suffer from, the sum is horrifying. I'm so scared, I can't think straight. But I have to pull myself together and go back to work. I only came home to make sure this call was completely private. Oh, and here's more bad news. The loss of our health insurance terminates the fifty thousand dollars in life insurance you would have received upon my death from unnatural causes. I'm sorry."

"Oh, Serg. Don't be silly." My eyes prickled. "Right now, we have to determine how best to buy you AZT." Since Sergio's diagnosis two years ago, AZT was still the only medication to delay the reproduction of the AIDS virus. No amount of international pharmaceutical research had yet produced a better option. "Could we buy AZT cheaper in bulk?" My heart thudded.

"I doubt it."

The cuckoo clock in the upstairs hallway shrilled its midday song. "I—I have to go." My throat hurt to swallow. "Or I'll be late for the carpool. Can you call back?"

"No. Let's not rack up the phone bill. I'll call you tomorrow, once I know my flight schedule."

On the way to the school, my biggest realization was that I couldn't confront Jaime León anymore. With Sergio in such deep trouble, he would need every friend he had, and I couldn't let my own emotional satisfaction take precedence over his welfare.

On the ride home, in the rearview mirror, I watched Pia and Abril prattle with their carpool schoolmates, their very innocence my cruel reminder that the world hadn't stopped turning because Sergio's and my universe had collapsed.

At home, I waited for the children to skip into the kitchen to be served lunch by Dulci before I headed for the porch. Freeing my ponytail, I kicked off my sandals, soothed by the perfume of jasmine. Dulci knew Sergio was coming home. *But what will I tell Armand tonight?* I threw my head back on a canvas cushion and willed myself not to cry, fearing the children would catch me. *Could Dr. Ritter manage Sergio's symptoms without AZT pills?*

Time stopped until Dulci appeared around the far corner of the porch to spray water on a riot of magenta, mauve, and tangerine bougainvillea topping the perimeter wall of my colorful garden. Didima's wristwatch told me I had eaten up three hours in total limbo, and my body tensed.

"Hey, Duls. Can you start the children's bath, please?"

Dulci jumped. "Señora Noor. How come you're not in bed reading?" She dropped the garden hose. "If he loves you, he'll understand."

Dulci, of course, meant Armand. In her world of soap operas, the day's episode ended with a perfect segue into the next episode. But, my next episode was a blank. For instance, *What will I say to Pia and Abril once I walk into their bathroom? "Hey, guys, you won't go to LA for your fall break. Maybe you'll never go back to LA ever, or Disneyland, which you can't stop talking of."* They were seven and six. *How can I tell them their papá will come home and become sicker and sicker and I can't do anything for him?* And I had yet to factor in Armand's existence in the midst of it all. I glanced at my garden, so absurdly bright and beautiful compared to my reality.

Outside the children's bathroom, I pasted on a smile and swung into the warm, humid aroma of Johnson's baby shampoo.

One look at my daughters, and I knew if I brought up Sergio's return, they would sense my distress with that uncanny radar children seemed to possess.

Hearing me come in, Pia cracked open an eye and waved a dripping hand.

I kissed Abril's dark, wet head.

"*Hola, amorcito.*"

"Mamá," Abril said in Spanish. She wagged a wet finger between her sister and herself. "Why don't you ever get in with us?"

"Where would I fit, amor?" I replied, also in Spanish.

"Hey, Pia, time to get out." Dulci pushed aside the shower curtain and extended a pair of fluffy pink towels. "Abril will catch a cold."

"I can't." Pia skipped in place. "I have shampoo in my hair."

"Nonsense." Dulci hid a smile.

"If you come on out this second, I'll sing you an extra song in bed," I negotiated, desperate to talk to Armand.

In answer, Pia bent and slapped the bathwater, splashing it hard.

"Mamá!" wailed Abril.

"Pia, *basta!*" I scolded. God, they were so damn innocent. *How could I tell them anything?*

Pia laughed and climbed out to rain on the bath rug. She grabbed a towel from Dulci's arm and draped it around herself.

"Come here. Let me dry your hair." I pulled Pia to me. "You'll take forever." I massaged Pia's head with the second towel. "Hey, stand still, or your tangles will hurt." I seized Pia's hairbrush from the marble countertop. "Here, aim the dryer to your head while I brush."

The bathroom suffused with the smell of hot damp hair while my thoughts torpedoed in opposite directions. Each time I processed my phone call with Sergio, yet another implication hit me. Now it was the termination of the built-in life insurance Sergio had lost along with his health insurance coverage. *What will I do without those fifty thousand dollars if Sergio dies?* We didn't have any savings. That was why Sergio had opted to build the house piecemeal but mortgage-free by having us live with his horrid mother for two endless years.

Perhaps I can secure a job to bolster Sergio's income in Lima? A tightness set in at the nape of my neck. I would phone Dick McBee at the Roosevelt the next day. *Maybe they can rehire me as a substitute teacher? How will I tackle the reality avalanching onto my shoulders?*

After their baths, I crawled into bed with Abril, who smelled of baby soap, Jean Naté body splash, and blow-dried hair. Ignoring my headache, I sang the children six songs each from the *Sound of Music*, encouraging them to sing along with me. Afterward, I kissed each one goodnight and crept out of their room. I knew Armand was in the kitchen the minute I tiptoed around the sharp U of the stairwell. No one slurped water louder than he did.

At the kitchen table, Armand held out his glass for Dulci to pour more water into from a silver pitcher. Their shadows merged in a gray paper cutout on the cream marble floor. Both glanced up as I walked in, squeaking the kitchen door.

"Hola, amor," he whispered. "Dulci says you put pisco and cloves in the *carapulcra*. I swear you cook Peruvian food better than my mother does." Carapulcra was Armand's favorite Peruvian highland dish of desiccated mountain potatoes in peanut sauce.

"How was school today?"

"I painted a still life all afternoon and handed in the paper you wrote on Catholic art in the Middle Ages. If my Art History professor ever catches wind of who writes my papers, I'll be expelled."

"He won't." I remembered the homework Sergio had done for me once upon a time, long ago.

"Señora Noor, can I heat you carapulcra?" Dulci tapped her forearm with an index finger. "Shouldn't you eat at least one spoonful of food today?"

"I can't, Duls. I'm so upset, it hurts to even swallow."

"Then, can I go do my homework?" Dulci was only in the ninth grade, despite being twenty-one years old, due to her sporadic education until coming to Lima.

"Of course. Go do it." Everybody except I could attend school, aspire to degrees, and move forward in life. How unbelievable it would be if I had a project to finish, homework to do, a paper to write, and that was my paramount problem. *Why have I never guessed that when I help Pia, Abril, Dulci, or Armand with homework, it's my own truncated dream I'm trying to resurrect? My own aspirations I fulfill through them?*

Armand waited for Dulci to leave. "What's upsetting you?"

I closed my eyes and clutched my head at the temples.

"What is it?" Armand dropped his fork and gripped the edge of the kitchen table. "Please don't tell me you have to go back to Los Angeles."

"It's worse."

"Amor. What could be worse?" Armand forgot to keep his voice down.

"Shhh." I put a finger to my lips. "You'll wake up the children." I told Armand the chilling news about Sergio's circumstances and the precarity of his remaining in the US.

Armand rubbed his eyes, trying, like me, to absorb it all. At last, he ventured, "When does he arrive?"

"I'll know tomorrow. But whatever that date is, I'll have to go to Los Angeles without the children to help him pack up."

"Why?"

"Because he's too weak to do it on his own."

"So what does that mean for us?"

"I've asked myself that question all day, and I don't have an answer." I placed my elbows on the table to support my aching head. "I don't know." I looked back up. "All I know is I want to be in your arms right now."

Armand got out of his chair so quickly the water bubbles inside his glass on the kitchen table rocked to the surface. "Get up." He scooped me into his arms. As he climbed the stairs, I hid my face in the crook between his neck and shoulder, touching the warmth of him, smelling the lavender of the soap he must have used to take a shower at his mom's home that morning.

In the bedroom, he placed me on the bed and switched off the nightstand lamp. In the darkness, he held me for a long time, letting me cry. "Sleep," he whispered, kissing my forehead. "You need the rest. Tomorrow will be another day."

51

Four days later, Armand and I sat down to dinner at the kitchen table, both pretending it was another regular evening in our lives. "How was school today?" I served myself the carapulcra Dulci had prepared for Armand. *I want to hug you. I want to scream I can't stand that this is our very last dinner together. I want to break down and cry.*

"We spent the day outdoors painting whatever we wanted."

"And what did you choose?" *Keep it together because stating the obvious won't solve anything.*

"I painted a bunch of roses up close at the rose farm. I knew you'd like that."

My throat constricted, and I drank water to ease the pain. "You know me so well." *How will I face losing you? I can't stand it. God, please help me.*

Upstairs in the bedroom, we undressed like an old married couple.

Armand caught my arm. "Hey, so will you see me with him back? This must be the fifth time I've asked, but you never answer me."

I dimmed my bed lamp and got under the covers. "I can't." I faced the cold reality at last. "What will I say to him?"

"So basically, we're done. This is it for us. That's what you're saying, isn't it?" Armand got into bed beside me.

I nodded, rubbing my forehead.

"And you're going to let him get away with it. Like he got away with getting AIDS and nearly giving it to you."

"Amor, are you going to let our last memory together be a fight?"

"Easy for you to say. I'm not leaving you. You're leaving me."

"Amor, I'm not *leaving* you. But this is Sergio's home. He is the father of my children, and he needs my help. I can't not give it to him."

"So I'm getting the heave-ho."

"Amor, do you think I can live without you? But I need time to figure it out."

"Promise me you won't drop me and forget I exist."

In the dimness, my tears spilled as I pulled him to me. "Shut up and make love to me, okay?" I whispered. "Please. Make me forget tomorrow is three hours away."

"Switch off the lamp. Let me see your face by moonlight. I want to remember your body bathed in it."

Two hours later, after Armand left, I cried myself to sleep, knowing I had no way of seeing him with Sergio in the house. Neither Armand nor I had cell phones, and during the hours I did the children's carpool, which could have been my window to see him, Armand was miles away, attending university. I saw no way around those obstacles right then.

The next morning, at six o'clock, Pia threw herself on my bed with, "Why, Mamá, why? Why do you have to go to Los Angeles today? How will I celebrate my birthday tomorrow without you? Are you sure we can't come with you? Can't you leave on Monday, when I'm in school and my birthday is over?"

"Will you go to Disneyland without us?" interrupted Abril.

"Of course not, amor." I opened my arms to Abril. "I have to pack. Papá's too sick to do it alone. But next Friday, when the two of you come home from school, we'll be back here already. And let me tell you the bonus." I held my hand out to Pia. "I'll bring you two birthday presents instead of one for missing your birthday."

"Can you also bring me lots of Häagen-Dazs ice cream? Bring me orange-cream popsicles. They're my favorite."

"Amor." I laughed. "How can I bring back ice cream? It'll melt into a huge mess."

"Then what will you bring me?" insisted Pia.

"I'll buy two packets of every candy I see at Ralph's?"

"Plus two birthday presents?"

"Yes."

At eight o'clock in the evening, I dropped the children at my mother-in-law's and raced to pick up Armand from outside his mother's home. He would bring the car back to Valle Hermoso and park it in my garage. Leaving it at the airport was out of the question since the Shining Path terrorists' target selection for bombing was random. They didn't care if they killed civilians or government officials. They were happy as long as they killed someone to reach the newspaper headlines.

At the airport, check-in complete, Armand pulled me to him, pressing my head to his chest. "He won't separate us," he whispered into my hair.

I pictured a previous embrace in a dark South Extension back alley. Chirag had been eighteen, and I, seventeen, when he said, "Nothing will ever come between our love." Today, at thirty, it was impossible to be that naïve. *But what right do I have to besmirch Armand's hopes with my cynicism?* I lifted my face for him to kiss me.

I joined the immigration line, dry-eyed and dry throated. In my last glimpse of Armand, his head was bent under the harsh phosphorescent airport illumination, left hand swatting something on his right forearm. Desperate to exchange one final glance, I stalled the line, willing him to meet my eyes. We exchanged a fleeting wave, and I was gone.

What can I do with this feeling of my heart breaking in two? One piece for Armand and the other for Sergio? It was always excruciatingly painful to see Sergio, thinner, more deteriorated than the time before. *Can I confess to him about Armand? Would he understand? Why, we haven't been together for years—plus, wasn't Sergio the one to reject me during our makeup sex sojourn two Januarys ago?* But deep inside, I knew he wouldn't be happy to know of Armand. And I couldn't hurt him while he was so sick. *But what about my heart? Why do my needs always have to get shelved... for Didima's benefit, my mother's benefit, for Sergio's benefit, for the children's benefit? Who takes care of what I feel? No one.* I had to play everyone else's caretaker, but only Armand took care of me, and I was losing him. *Why is life so unfair? Always?*

GERANIUMS

52

SERGIO AND I LANDED IN Lima at the end of March.

From the back seat of his brother's car, Sergio said, "Does Lima look dirtier than when I left it two years ago, or is it just me?"

Carlos smiled. "Each time I travel outside Peru, I daydream of how Lima could use a good rainstorm to wash it clean, but of course, it never happens."

I took Sergio's hand and whispered, "You did buy a reasonable supply of AZT pills, right?"

"I didn't have to. Once my doctors heard of my health insurance debacle, they pooled resources and collected sample pills in the little time I had left. I suspect Dr. Akil, my lung specialist, bought his contribution at a pharmacy, but when I asked, he insisted they were 'samples.' I'll miss those doctors."

"So how many AZT pills do you have?"

"Three hundred and twenty-one."

"That's so little if you take six a day."

"I'm trying not to think of it."

At home in Valle Hermoso, I said, "I've fixed up the study downstairs for you because who knows how long you'll have the strength to tackle the stairs."

Sergio's eyes widened. "What? No! I want to be upstairs with you."

"I know, Serg, but upstairs, you'll have to climb in and out of our bathtub.

The study bathroom has a shower stall. What'll we do if you slip and fall and break a bone?" What I didn't say was how fearful I felt of living with Sergio again. It was inexplicable, since in Los Angeles, I had shared a bed with Sergio and both the children and I had used common wet surfaces with him, wearing flip-flops for protection. However, the permanence of Lima brought to mind every caution specified by the doctors in the United States, and those of Dr. Ritter, who currently believed that trace amounts of the virus were present in a patient's semen, saliva, sweat, and even tears. All it took was one virus to touch one scratch on another person's body, and the deed was done.

The following afternoon, Nila came by, vociferous in her insistence that Sergio be seen at a private clinic by a doctor other than Dr. Ritter. "He doesn't have a bedside manner," she said. "You have the savings for private care. Use it to receive the best treatment possible."

Upon her departure, I confronted Sergio. "Serg, you have what? Five thousand? Ten thousand in savings? How long will that pay for private care? Dr. Ritter has never failed you, so talk to him first."

During Sergio's first checkup, I brought up the subject, and Dr. Ritter said, "Sergio—at some point, you will get worse, and we have to think of your hospital care. I am linked to both public and private care in Lima, since apart from being the lead oncologist at the Clínica Internacional, I am also the director of oncology and infectious diseases at the Rebagliati State Hospital. Therefore, treatmentwise, I can assure you that any private clinic, including the Clínica Internacional, doesn't offer one extra benefit except the perk of a better location and better room service. As such, you would be smarter not to fritter what little money you have on private care, because as soon as your money runs out, private clinics will kick you out within the hour, and that won't serve you well when you are in actual, desperate need of treatment."

"Doctor," I said, "do you see outpatients at the Rebagliati?"

"No. Why? Up on the oncology floor, patients are so vulnerable that none of the doctors there see any other patients but the inpatients. Otherwise, we'd be bringing them more infections."

"Because with our health insurance gone, money is a very big constraint for us... so I was wondering if Sergio could see you at the hospital to save us paying your forty-dollar consulting fee for his monthly checkups."

"Even if I *did* see outpatients there, I wouldn't recommend Sergio expose himself in that fashion. His immune system wouldn't protect him from all the cases of flu and other common diseases that people from all over Peru come to the Rebagliati for, since it's the largest free hospital in the country."

On the way home, Sergio said, "I'll do as Dr. Ritter says, not because I like it but because I trust him."

I took my eyes off the windshield. "Dr. Ritter has never steered you wrong. But what will you say to Nila when she insists on private care again?"

"I'll think of something."

I smiled a bitter smile. "It's easy for her to insist. She has Eduardo to depend on a hundred percent. Meanwhile, I will be left alone to fend for myself and the children if you should die. That possibility keeps me awake most nights because I can never find an answer to what will happen to us if you should really die."

"I'm not there yet, so please, let's not bring the future to today. I don't need the depression."

I placed my free hand on his. "I'm sorry. I won't mention it again."

With Sergio home, I couldn't phone Armand, and the days slipped by, becoming three weeks, while Armand was probably convinced I had deleted him. I was driving past Eva Nalvarte's neighborhood while doing the carpool when it occurred to me I could use Eva as our go-between. On the way home, I stopped at her place.

"Jesus, Noor, I've been wanting to call you myself, but Armand won't let me."

"Eva, tell him I love him. Tell him not to leave me." Tears trickled down my cheeks. "I don't know what to do to see Armand with Sergio home all the time."

"Why don't you invite us all to tea? Tell Sergio you made new friends while he was gone and that you'd like him to meet them."

"What a simple idea. Why didn't I think of it?"

"Because you're under too much stress. Cancer isn't an easy disease."

And her words reminded me of how, besides Sergio's family, no one knew of his true diagnosis except Armand.

Another week passed.

"Serg, I want you to meet some new friends of mine. They've been amazing to the kids and me while you were gone. Eva has a beach house the kids love to go to."

"And how did you meet her?"

"Through a student of mine at the Roosevelt."

"What is her name? How come you've never mentioned this student to me?"

Feeling corralled, I said, "It's not a her. It's a him. His name is Armand."

Sergio didn't comment on that, but I knew I had set the wheels turning in his head. Yet if I didn't introduce him to Armand and his gang, I would never see him. So it was a risk I had to take, or else I would lose Armand altogether.

Of course, I couldn't *say* any of that to Armand when I called him and pretended he was a friend. Short of talking to him in front of Sergio, I had no way around that obstacle, either, since Sergio could get curious and pick up the phone extension in the study at any time.

The coming weekend, Eva, Salvador, Karina, and Armand arrived for tea to "meet Noor's husband."

After introductions, I sat as far away from Armand as possible. *Will Sergio notice the tension in my body?*

I relaxed my face as Armand exclaimed, "Seeing you in person, I can tell now that the portrait Noor's mother painted of you is pretty staggering. It's tough to capture a subject's exact expression with the broad strokes she uses."

"You must show him the portrait of me you've painted." Instantly, I knew I had said the wrong thing.

"Oh." Sergio crossed his hands over his knees. "You painted Noor? I must see this painting."

"It was a class assignment." Karina tried to save the day. "We all painted someone."

"They'll paint me next, right?" Eva smiled at everybody present.

"When did you sit for Armand?" Sergio's smile was taut. "How come you never told me of it?"

"I didn't. He did it from photographs of mine when I was with you in Los Angeles. Until the insurance fiasco occurred, I meant to ask you if we could pay him to paint the children."

"I wouldn't take money from you." Armand looked at me. "I'll paint them next summer." He ran a nervous hand through his tousle of brownish-gold hair.

What in God's name possessed me to suggest this tea party? I steered the conversation to Eva's stuffed-toys business, but Sergio was not to be deterred. I knew by the way Sergio's eyes assessed Armand that his questions about Salvador's architecture major were a venue to probe Armand. "Have any of you been to Paris?

You have to see Paris to absorb Renaissance architecture." Sergio immediately learned of Armand's adolescence spent in Europe.

An hour passed.

No sooner did the door close behind the visitors, Sergio caught my arm. "How long have you been with Armand?"

Like a sheep being herded by a sheepdog, I stuttered, "Y-you got your AIDS from someone, Serg. I think I have a right to a boyfriend, too, no?"

"Is this your way of punishing me for telling you how I got AIDS?"

"No. I would never do that to you. But this is my answer to the reality that we haven't been a couple in years, and you would have divorced me without an AIDS diagnosis."

"Is that why I sleep in the study?" Sergio gained color.

"No. But the truth is the truth, and I can't change it."

"It'll be nice to hear what your mother has to say about that." Sergio collapsed on his bed and threw a blanket over his legs.

At the mention of my mother, my bottom lip curled. "You think I care what my *mother* has to say? Besides, if you do—do tell her of your AIDS diagnosis. I'm sick of inventing how your cancer is progressing each time she calls and asks for details, while she cross-examines my story because I forgot whatever I said the last time she called."

"Where do the two of you do it?" Sergio's glance was questioning.

Instant galaxies swirled in my vision of the sofa in the drawing room, my garden, my bedroom, my bathroom, and the cement-slab bunk beds at Eva's beach house, but I kept quiet.

"I'll feel a lot better if you tell me how the two of you met and how it happened," persisted Sergio.

How can I refuse when, in a peculiar way, telling him would lessen my guilt? I took the French armchair next to his bed and told him the story.

"And how is the sex?" Sergio stared at me.

"What? Why would you ask me that?"

"Because they say women in their thirties know what they want. You never did with me."

I fought to keep my voice steady. "I don't think—" then, as if coming into my own, I calmed down, and my voice came out steadier. "I don't think it's your business." But my eyes wavered when Sergio looked like I had slapped him. I wanted to say, *You brought AIDS into our midst*, but I kept quiet. Hurting Sergio more than he must already hurt inside didn't make me stronger. It made me meaner, and I had never been mean to anybody on purpose.

The next day, I raced to Eva's. "He knows," I reported. "He confronted me about Armand the minute you guys left the house."

"Yes, he knew it the minute we came *into* the house."

"But you suggested it! That's why I had the tea party."

Eva bit her bottom lip. "I was wrong. I shouldn't have underestimated Sergio's intelligence."

"So now what do I do?"

"I don't know. I'm not giving you any more advice that might go further south."

On my own, I didn't know what to do except be honest. I waited two more days and practiced saying it in the mirror. Either way, my face flushed when I said, "Serg, now that you know the truth, can I see Armand sometimes?"

Sergio's smile twisted. "If I say no, you'll see him on the sly."

"That's so unfair!" I slapped the French armchair. "Because *I* suggested we patch things up, until this whole AIDS business happened, and *you* refused. Instead, you rubbed divorce papers in my face, knowing full well I didn't want one. So why are you laying a guilt trip on me now?"

"Because I hate it." Sergio's teeth clenched, and his eyes glistened. "I hate it that you have a boyfriend. I know it isn't fair. I know what I said, but I still hate it."

"So you're telling me not to see him, aren't you?"

"No. No. Do whatever you want." Sergio gazed out the study's picture window. "I can't stop you."

How typical of Sergio to play the victim card because he didn't have the power anymore. *Where was that card when I used to beg him to drop me at Carla's to study on weekends, back when I had a university to go to? And when he told me to take buses to university, all because I had the temerity to want a degree?* No. I would stand my ground for once. If Sergio were well, he would have left me by then. I owed myself the relief of seeing Armand.

53

My window of time to see Armand was on weekends. I chose Saturday over Sunday because Sunday was Dulci's day off and I couldn't leave Sergio in charge of the children. *What if they have an accident and need first aid?*

On the day I called Armand to tell him I would see him, he asked, "What will you tell Sergio?"

Conscious that Sergio could be listening, I replied, "I'll tell you when I see you."

On said Saturday, Sergio had known for days I would see Armand at eleven that morning. Regardless, his eyes glistened with tears when I announced I was leaving the house. Knowing I would cry, too, unless I left, I ran out of the house to find Armand waiting in his beat-up station wagon by the curb.

"How long do you have?" he asked.

"Enough time to grab an ice cream maybe?"

Armand glanced away. "So, how did he discover I existed?"

I told him the full story, trying not to feel guilty toward Sergio *or* Armand.

"Good!" said Armand. "Now he knows what it feels like to find out his partner is cheating on him like he cheated on her."

"In our case, it isn't that simple, is it? Neither one of us was cheating on the other, since we weren't even together, but Sergio and I have a very weird bond that no outsider understands. We love each other and hate each other, and it flip-flops, so we hurt each other and care for each other, and it's an absolute snarl of emotions."

"You're right. I don't understand it."

"Like I don't understand your family dynamics."

"How can you defend him?"

I shrugged. "Don't ask me what I feel for him. It's the same as me asking you if you love your parents."

"Eva invited you and the kids to the beach."

"Amor, the kids and I can't go with you to the beach while Sergio lies home alone, sick."

"Why not? He wasn't thinking of you when he went to that party and got AIDS."

"I know, amor. But I can't be that cruel to him."

"I miss you."

"I miss you too. At night, I lie awake imagining you beside me."

Back at home, Sergio attacked me with, "So, how was your date?"

"Serg, one hour with a friend at an ice cream parlor isn't much of a date, now, is it?"

"Don't insult me by calling him a friend when he is your lover."

"Right, but we didn't make love in the middle of the ice cream parlor."

"I'm sorry. I shouldn't have asked the question."

"Exactly. The same as I don't say a word when you hustle me to stay upstairs when Nila visits you for hours. I also never ask you what you two talked about… nor do you ever divulge what you and dear old Jaime discuss when he visits you and you close the study door because your conversation has to be so ultra-private."

After that exchange, Sergio took refuge in his polite-stranger act so I wouldn't know what he was thinking. Convinced that it was for the best, I followed suit, though I could never not feel guilty about how Sergio hated Armand's existence in my life. Yet for once, I was not ready to back down. Not ready to hurt Armand either by stopping seeing him. After all, Sergio wouldn't listen to me if I said I didn't want Nila or Jaime coming to the house.

By the following month, Armand and I had not made love in a hundred days.

"What if you rented a room in San Isidro?" I bit my bottom lip.

"When would we meet there? You never go anywhere without Sergio knowing."

"Christ. You're right. I can't rub it in his face that I'm spending hours and hours with you."

"See? It's always about his feelings, never mine."

"Amor, you're not dying. He is. And Sergio had the shittiest childhood anyone can have. I can't be cruel to him."

"So, what excuse would you give him for being gone for so long if we did rent a room?"

"I could say I'm visiting Carla with Pia and Abril. Once I dropped them, I'd come see you. San Isidro and Magdalena aren't far apart by car."

"What about a motel?"

"A motel? Did you say *motel*? I would feel like a whore! Have you ever been to a motel?" *It wouldn't be the same as going to a five-star hotel with Chirag, but I can't say that to Armand.*

"Not unless you count my brothel visit in Madrid."

"No. I hate the idea. Besides, with all this terrorist activity, they'd register our names, photocopy our IDs, and with your last name, they'd associate you with your dad in one second. What would we do if they abducted you for a ransom? I can already see the newspaper headlines. 'Prominent industrialist's son caught with his pants down screwing Indian wife of Peruvian diplomat.'"

"I get it." Armand waved his arms crosswise. "Bad idea."

"Yes. But where's the money to rent a room?"

"I'll borrow the money from Salvador and pay him back little by little from the stipend my dad sends me to buy art supplies." Armand's stipend was three hundred dollars a month. His father paid Armand's mother a five-thousand-dollar alimony, so he didn't see why Armand couldn't ask his mother for money if he needed more, and Armand wasn't the asking kind.

In theory, it should have been easy for Armand to find us a room. The newspapers overflowed with notices of rooms for rent from people who craved the extra income. In practice, no one agreed to rent to a twenty-one-year-old who didn't work for a living. The questions came in rapid-fire whenever Armand showed up for any appointment. Would his parents be the guarantors? Would he live there? Oh, he wouldn't? Then why did he need the room?

A month passed until one landlord agreed to rent Armand a room on the third floor of his house in San Isidro, right next to the Parque El Olivar. On Saturday, Armand showed me the room without a stick of furniture at the end of a rabbit's warren, past five successive grilled barricades with locks. "Here are the duplicates for you." He handed me a steel key ring.

"Are you happy?" I asked after an hour of lovemaking on bare boards. I rubbed the tip of my nose against his, content just to be near him outside the confines of his car.

Armand hugged me hard. "When can we do this again?"

"Next Saturday. I'll take the kids to Carla's. Pray it works."

"And I promise I'll see to a bed here. I bet Eva can come up with a solution."

On Saturday, Carla's mother talked forever. I raced to our hideout in San Isidro, two hours late.

My tires screeched around the last corner, convinced Armand must have already left. But he sat cross-legged, leaning on his new landlord's grilled garage enclosure.

My heart still thudded even as I parked the car.

In the room, we fell upon each other on a tattered mattress from Eva's attic, ignoring its stench of mouse droppings and urine—never mind bedsheets or a pillow.

In between kisses, Armand said, "This proves I would love you even if we lived in a dumpster."

"Oh, amor." I moaned as he kissed my throat. "Why did I take so long to find this?"

"Find what?" Armand rose on his elbows to push aside the curtain of my dusky hair and lick my hardened nipples.

"You." I embraced him. "The joy of being loved by you."

I discovered why the landlord had been eager to rent Armand the room as soon as I used the bathroom. "Guess what?" I fell back on the mattress beside him. "I'm betting this place has never had water, because even the toilet bowl is dry."

After school carpool the next morning, I borrowed two five-gallon pails from Eva. I filled them from an outdoor faucet in the landlord's courtyard and carried them, spilling, up three flights of stairs, past the unlocking and locking, to our room, along with two old bedsheets and a pillow Dulci had smuggled into the car late at night.

But after all my efforts, Armand and I couldn't go to the room during the four following Saturdays, sabotaged by a college study group, a children's parent-teacher meeting, a lunch Xenobia Santander arranged to welcome Sergio back, and lastly, a weekend party hosted by Armand's mother in her ex-husband's country estate.

Each Friday, I cried at night, knowing my day to see Armand was prime weekend time. If I wasn't busy, he was. *Does he miss me as much as I miss him?* My plight was that much harder because what could I say to the guests at my mother-in-law's party: *I'm sad I can't see my boyfriend?* Neither could I show my frustration to the children, who were delighted I would meet their teachers.

As the weeks morphed into months, that empty room became a symbol of my lack of a relationship with Armand.

54

Between March and the end of June 1992, Sergio lost twenty more pounds. He scratched a mosquito bite into becoming an open wound on his right gluteus because his immune system couldn't heal the sore spot. That tiny sore, which would have cauterized itself within hours on a healthy body, progressed from the size of a peppercorn to a penny then a quarter and, in less than a month, a lime. For fifteen days, Sergio continued to shower, as usual, after which I wiped him, protected by latex gloves, to dress the bleeding patch with antibiotic ointment and a gauze bandage.

During his following monthly checkup, Dr. Ritter forbade showers. "Unsterilized running water will endanger other parts of your body," he told Sergio. "It's also a needless way to expose Noor to AIDS."

After that, I sponge-bathed Sergio. Washing his hair was a laborious task I addressed twice a week at our kitchen sink. With the showers gone, Sergio and I had more to discuss around his physical needs, but we didn't share any private feelings. Our relationship reduced to a parody, where I would sponge him and wash his hair before he received visitors. In return, he got more used to the hour I took to see Armand, unless I "visited Carla with Pia and Abril," which was seldom.

On the morning of July 28, the Peruvian national day, Dulci had the day off, and the children were on their short winter vacation, and therefore, it was my opportunity to sleep in. I wasn't ready for Abril to burst into my bedroom, crying hysterically, shouting, "Mamá, Papá is dead. Mamá—wake up. Papá is dead!"

Sleep-ridden, I dashed down the stairwell, terrified of what Abril was blubbering. In the study, I stopped short and dove to the floor next to the study bookshelves, shrieking, "Serg! Serg!"

I shook Sergio's inert shoulders, but he was unresponsive. Heart pounding, I rolled Sergio's body faceup and kneeled to place my ear against his chest.

His heart was still beating.

"Abril, baby, he's not dead." I pulled Abril down to hug her. "Hush, he's going to be fine. Now, be a good girl, and go sit on the armchair while I call the doctor. Papá fainted. He isn't dead. Go."

Despite my assurances to Abril, my hand shook as I dialed Dr. Ritter's home number. No one answered on a holiday weekend. Next, I ran to the bathroom, bounded back, and sprinkled cold water on Sergio's face. He blinked.

As soon as he blinked, Abril dropped to the floor beside him, hugging him, kissing him. "*Papito, ¿estás bien?*"

"*Sí, hijita, sí, estoy bien. Cálmate.*"

"Oh, Serg!" I smoothed the untidy waves crowding his forehead.

"What's going on?"

"You tell me." My voice was husky. "I found you facedown on the floor."

Sergio rubbed his eyes and gazed at the daylight framed by the picture window. "I remember now."

"Remember what?"

"I haven't mentioned this because I don't want to sound crazy, but for a month, I've been waking up at night with my heart racing. Then I see my liver dripping blood, perched on a bookshelf, always out of my reach. Usually, the hallucination goes away if I close my eyes and breathe for a while. But last night was different. I knew that if I didn't grab my liver and put it back inside me, I'd die. So I got up, but I became so dizzy I fell back on the bed. To avoid falling again, I crawled to the bookshelves, stood up, and jumped. That's all I know. I must have fainted."

"We're taking you to the doctor's. Abril found you on the floor, which is why she is in hysterics. Abril, come here. Help me put Papá back in bed." I placed Sergio's bony arm around my shoulder. "I'll get the children dressed. Can you dress yourself? Otherwise, I'll help you after."

"But isn't today the twenty-eighth? No doctors' office will be opened today." Sergio slumped on his bed.

"All the more reason to take you to the emergency room while it's daylight. I can't deal with this at night all alone. Not with the midnight-to-six-a.m. curfew that we don't notice because we never go anywhere."

The government-mandated curfew was only a month old, but the population of Lima loved it since it had dramatically lessened terrorist-instigated property destruction. Until then, it had not impacted my family's existence, so I hadn't given it much thought. However, suddenly, it was scary to think of what I could or could not do if Sergio needed medical help on some unexpected night.

Within the hour, I drove my whole family to my mother-in-law's in San Isidro to drop the children there. As much as I hated her, I went upstairs with Pia and Abril, explained what had happened and where I was taking Sergio.

Instead of thanking me, Xenobia Santander said, "Call me with an update as soon as possible."

I left without another word because being rude to the harpy was not in my family's best interest.

In the car, Sergio appeared so pale I said, "Hey, you're not going to faint on me in the car, are you?"

"No, I feel fine. I ate half the sandwich you packed me."

Our only free care option was the Rebagliati State Employee's Hospital, where Dr. Ritter was the head of the oncology department. If Sergio got admitted that day, Dr. Ritter could examine him in the morning because the next day was a Wednesday.

Grateful that Sergio knew the way to the downtown location, I dropped him at the ER entrance because I had to find the hospital's parking area. Wherever it was, it would be a longer walk than Sergio could handle, never mind the winter garua drizzle that made it feel ten times colder than it really was due to the ninety-six percent humidity.

In the ER's dingy waiting room, I found Sergio sitting on the grungy floor because every other available seating option was taken. Seeing him so diminished, I swallowed a lump in my throat. Poor Sergio was so much more status-conscious than I was. Wishing I'd had the foresight to bring a cushion, I went back out and bought five of the cheapest scandal sheets I could find to act as a barrier between Sergio and the floor.

"Here, let me place these newspapers under you to act as a cushion."

I hoisted my husband to his feet. After that, I sat down beside him, taking his cold hand in my own—few buildings in Peru had central heating.

"This is awful. I just want to be back home in bed." Sergio looked ready to cry.

"I know, my darling, but if you faint in the middle of the night and I don't know about it, that'll go worse for you."

Sergio's eyes filled with tears. "You haven't said 'my darling' to me in so long."

His words brought abrupt tears to my eyes. "Serg, the fact that I have a lover doesn't mean I don't love you. I don't know how many times you have cheated on me or with whom, but you love me, too, don't you? That's what Magda told me in Los Angeles. That you loved me. Is it true?"

Sergio nodded, squeezing my hand.

I told him my plan to get Dr. Ritter to see him the next day. So we sat there, two lost souls, united by time, space, and two children, until Sergio got called in for a triage assessment three hours later.

"Señora, he has AIDS," I told the triage nurse. "Please help us. He is super weak and exhausted, and he needs to lie on a bed."

"I'll see if a doctor can examine him earlier." The nurse's voice was filled with sympathy.

Notwithstanding, it was five o'clock before Sergio was admitted into the infectious diseases ward on the seventh floor. We had arrived at the hospital at ten in the morning. An orderly wheeled Sergio into a room in a wheelchair. *Is Sergio comparing our threadbare surroundings to the opulence of the American hospitals he was used to?* At least the ward was scrupulously clean.

"Go call my mother." Sergio gave me a beseeching glance. "She must be worried."

"I will. And I'll find some food for us to eat. I'm dying of hunger."

Down in the lobby, I forced myself to be polite to Xenobia Santander on the phone, telling her I would spend the night in the hospital with Sergio. "I'll call you as soon as a doctor sees him." I didn't tell her I hoped that doctor would be Dr. Ritter, since Xenobia hated him.

That evening, when an intern doctor came around at seven p.m., I begged him to let Dr. Ritter know Sergio was in the hospital waiting to see him.

Later at night, when Sergio was asleep, I lay down on the linoleum floor because my body couldn't take the discomfort of the one metal chair the room provided for visitors. In the darkness, at last, I was free to contemplate the enormity of the day's events, free to worry over what might really be the matter with Sergio, free to freak out that this was perhaps the end. Sergio and I had never discussed him dying—it had always been a nebulous future event. *What will happen if he dies?*

Despite my worries, I fell asleep. The night nurse's visit woke both of us up at three a.m. when she came in to take Sergio's vitals.

After she left, Sergio said, "Come lie on the bed with me. I don't take up much space these days."

That was how Dr. Ritter found us, asleep next to each other at seven in the morning. "What is going on, Sergio? I read your chart. Fortunately, you don't have a temperature."

Seeing the doctor, I sprang out of the bed, explaining what had happened at home the previous morning.

Dr. Ritter placed a hand on Sergio's forearm but looked at me. "This is dementia setting in. The AIDS virus has infected Sergio's brain. When he's anxious, the anxiety alone might provoke a heart attack. He shouldn't be alone at night. But he's free to get discharged and go home. All we can do is manage his symptoms. No medication exists for this type of dementia."

On the way home, we picked up Pia and Abril, assuring them and Xenobia Santander that Sergio was fine. This was our challenge to tackle, not theirs.

Back in the house, I placed Sergio's arm around my shoulders to help him climb the stairs to the master bedroom so he could sleep next to me.

But on the sixth step, Sergio panted, "I can't do this. I'm too tired."

From then on, each night, I came down to check on Sergio every time I awoke up for a bathroom break. In the mornings, I woke at five o'clock so the children would never walk in on Sergio.

Three days after Sergio's hospital visit, I said, "Serg, that hospital visit really frightened me. What is our money situation?"

"Bad. We're going through my Los Angeles savings like water because my salary in Lima is a joke."

I wanted to say, *Well, when were you going to tell me that?* But I said, "Tell me a little more than that, no? How are you for AZT pills and doctor's visits besides food money?"

"Our worst expense is the children's school fees at five hundred dollars for the two of them. Add everything else, and we are six or seven hundred short each month. That's where my savings have been going, so I can't even think of buying more AZT at ten dollars a pill."

"I should call the Roosevelt to see if they have any need for a substitute teacher."

"If you start teaching and I need emergency help, it will give you a bad rap as an unreliable worker. You don't need that reputation for when you'll truly need a job."

"You mean if you die, don't you?" The chill of those words swept through my heart like a blizzard.

"It's a possibility we have to face."

No. You don't have to face it. I'll have to face it. Like the aftermath of Didima's death. Those who die are the lucky ones who escape. It's those who live on that have to deal with the messes that you people leave behind. "What can we do to save money?"

"Nothing we do is extravagant."

"So how much do we have right now?"

"A little more than two thousand until my salary and the association stipend come in."

That night, I couldn't sleep or think or reason. The next morning, I called the Villa Maria School to ask if I could see the headmistress.

In the afternoon, I spoke to Mother Alvarez-Calderón. "*Madre*, I need to tell you the truth." Without preamble, I explained Sergio's diagnosis and how he was probably going to die. I spoke for twenty minutes straight, ending with, "If you tell anyone what I am telling you, my husband could lose his job, though I suspect that those who could have dealt him a blow already did so by making him lose his health insurance. But right now, I need you to please lower the children's school fees. Otherwise, a time will come that I won't be able to pay it anyway."

"Let me talk to our finance department and call you."

55

On August 6, I brought the children home from their first day of school after the short winter vacation, when Sergio asked from the study, "Amor, can you come in here?" He handed me a formal manila envelope.

"What is it?" I fumbled out a card. It had been a long time since anyone had invited us anywhere.

"Read it."

My cheeks warmed in anger as I read an invitation to tea with the secretary-general. "I'm not going." I threw the card on Sergio's blanket-covered legs. Since Sergio's ignominious return from Los Angeles, I had insisted on dressing in torn jeans and flip-flops to do paperwork at the foreign office. And whenever Sergio objected, my lips thinned. "Why? What will they do? Stop giving you your measly three-hundred-sixty-dollar government salary? Or the one-thousand-dollar stipend from the Diplomatic Association? After all your years of service, they've treated you like used toilet paper, and you care I *dress* properly for them? You're a fool."

"It says RSVP."

"I can always tear up the card and send the pieces back as my answer."

"Are you *trying* to get the foreign office to sack me for insubordination, or are you just stupid? Normally, I wouldn't care if you didn't go, *but the invitation is only for you*, and it's signed by the secretary-general himself. To me and any other career diplomat, he is more important than the foreign minister because he's not a political appointee. Even though I haven't been to work in months, the man is still my boss. If you don't answer, I'll have to."

I scowled and scribbled an irate *yes* on the RSVP line of the invitation. Then I threw the card at Sergio and stormed out of the study.

Upstairs, I landed facedown on my bed, teeth gritting. It didn't matter what

I did or where I was. I never had free will. In India, my will had been subjugated to my mother's, and to escape that, I had been idiot enough to exchange my mother's despotism for the rigors of Sergio's diplomatic lifestyle. God, how I would love to tell the secretary-general off, but the real reason I was angry was because I knew I couldn't do that to Sergio. He already had enough to deal with. I couldn't harm him in his workplace. *Yet will I be able to control my temper when I'm face-to-face with the blessed secretary-general?*

On the afternoon of the scheduled tea, I clattered down the stairs in high heels and entered the study dressed in a pale-pink alpaca suit I had sewn years earlier.

Sergio extended a trembling hand. "I was afraid the whole morning of what you would choose to wear." His voice quavered.

My eyes grew moist as I squeezed his hand. "I didn't dress for *them*," I hissed. "I dressed for *you*. I promise I'll be on my best behavior, never mind what the stupid secretary-general says to me. Okay?"

"That perfume is Eau de Givenchy, isn't it? Do you remember where we bought it?"

"Of course I do. It was in that little shop in Èze on our way to Monte Carlo during our honeymoon."

We heard the doorbell peal in one nonstop ring, and simultaneous thumps heralded the children coming home from school. Dulci rushed to open the outer door. No carpool parent ever left the premises until the children were indoors.

"Mamá." Abril tripped in. "You look beautiful. Where are you going?"

"To Papá's office, amor."

Pia dropped her schoolbag with a thump.

"Pia, go put your schoolbag in your room. Now. It isn't Dulci's job to carry your schoolbag to your room. It's your job, and you know it."

"Señora Noor, a car from Señor Sergio's office is already waiting." Dulci's fingers poised on the study door. "The driver waved to me as the children came in."

"Go." Sergio ran a hand through his greasy hair and held his fingers to his nose. "Or you'll arrive late."

"Yes, I know I have to wash your hair. I'll do it when I come back. No—that'll be too late. Tomorrow morning, after the carpool?"

I slipped into the back seat of the waiting limousine, struck again by the absurdity and hypocrisy of the foreign office to have me go drink *tea with the secretary-general* while Sergio lay dying without adequate medication. I gripped the polished interior door handle of the expensive car, praying I would keep it together at the meeting.

In Torre Tagle Mansion, the headquarters of the Peruvian foreign office, I stewed as I walked into the secretary-general's vast football field of an office. However sincere my promise to Sergio about controlling my temper, the eighteenth-century edifice screamed its decadent show of pomp and wealth, rubbing in that it was the lack of money that limited Sergio to two AZT pills a day when he required six or eight just to stay alive.

I barely acknowledged the polite smile of a spritely, white-haired secretary-general who introduced himself as Ambassador Rodrigo Duarte inside his stately office. The ambassador adjusted his gold-rimmed bifocals as he poured us coffee from a porcelain set arranged on an antique silver tray placed atop a majestic coffee table in one corner of the office.

My fingers bunched into fists as I said in perfect Spanish, "*Señor Embajador*, is there a point to this meeting?"

For a second, Ambassador Duarte appeared aghast, but he busied himself handing me a cup and a couple of *alfajor* cookies on a miniature china plate. Of course, the foreign office would serve alfajores. Alfajores, with their rich pastry dough and milky, cinnamon-flavored caramel filling, were the ultimate symbol of old-style Peruvian class and decorum. That decorum had to be preserved for everything except health insurance for sick diplomats.

The secretary-general faced me, fingers laced on his lap. "What do you expect from us, señora?"

"Expect, Señor Embajador?" *Does he think I'll sit here and play his pretend game to assuage the foreign office's guilty conscience?* "After the way this institution has treated my husband?" *Oh, Lord. I shouldn't have said that.*

"My, señora. You are direct, aren't you?" The secretary-general straightened with a nervous laugh.

"Would you prefer I pretended otherwise, señor?" *What's the point of trying to mask my feelings? They are already out in the open, so help me, God.* I smiled a wry smile and bit into an alfajor cookie, tasting its rich, creamy center.

"I arranged this meeting, señora"—the ambassador paused—"to inform you the foreign office is creating a job for you. You studied translation and interpretation, I understand?"

"Yes, Embajador, but I don't have a college degree from anywhere. I never finished my studies in India or here. Besides, I don't believe in any promise this office makes."

"How many years of college did you finish?"

"Five. Isn't that a joke? Five years of perfect grades in two countries and no degree to show for it."

The ambassador smiled. "Señora, your Spanish is flawless." He sipped his coffee.

"So, when can I start working?"

"I don't know, señora. This job has to be created, so it won't materialize overnight."

I stood up. "And you couldn't tell me this over the phone? You had to play this whole charade of a tea party to tell me that *someday, maybe,* this foreign office might create a job for me?"

"I presumed you would want to know."

"Well, I know now." I left the secretary-general's office without a backward glance.

At home, Sergio asked, "How did it go?"

"Great." I didn't dare tell Sergio I had walked out on the secretary-general. "The whole darn tea party was to tell me that *someday, maybe,* the foreign office would create a translation job for me."

"Did the secretary-general say when?"

"Nope."

"Did he tell you how much they would pay you?"

"Nope."

"So, what did he tell you?"

"Basically *nothing.* But that's how the games of politics and diplomacy are played, isn't it? All show and little content? Meanwhile, you lie here dying bit by bit, day by day."

The very next day, the Villa Maria School called. Headmistress Mother Alvarez-Calderón came on the line. "Señora Santander, our finance department has awarded each of your children half a scholarship. I hope that will help your family."

"Oh, Mother Alvarez-Calderón, of course it will. If I were standing in front of you, I would hug you."

I tripped down the stairs to tell Sergio the news.

"What did you say to her?" He looked apprehensive.

"I told her the truth."

"You shouldn't have done that."

"Serg, do you seriously think the powers that be in the foreign office don't already know all the diagnoses of the seven sick diplomats who got excluded from the new insurance package?"

"We don't know that for sure."

"Well, I wasn't going to sit by and watch our resources dwindle to zero without acting to reverse it."

"I'm sorry. The first thing I should have said was a thank-you."

Ten days later, when I came home from the morning carpool, Sergio looked extra pale. "The secretary-general himself called and asked to speak to you. When I asked him what it was about, he said, 'Tell her to call me,' and gave me a direct number. Is there something you are not telling me?"

"No," I lied. "We parted on the best of terms."

"Here's the phone number." Sergio shifted to one side of his bed as if making space so I would sit and call the secretary-general from his phone extension.

But I took the scrap of notepaper and left. Upstairs, I dialed the number, rubbing my eyes.

The secretary-general picked up the phone on the third ring. "Señora, would you be kind enough to indulge an old man and come have another cup of coffee with me?"

"Why, señor? Has the foreign office created that job for me?"

"No, not yet. But they are working on it."

"Then what is it? Are you in the mood for more pretense?"

"Yes. Now will you come over, or do I have to come to your house to see you?"

"No. I'll come over. Can I come right now?"

"Two this afternoon would be better."

"As long as you know that if I get angry enough, I *will* walk out on you again."

"Señora, I never suspected Indian women were so fiery. I assumed they were submissive."

"Yeah. That's why I left. Because I didn't fit inside India, and India didn't fit inside me."

In the secretary-general's office that afternoon, I said, "Señor, I'm sorry I was so rude to you last week. But I feel so helpless. My husband is dying, and I am powerless to help him."

"Nonsense. Please don't apologize to me. May I call you Noor? You could be my daughter."

"Yes."

The secretary-general waved his hands. "My wife could be in your place. In my thirty-plus years of service within this office, I have seen many injustices, but this one outdoes all the rest." The ambassador pointed to his antique desk the size of a ping-pong table. "That colonial monstrosity tells me every day that though I am secretary-general today, I could be out on the street tomorrow. It's how fickle politics are."

"That's what Sergio explained to me the day he lost his health insurance."

"Please tell him I understand what he meant. I don't know him well, since we never worked together, but I do know his reputation. He was among the best. Tell him I said that." Ambassador Duarte strode to his desk, grabbed a manila envelope, and came back to hand it to me.

"What is it, another invitation?" I tore open the stiff, embossed rectangle. "Embajador." I stared up at the standing secretary-general, "I've met you. I like you because my rudeness didn't faze you, but I won't agree to meet anyone else."

Ambassador Duarte smiled. "I like you too."

I peeped into the envelope and saw a wad of crisp dollar bills and a greeting card. Eyes wide, heart thumping, I pulled out the card, dumbfounded.

It read:

Dear Sergio,

Here are two thousand US dollars from us to you.

The card had a million initials on it.

I glanced at the secretary-general again.

"This," he said, "is what I canvassed for you after you walked out on me last week. I talked to my assistant, and he came up with the idea to petition our entire workforce to help the seven families in distress due to the insurance debacle. The gesture is extra special because even the diplomats at home contributed to this pot. I hope it will help."

How many AZT pills will two thousand dollars buy? That was what my life had shrunk to—calculating the number of AZT pills before I could experience gratitude. "Embajador." My voice came out hoarse. "Would you find me uncouth if I hugged you? I can't think of anything appropriate to say." I bit my lower lip.

Ambassador Duarte pulled me to my feet and embraced me. "Don't be silly. I don't need words for you to tell me how you feel."

"Oh, señor, I don't know how much chemotherapy this money will buy, but I'm relieved to know it will save Sergio's life one treatment at a time. So my children will still have a father to call papá… until they don't."

56

AT HOME, I TOLD SERGIO the real story behind the two-thousand-dollar gift. Only his aghast expression told me the enormity of my rudeness to the second-in-command of the Peruvian foreign service.

"It's true that fools rush in where angels fear to tread," Sergio said. "No one in their right mind would ever be rude to a secretary-general. Never mind the reprisals that behavior would bring."

"Why? He's a human being the same as the rest of us."

"Spoken like someone who has never had a real job."

"I thought you'd appreciate receiving two thousand dollars."

"I *do* appreciate it! But what I *really* thank God for is that *you didn't cost me my job*!"

"When can you tell Nila to go to Miami and buy you more AZT?"

Sergio shook his head. "No. We need this money for expenses here. My fainting spell taught me that. If I die, I can't leave you with nothing."

"No. If dying is the criterion, AZT will keep you alive longer. Get the AZT."

"It won't really. Not unless I take it properly, which I can't do because it's so expensive. Two thousand dollars will buy two hundred AZT pills. At six or eight pills a day, that is a month's supply. It's better this way."

My eyes filled with tears. "No, it isn't. What you're saying is that one month more or one month less doesn't matter because we have no money for more AZT to actually help you."

Sergio looked away then focused on me. "I had forgotten how you Indians really call a spade a spade."

The following day, after carpool, I helped Sergio to the kitchen sink and massaged shampoo on his scalp while we both bent over at such an odd angle, my right arm ached from sustaining the weight of his head.

He asked, "Can you please buy me Johnson's baby shampoo? This Selsun Blue feels like detergent on my head."

Instantly, Pia and Abril and their innocent bath routine came to mind. "I bought this Selsun anti-dandruff because you asked for it. We have Johnson's upstairs in the children's bathroom. Should I go get it? It's running low though. I have to buy more."

"No, not this time. Next time."

I rinsed his hair. "I'll need more money. Imported shampoos are expensive."

Sergio twisted his head to meet my eyes. "Perhaps if you didn't squander our money on your dates with Armand, you wouldn't need more money."

"What?" I nearly dropped his head. "Armand never lets me spend a penny while we're out. He knows how little we have." *I already feel guilty enough about seeing Armand. Why does he have to make it worse? I won't let him do this to me.* My voice rose as I wrapped a towel around Sergio's hair. "And while we're on the subject of money, exactly what will happen to the kids and me if you do die? I mean, where am I supposed to receive a pension?"

"The foreign office will see to it." Sergio walked away, slow and stiff, as if resigned to his fate, despite my penchant for saying "if" instead of "when."

I followed him, fuming from what he had implied about Armand. "Have you filled out any forms?" I insisted.

"No." Sergio sounded uncertain.

"Then how do you know? Have you talked to anybody?"

Sergio shook his head.

Resigned to die yet ruled by denial. What can I do with him? "Well, I suggest you do so because if you don't, I will." Frustrated, I switched on the hair dryer waiting on Sergio's nightstand with a loud click.

I did not wait for Sergio to discover the details of how I would receive a pension if he died on me. I went to the foreign office myself. Questions posed to the right department the following week revealed that as Sergio's widow, I would be eligible for only ninety-three percent of Sergio's monthly government salary of three hundred and sixty American dollars, in Peruvian currency, upon his death. That was because he had completed twenty-three of the twenty-five years of required government service. More distressing, though, was to learn that if Sergio died that day, I wouldn't receive a dime, since he'd never *registered* his diplomatic academy diploma within the record-keeping department of the foreign office.

"Tell me what to do, señor." I stood outside the wooden hatch of the record-keeping department, fighting back the panic in my voice. "Tell me, and I'll do it."

"Sorry, señora. He didn't do it in time."

"Señor, he's still *alive*." I resisted the urge to scream at the man. "Explain to me what he has to do, and he'll do it."

"Bring me his graduation diploma updated with the signature and seal of the present academy rector."

"Thank you for your kindness, señor. I'll do that and come back."

When confronted at home, Sergio explained he had never collected his graduation diploma. "Back in my time, no one received their diplomas on graduation day because the bloody things took a month to prepare."

My sobs overcame me when the academy rector's receptionist said he refused to accept my phone call without giving any reason for it.

"Write him a notarized letter, señora," the receptionist whispered kindly. "He can't ignore that."

Three weeks later, I walked out of the Peruvian Diplomatic Academy in Jesus Maria, holding the first physical copy of Sergio's graduation diploma, signed and sealed by the rector.

At our garage door, I blew the car horn, excited to go in and show Sergio his diploma. Thirty seconds passed. *Where is Dulci?* I put a fist to my heart. *Why isn't she opening the garage door?*

I tore out of the car. Shaky fingers unlocked the main entrance. Inside, the thumping, bumping dance of the clothes dryer emerged from the laundry room to reveal Dulci's whereabouts.

I heaved a sigh of relief and called, "Serg?"

But he didn't reply.

My hand swung open the door into the house, and instantly, the downstairs hallway pitched like a boat in front of my eyes. The foulness took a couple of seconds to hit my nostrils. In my high heels, I sidestepped uneven blotches of feces on the marble floor, following them into the study. Sergio sat hunched on his bed, wrapped in his blue-and-white-striped kimono dressing gown, which was marked by more feces. His sleeves, the French armchair at the foot of his bed, and the library shelves were all stained, while a heap of dirty pajamas lay discarded on the *Darjazin* rug.

Did he do this on purpose? Why would he do such a thing? "What the devil happened here?"

"I-I lost control and dirtied my pajamas," Sergio said.

I glanced around and knew he was lying. I lunged toward Sergio, fury shimmering around me like heat off a tarred roof. "How did it smear everywhere? I told you to use the bedpan. Why didn't you use it?" We still had around a dozen adult diapers left over from Los Angeles, but Sergio used those on Sundays to go visit his mother.

"Because I believed I could reach the bathroom." Sergio half raised his arms as if I might hit him. "I'm sorry."

I burst into tears and shook my head. "I know you're lying." I sobbed. "You did this on purpose. Tell me why."

Sergio started crying too. "Because I'm angry, and I'm alone, and I'm helpless. I'm angry you have a lover. I'm angry I'm dying. I'm angry because soon, my children won't have a father anymore. I'm angry because all my life, I have struggled and fought and clawed my way up every ladder, and for what? For this end?"

His outburst wilted my anger like a rose in a bonfire. Sergio was as much my victim as I was his. A cat and a mouse trapped on the same raft, facing the same storm, only sometimes he was the cat, and at other times, he was the mouse. Neither of us had control over who was what, when.

"Señora Noor?" Dulci called.

"In here, Duls." I wiped my tears on the sleeve of my tweed jacket.

Dulci appeared at the doorway and gasped, looking from me to Sergio and back. "I can clean the study while you bathe the señor," she volunteered.

"No." I jumped. "Don't come in here."

Dulci knew she wasn't supposed to touch Sergio, but she assumed it was for his safety, not hers.

Tiredly, I plodded up the stairs to change, recalling New Year's Eve of 1974. That day, Didima had come home from another hospitalization as frail as an injured bird.

At ten p.m., I switched off the light in our bedroom, ready to go to sleep, happy Didima was alive. I would greet New Year's Day at home in my own bed instead of on an uncomfortable hospital armchair.

"Noor Shona?"

"Didima?" I said in the shadowy darkness.

"Shona, take me to the bathroom. I've got to go right now."

I shot out of bed. "Hold me so you don't fall, okay? Take tiny steps." By the door, I flicked on the light switch again. An icy gust of January wind blasted us as I unlatched the door to the veranda we had to traverse to reach the bathroom. Biting my bottom lip, I placed Didima's hands on that door. "Hold on for a sec. I have to grab your shawl." I dove to snatch the shawl at the foot of her bed.

In those seconds, independent-minded Didima took two fateful steps forward and lost her balance.

I lunged to the floor. "Didima! Didima, are you okay?"

"I dirtied my nightdress."

"What do you mean?"

A freezing whoosh of winter wind blew through the bare branches of our garden while the veranda's washbasin sang *drip-drop, drip-drop*. I lifted the edge of Didima's white flannel nightdress, and the stench told me what Didima was trying to say.

Shivering, I grabbed Didima by the underarms and heaved. Another frigid windblast. "Didima, you're too heavy. Help me."

My back and legs protested as I wrapped my arms around Didima's waist. Didima crawled back into our room, and we deposited her on a plastic imitation-cane chair.

In our kitchen, I filled a large pot with water to put on the stove. In the firelight, my breath clouded in puffs as I soaked kitchen rags to boil.

The New Year's dawn was light in the sky when I finished sponging Didima down. I spent that New Year's morning laundering dirty linen and scrubbing the imitation-cane chair with Sunlight soap and our garden hose. Afterward, I had washed my hands with bleach, but my fingernails had continued to smell of Didima's excrement, as if to emphasize our unshakable connection.

***

At the head of the stairs, in front of my bedroom, I collapsed on the cold marble of the second-floor landing and wiped my eyes again. Today, at least I wasn't twelve years old, it wasn't midnight, and I could count on hot water. Didima had been so poor, I had never even *seen* rubber gloves as a child. I supposed I should thank God I possessed those now.

57

THE NEXT MORNING, I DIALED Armand's number. "Hi, I—"

"Let me guess. You won't see me today."

I didn't tell Armand what Sergio had done because he wouldn't understand Sergio's pain or his frustration. Twenty-one was too young for him to assimilate how complex my allegiance with my husband was. "Yes, but it isn't Sergio's fault. It's Dulci's," I lied. "She left today because her brother has appendicitis. I can't leave the kids alone with Sergio."

"Last Saturday it was another reason, and the Saturday before, a different reason. I cancel everything to see you, then you cancel on me."

"I can see you tomorrow afternoon in our room. I'm taking Sergio and the kids to his mother's."

"I won't be there."

"Where will you go?"

"To Eva's, with Salvador and Karina. I'm invited to the beach, with or without you."

"I'll wait in Olivar Park near the room anyway. In case you come back from the beach."

He hung up.

Why can't he understand how strapped I am? Am I losing him? No. To me, everything appears the color of mud these days. I will wait for him in the park... and he will come.

On Sunday afternoon, it was well past three o'clock when I parked our car under my mother-in-law's apartment. While Horacio helped Sergio up the one short flight of stairs, I walked away, pretending I would meet Armand for certain. Around the corner, sturdy pumps hurried toward Olivar Park. On Sundays, San

Isidro always fell deathly silent except for the occasional rumble of a lone bus belching gray diesel fumes to match the gray sky, which matched my mood.

Armand wasn't at the park when I arrived. *He'll come*, I kept telling myself. I should have brought a book, but I hadn't. I lay down on the grass under a familiar olive tree and contemplated the sky through the fronds of its pointy leaves. *Does this olive tree remember my studying out here so desperately to get that degree? A degree that's now a million miles further away than it was three years ago?* I *would* get that degree. It was just a question of when, but that reiteration rang suspiciously hollow, regardless of how much I wanted to believe it.

"Hi." Armand surprised me, approaching from behind.

I sprang up. "You came! I knew you would come."

"I didn't go to the beach." Armand didn't greet me with a kiss.

I searched his face for answers but didn't receive any. "Your eyes look red. Are you okay? Why didn't you go to the beach?"

"I stayed to talk to you."

God, please. I can't face another argument. All I want is the relief of your arms for a while. "About what?"

"Do you want to talk here or in the room?" He dangled the key ring in front of me.

"Let's talk here." *Surely, he won't pick a fight in a public place?*

Armand lowered himself to the grass, opposite me, crossing his legs. "I can't do this anymore, Noor." He glanced at his hands.

"Do what?" My defensive hackles rose.

"Be with you." Armand looked back up.

"I know why your eyes are red!" I exclaimed. "You've been drinking, haven't you? Why? To find the courage to ditch me at the hardest juncture of my life? So afterward, you can say you didn't know what you were doing?" *Will he leave me? Hanging high and dry when I need his support so much?*

"No." Armand stared at me with green fire. "To find the courage to tell you I hate what you've converted our relationship into. Ever since Sergio came back, it's been all about him. You don't give a rat's ass how I feel because I'm not dying."

I wanted to beg him to not do this to me. Beg him to stay with me, to see it through, but I couldn't. My pride wouldn't let me. "Are you done? Because if not, I have two hours to kill. I can sit here and listen to as many of your complaints as you want."

"No, I'm not," Armand hissed, casting a quick look at other parkgoers. "I don't want to listen to you on the phone each night repeating how Sergio's mediocre family wants to spend what little he has in savings on his treatment here."

"I'm sorry." I jumped to my feet. "I'm so darn busy trying not to catch AIDS, I forgot to consider your feelings. I forgot that unless it's about you or your homework or your friends at the beach, it doesn't matter. What does one son of a bitch dying of AIDS, who by the way, happens to be the father of my children, matter compared to your needs?"

"See? This is how it is." Armand jumped to his feet, too, and punched the olive tree trunk. "One minute, he's a monster, and the next, he becomes your dying husband, and you love him."

"Yes, for me, he's all of those things. You don't like your father or mother, but you do love them, don't you? You hate it when your mother's gone for six months at a time but comes back to impose birthdays and Mother's Day and Christmas celebrations on you. You complain to me, but you play along. How's this different?"

"I don't care. I can't be with you anymore."

Sizzling in anger, I snatched my purse off the grass. "Right," I said through my teeth, shame washing all over me. The shame of dating a younger person. The shame of having been needy enough to succumb to it. "Don't let me keep you here for another minute. I'm sorry I wasted this much of your time."

"I didn't ask you to leave."

"Right. Then what *did* you ask? I know you're young. I know I should never have depended on you the way I did. Now you're making me pay for it."

"I'm sorry I'm letting you down."

"Sure, you are. That's why you're doing this, aren't you?"

"I'll just go. Because whatever I say won't sound right."

"Yes. Please go, and I'll try to forget I ever met you." I walked away so I wouldn't see Armand leave me, so he wouldn't see the raw pain in my eyes.

On my walk back to my mother-in-law's, I had no tears left to wring out of my head. Of course Armand had left me. *I loved him, didn't I? In my life, love always leads to loss. How did I forget that detail? Why did I ever think I wouldn't lose Armand the way I lost Chirag?* It was never the characters, but the circumstances. They won until they became the fabric of fiction, like in *Romeo and Juliet* or *Anthony and Cleopatra* or *Tristan and Isolde* or my all-time favorite, *Love Story*, that I had identified with so much, once upon a time.

It wasn't me Armand didn't love. It was Sergio and his obstructive presence. *Yet what can I do?* I belonged to Sergio long before Armand came along and stole my heart. That was what Armand never understood—the invisible chains shackling me to Sergio, his past, my past, and the children we shared. It was a salt monolith no amount of tears could dissolve.

The following morning, I watched the carpool children enter through the Villa Maria's portal. With nowhere else to go, I drove over to Eva's house in San Borja.

"*Armand* ditched you?" Eva let me in and got back into bed. Her hand petted the flank of her malamute, Yorgi, with his Mickey Mouse forehead, lying beside her on the covers. "I saw this coming a while ago." She patted a spot for me to sit.

"Why didn't you warn me?" I wiped my eyes with a corner of Eva's bedsheet.

"Because the collision was happening in slow motion. I know you're bitter right now, but this isn't Armand's fault any more than it is yours. It's the situation. It was always untenable. I could sit here and say, 'Armand shouldn't have met Sergio, or this or that, but in the end, the outcome would always have been the same."

"No. If I had possessed the brains to keep them apart, Armand wouldn't have broken up with me, nor would Sergio be punishing me over my relationship."

"Noor. Be real. If Sergio hadn't met Armand, you would never have had the opportunity to see him anyway. That, too, would have broken up your relationship. You have to understand who you're dealing with here. Armand is not an ordinary twenty-one-year—"

"Eva." I rolled my eyes. "Say something I don't know."

"No. You're missing my point. You don't want to hear this, but Armand chose you because he needed a mother as much as he needed a girlfriend. Don't you see the writing on the wall? He had tons of girls his own age to choose from at his university. Pretty girls, young girls, girls such as Karina. And he isn't lacking in good looks, so that wasn't the problem. Why did he go so far out of his way to pursue you?

"He did it because the first time he butted heads with you at the Roosevelt, you didn't condone his actions. But you also didn't report him to the school authorities. Instead, you forced him to take responsibility. Real, true responsibility. It was more attention than he had ever received from either of his parents.

Ever. He didn't have their attention even when he struggled as a child—he had tutors... but he had your attention.

"Don't you see what is happening? He can't take this relationship anymore because he doesn't have your direct attention. You can't blame him for being the product of his circumstances any more than you can blame yourself for being the product of your circumstances. But please don't sit here and condemn him—"

I burst into tears. "Tell me what to do, Eva," I sobbed. "I am falling apart here. I can't take the pain of him ditching me when I need him more than ever."

"Noor. You have to girdle up and take it. You don't have the luxury of being twenty-one. You're thirty. You have two little children who depend on you, and a sick husband. They are your first priority, period. When you think of Armand, don't do it in anger. Appreciate how much he did for you while he was around. If this is any consolation—like he left you, I can guarantee he'll come back, because he loves you too. But his coming back will simulate a child returning to its mother. Armand is a sweetheart, but he isn't the rock you need, and he'll never become that rock, either, because he'll always lack those nine years of experience you have over him, besides the trauma of his dysfunctional childhood. But when he does return, *you'll* have to choose. If you take him back, know that he will leave you again. Otherwise, choose better this time around, and let him go. I know you love him. He loves you, too, but he isn't what you need in a partner. You require someone older and stronger who can support you and your two girls. That person is not Armand."

I drove away from Eva's house convinced Eva was right. I loved Armand because he wasn't normal. He was as extravagant as a rich, gooey chocolate cake. But I couldn't live on cake, and it hurt like hell. I had to muscle up and focus on Sergio and Pia and Abril because they were my responsibility, the same as tending to Didima had been my responsibility, fair or not.

Back at the house, I let my purse and keys fall to the floor of the downstairs hallway, as if my body couldn't take the struggle any longer.

Hearing me come in, Sergio called out from the study, "My head itches. Can you wash my hair?"

"Sure." He was all I had left. I struggled to control my exhaustion and tears. "I'll come for you in a minute. Let me change."

I picked up my fallen purse and keys.

Upstairs, I stared at my tear-blotched face in the master bathroom mirror.

What has my life come to? I had to get my act together. I had to. A splash of cold water on my face helped. I wiped off the water and headed back downstairs.

Sergio registered my ravaged face. "Armand hasn't called, has he? Are the two of you okay?"

"We broke up." *That should make you happy.*

"What happened?" Sergio's tone of concern sounded false, and it sandpapered my raw nerves.

"Nothing I want to share. But if it serves as any consolation, he's gone. I guess I discovered I couldn't have a husband and a boyfriend all at once."

"I'm sorry."

Again that false concern, as if I'm too stupid to detect it. "Serg. It's okay." I swallowed the obstinate lump in my throat. "You don't have to pretend you're sorry. We're all human here, and we love, and we hate, and we make mistakes." I wanted to add he had made the biggest mistake of all, contracting AIDS through irresponsible sex, *But to what point?* Hurting Sergio wouldn't lessen my pain, the pain of knowing that if he had been well and divorced me, I might have had a chance with Armand. *Will Armand come back to me, like Eva said? What will I do if he does? What will I do if he doesn't?*

58

That afternoon, I left Valle Hermoso again to do the children's carpool. On the way home, my stomach heaved so hard I stepped on the accelerator to get home before I ended up vomiting all over myself. On our patio, I leapt from the car to retch in dry heaves on the flagstones, only then remembering that I had nothing in my stomach to vomit. Instead, a thin stream of bright-yellow bile stained the gray stones while Pia wrenched out of the car and hugged me from behind.

"¿Qué pasa, Mamita? ¿Qué pasa? ¿Estás bien?"

My head sank to my knees, and I broke into loud, racking sobs. I disengaged from Pia's hug and charged up the stairs to land on my bed, facedown to muffle my crying.

My eight-year-old chased after me, a glass of water in hand. "Mamá, *Mamita*, have this water."

But I couldn't take my face off the bedcover as Pia lay beside me and put an arm around my waist. I clamped a palm on my own wailing to sit up and hug my child with my free arm. "Mmm, *mmmi amor*, I'll be fine. Go have lunch."

"But, Mamá, I want to be with you. You're not well."

I took stock of Pia's scared face and forced a smile. "I am, sweetie. I am. I just n-need to sleep. I didn't sleep well last night. Go have your lunch." *Can Sergio hear me from downstairs? What will he attribute my breakdown to?*

Once Pia left, I rummaged through my nightstand drawer for my bottle of antianxiety pills. I shook out six tablets instead of my normal dose of one and rushed to the bathroom sink to gulp them. Then I dove under my eiderdown quilt, muzzled a pillow over my mouth to wail again, and waited for sleep to take over.

Given the ratio of body mass to quantity of medication, I could have slept through the next day as well, were it not for Dulci and Pia, who shook me awake at dawn. I stirred, my mind adrift on a sea of clouds.

Pia's head poked right through those clouds. "*Mamá, te toca el pool.* You have to do the carpool."

I tried to open my eyes, but my eyelids were sealed. I attempted to clutch Pia's hand outspread on my chest, but my arm remained rooted to the bed. Pia's fingers parted my right eyelid, and the child's face emerged in wide-angled view. I heard Dulci draw back the curtains, and I endeavored to turn my head but couldn't.

"*¿Mamita?*" Pia's smile trembled. "*¿Estás bien?*"

"*Sí*," I croaked, moving eyes inside the rock that was my head. I had to get up. If the children missed school on my account, Sergio would report that to his family, and it would provide them with more fodder to gossip about. Holding on to that thought, I fought the weights securing me to the bed.

I didn't know if Sergio had told his mother and Nila of Armand's existence in my life, but I assumed he had. Mostly, I didn't see Nila, since Sergio requested I remain upstairs when she visited him, so it was hard to tell what she knew and what she didn't, but I had not forgotten her wishing me dead in Miami. With my head thus loaded, I had developed a royal migraine by the time I came home from the carpool.

Migraine and all, I washed Sergio's hair at eleven, grateful I didn't have to do an afternoon carpool. But that relief evaporated by one o'clock, when a knock on the outside door revealed Nila walking in. She didn't catch me policing her through my bedroom French doors. I would have to remain trapped upstairs for who knew how long. Tormented as I felt, I couldn't even read, so I lay in bed and replayed Armand ditching me until tears took over and I had to muffle my sobs so Sergio and Nila wouldn't hear me from the study.

At two, the children came home from school, giving me the excuse to focus on them rather than my own drama. After lunch in the kitchen with Dulci, they came upstairs, and I went into their room. "Abril, show me what homework you have. My head hurts, so I want to help you now if you need it."

"Mamá," Pia protested. "I need help first. Today, we learned what a composition is, and I have to write one."

"Of course, amor. What is the topic? You know what a topic is, right?"

Dulci came to the door. "Señora Noor, Señor Sergio's sister wants to speak to you."

My heart felt like it crashed against my ribs. "Did she say why?"

"Not to me. I'm just the maid." Dulci smiled wryly.

"Then help Pia, Duls, until I get back."

I was halfway down the stairwell when Nila, standing at the bottom, looked up. "Shall we go for a walk?"

"Sure." I gave Nila a nervous nod. "I was helping Pia with homework, but I can walk with you for a bit. Let me put on a pair of shoes and a heavier sweater. It's never this cold in September."

In silence, Nila headed downhill toward the Jesuit school footpath lined with Australian eucalyptus, which always reminded me of the Lodhi Gardens in New Delhi. I plucked a leaf and rubbed it between my palms to inhale the scent. For me it evoked the Vicks VapoRub salve Didima used to rub on my chest whenever I suffered a cold as a child.

Nila's suede boots rang on the concrete pavement. Abruptly, Nila asked, "Do you want to return to school? What would you study this time?"

"I can't. We don't have the money."

She changed her question. "How is my brother doing?"

My lips pursed. "I don't know. He doesn't receive the care he did in the States."

"Is it hard for you to tend to him?"

"It's hard to deal with the wound on his hip because it won't heal."

"What wound?"

"Oh, Sergio didn't tell you? He scratched a mosquito bite on his right hip, and the spot became a sore. Now the sore is the size of an orange. Dr. Ritter says it's a huge infection risk for him and me. That's why I sponge bathe him and wash his hair at the kitchen sink."

"And that's hard, right?" she demanded.

"Yes."

"Then go back to India. We'll look after Sergio and the girls." Nila said this as if she had achieved her objective.

"What did you say?" I halted to crush the eucalyptus leaf between my fingers.

"I said, go back to India." That time Nila didn't bother to disguise her hostility. "That's where you belong, and that's where you should be."

"Are you saying this because of what I did in Miami?"

"No, Noor. I'm saying this because it's time you left our family."

I stared at her. *Their family? I don't have any connection to Pia and Abril? Besides, who's the one taking care of Sergio and exposing herself to AIDS every day?* But instead of saying anything, I ran back to the house.

At our door, I thumped on it like a lunatic until Dulci ran out to see what was wrong. I brushed past the young girl to charge into the study. "You dick! You sent your *sister* to chase me out of Lima when I'm the one who bathes you, dresses your wound, and cleans your shit each day? You want me gone so if you die, my children will live with your horrid relatives and not me because I'm not good enough?"

Sergio's left eye developed a tic. "Noor, lower your voice. Calm down. These days, I don't know what I do or say."

"Calm *down*? I'll calm down once you're dead. Do you hear me? And here I am, the idiot who never blames you for bringing AIDS into our lives. So now you listen to me. You and your nasty family will take my kids away from me over my dead body. Is that clear?"

"Noor, listen. Listen to me." Sergio's voice shook as his eyes became wet, looking wide and panicked.

I trembled. "I haven't forgotten how you threatened to leave me behind in India and bring the kids to Peru." I ran out of the study and up the stairs, shouting, "Tell your *sister* to sponge-bathe you today and to dress your disgusting AIDS-infested wound because I'm taking the kids to Carla's for the rest of the weekend." Upstairs, I hollered, "Homework is over! Come on, you two. Let's go to Carla's."

"No!" said Pia. "I don't want to go to Carla's. I want to go to Auntie Eva's at the beach. With Armand. We haven't been to the beach once since Papá came home. I hate it."

"I want to stay home and watch my *Cinderella* video with you," Abril complained. "I don't want to go to Carla's either." She copied her sister.

"Well, you don't have a choice." I yanked Abril to her feet.

"Mamá, you're hurting me!"

"Get up and come with me. Now! Both of you."

Pia began to cry. "You always do this. Tell us where to go and what to do. You weren't this awful when Papá was in Los Angeles. You're horrible now!"

"I'm sorry. I'm sorry I've become this way. Now, be a good girl, and hurry up and come with me."

Nila reentered the patio as I bundled the children into the car. Without glancing at her, I shot out of the house, controlling tears lest the children asked why I was crying.

Ten minutes passed. I noticed how my right fist was throbbing on my lap. Unclenching my fingers revealed the remains of the Australian eucalyptus leaf. Again, I remembered Didima and chest rubs with Vicks VapoRub. But Didima was long dead, and soon, Sergio might be too. That possibility punctured the anger in my head, releasing it like air out of a tire. But I drove on, unwilling to reencounter Nila.

"What is it?" Abril craned her neck.

I handed the child the crushed leaf. "Smell it. Tell me what it reminds you of."

"*Huele a beebaporoob.*" Abril handed Pia the mangled leaf.

The Peruvian distortion of the English proper noun put a grimace on my lips. I needed to teach my children my comfort language. Both Pia and Abril wrote some English, but other than the songs I sang to them, which they knew by heart, they couldn't say one English phrase right. That equation bothered me deeply, since English was the world language, but I had so much else on my plate, I couldn't even think to address it.

At Carla's, the reality of my sick husband being my responsibility simmered in my brain. After dark, I left the children to enjoy the relief of a weekend away from the turbulence of our home and drove away, though the Bustos would gladly have accommodated me in their crowded Magdalena townhouse, had I asked.

By then, Nila would be long gone. Dulci would soon go to bed, and Sergio couldn't be alone.

When Dulci let me into the house, the study lights were on.

From the hallway, Sergio said, "Noor?"

Reluctantly, I went into the study.

"What happened between you and Nila? She wouldn't tell me."

I smiled. "She told me to go back to India, where I belong. Leaving Pia and Abril here with you and your family, of course."

"She didn't mean it."

"Actually, she did. And I'm not sure you didn't put her up to it."

"I swear I didn't."

"Well, what else would you swear?" I swerved to hide my tears and headed up the stairwell.

Behind me, Dulci followed.

"What is it, Duls?"

"Today, Señor Sergio realized how much you do for him."

"Why? What happened?"

"His sister decided to sponge him down, and after she finished, I had to remove the rug from next to the señor's bed because she wet the whole thing."

"And his wound? Did she clean and dress that?"

"No. She left it all wet. After she left, Señor Sergio requested I change it like you do every day. He said, 'I don't know if Señora Noor will come home tonight, Dulci. And without her, I can't change it, because I can't see it.'"

"What? Oh my God!" *Will Dulci be the next AIDS victim in the house?* I shouldn't have left. I placed a hand on my chest. "Did you wear gloves?"

"No. I forgot."

"Dulci! Show me your hands. Do you have any open sores?"

Dulci spread her fingers, turning her palms up. "I don't think so."

"Did you touch the raw part of his wound?" *Say no. Please say no.* My fingers tensed into two tight balls.

"I don't remember. I patted it dry with a piece of gauze, spread antibiotic ointment, and dressed it back up."

"Did you spread the antibiotic with your finger?" My heart beat like a drum. I didn't need this. *God! Why did I leave the house?*

"No. I did it with the same piece of gauze I used to dry the wound."

I put my arm around Dulci's shoulders and squeezed them. "Go down, and go to sleep. We could both use the rest."

Saturday came, uncaring of my broken heart or somber mood, and a watery sun shone all morning. Seeing it, Sergio asked to sit on the porch. Once he got tired, I helped him, his gait wobbly, his passage halting, back to the study for his ablutions. To touch him was disconcerting. Through the blue-and-white kimono sleeve, the flesh above his elbow hung so loose, it felt as if it would come off if I pulled on it.

I undressed him and squeezed the sponge in my hand, the silence between us marked. Sergio's face had sharpened to a gauntness that was transparent. If

I looked long enough, I would see his thin, tainted blood within veins astride bones as bleached and porous as the bones I remembered see-ing scattered in the wheat fields adjacent to the Loreto Convent School towards the end of every winter during my childhood. Each time I moved his limbs, Sergio's tendons stood out in stunning articulation at the ends of each desiccated muscle to out-line their attachment to the bone, making my husband resemble Christ on the cross.

For once, he didn't complain about the asperity of my gloved hands as I wiped and dressed his upper body. While I addressed the wound on his right hip, Sergio shivered despite the two area heaters, which had me perspiring as if we were in a sauna. Though the wound emitted no smell nor bled each day, it unnerved me to watch how its ragged edges ate away at the healthy flesh around it, a strange carnivorous being.

On Monday morning, I volunteered to carpool for a parent who required emer-gency medical attention. I lost my composure when a metallic-brown Volvo sta-tion wagon shot in front of my car at the four-way intersection of the Mercado de Surquillo. My fingers tightened on the steering wheel, and Abril's voice faded inside my head. *Was that Armand? Why is he so far from home, this early? His university is in the opposite direction. Did Armand sleep with another girl? Is it that easy for him to forget me already?* In my imagination, I invented a relationship between Armand and a new girl, one much younger than me. I saw him laugh at the new girl's jokes, praise her cooking, and make love to her perfect body. When the tears in my eyes blurred the road, I stopped the car before I crashed it with five innocent six-year-old passengers.

At home, I lay in bed, my whole being burning with hatred toward the Santanders. I developed goosebumps at the sound of Nila arriving after lunch but forced myself to breathe. *Why do I seek acquittal from any member of Sergio's family?* I was the foreign outsider who Sergio had married, and all his misfor-tunes were my fault.

The showdown would come if Sergio died. My eyes stung with anger. *The Santanders will not take my children away from me. They will discover who I am if they try.*

IRISES

59

Lima, September 1992

THE MOON WAS HIGH IN the dawning sky when I sat up in bed, blinking at the lucidity of the dream I had just had. *Am I losing my mind, like Sergio?* But the dream's message persisted. The sooner Sergio died, the more chances that his will and testament would leave me half his estate and Pia and Abril the rest. *Contrarily, if he lives long enough to alter his will, who knows what scheme he and his conniving family will hatch to take my children away from me?*

It didn't matter that I tended to Sergio day after day. If it suited his family's purpose, Sergio was capable of separating me from my children. *Why else would he have intimated leaving me behind in India and taking Pia and Abril away from me five years ago? Would he have had the gall to think that, let alone say it, if I had had an influential father like Dadu?* Of course not.

But Sergio had said it because he could. The same as Nila had said what she had said because she could. The same as a nineteen-year-old had talked himself into my life because he could. Because when they looked at me, they saw no more than a dragonfly to nail to the drawing board of their own interests with one jab of a thumbtack straight through my heart. In the grand scheme of Sergio's life, I didn't matter. Period. Even on his deathbed, I didn't matter, though I had borne his children. Pia and Abril were half of me as much as they were half of Sergio, but that didn't count for the Santanders.

I swung out of bed, my life playing out like a movie inside my head. *What about me invites abuse?* Whatever it was, my stepfather had spotted it in me like a signpost, daring to molest me with my mother sleeping on the floor in plain sight. That same quality had propelled my mother to dump the care of Didima on my shoulders since I was twelve years old. From that year on, I had become Didima's caretaker while my mother had played Florence Nightingale to her ailing husband, whose drinking and driving made him smash his motorcycle into the leg of a defenseless teenager, maiming the boy for life.

That weakness in me had been Rajat's opening to con me into having sex with him, impregnate me, then encourage me to abort the consequences of his action. It had also been Sergio's incentive to marry me to have the children he had wanted. And that same character flaw had encouraged Armand to hang around me like a bee at a greenhouse door until I had let him in to get what he had wanted from me all along.

But I would end the vicious cycle. I would kill Sergio before he or his family could take my children away from me. It was that simple.

Killing Sergio would be frighteningly easy. The streets of Lima had no sewers because, of course, *it never rained there*. Therefore, I intended to find the filthiest puddle I could and take the water home to mix in with Sergio's food. It was the ghastliest act I could think to do. The nature of his weakened immune system would accomplish the rest.

Dulci's mouth rounded in an O as I entered the kitchen, fully dressed at six thirty, purse strap slung over one shoulder.

"How come you're up so early? What's the matter?" She searched my face for an answer.

"Nothing." Anxious fingers groped inside my purse to touch the empty Centrum vitamin bottle I had hidden there.

On my way out of the house, I rolled down the car window. "Duls, tell him I won't come home until I fetch the kids in the afternoon. I'm visiting Carla."

"Good for you," muttered Dulci. "That way you might miss his witch of a sister when she comes to visit."

At the Villa Maria, I deposited my young charges at the school doorway. To complete my task, I had to reach the Mercado Central in the center of Lima, the old city marketplace, like Chandni Chowk in Old Delhi. But I didn't know how to drive there, and leaving the car in front of the school was out of the question. As soon as I left, thieves would strip it or steal it within minutes of my departure.

So I found a spot inside a parking garage a mile away from the school, grudging the money it would cost. I stuffed my Centrum bottle in a cheap vinyl shopping bag and locked my purse in the trunk. My feet racewalked to the Avenida Petit Thouars.

Taking a bus in Lima was an adventure I had mastered from my college days there. In an hour, I alighted on Avenida Abancay, focused on crossing the busy avenue chockablock with buses, cars, diesel fumes, and exhaust smoke to access the Mercado Central on the other side.

The sight of the mercado evoked sharp and distinct memories of those Sunday-afternoon trips from four years ago, when Sergio had brought the children and me to Chinatown for dumplings to relieve his mother of our unwanted presence for a few hours. But that was one among my husband's many personas. What I *did* know was that one of those Sergios had used me to have children so no one would suspect he was bisexual and he wouldn't shame himself or his family. But once he had achieved his goal, I became expendable.

Coming to the mercado always stirred me. On the one hand, its curious smell of dust saturated with dampness and wood smoke and the pretty, colonial architecture on the Congress Plaza told me I was in faraway Peru. That feeling was heightened by its people, grim-faced and fearful due to the climate of terrorism mixed in with poverty, hurrying along, never meeting the eyes, belongings hugged to their chests for fear of bag snatching—but then, the odors of sweat, putrefaction, and rubbish on the street reminded me of India and home, and my heart would wrestle with my decision to leave my own country only to never belong in Peru either.

Stop! Today of all days, I couldn't do that to myself. I needed to focus.

I walked, slowed by the sheer volume of humanity. My eyes fell on the barricaded Inquisition building ahead. Sergio had explained that it was off limits, not owing to disrepair but because the government couldn't decide if it wanted people to see the unspeakable torture instruments it housed, plus the bad vibes of all those who had died in the building in underground chambers.

I shivered and glanced away, and the first thing I saw was an old lady walking her *pet sheep* through the madness. The sheared animal wore a phosphorescent-yellow T-shirt to protect it from the dank September cold. Its random presence reminded me of Sergio's Pneumocystis carinii sheep pneumonia he had suffered three bouts of in Los Angeles.

Am I really going to kill Sergio? Immediately, my heart tightened with opposing emotions. It was either that or risk losing my children to the Santanders. Whether it was his dementia or his intent to take Pia and Abril away from me, Sergio would side with his family. And *they* wouldn't hesitate to drown me if they needed to. I couldn't—I *wouldn't* allow that.

What I *would* find was a street called Calle Ayacucho. It was the dirtiest street in the market, where caged animals were sold. *But where is it?* I clutched my vinyl shopping bag to my chest and approached the lady with the pet sheep.

"Señora, where is Calle Ayacucho?"

The lady pointed to the left. "Down the side of the congress building."

But as I hurried into the street she had indicated, I saw faded-pink two-story row housing, not animals for sale. At least the street was a pedestrian street, so no traffic to contend with, but time was frittering by, and I had to get back to the Villa Maria to do the afternoon carpool. My hands clenched. *Was that animal-selling street scrapped? Or did I remember the incorrect name?* Around me, people thronged, but they didn't appear approachable. Yet I had a mission, and I couldn't fail.

I walked on. In the middle of the busy street, an old lady hunched behind a plastic table. She was so old her hands resembled dirty claws inside torn woolen gloves, and I didn't know if she could see out of her rheumy eyes. She sold wooden rosaries, incense, dried frogs, and desiccated lizards to unite Catholicism from Spain with black magic from the Amazon jungles.

"Señora!" I bent to her level and raised my voice, as if to assume she was deaf as well. "Where do they sell animals?" From that distance, I could smell her rotted teeth.

"Here." She pointed behind one shoulder. "Further down."

Relief.

But further down proved to be a new street altogether. Calle Ayacucho had two parts, a fact no one had mentioned to me. I hurried into the street with cages stacked upon each other, besieged by the smell of animal fur, stale urine, and the warm, milky scent of puppies. But the sour odors of unwashed human bodies, decayed wood, and humid woolen clothing overpowered the former. I fought my way past the staring eyes of puppies, kittens, birds, rabbits, and guinea pigs, ignoring the desperate writhing within cloth bags stuffed with wild snakes from the Amazon jungle. Vendors urged me to buy a rabbit for my stew pot. A guinea pig for a succulent family roast.

Suddenly, my heart jolted, and I missed my footing and stumbled. Toward the end of the street, a puddle glistened next to the footpath where a gutter should have been but wasn't. Alongside it stood the stacked cages of flapping jungle parrots.

Parrots...

Lima didn't have the wild parrots of my Calcutta childhood. In my memory, every summer lunch at our Jodpur Park townhouse included the raucous company of parrots feeding on the plate-sized sunflower heads in Baba's vegetable garden. My pace quickened to reach the cages of the jungle parrots. I had a mental image of entering our home in Valle Hermoso with a hundred parrots to set free. Yet for each bird I freed, dozens more would be captured. *They need to wise up to their reality and charge the world head-on, like me.*

At last, I stopped in front of the elongated puddle and refused to look at the parrot cages to my right. Within my own shapeless midday shadow, my evil quest stared back up at me. Its gray-brown surface reflected the colors of the rainbow in droplets of grease on its stagnant surface. *If this doesn't kill Sergio, nothing will.* Behind me, the pale-pink façade of the Church of Santa Rosa urged me to reflect and reconsider what I was doing. As if to mock me, the Palace of Justice stood at a diagonal, asking where the justice was in what would happen to me if I didn't kill Sergio. And right next to me, a beady-eyed vendor, bright in his winter clothing and woolen mountain hat, gums bleeding from the coca leaves he chewed, waited for me to inquire the price of his parrots. Meanwhile, time ticked by, and I had to hurry to get back to do the afternoon carpool.

Without further ado, I fished out my Centrum bottle and unscrewed the childproof cap. My hand hovered over the cesspool to cast a thick question-mark shadow on its oily surface. I closed my eyes and dunked it, wiping the foul-smelling residue with a corner of my blouse.

On the carpool ride home, Pia sniffed and asked, "Mamá, what's that horrible smell?"

"Nothing, amor. I tripped and fell into a dirty pothole. That's why the edge of my blouse is filthy, see?" Thank goodness it was all Pia noticed and not that I had arrived dangerously late for the carpool, again. I hated that in the end, I had to kill Sergio, but losing Pia and Abril to the Santanders was not going to happen.

At three p.m., the modulated tenor of Nila's voice from the study did not disturb me. After more than a week, I focused on a P. G. Wodehouse farce and laughed out loud at the impossible antics of its main character, Lord Emsworth of Blandings Castle, whom I loved like a favorite uncle. I heard the usual squabble coming from the children's room while Dulci played the referee.

I went in to settle the fight. "What's the problem, amor?" I smiled at Pia.

"Tell Dulci to help me with my math homework before she does social studies with Abril."

"Come on. Let Duls help Abril. I'll help you with math."

An hour later, Dulci came into my bedroom and shut the door.

"*¿Qué pasa, Dulcita?*"

Dulci leaned on the door, hands behind her back. "Armand called while you were gone to Carla's."

My heart changed rhythm at the sound of his name, but I kept quiet.

"I didn't tell you earlier in case you started crying," continued Dulci. "You freaked the children out last week."

"What did he want?" I stared past the French doors of the bedroom at the upper outline of the Jesuit school with its one bell tower.

"He asked to speak to you."

My mouth warped. "Did you ask why? Was it for a homework question? That's all he ever needed me for, didn't he? The purpose I served in his life? To be the mommy who kept him in line because his own mother never did."

"I don't know." Dulci crossed her arms. "But he sounded pretty depressed."

"Duls—if Armand calls again, tell him I'm not home. No—don't even tell me he called." How easy it would be if I could forget him. But what Eva had said was true. To him, I had been part girlfriend and part mother, and I wasn't ready to play that part. *Sorry, Armand. Go find yourself a different mother. I have my own kids to save.*

Dulci shook her hands. "I almost didn't tell you this time, but then I doubted myself."

"Well, I'm your *patrona*, and I'm telling you never to tell me if he calls."

At dusk, on the heels of Nila's visit, I went into Sergio's study. "Do you want a sponge down?" I wanted to say, *What? Nila didn't offer to sponge you again? Or leave your AIDS-infested dressing all wet and soggy so she wouldn't expose herself to your disease? No. That's my job because I'm the poor, expendable immigrant from far-off India. Who cares if I contract AIDS? Nobody.* But I stood still, like hired help, thinking of Sergio's hypocritical immediate family.

Those days, except Nila, no one but Jaime León came to visit Sergio. Them and Horacio, the adopted godson. Even Sergio's harpy mother's excuse was that she didn't have a ride to come see him. And Carlos, who lived next door, dropped in every ten days or so but never entered the study, where Sergio lay. He talked to his brother in hurried phrases from its doorway, hands inside black leather gloves, as if Sergio's AIDS might become airborne and infect him. Only Horacio came by on most Wednesday mornings with the faithfulness of a rescued pet, bearing an offering of two packets of soda crackers, the meager gift he could afford on his salary as Nila's unofficial house cleaner. Lost in my reflections, I jerked when Sergio attempted pleasantness.

"How was your visit with Carla?"

"What?"

"I said, how is Carla? You visited her today, right?"

Christ. I had forgotten my lie to Dulci that morning. "She's fine." To cover up the lie, I hurried on. "Do you want a sponge bath or not?"

"No, just change my dressing. What route did you take to Magdalena? Nila said the whole back section behind the Golf Club is dug up."

Nonplussed, I grappled to reply. "I don't know the names of the streets around there, but I recognized where I was when a side street threw me out onto the Avenida Marina." Hoping my answer made sense, I pulled on a pair of disposable gloves. Once I killed him, neither he nor his family would ever be able to scare me again. Or steal Pia and Abril from me. The sorry lot of them simply didn't know it yet, so they were lording over me. But tomorrow, I would end my misery.

60

After carpool in the morning, I lay dressed on my bed and stared at the Jesuit school tower piercing the sky above the perimeter wall of our house. The Jesuit's bell would peal any minute to mark Sergio's lunch hour.

Do I have the guts to kill him?

Immediately, the image of Nila in the downstairs hallway asking to go for a walk flared in my mind, and my eyes smarted. I angrily passed a shirtsleeve over their moistness and glanced at my antique dressing table. The bottleful of filthy water rested right inside its left drawer.

Too impatient to wait for the Jesuit's bell, I pulled out my nefarious cargo and trotted down the stone staircase, smelling the rich aroma of yellow-orange Peruvian pumpkin soup, Sergio's favorite.

"Duls." I wedged a gray plastic doorstop under the kitchen door to conceal the vitamin bottle behind it. "Is the soup ready?"

"Yes." Dulci poured chilled cream into the steaming concoction. "I'm serving him."

"Well, let me do it because I have to ask him for grocery money. You know how he hates that, so it'll go better over food. Go catch up with your ironing." I selected a black ceramic soup bowl out of a kitchen cabinet.

Heart beating hard, I waited to hear Dulci unfold the ironing board in the laundry room. On tiptoe, I retrieved the plastic bottle from behind the immobilized wooden door. Right then, the Jesuit bell tolled twelve times. *Ouch. How should I interpret that? As a sign from God or the devil? Will I go to hell for doing this?* Well, if I went to hell, I would take Pia and Abril there with me.

I placed the Centrum bottle on the marble countertop to click-click open the childproof bottle cap. Out flew the horrific stench from the cesspool at the Mercado Central. My hand shook as six drops of noxious brown sludge landed in the empty soup bowl. On top of it, I ladled three scoops of steaming pumpkin soup with a trembling hand and stirred. I raised the bowl to my nose. *What if Sergio smells my tampering? Or doesn't eat today, as on so many other afternoons? Then you'll do this again tomorrow. Sergio and his family will not take Pia and Abril away from you. Now or ever.* I hid the vitamin bottle under the kitchen sink amidst cleaning agents.

The study had a stale dog-blanket smell from closed windows. On the surface of Sergio's black-lacquered desk, the ghost-pale shadow of a stray bougainvillea bough swayed. I absorbed Sergio in one long gaze. My husband's emaciated body was propped up by several pillows on the narrow twin bed, reading glasses poised low on his nose. A leather-bound copy of five *National Geographic* magazines rested on pronounced knees under silk pajamas. One hand thumbed its cream-colored pages while the other staved a yawn.

Seeing me, Sergio snapped his mouth shut. He removed his glasses and smiled. "Is that my pumpkin soup?" His lips puckered as he cracked his knuckles like dry toast. Arms rose with trembling palms up.

At that precise moment, the whole room expanded in my vision, and Sergio receded to the far end of a transparent tunnel. My hands, followed by my arms, grew numb, becoming two blocks of ice until I didn't feel the soup bowl anymore. Soup and bowl crashed to the Darjazin rug in a frightful orange mess. I broke into loud sobs and curled around Sergio's soup-soiled black suede Gucci bedroom slippers as if waking from a nightmare.

This is Sergio, the person who removed me from India. The father of my two children. How did I even conceive of killing him? He's dying anyway. Do I really want the karma of killing the one man who has stood by me more than any other man in my life?

Slowly, Sergio moved to get off the bed. "Are you okay?"

My crying brought Dulci from the laundry room. Bawling, I struggled to my feet and rushed past her.

Upstairs, I sobbed as I stepped out of my dirty clothes. I snorted in a runny nose and staggered into the bathroom to turn on the shower. I couldn't be late for carpool. Hysterical laughter bounced off the bathroom walls until the tears resumed. Once I came back, I had to wash Sergio's hair. My day had no room for the luxury of madness.

When I came downstairs, Sergio asked, "What happened to you? Are you okay?"

"I don't know. I think I was near fainting. My arms went numb. Did you eat? Did Dulci serve you more soup?"

"Yes. She's washing the rug right now."

At the Villa Maria, I approached Pia's teacher. "Marianna, can I write a letter to the school and specify that *no one* other than the carpool parents can ever pick up my children?"

"You don't have to. Since the terrorism escalated ten years ago, the school pays us extra to staff our classes until the last student is gone. If the administration ever received a complaint from a parent about this, we could lose our jobs, so don't worry."

But I did worry. I waited until Nila arrived at the house. Then I phoned Frida, knowing that Sergio wouldn't listen on the phone extension with his sister present. "Frids, I haven't had a chance to tell you this, but five days ago, Nila told me to leave the country and go home to India without Pia and Abril."

"What?"

"Yes. Don't ask how I've been." I pleated the edge of my T-shirt.

"*Dios mío*—haven't I taught you that attack is the best form of defense? You should have slapped her face. I know I would have slapped her. What did you say?"

"Nothing to her, but I lost it on Sergio. I screamed every insult I could at him and stormed out of the house with the kids." I let the T-shirt go and traced the pattern of my bedspread with an index finger.

"She's bluffing. No one can take your kids away from you. The law wouldn't let them."

"What law? The law that made the police ask you why on earth you stopped at a red traffic signal last Christmas, when you got mugged? What would stop Nila from kidnapping my children after Sergio dies?"

"Hey, stop being paranoid. How could she kidnap the children when they never leave home without you?"

"Yes. But what if the kidnapping happened at *la Vieja Bruja's* house?" I referred to our mother-in-law by the nickname of "old witch" we had given her together. "Nila knows I have no money to hire a lawyer."

"Jesus, calm down. Nila would have to prove you abandoned them. That's why she told *you* to leave the country, the clever bitch. She'd also have to prove you were an incompetent mother, and trust me, *I'll* give evidence you're not."

"How do you know this?"

"Because, I've told you this before—my dad's best friend is a lawyer. If the Santanders ever do any such thing, I promise my dad's friend will represent you for free, okay? Now can you stop worrying the sky will fall on your head?"

"Easy for you to say. You aren't alone in a foreign country with a bunch of jackals like the Santanders on your tail. How would *you* feel if someone threatened to take your kids away from you?" My fingers clenched even saying that out loud.

"I would kill them."

Exactly. But I didn't admit to that.

In the evening, after Nila left, I went to the study to check if Sergio wanted dinner.

"No. Can you sponge me down instead? I'm cold and sweaty."

My head cocked. "How can you be cold when this room is boiling with two area heaters?"

"I'm probably developing pneumonia."

My heart lurched. "Why? You don't have a cough or shallow breath." *If killing him was what I wanted to do this morning, why do I now have such a fierce desire to protect him? Why can I never control what I feel for Sergio? Literature claims love and hate are two sides of the same coin. Is that why Serg and I veer in and out of meanness and kindness toward each other without missing a beat?*

"Because I am sweating. Whenever I got pneumonia in Los Angeles, I would sweat profusely during the days prior."

"Do you have a fever? I can't tell in this heat." I placed an exposed wrist on Sergio's damp forehead.

"I never ran a temperature, but the pneumonia was always there."

"I'll call for Dr. Ritter to come by." I wiped my temple with the same wrist.

"No. That'll be an extra expense. Tomorrow morning, take me back to the Rebagliati's emergency room. Dr. Ritter said not to waste time if I felt anything abnormal."

"So let's go there right now."

"No. I'm exhausted. Whenever Nila comes, she stays too long, but I can't say that to her face. Right now, even the thought of a sleepless night in that dingy emergency room makes me want to cry."

Without intending to, I hugged Sergio's frail, sitting form. God forbid I should ever feel that dependent on anybody, or that fragile. Dr. Ritter claimed the actual treatment in the Rebagliati was as good as any private hospital in Lima. *But will his team be able to cure Sergio's special brand of pneumonia?*

61

In the morning, Sergio said, "Each breath feels as though my lungs are being poked by nails. When will the kids leave? How fast can you drive me to the Rebagliati?"

"I don't have carpool today, so you see the kids off. I'll go get ready."

In the Rebagliati Hospital emergency waiting room, I begged the triage nurse, who remembered me from Sergio's last visit, to assign Sergio a stretcher to lie on. "He probably has pneumonia. If we sit on the cold floor, he'll only get worse."

Once Sergio was settled, I dashed to the lobby to call my mother-in-law to have her send either Nila or Carlos or Horacio over as soon as possible. Instinct told me that Sergio would be in the hospital a lot longer than the last time, and I couldn't accompany him indefinitely. But someone had to come and replace me before I could head home to put the children to bed that evening.

"Horacio won't be home until six," Xenobia Santander said, not even mentioning Nila or Carlos. "He has enrolled in a hairdressing course. I'll send him over then."

Throughout that day, I stood by Sergio's stretcher, tending to him as best I could. Our nightmare challenge happened every time Sergio needed to use the bathroom. I wouldn't let him sit on any public toilet seat, and he was too weak to poise to address his needs. Therefore, each time, we squeezed into the men's bathroom together, and I held him, cleaned him, redressed him, and brought him back to the stretcher. That was why I couldn't leave him alone to fend for himself, but no one showed even after seven in the evening. By that time, I was trapped between a rock and a hard place—desperate to go home and reassure the children, who had sounded distinctly unhappy on the phone when I had called them in the afternoon, and equally reluctant to abandon Sergio.

On my last call to Xenobia Santander, again she didn't deign to mention

Sergio's siblings, instead she reported, "I don't know where Horacio is. He should have been home by now." At seven thirty, I felt desperate. "Serg, I have to go home and check on the children. I'll do it as soon as I can and come back here. The triage nurse is a new one, but I've convinced her to help you to the bathroom if you should need it. Hang in there, won't you?"

Sergio nodded, eyes scared, the expression on his face so vulnerable. I looked away before he caught my eyes glistening. On the way home, I reflected on how Sergio's immediate family members were strictly good-time visitors. Not one of them had any interest in actually participating in the reality of his care. That burden fell only on the shoulders of expendable people like Horacio and myself, *if* I managed to enlist his help.

At home, I hugged and kissed Pia and Abril and sang them their bedtime songs, sick with worry that Sergio was alone and untended. Once I closed the children's bedroom door, a frantic call to Xenobia Santander's revealed Horacio was finally home.

"So when can he go to the hospital?" I chewed the inside corner of my lips, afraid I would draw blood if I wasn't careful.

"It'll go faster if you come fetch him and take him there." My mother-in-law sounded sarcastic.

"I'll be there as fast as I can." I didn't bother to ask why Nila, who lived five minutes away from my mother-in-law's, couldn't do her "favorite" brother the kindness.

Carrying a Tupperware of oatmeal porridge for Sergio, I charged out of the house. At that hour, even if he was admitted into a ward, he had missed the eight-o'clock Rebagliati dinnertime window. He wouldn't receive any food until breakfast the next day. And Sergio couldn't afford to lose yet more weight.

The ride from our house to San Isidro, even with the lighter nighttime traffic, took forty minutes. From there to the hospital car park and the long walk to the ER waiting room put me beside Sergio at eleven at night. At least he was inside the ER, but a doctor hadn't seen him yet. Nor would any doc-tor give him the meds he might need until Dr. Ritter saw him the next morn-ing. I knew that from our last visit. In Lima, the general doctors didn't know enough about AIDS patients and their needs, so they left the cases up to the specialists. Our only reason for coming to the ER was to get Sergio admitted into the hospital.

"Stay the night with me." Sergio gave me a pleading look.

"I can't." My voice quavered. "I can't inform the carpool group at this hour that I won't do the carpool tomorrow. With the curfew restrictions, I won't reach home in time to swing it if I stay the night with you. And I can't afford to antagonize that nasty carpool mother, Vera Gamarra. She'll be only too happy to kick me out, then I'll have a worse problem, especially with you in the hospital."

A light went out in Sergio's eyes when I said that.

To cheer him up, I said, "Let me go ask the nurse about the status of a room for you. Here, eat this oatmeal, meanwhile."

"They are cleaning the room," the nurse said. "He will be admitted within the next twenty minutes."

But the next twenty minutes stretched into an hour. By the time Sergio was settled in bed, with Horacio there for his nighttime care, it was twelve thirty a.m. The curfew began at midnight.

I drove away from the hospital, unnerved by how deserted Avenida Manuel Segura was. Usually, the avenue outside the hospital was packed with traffic. Feeling like a moving lighthouse, I drove slowly, praying the curfew police wouldn't arrest me if I was caught driving without the appropriate permit.

I drove for under an hour without incident. Five minutes shy of home in Valle Hermoso, after I got off Avenida Benavides, my heart relaxed, and I yawned as I passed the Jesuit school entrance.

As if waiting to ambush me, a police vehicle shot out from within the school compound as I was one house short of my garage door. Two police officers ejected from the vehicle, one aiming a rifle at my windshield, the other screaming, "Stop your car!"

I complied, my heart a huge obstruction inside my mouth as I rolled down my window.

"Explain yourself!" shouted the policeman with the gun.

"Show us your curfew permit!" barked the other one.

"I don't have one." I stuttered why I was out at all, pointing to my garage door. "This is where I live. I'm sure the Jesuit school guard has seen me before."

"I'm sorry. You're coming with us to the Monterrico Police Station. Explain yourself to the police chief in the morning."

Remembering Frida telling me how she had bribed her way out of several traffic tickets, I gripped the steering wheel to stop my hands from shaking. "If you let me go to my house"—again I pointed to our garage door—"I'll give you a hundred dollars. It's all I have at home. Divide the money fifty-fifty. Or else I can come with you to the police station. It's up to you. But if you help me, you will have done a good deed because my husband is in the hospital with cancer. He doesn't need to face this problem right now." For the first time, I took stock of how young the gun-holding policeman was. If I wasn't dead scared myself, I would say he appeared as scared as I felt. The other one was older, fatter, and of native descent. His glance was shrewd. "Make it two hundred. Look how big your house is. You're a rich lady."

"I don't have two hundred. But I'll give you everything I have if you let me go."

"How much do you have on you?"

My hands grew moist counting the fifty nuevos soles Sergio had given me yesterday for grocery shopping. "Take it." I thrust the money out the car window.

"Go home and get the rest." The fat policeman pocketed the money.

All I had in my walk-in closet were one hundred twenty-six dollars. Knowing I had no choice and that I was lucky to even have access to offer the money, I raced back out and handed the money to the older policeman.

"Let this be your lesson, señora. Other policemen would have charged you a lot more."

I felt like saying, *So would you, you self serving rat, but you can smell that I have no more, which is why you're settling.* "Thank you, *Señor Policia*. You are indeed a very kind man."

Minutes later, I fell into bed, aware that I had created a worse problem. I didn't have enough gas to do the carpool, nor did I have a single cent left with which to purchase any. That worry took care of the rest of my night, and I didn't sleep a wink. At six thirty, I called Pauly Kozinski to explain my predicament.

He said, "Oh, Noor, I'm so sorry. Police corruption is the norm here because their average yearly salary is six thousand dollars, and no one can live on that. Come fetch Marianna first. I'll give you money for gas." Marianna was Pauly's daughter, who was in the second grade with Pia.

In the hospital, I explained everything to Sergio at nine in the morning.

He said, "And I have more bad news."

My toes clenched. "What?"

"When Dr. Ritter saw me, he said I not only have pneumonia, I also have a bad case of staphylococcus. He told me to tell you to go find him when you arrived."

"Can he treat whatever you have?" I placed a hand on Sergio's forehead and smoothed back his untidy hair. *Does he have more white strands than a week ago?*

"He ordered a slew of blood tests."

I ran out to hunt down Dr. Ritter. He was doing paperwork in a cramped little office crowded with test results and to-do lists hanging from every wall surface.

"I'm sorry" was the first thing he said.

"How long will he be in here, do you think?"

"I don't know, Noor. I don't know if he'll ever go home again."

My unshed tears blurred Dr. Ritter's face. "Can the kids visit him this afternoon? They are pretty upset, and I know seeing Sergio will calm them."

Dr. Ritter shook his head. "Children aren't allowed in this ward. Patients in here have such compromised immune systems, they can't be exposed to the panoply of common germs schoolchildren carry on their persons."

My heart converted to a large chunk of lead in my chest.

Within the next two days, however, I chose to feel hope when Sergio's condition improved after his body was barraged by a combination of antibiotics to combat the presence of Pneumocystis carinii and the bad staphylococcus infection.

At home at bedtime every day, I told the children that he was getting better. But in the hospital, that fairytale was negated by Dr. Ritter instructing Sergio to leave his bed and walk twenty steps, three times a day.

In Sergio's condition, even five steps, supported by either Horacio or me, were an excruciating, knee-trembling ordeal he couldn't comply with. He cried through each attempt at it and complained how the floor seemed miles away and his legs behaved like cement posts. And with him, Horacio and I cried, too, because it was so hard to watch.

How can this be happening to Sergio at age forty-six?

By day three in the afternoon, no family member of Sergio's nor Jaime León had dropped in to see him.

Overcome by what I was basically facing alone, except for Horacio, I said, "Serg, you better tell me what to expect if you don't survive this. Tell me where your will is and what it says. Don't leave me to face any surprises, especially with you gone."

Sergio's look told me that the possibility of dying hadn't occurred to him. "There *are* no surprises. The will leaves you fifty percent of my estate, and the children receive twenty-five percent each. And Nila is the executor. If I die, she will activate the will, and I have designated her to be the next of kin for Pia and Abril if something happens to you."

"What? Absolutely not!"

"What? Why not?"

"Serg, since the shoplifting incident, Nila hates my guts. You *will not* leave me at her mercy without you to buffer me from her hatred. And I will decide where my children go next if I'm dying."

"But that's how I wrote the will."

"Then you need to change it."

"And how can I do that while I'm stuck here?"

"I don't care. Tell me where the will is and what to do. I'll go do it. *I won't let you subject me to Nila. Sorry.*"

"It's in our walk-in closet, inside my locked drawer, but I don't know what you can do with it unless I'm present. Take it to a notary public. Here in Peru, notaries are a big deal with law degrees and law offices. See what a notary says. A notary would have to sign off on any change. That much I know."

"Can you hang in there by yourself today while I go sort this out? The last person I want to deal with is Nila if you do die."

"Fine. I'll help you in any way I can, if it's even possible."

Three hours later, I stood in front of Notary Public Attorney Maruja Denegri in her Miraflores office, crying, as I explained my circumstances, AIDS included. "You have to help me, señora," I said to the elderly Maruja, in her posh gray tweed suit that matched her short gray curls. "I am all alone in this country except for my two little children and a husband who might not survive this hospitalization."

"The problem is very unusual." Attorney Denegri's expression was sympathetic. "I need ten minutes to consult two other notary publics I trust. I promise I'll do my best to help you."

For those ten minutes, I was seven years old again, sitting in a cold waiting room, alone, hungry, and tired, with Didima hospitalized for her first heart attack, complicated by the presence of multiple gallstones *and* kidney stones. Waiting to hear if she had survived her operation, I prayed to God for the first time outside the Loreto Convent School assembly, begging him not to kill Didima. Thinking of her, I couldn't decide which was more painful, the present or the past, when Attorney Denegri came back out of her office. "Señora, what's your husband's phone number? He has to corroborate what you told me."

"Let me call the hospital. The Rebagliati doesn't have phone extensions in the patient rooms. But the nurse knows me, and maybe she can help Sergio to the phone. He can't walk the distance by himself." I teared up again.

After Attorney Denegri was satisfied, she said, "You have to name a new executor eighteen or older."

"Carla Bustos," I said without hesitation. "She's twenty-one."

"I'll need a day to redraft the will. Can Carla Bustos come here with you tomorrow afternoon? We close at five."

"Yes."

In the hospital the next day, I gripped Sergio's hand. "Thank you for helping me fix this. If you do die, the less I have to deal with your family, the happier I'll be."

"Noor, I'm not dead yet. It may not come to that. I am getting better."

"Yes. Yes, you are." I squeezed his hand and refrained from pointing out that he could barely walk anymore. *Hasn't he noticed?* "But please understand how scared I am. For the last ten years, I have never lived in a world where I didn't have you to depend on. And you are crumbling before my eyes, and I can't do a damn thing to help you."

"Can you spare me your Indian directness? I can't take it right now."

"I'm sorry."

At four in the afternoon, I picked up Carla waiting for me outside the UNIFE gate because she hadn't wanted to cut class. I was not ready for all the emotions the sight of the all-girls university stirred inside me. *This December, Carla and her whole gang will have completed degrees... whereas by then, I might be a widow.*

Inside the car, Carla said, "Amiga, can you buy me a sandwich? I'm hungry."

"Of course. But can I do that after we finish with the notary in Miraflores? Her office closes at five."

From Carla's perspective, I was rich because I had a house and a car and my husband was a diplomat. And perhaps I was rich, compared to her family, but that didn't mean I had floating cash. *Yet what can I say to her? No, I won't buy you a sandwich when you're helping me escape dealing with my unloving, uncaring sister-in-law, Nila?*

Given the rush hour traffic, we reached Miraflores with ten minutes to spare. With all the formalities to complete, the main door of the notary office had already been closed to the public for twenty minutes before Carla and I left the premises. I would take the will to the hospital as soon as I bought Carla food. Once Sergio signed the revised will, Nila would have no power over me.

In downtown Miraflores, the only parking spot I found was in front of an ice cream parlor. Inside, Carla ordered a sandwich and an ice cream cone. "Amiga, can you drop me home please? Midterm exams start tomorrow, and no direct buses go from Miraflores to Magdalena."

I wanted to scream, *Car, my husband is dying, and you can't catch two buses home*? But I said, "Of course. Can you eat your ice cream cone in the car, though?" I told her of my curfew experience.

In Magdalena, forty minutes later, I said, "Car, can you please call Dulci and tell her to put the kids to bed? All they'll do is worry and fight Dulci, wanting to wait up for me, and tomorrow is a school day."

"I'll try. Our neighbor's phone wasn't working, the last I know."

Within the hospital, I ran down the seventh-floor corridor to Sergio's room, frantic to head homeward well before the curfew. In there, just the hopelessness on Horacio's face stopped me short. "What? What's wrong?"

"My *padrino* went into a coma."

"What? He was fine this afternoon when I left!" My eyes shot to the right to take in Sergio lying faceup. "Are you sure he's in a coma? He seems asleep." I placed a hand on Sergio's forehead, too shocked to react.

"I don't know, Naña." Concern rendered Horacio's voice higher-pitched than usual. "But it's what the nurse said at seven when she took his vitals. When I came in at six forty-five, I assumed my padrino was napping, so I didn't try to wake him."

I ran to the nurse's desk.

"He didn't wake up, señora, when I took his vitals. That is never a good sign. But don't take my word for it. We'll see what Dr. Ritter says when he comes in tomorrow morning."

In stark contrast to how I had rushed in, I left the hospital in a slow daze, the new will unsigned. *Would Sergio have been awake if I hadn't taken the detour to drop Carla home?*

Driving to Valle Hermoso, tears trickled down my cheeks. I would have to lie to Pia and Abril the next morning when they woke up and asked, "How is Papá doing?" If Sergio didn't wake up from this coma, his last interaction with the children would have been him saying goodbye to them on their way to school four days ago. As for me, I couldn't remember what we had said to each other that afternoon before I had rushed off to pick up Carla.

At home, the kitchen clock showed ten thirty as I drank a glass of warm milk with honey. Dulci put away the stew I didn't eat. "Your mother called from India three times, but since she doesn't understand what I say and I don't understand her, she's sure to call again. Señor Jaime León called, too, but I guess it's too late for you to call him back."

At the sound of Jaime's name, my stomach knotted, robbing me of the calming effect of the warm milk. I went up the stairwell, determined not to call Jaime back, then or ever. The best I could do for Sergio's sake was avoid him altogether. If I spoke to him or came face-to-face with him, I knew I couldn't control the confrontation that would follow, and Sergio wouldn't want that. As for my mother, she would call back. I didn't intend to waste the money we didn't have to call her.

When the phone rang at three a.m., it frightened me into scratching my cheek in my haste to lift the receiver in case the hospital was calling.

"Shona!" my mother said in her high, little-girl voice. "Where have you been? It's impossible to get a hold of you."

I rubbed my eyes. "In the hospital, Ma. Sergio is in the hospital."

"Why? What's wrong with him? Is his cancer worse?"

"Ma. Sergio never had cancer. He has AIDS. And he went into a coma this evening." I rubbed the scratch on my cheek, and it stung worse.

"What?"

"Yes. He never wanted to tell you the truth, but now I'm telling you."

"So what will you do if he dies?"

I rubbed my forehead. "I have no earthly idea."

"Come home. We'll take care of you and the girls."

My mother's words were so ludicrous I had to smile. "To you and your pedophile husband? So he can molest Pia and Abril like he molested me? That would thrill him."

"Noor!" My mother's voice grew shrill. "You know that was a lie. Robu is not a child molester."

"Right, Ma. But the main reason I married Sergio was to escape him and you… so no. Whatever I do, I won't come back to India. Now I'm going to hang up because it's three in the morning here, and I am extremely tired." I hung up, not letting my mother say any more. But of course, that phone call was the end of my sleep for the night.

62

AT SIX O'CLOCK, I KISSED the children awake and told them I was going to the hospital. To my relief, sleep-ridden as they were, they didn't ask, "How is Papá?" and I didn't tell.

At seven o'clock, when Dr. Ritter came to Sergio's bedside, instead of speaking, he flipped back the blanket and sheet covering Sergio's body.

"What are you searching for?" I stared at him through itchy, burning eyes.

"Diarrhea."

"How will you tell if he's in a coma?" My chest tensed to even say those words.

"In a minute." The doctor withdrew a pencil-sized flashlight from his white jacket pocket. Gently, he turned Sergio's head toward him and parted one eyelid to point in a sharp spear of light. "He is because his pupil doesn't respond to light."

My own eyes filled with tears. "Can you tell if he'll come out of it?"

"I can't say. He has progressive dementia and the Pneumocystis carinii pneumonia and the staph infection. No one can predict what else may develop inside his body."

"If he were in Los Angeles, they would have washed the pneumonia out of his lungs."

"I know. But if it is of any consolation to you—no hospital in Peru has that technology, so he isn't being shortchanged here."

"So, is this the end?" I wiped my eyes. "Will he never wake up?"

"I could be wrong, but I don't think so. In the last stage, AIDS patients suffer a colossal bout of diarrhea, which makes them collapse from dehydration. Sergio isn't at that stage yet, but it doesn't mean he will recover from this coma either. All I can rationally do is leave his hydration and antibiotic treatment in place."

On day three of his coma, Sergio lay faceup on the hospital bed while I sprawled in an untidy heap on the one narrow green metal chair for visitors in his room, head thrown against the wall-to-wall window, an empty barrel of tears. My eyes burned under puffy lids as I stared at the busy Avenida Manuel Segura far below. Traffic, pedestrians, a flashing ambulance jolted along, making sounds I could not hear through the sealed window expanse, just as surely as they didn't even know I existed, never mind my pain or powerlessness.

Did I really contemplate killing Sergio, as defenseless as he is? How far can fear and paranoia drive people until they lose their minds? The judge in Miami had said near-total loss of control made one do strange things, and for me, the possibility of losing my children was not near-total loss—it was total loss. Until having Pia and Abril, I had been no more than a dancer on quicksand—jumping from solution to solution throughout my short life. Then they came along, and I had more to think of than just me. Those two precious children were so much more than anchors stabilizing me—they were my motivation to wake up each day, my reason to live.

The decision to take on a boyfriend hadn't changed that any more than Sergio's foray into casual sex had changed his being Pia and Abril's father. That was what my in-laws didn't understand when they told me to leave my children behind and return to India.

What will I tell the children if Sergio dies in this hospital? My heart thudded. *What will I do without him? Where will I find a job? Why haven't I phoned Dick McBee at the Roosevelt for a job possibility yet?* God, I had to focus and regroup. Whether Sergio survived his hospitalization or not, I needed a plan. His bank account contained one thousand dollars and change until he received his next salary—if he lived to receive it. I leapt to my feet and sprinted to a public telephone in the hospital lobby.

"Dick, listen—" I said after preliminaries.

"How is your husband?" cut in the assistant headmaster of the Roosevelt School. "Cancer isn't easy. I know because I watched my brother die of it."

"Oh, Dick, he's dying." I gulped.

"You don't know that. What does the doctor say?"

"Sergio is in a coma. The doctor doesn't know if he'll come out of it."

"Oh, Noor, I'm so sorry. How can I help?"

"I need a job."

"You know I can't give you a real job without a college degree. What I *can* do is place you among the first five people they call for substitute teaching because we were happy with your last performance."

"That's more than I have now, so thanks."

"Are you available this coming Monday? We need a sub for a month."

"I can't right now. I spend my days at the hospital. I couldn't bear it if he died in my absence."

"Sorry," Dick McBee apologized. "That was crass of me. It was on my mind because the secretary called me about it right before your call. Keep me posted."

On the ride back to the seventh floor, I daydreamed of Sergio being awake when I got there. I ran into his hospital room then stopped short, as if hit by a blunt object.

Sergio's position hadn't changed, but his mouth had fallen open like a gaping hole, and worse, his eyelids blinked unevenly. I hustled in the duty nurse. The nurse stared at Sergio, and I watched her observe his forehead, as smooth as a blank canvas, with not a wrinkle to betray a thought behind it.

"He's still in a coma." The nurse lifted Sergio's stubbled jaw to close his mouth but to no effect. "I'll call Dr. Ritter."

"It's my fault." My eyes welled. "I left him alone to use the telephone down in the lobby."

"That's nonsense. Stop blaming yourself. His condition is beyond anyone's control. Let me go call the doctor."

Since I could see Serg's room from the nurse's station, I asked, "Can I speak to him too?"

"Come on."

Alberto Ritter chided me from the other end of the telephone line. "Noor, stop blaming yourself for every change in his condition. What happens next is between him and God. I have done everything a doctor can in this country."

"But have you ever seen a coma patient with his eyes and mouth open?"

"No. But AIDS is new territory even for us doctors. So who says I've seen it all?"

When Horacio arrived at seven p.m., I shut Sergio's eyes and held his mouth closed, but my husband had traveled beyond the laws of biophysics.

On my way home, I prayed, *"Please, God, please don't let him die."*

The following morning, Horacio's eyes were swollen slits in his face from crying.

I looked at Sergio. "Can you imagine how dry his throat must be? I shut his jaw to no avail. You know what? I'm giving him water."

"But how will he drink it?" Horacio objected. "He's in a coma. What if he chokes?"

"I don't know, but I intend to try because I can't stand to see him like this and not do *something*. You hold his head, and I'll trickle water down his throat from my bottle."

Coma or not, Sergio's gullet responded by reflex action as I poured an experimental thread of water into his gaping mouth. He swallowed two inches from my water bottle in the span of ten minutes. Emboldened by success, I instructed Horacio to lay Sergio's head back on the pillow. After that, Horacio took the metal chair, and I sat on the floor with my back against the sealed window.

Presently, Sergio's eyes rolled backward, and my heart slammed. I glanced at Horacio, who began to tear. Sergio's eyelids closed, and his mouth shut as if after a yawn. Both Horacio and I were too scared to utter a sound as we observed Sergio, apparently asleep. His head moved to the rhythm of tired grunts.

Ten minutes passed.

Sergio stirred and hiccupped. His eyes fluttered open, focused. He stared at us one at a time. "Horacio, won't you be late for school?" His voice sounded as scratchy as the bark of an old lantana bush.

I jumped to my feet and took Sergio's hand, kissing his cold fingers. "He doesn't have school today, darling." I cleared the hoarseness in my throat. "You lost three days in a coma." Tears spilled.

"Yes, padrino, you've been out of it since the night of the twenty-eighth. Now I can tell people I've seen a miracle." Horacio wiped his eyes.

"*Hijo.*" Sergio's voice was weak. "Don't be so *huachafo*—tacky."

We all laughed unsteadily.

Then he said, "Did you resolve the will issue? Did I sign it? I can't remember."

I shook my head. "I have it here. Sign it please?"

"Of course. Then take it back for the notary public to stamp my signature."

"I'll do that tomorrow because I don't have carpool in the morning."

After that, I couldn't control the foolish smile tugging at the corners of my mouth. I sat beside Sergio on the hospital bed and held his hand as the spring sun traveled from the back of the hospital building to the front and brightened a wedge of pale-blue sky. His fingers in my grip felt as if the slightest pressure would snap them.

"That sky reminds me of the wool you bought me in Nice on our honeymoon."

"Does it?" Sergio's eyes lit up. "Because it reminds me of the dress you wore on the day I knelt to the ground in the Presidential Palace rose garden to tell you how happy I was you loved me." His eyes blinked with tears.

"How simple life was back then, wasn't it?" My hand tightened around his.

Our day threaded by on a tapestry of memories, each as delicate as the tiny lace flowers I had sewn on our children's gauze crib netting before Pia's birth.

"Why do you take this much trouble?" Sergio had asked in bed one night, both of us on our last legs after attending a cocktail party and a sit-down dinner. "The kids won't remember. Doesn't your belly hurt, bent over like that?"

I had smiled without taking my eyes off my needlework. "So they'll think they're looking at the stars. You know that saying, 'Shoot for the moon even if you miss, you'll land among the stars.'?"

The light and shadows in the hospital room had already changed when Sergio took my hand. He was about to speak when the nurse came in to say that Abril was on the phone to speak to her papá. Leaning on me, Sergio walked to the nurse's station. As he talked, the cityscape outside the window of the seventh-floor foyer swam in my eyes. Slanting bars of sunlight touched the corners of Sergio's bare ankles, his feet tucked inside his Gucci bedroom slippers on the diamond-patterned linoleum floor.

"I'll be home soon, amorcito," he said to our seven-year-old, and my throat choked with hope.

On the fifth evening of Sergio's recovery, he and I sat side by side on his hospital bed, fingers laced. Before Sergio saw them, I spotted my mother-in-law, Nila, and three other visitors stop dead at the sight of our intertwined hands.

Señora Santander's forehead creased, and she looked at Nila. Her eyes said, *Could I be seeing this?*

Nila shrugged. Her eyes said, *Well, Mamá, Sergio is a big boy.*

Either way, I don't like it one bit, Señora Santander's eyes said, her mouth pressed into a thin wine-colored line.

My hand tensed in Sergio's grasp.

"What is it?" He searched my face.

In that second, Nila walked into the room with her hurried, high-heeled gait. "*Hermanito*," she bubbled. "Look who has come to visit you."

Sergio smiled at his family but tightened his hold on my hand as if to show his mother and sister where his loyalties lay. He looked me straight in the eyes. "Darling," he said for his visitors to hear, "go home. The children need you more than I do."

"The children are fine," I protested. "Dulci will serve them dinner. I want to stay here with you."

Sergio pulled me toward him, giving me a kiss on the forehead. "We'll have the whole of tomorrow together. Go home for now, and let me visit with my family. It'll be better that way."

I left Sergio and his visitors, my movements jerky, footsteps uncoordinated, deeply resentful of their intrusion upon what I considered my time with my husband. Thus preoccupied, I drove out of the carpark straight into the traffic without looking left or right, causing a tractor trailer to brake so hard its rear end nearly overturned and the avenida drowned in car horns while drivers stuck their heads out of car windows and cursed me to high heaven until everyone righted their speed.

An hour later, I lay in my own bed, one arm around each child. "You two sing to me tonight. I'm so sleepy." Once the children left, I swallowed two anti-anxiety tablets.

My uneasy slumber was shattered by the loud ringing of the phone on the night table. I peered at the phosphorescent numbers of the digital clock on Sergio's nightstand. Twelve thirty. I snatched up the phone receiver. "Horacio? Is that you? What's the matter? Is he okay?"

"Yes, Naña Noor. He's okay, but he wants Coca-Cola right now. Maybe he's delirious, because he's been begging me to call you for the last hour to tell you to bring him Coca-Cola."

"I can't." I glanced at the darkened edges around my bedroom curtains. "Not with the midnight curfew. If I'm caught driving around, I'll be arrested. Why can't you buy him a Coke at the hospital cafeteria?"

"Because it's past midnight, and the cafeteria closes at nine. Besides, I don't have enough money."

"Call Nila. Do you know if she has papers to drive during curfew hours? Maybe she can bring him the Coke."

"I've offered him that, but he doesn't want to see Naña Nila. He wants you.

And he keeps repeating your name, saying, 'Noor. I want to see Noor. Tell her to come, Horacio. Go call Noor, and tell her to come see me. Why isn't she coming?' And then he starts all over again."

My eyes teared up in the darkness. "Tell him I'll bring him Coke right after the curfew ends at six in the morning," I rasped. "I don't have carpool tomorrow. I can leave the house at six."

"I'll try, Naña."

I hung up and swallowed a huge knot in my throat. *Why is life so difficult? Why is there a curfew right when I need to go to the hospital?* All Sergio wanted was a Coca-Cola, and I couldn't give it to him. How cruel life was in such an impersonal way. I lay back down, tears making a wet patch on my pillow.

I closed my eyes, but it was as if my mind had been switched on and I couldn't switch it off. *Why does Sergio want to see me and not Nila? He's certainly close enough to his sister. Yet all through his stay in Los Angeles, he never once professed a desire to see his family. His one angst was always to see me—me with the children or me without the children but always me. Why?* That question plagued me, and I remembered Magda's words. "He loves you, Noor," she had said.

In the hallway, the cuckoo clock cheeped every fifteen minutes, making me feel like a sparrow trapped in a church building, flying from window to window without a way out but seeing a different landscape each time. *What if I've read Sergio wrong for all these years?*

How easy it had been to paint him the villain because to put any effort into my relationship with Sergio would have obligated me to admit how much I needed him and depended on him. And that would have left me vulnerable—as vulnerable as I had felt when Dadu had died, and Baba had left, and Didima had died, then I had lost Chirag as well.

Back in our lives in New Delhi, it had seemed as if Sergio was threatening to take the children away from me, but had he? I wouldn't be sitting in Peru today if he had. What if he had used reverse psychology to goad me into coming to Peru with him when he knew our marriage was crumbling? If that was the case, his plan had certainly worked. And how will I know any different unless I ask him? As if to torture me, the lens through which I had always judged Sergio's actions inverted to show me the facts in the opposite light. *For sure, he had been reluctant to have me attend university here, but had he ever stopped me? He could also have divorced me anytime once we were in Lima, but he never did. Why?* I wanted to know. Yes, he had been mean to me on many occasions, but his meanness died with his words. I thought of the chocolate cookies he bought me every other day whether we were talking to each other or not.

Too late, I realized why I had sought Armand's company. Because focusing on him kept me from facing that Sergio was dying. Because Armand's presence or absence couldn't rock my boat, whereas Sergio's absence would sink it. And owning that truth thrust a dagger into my heart.

Yes, Sergio was likely on his deathbed, but if we could answer some of each other's questions, it would provide us both with a better understanding of what our marriage had meant in our lives as individuals—afford us a chance to heal what we could of our wounds.

On that note, I must have dozed off, because the alarm startled me at five thirty.

63

AT SIX THIRTY, I HURRIED into Sergio's hospital room, a two-liter Coca-Cola bottle hugged to my chest. Inside, just the sag of Horacio's shoulders made me glance at Sergio. He was in another coma—that time, though, he didn't blink—he breathed hard, eyes staring wide-open at nothing, jaw agape for the second time.

Oh my God. How long until his corneas dry out? What if Sergio wakes up blind?

Furthermore, three iridescent horseflies circled poor Sergio's face like vultures.

I shooed them away and shut Sergio's eyelids, but of course, his body wouldn't obey me. My other hand placed the useless Coca-Cola bottle on the chipped green surface of the rolling dining table. "When did this happen?" I folded into the hospital room's metal chair and looked at Horacio.

"He was conscious when the night nurse visited at three."

I stared out the picture window, thinking of how much I had banked on a conversation with my husband, a conversation that would have helped the rest of the life I might have to live without him.

"Naña, will you help me change his bottom sheet? He dirtied it with a diarrhea attack an hour ago."

I became conscious of a dull, medicine-laden smell and raised a corner of the blanket and sheet covering Sergio. Underneath skulked such a dreadful stench that my mind raced to Dr. Ritter's warning about diarrhea preceding death, and it felt as if my heart stopped beating, then crashed back into action.

I dropped the covers, understanding the presence of the horseflies. My forefinger sliced the air sideways, anger making my voice shrill. "Why didn't the nurse change the sheets when this happened?"

"She said it was the orderly's job, and he doesn't reach this ward until nine."

"So where did you get the new sheet?"

"From the nurse. I begged and begged her for it so you and I could change it once you got here."

Since the nurse didn't have gloves to spare, we changed the sheet barehanded, gagging as we pushed and pulled on Sergio's inert body, praying the activity would snap him out of his unnerving state.

While Horacio wiped his godfather's back clean, I ran to beg for fresh gauze to redress Sergio's hip wound. *Will this diarrhea infect it?*

I peered into Sergio's gaping mouth. What should have been pink looked a sallow rose. Behind his front teeth, his tongue lay coated with a white fur, slack and round, crinkled along the middle until it disappeared down his throat. His molars had gone jet-black. Only his throat was alive with the sound of his gargled breathing. With each intake, his epiglottis vibrated while the cavity behind the bell-shaped nodule was crisscrossed with slimy green seaweedlike projections that stretched into thin arcs each time air passed through but never broke to clear the passageway.

Inside me, something felt like it would burst if I didn't act to reverse the situation. Sergio couldn't leave me hanging that badly. He couldn't. Not with all the questions I had to ask him. *Please, dear God, let me talk to him one more time. Allow us to have that conversation that will provide the closure we so need. Please.* I turned to Horacio. "Shall we try water again?"

Horacio's face brightened. "Yes, let's."

I sought my water bottle, envisioning wild images of Sergio healthy enough to go home. From the bud of imagination, hope that he might once again share priceless moments with the children, especially Abril, bloomed like a sunflower. *Maybe we can have lunch one day?* I would prepare him fried fish. He talked nonstop of fried fish from his childhood spent with his aunt in the seaside district of Callao but never had the stomach to eat it since getting sick.

"Hold his head steady, Horacio." I poured a trickle of water down his throat.

Time paused.

A window of pure expectation opened in the universe. Both Horacio and I watched Sergio's face for a miracle. Instead, Sergio's whole body arched. He twitched and emitted two last gasps. His face blanched from pale to lifeless, and he ceased to breathe.

We stood stunned, both of us staring at Sergio's unblinking eyes. The silence in the room grew deafening. A greedy horsefly circled Sergio's open mouth.

I croaked, "Horacio, go find the nurse," as I chased the scavenger away.

The duty nurse scuttled in and paused at the sight of Sergio. She grasped his limp wrist and stared at the luminous dial of her electronic wristwatch. Thirty seconds passed. She said to no one in particular, "Today is Monday, October 6, 1992, 6:59 a.m. Señor Sergio Santander just expired." She met Horacio's and my anxious gazes. "I'll call the resident so he can sign off on this. "*Lo siento mucho.* I am so sorry."

I couldn't tell whether it was fifteen minutes or forty-five while I sat on the lone metal chair in the hospital room, unable to process that Sergio would never wake up again, talk to me again, call Abril again, or ever drink another glass of Coca-Cola. The finality of his death wouldn't register in my brain. I was sitting there, and he was on the bed. He would wake back up—that was what my psyche told me over and over again until two hospital orderlies trundled in a gurney and positioned it parallel to Sergio's bed. My whole body slumped as they transferred Sergio to the new surface, sheets, blankets, and all, without one glance at either Horacio or myself. When the first orderly fanned a fresh white sheet to cover Sergio from head to toe, I controlled the urge to jump up and scream that he would suffocate my husband, the rational part of me aware that Serg wasn't breathing anymore anyway.

But as the second orderly wheeled Sergio out, I came to life, heart beating in panic as I chased after the duo. "Where are you taking him?" I clutched the moving gurney, trying to stop it—without success.

"To the morgue." The orderly took the corner without a break in stride.

"We'll come with you." I ran beside him.

By that time, Horacio had joined me, and we trotted alongside the orderly as he pushed Sergio into an elevator marked *Restricted Service, for Internal Use Only*. As the four of us traveled to the basement, I couldn't accept how I was losing all control over the circumstances, and Sergio, with each advancing second.

When the elevator doors opened, the orderly propelled the gurney with Sergio on it at such a pace, it squealed around two corners before I registered the smell of formaldehyde and saw cavernous offices marked *Archivos*, *Imprenta*, and *Historia Clínica* flit past as we raced to stay abreast. The corridor slanted down into scary darkness. I saw a wall ahead next to a doorway marked *Morgue*, but it had overflowed to three gurneys parked by the wall outside it, covered from top to bottom like Sergio, shipwrecks marooned on the island of death. The orderly positioned Sergio behind the third gurney, then it hit me—that *this* was the end. Sergio was dead, gone and truly beyond my reach.

As though getting rid of cracker crumbs, the orderly brushed his hands.

"Señora, you have to leave now. I'll show you to the elevator, or else you'll get lost down here."

"I can't leave." I planted my feet apart and crossed my arms. I couldn't leave Sergio alone out there. I couldn't.

Horacio tugged at my elbow.

"No! I'm not leaving. A minute—give me a minute to say a prayer for him," I pleaded.

The orderly flicked his wristwatch.

I placed two trembling hands on Sergio's head and heart. Eyes closed, I muttered the Our Father for Sergio.

Horacio took my hand and pulled again.

We hurried behind the orderly while every fiber in my body screamed not to abandon Sergio, but since that morning, life had run on fast-forward and swept me along like a doll in a flood, and the flood wasn't stopping.

Inside the elevator, I pressed the button to the seventh floor, knowing I had left my anchor behind in the basement. *What will I do without Sergio? What will happen to me and the children? What move will his family spring on me now?*

As if in reply, I found Sergio's brother, Carlos, waiting in Sergio's ex-hospital room. Next to him, the duty nurse shuffled a stack of papers. *Who called Carlos? I certainly hadn't.*

The nurse pushed the papers into my hands. "Sorry, but can you fill these out? They are for the death certificate and the autopsy."

Carlos followed with, "Do you know who will pay for my brother's funeral? We need a coffin."

I stared at Carlos. *Will the thousand dollars in Sergio's account do? But if I spend that on Sergio's funeral, what will I use to buy the children food?* I walked to the reception desk. "Could I please use the telephone for one last outgoing call?"

In sympathetic silence, the duty nurse pushed the touch-tone phone toward me.

I dialed a number I knew by heart. Juan Arciniega was the latest young diplomat who had assisted me with the snarl of Sergio's pension in the administration department of the foreign office.

"Señor Arciniega." My voice was stony. "This is Noor Santander. My husband just died, and his brother asked me who would pay for his funeral. Would you happen to know what I should do next?"

"Señora Santander, I'm truly sorry to hear that. I never worked with Minister-Counselor Santander personally, so I didn't know him, but I knew his reputation. Please allow me to place you on hold. I'll consult the department head. I promise I'll have an answer for you. Don't hang up."

I stood by that telephone, a robot, receiver dangling from one hand while I waited to be told what to do.

"Señora Santander?" Seldom had a familiar voice reassured me more. Juan Arciniega said, "Our department head, Ambassador Mauricio Carillo, informed me of a standing disposition from the secretary-general's office with regard to the case of Señor Santander. The foreign office will pay for his funeral expenses. I'd like you to understand, señora, this is highly unusual. Our bylaws only cover the funerals of career ambassadors. Please call me if you have further questions—and save every receipt for us to pay the expenses. And, señora? Again, I'm so sorry for your loss." His words brought home how Sergio's brother hadn't seen fit to offer me his condolences because I didn't deserve the sympathy.

The next thing I knew, I clung to Horacio's forearm as we crossed the jam-packed Avenida Manuel Segura outside the Rebagliati Hospital. Thank God the children would be in school until two o'clock and I didn't have carpool. Instead, caught in the discordance of buses, cars, people, and an overabundance of smells, I couldn't recall *who* had dictated my next move, but I had one instruction straight. I had to buy a coffin and deliver the receipt to Carlos, who would stay at the hospital and see to the autopsy and the embalming of Sergio's body, a standard procedure in Peru. Since I had no cash on me, nor possessed a checkbook, and much less a credit card, a receipt was my only option.

"Horacio?" I awoke from a daze. "Why do we need a coffin if Sergio will be cremated?"

"I don't know, Naña. I've never seen a cremation. Maybe they burn the body in a coffin like they bury people in coffins? Naña. Naña Noor. Stop!"

"What? What is it?" I tightened my viselike grip on the young man's forearm. My other hand squeezed my purse to my chest as if to defend my heart.

"The coffin shop, we passed it. See where it says *Ataúdes*?"

We both retraced our steps and entered a narrow hallway that led to several shop entrances. We pushed the door of the one with the word Ataudes stenciled in black letters on its beveled-glass pane. My head swam in the smells of varnish, wood, and incense that wafted from dozens of coffins—on the floor, on shelves, on platforms, opened, closed, vertical, horizontal, different shapes, different colors, different linings, padded, puffed, opaque, and shiny—until I shut my eyes to escape it.

A salesman stood behind a cramped counter with a curved glass pane full of crucifix stickers. "Señora, may I help you?"

I opened my eyes. "Yes, I need a coffin."

Horacio and I drowned in a memorized sales pitch I had trouble comprehending.

"Señor." I placed palms over my ears. "Stop. I'm not Peruvian, so I don't understand a word you're saying. Can I buy a coffin that doesn't cost more than two or three hundred dollars? Plus, once we choose the right one, I can't pay for it. We'll have to phone my husband's office—they'll tell you how they'll pay for it."

An invisible shade dropped over the salesman's eyes. His tone changed. "Sorry, señora. I can't sell you what you won't pay for."

My body hardened into a seashell. "I didn't say I wouldn't pay for it. I said the foreign office of Peru would pay for it. Here." I dug out a scrap of paper from my purse and wrote a phone number, ignoring the salesman's waving arms. "Phone this number." I thrust the paper scrap through the hole in the glass pane above the counter. "Ask for a Señor Juan Arciniega. He'll confirm what I said."

"Why can't you pay for it?" The salesman looked sullen.

"Because when I left my house this morning, señor, I didn't think, 'Oh, I'd better go to the bank and withdraw money in case my husband dies today and I have a coffin to pay for.' Now, will you phone this number, or should I find another coffin shop?"

Back on the street, my body melted to jelly. I stopped midstride on the berm between opposing traffic. "Horacio, I can't do this. Here is the receipt for the coffin. Take it to Carlos. I'm going home."

"But what if Señor Carlos wants to speak to you?" Horacio shifted uneasily.

"To say what? Sergio is lying dead in that hospital basement. Do you think I care what Carlos might say to me?" I headed toward the hospital's carpark. Halfway down, I ran back to Horacio and pulled on his T-shirt from behind. "Hey," I panted. "Tell Carlos I don't want a wake. Sergio hated wakes. Carlos must know this already, but tell him I said so anyway."

As I walked, I stared at passersby, feeling as if my whole body was skinned raw. *Can people tell I just became a widow? Lost my very anchor? That I don't know how I'll find the wherewithal to drive home, let alone tell the children their father died?* This was worse than Didima dying because this time, I had Pia and Abril to take care of, defend, protect. I could not fall apart. Not then. Not ever. My children needed me too much.

64

On my way home, my knuckles glowed white on the steering wheel. In Valle Hermoso, Dulci opened the garage door. "Are you okay? You look terrible."

I parked the car. When I let go of the steering wheel, my fingers became maroon crescents, cramping in opposite directions. Flexing through the pain, I stepped out into the smell of fried hot dogs and fresh french fries, the children's special treat. "Duls, he just died. I don't know what I'll tell Pia and Abril when they come home from school." I dug my thumb and forefinger into my eyelids so hard, silvery rings danced in the darkness. I blinked to readjust to the light.

Dulci's eyes rounded. "They're not expecting this. All Abril talked of this morning was what she would tell her papá when she called him in the afternoon."

I rubbed my eyes again, clutched my hair back, and glanced at the sky. "Thank God they aren't home yet. I hope Frida's home. Maybe she can tell me what to say. Make me a coffee, Duls, please? I'll phone her."

Dulci placed her hand on my forearm. "You call her. I'll get you coffee."

Frida had already heard the news from Carlos. She rushed over to be with me as I sank into a porch chair, sipping coffee, Sergio's death overtaking me with the surety of a glacier in motion.

Frida hugged me and took another porch chair.

"What do I say to the kids?"

"Don't say anything, not today. Let's talk to my mom. She's been a school social worker all her life. I'll call her now. I have my cell phone."

Frida's mother asked to talk to me right away. "*Hijita*, I'm so sorry this happened, but we all knew it was coming, didn't we? And that's it—we knew. The children didn't. That's why it's best not to reveal it to them today, while you yourself aren't in control. Sleep on it, and tomorrow will be another day. Also, please don't expose the children to his *velorio* wake, they—"

"What velorio? There won't be one," I interrupted.

"Yes, there will, Noor," Frida said gently. "You can't stop it."

I dropped the cell phone on the porch table and shot to my feet. "That's *bullshit*! Sergio specifically didn't want a velorio. Let me call Carlos."

Frida got up, took me by the shoulders, and pushed me back into the chair. "Hey, you won't win this one. La vieja, his old bat of a mother, wants it. Velorios are too entrenched in this culture, so it doesn't matter what Sergio desired. He's dead, so he can't stop it."

"Hello? Hello?" crackled the cell phone on the porch table.

"Hello? Yes, sorry, señora." I jammed the phone back to my ear, anger prickling beads of sweat on my forehead. "This is the ultimate joke. It's Sergio's funeral, and *his* wish is the last consideration, but Frida's right. He's dead, so he won't care. Come to think of it, nothing matters—"

"Noor, Noor, listen to me, hijita. Don't take the children to this velorio. In Pia's and Abril's memories, their father should be alive, sharing experiences with them, not lying dead and stiff inside a coffin. Please trust me on this one."

"I will, señora, of course I will. I don't want this to be any more traumatic for my children than necessary. Even I don't want to go to the rotten velorio. God, how I hate my mother-in-law."

Frida stayed to answer the door when Pia and Abril thumped on it. She let them in with a broad smile and kissed their warm pink cheeks as they dropped their schoolbags on the patio flagstones.

Automatically, I said, "Hey, you two, pick up your schoolbags," as Frida ushered them forward. "How was school today?"

Undeterred, Abril asked, "*¿Por qué estás en casa, Mamá?* Why are you home?" The frown on her young forehead broke my heart.

"Because your papá is having an operation." I recalled the autopsy consent form I had signed. "So I decided to come home and be with you instead." I collected the two schoolbags.

"Will it make him all better?" Pia pushed the door into the house, untidy golden head swiveled to address me.

"I don't know, amor. We'll see." My voice faltered.

"Pia, that is in God's hands," interrupted Frida. "Your mamá can't predict what will happen to your papá."

"He'll come home soon," insisted Abril. "He told me so."

I dropped the schoolbags to pull my seven-year-old into an embrace. "Who'll watch *Robin Hood* with me after you two do your homework?"

"Why can't we watch it before homework?" Pia asked.

"Pia." I wagged a warning finger. "You always give your sister all the bad ideas. Go in and eat lunch with Dulci. It's hot dogs and french fries."

In the garden, I grabbed Frida's arm. "Hey, so I won't tell them today, but when *will* I tell them?"

"Tomorrow, after the wake and cremation. Carlos will be with us. We can tell them then. Together."

That night, I sang the children their bedtime songs, the world's meanest imposter, as I let them pray for God to cure their papá and send him home. A part of the truth had snuck up on me in the afternoon while I had nestled with Pia and Abril, watching *Robin Hood*, not registering a word. When I hadn't been a block of ice, I had wanted to jump up and run out of the house on bare feet and keep running.

At dawn, my eyes popped open. Sergio's digital clock glowed it was five fifteen. The word "afraid" blinked with neon precision on the billboard of my sleepy mind. Around my bedroom curtains, the sky leaked purple and indigo, heralding a dawn Sergio would never see again. Afraid was what I had been all those years. Afraid to admit any feelings for Sergio because, to me, that meant I could lose him, like I had lost Dadu, and Baba, and Didima, and Chirag. And when I had allowed myself to feel anything at all, I had hidden behind the word "pity" because pity wasn't love. So I had ached for his illness and his pain, safe in my pity for him, knowing that pity couldn't hurt me if he died. Yet there I was, hurting more than I had ever hurt in my life.

Oh my God. Where is Sergio? I have to see him. I have to talk to him one last time before he leaves me forever. I tossed back my bedcovers, drew back the curtains, and wrestled into clothes. *But where is he?* Yesterday, I had been so busy objecting to the velorio, I'd forgotten to ask Frida its location.

Frida. Of course. Frida would know. *But how can I phone Frida at five thirty in the morning? What will Carlos think?* Suddenly, it didn't matter what Carlos thought. I dialed their number with a shaky finger.

"F-Frida? Where is he? I have to see him."

"Who? Sergio?"

"Yes. Don't ask me why. I just have to—"

"You don't have carpool today?"

"No. I'll wake up Dulci and tell her to keep the children from worrying about why I'm not around this early."

"Okay, dress up and come on out," whispered Frida. "We'll leave at six sharp, when the curfew ends."

At our doorstep, clouds had descended in a shroud over every house, every treetop, and even on the bare brown hill. Shivering, rubbing my bare arms, too jittery to go back in and fetch a sweater, I stared at Frida's automatic garage door. The air smelled damp as the door rose.

"Where is he?" I fought with the seat belt as I got into her Toyota station wagon.

"In a *velatorio* at the Virgen de Fátima church." Frida focused on the road.

"D-do you k-know where it is?"

"Of course I do."

Unlike me, born and brought up in Lima, Frida knew the city so well she avoided the main arteries. As she sped through the secluded inner streets of Miraflores, I reflected on how even terrorism hadn't been able to eliminate a certain detail of the city. It was Lima's bakeries. They crisscrossed all neighborhoods because, since colonial days, people in Lima only bought their bread at local bakeries. And no mixture of flour and leavening I had ever tasted was fluffier, crisper, or more aromatic than the buns of Peruvian *pan francés*.

A long time ago, when Sergio had been well, his weekend breakfasts with the children revolved around fresh-baked pan francés, which he would stuff with Peruvian *queso fresco*—cottage cheese—and black olives, *jamon inglés*—English ham—along with fried eggs, his favorite breakfast-egg choice in the world.

How strange that Serg could have died anytime in this terrorist-ridden city from a bomb blast, but instead, he had died a day at a time. I glanced at my hands in my lap and reflected on how little I had helped him. That realization crushed me.

Twenty-five minutes into our ride, I sniffed the air. "I smell the sea. Are we near the sea?"

"Yes."

Within minutes, Frida parked her white station wagon behind the Virgen de Fátima church building, in front of a pretty oval park. "The velatorios are right here, by the Parque Domodosola."

I stared at the park, sculptured on top of an ancient landslide with a spectacular view of the ocean. At that hour, its stunted, misshapen trees and cooing mourning doves accentuated its stillness, submerged as it was in numinous sea fog. To its left, Miraflores diffused into the crescent of Chorrillos, where both districts hugged the blue coastline like a gray sickle. In the distance, the thin line of a pier pierced the water, a lone pin on an ultramarine pincushion. To the park's right were high-rise apartments with backdrops of sea waves instead of city traffic, a sea breeze in place of fumes. Peace was always a privilege of the rich.

I shut the passenger-side door of Frida's station wagon with a loud, metallic thud. My jeans brushed a flowerless geranium bush whose ebullient spring growth spilled out of the park. The noise caused a mourning dove to pause on the dewy grass and stare at me with unblinking, blue-rimmed eyes. I plucked a geranium leaf, remembering Didima. I crushed the severed geranium green and held it to my nose, aching for how much Didima had loved the smell, as I followed Frida across the street to a wooden doorway. Inside, Frida pulled me to a room on the right.

The velatorio, or wake room, was a large chamber with a ceiling of exposed wooden beams that converged into a skylight. Two dark-blue vinyl-covered benches with padded backrests jutted from opposite walls. On the central wall hung a life-sized crucifix with a statue of Christ dressed in a toga. Underneath him, the coffin I had purchased rested raised on a special stand. The first detail to jar on my nerves was the profusion of colored floral wreaths encircling the wooden casket. In India, the Hindu color of death and grieving was white. I tried not to mind and focused on the smoldering smell of frankincense combined with the fresher scent of the seasonal blooms.

One wreath of vibrant-purple irises, however, transported me to a bed in a New Delhi maternity clinic in 1984. Dressed in a pink bed jacket, I had waited for breakfast, as I hadn't eaten since lunchtime the day before, when my water broke. But in place of breakfast, in walked a delivery boy carrying the largest flower arrangement I had ever seen, dominated by full-lipped irises. *Who had sent me such a beautiful bouquet?*

I had never seen a real iris, only heard enthralling stories about them from Didima, who showed me a faded tray cloth with matching napkins she had embroidered many years ago. Didima said she had woken up to a field of irises on the Dal Lake in Kashmir one day, where Dadu used to vacation with his young family. Those irises had Didima banish Dadu from their houseboat. "Don't come back until you bring me cloth and embroidery threads to capture this scene," she had told him.

My eyes pooled as the delivery boy handed me the bouquet and I smelled the delicate fragrance of those irises. The bouquet contained a card in which Sergio had written:

My darling, I wanted to give you pink peonies for Pia's birth (since you always mention peonies, from reading Peony *by Pearl S. Buck), but they weren't in bloom yet in Kashmir. So I had them ship these irises for you because they were my favorite flowers in Japan. Someday, I'll show you both peonies and irises galore. For now, enjoy these.*

Love you, Sergio

P.S. I'm the happiest man on earth!

***

I looked at the closed coffin. For me and every other Hindu Indian on earth, colors meant life. They denoted a celebration of spring and youth and comedy. *Why would anyone place colored flowers next to a coffin?* Now I understood why Hindus mourned death in white clothes and with white flowers, like at Dadu's wake. White epitomized discretion and respect. It allowed each mourner the privacy to experience pain without public display.

Again, I crushed the geranium leaf in my hand and held it to my nose. "Who sent the flowers?"

"I've no idea." Frida shrugged in her offhanded way. "Should I check the cards?"

"No. I want to see Sergio."

The casket, which had seemed so huge in the coffin shop, appeared puny and narrow. *How did poor Sergio even fit in it?* Frida creaked open the heavy lid to release the combined odors of metal, new cloth, and pinewood. Inside, Sergio lay dressed in a light-blue hand-finished summer suit and a claret raw-silk tie, clothes he had purchased in Tokyo in the seventies. The sight of him paralyzed me. I remembered Didima's face in death, lips contorted to one side, eyes buried at an angle inside her forehead, and one hand grappling at her throat.

In my mind, a question erupted. *Who gave them this suit? It was among Sergio's favorites.* I grasped the cold edge of the coffin and received my second shock of the morning. Unlike poor Didima's, Sergio's face had been "fixed" to resemble a rigid mask. From that close, the seamstress in me saw how the mortician had sewn his eyelids shut and disguised the evidence with makeup.

Such is the power of the living over the dead.

Also, poor Sergio reeked of chemicals, but that smell mixed with the other smells in the coffin and the wake room. The pallor of his face had been layered with foundation and further brightened with rouge. His jaw, so obstinately distended in life, was clamped shut in death, lips stretched across those large, square, and prominent incisors but not well enough to hide the thin wire threaded between his teeth to hold his mouth shut.

With each shift of my head, the telltale wire winked and glinted in the daylight streaming down from the clerestory window. Painfully, I realized what Frida's mother had meant about sparing the children that terrifying sight of their father as a last memory. It was not Sergio—it was his remains. No one, myself included, needed that image inside their head. I reached to touch his face, hesitated, then withdrew.

A long time ago, Didima had placed her hand on Dadu's brow minutes before he had been taken away to be cremated. The anguish of touching his cold lifeless skin had become the tale of many a South Extension evening whenever Didima had felt sad and cried.

Beneath his face, Sergio's neck looked pitiful within the collar of a dress shirt now three sizes too large for him, as was the suit. Only his hands, folded on his chest, still looked perfect. Capable, midsized hands with wide, oval fingernails and defined half-moons, always clean and well-groomed, irrespective of what he was doing. Hands that had produced incomparable meals but could never hammer a nail straight into a wall. Sergio had always laughed that he had ten left thumbs for home-repair jobs. Memories tumbled forth in a waterfall—those hands chopping onions at the speed of light, washing dishes with an economy of movement a chef would envy, stirring a large pot full of a Portuguese chickpea dish with dried bacalhau codfish at Easter time, fussing with the children's hair on Sunday mornings, holding his Nikon camera while his daughters ran free in the Parque del Olivar, and now lying motionless, placed one on top of the other inside a coffin, lit by daylight that poured in through a roof window.

I floated in the void inside me, unmoored. Desperate for an anchor, again, I gripped the coffin edge. Eyes scrunched, I muttered the Our Father, prayed for Sergio's soul to be in heaven, begged for the courage to continue without him.

My unwilling fingers slid the groaning coffin lid forward and paused. I glanced at the mangled geranium foliage in my other hand. Kissing it, I placed it on Sergio's folded hands. I shut the coffin lid, and yet I did not cry.

65

At ten thirty a.m., I returned to the velatorio swathed in a black dress and a dove-gray silk scarf.

The Parque Domodosola appeared bright and impersonal, as if its morning persona had never existed. Its oval contour was crowded with parked cars while people thronged inside and outside the four wake rooms. I felt like an idiot wearing black, but I wore it because it was Sergio's country, not my own. If I had showed up wearing white, like a Hindu widow, the gossip would follow me to my grave. Like a dog kicked for another's amusement, I recalled when Xenobia Santander had labeled me a savage animal, all because I ate cauliflower stubs.

Inside the wake room, a variety of perfumes intermingled with the original odors in the room. On the right wall bench thronged people from Sergio's extended family, all allies of my mother-in-law. Their gazes devoured me as I walked in, but I refused to meet their eyes directly. Instead, I endured their looks impaling my stomach then drilling holes into my back as I gravitated to the vacant left bench.

Where the hell is Frida? Anytime now the questions will come: Where are Pia and Abril? Why didn't I bring them? Thank God Sergio would not be buried, and the farce would end at the culmination of the wretched wake he had so explicitly forbidden. If I had but one white rose with which to honor Sergio's death, it would have meant so much to me, but I hadn't thought to go buy one, and it was too late.

The velatorio was packed to the maximum with hyenas drawn in by the scent of death, faces I didn't even recognize, like those that had appeared only upon Didima's death.

At last, my mother-in-law walked in with Nila. Dressed for a party in black silk, she had a black lace scarf draped over her dyed and groomed brown hair and skin-colored tights with dainty high-heeled shoes. But instead of joining Nila, Xenobia sought me out with her eyes. "Where are the children?"

My heart picked up pace. "I didn't bring them." *Where in God's name is Frida? Is she staying away so the Santanders won't see the two of us hobnobbing?*

Xenobia headed straight for the coffin.

In utter disbelief, I watched her swing open the coffin lid.

"Oh, look, how did this get in here?" Her hand, with red-painted talons, grabbed something, and lightning-quick, out flew the wilted geranium leaf to land on the velatorio floor like a sodden feather. At the sight of that geranium leaf, I sprang to my feet and reached the coffin in two leaps, swinging the coffin lid shut.

Surprise rounded Xenobia's eyes. "I want the coffin lid open. That is how wakes are celebrated here."

"Right. And I want the coffin lid closed."

Without deigning to address me, she swung open the coffin lid again.

"Listen, you old witch. Sergio was my husband, and he expressly did not want a wake, but you vetoed his wish because he's dead and he couldn't stop you. Now either back off, or should I tell all your adoring fans what kind of a mother you were when you abandoned Sergio at age four to an aunt who whipped a little boy, day after day, year after year? Because I have nothing more to lose. Any support I ever had is lying dead in that coffin… and you won't desecrate Sergio's memory by letting people ogle at what this disease did to him. It's your call. Since this wake was your idea, I'll be happy to give all your attendees a reason to gossip for the next forty years."

"Mamá!" Nila rushed to her mother's aid, shooting me a dagger-thrust look. "Come on. This is not the place to confront her." She took Xenobia's arm and led her off to the right-side bench.

Can people see my body trembling? I sat back down alone on the left bench. *How would Pia and Abril have reacted, had they been here? Thank God they aren't. They, least of all, need to see Sergio lying shrunken and wasted, unable to guard the dignity that had so characterized him in life.*

From a distance, I observed Sergio's mother talking to Jaime León, who hadn't had the basic courtesy to come greet me, never mind offer me condolences. *What about a son's death in the West inspires a mother to style her hair, paint her lips, and stain her cheeks with rouge?* Instantly, I saw Didima's face on the day of Dadu's funeral, skin as waxen as a *mombatti* candle, eyes red rimmed, white sari pallu draped over her head, neck, arms, and ears stripped of jewelry, and her forehead conspicuously bereft of the traditional Hindu red teep dot.

Soon, too soon, Carlos came in to inform people to head for the crematorium, and that moment, too, rushed up on me. I stood but sat down again as Xenobia Santander readied for a stately exit. Even stocky and ample chested, the elderly lady cut an imposing figure, a peacock escorted by her bevy of peahens. She rose to her feet in her own cloud of expensive per-fume, thin lips pursed in a red diamond of disapproval as she readjusted the black lace scarf draped over her hairdo.

As if conscious of scrutiny, the entourage clattered out on expensive high heels, and casual treads mutilated the geranium leaf, kicked it, ground it into the tiled floor. And the more misshapen that pitiful piece of herb became, the worse I wanted to rescue it because, for me, that geranium foliage represented my relationship with Didima, and that day it also embodied my entire life with Sergio.

I waited until the room was near empty then dove to grab its remains.

Behind me, someone asked, "*¿Qué haces?*" It was Jaime León.

"*Nada.*" I tightened my fist around the unrecognizable verdant paste. "*No hago nada.* It's a bit of rubbish."

But Jaime held out his hand. "Give it to me. I'll chuck it." He smiled at me.

And that smile lit my brain on fire. "Listen, you twisted old man. Don't pretend you're my friend. You might not know it, but Sergio told me about the party at your house that infected him with HIV. It was the ultimate joke that Sergio considered you a father figure when you were his worst enemy."

Unbelievably, Jaime burst out laughing. "Is *that* what he told you? He didn't tell you I was his first lover at age sixteen? That because of my urging, he went to law school, or that I paid for his tuition, since his stenographer's salary went to support his mother?"

I bared my teeth. "Now why doesn't that surprise me, you sick, pedophilic reptile? *Of course* you would take advantage of a financially disadvantaged, fatherless boy like Sergio must have been as a teenager. Who else would you prey upon except a young boy who was extremely vulnerable? Now I despise you ten times more than I did five minutes ago—I hope you rot in hell when you die, you jerk—but know this, as I stand here. When Sergio went to India and got away from you and his toxic mother—he chose me. Because I represented a new beginning for him. And he loved me, and he had his two beautiful kids with me. I was always his shining star that represented something he did right in his life. His reason to be proud. You think he didn't notice that his family and you scurried away like rats when he needed you the most, and just his godson and I nursed him day and night while he was in the hospital?"

For the first time Jaime looked uncomfortable. "No one told me he was in the hospital."

"Good excuse. But perhaps it was for the best you didn't come to taint his last moments, so go forth and live your filthy life, and don't ever dare come near me again. Not that you will, because I have two little girls, not boys who you can dream of seducing." I strode out of that wake room momentarily feeling like a Titan for finally having defended Sergio from the rattlesnake that was Jaime, but then my shoulders slumped, remembering that Sergio didn't need my defense anymore.

Outside the *velatorio*, I dropped the sorry geranium corpse into my purse. High above, the sky had gone pale and a brisk breeze came by to lift my hair and fill my gray scarf like a sail. In the distance, the sea glittered and sparkled, reminding me of how Sergio had loved the icy temperature of the Pacific Ocean, grumbling that the Arabian Sea in Goa and the Mediterranean in Europe felt like warm soup on his skin. Inside my chest, a tightness made me wish he had never met a predator such as Jaime León and I prayed that wherever he was, he wasn't in pain anymore. Meanwhile, my psyche begged him close to cushion me from the frightening reality of his death.

A tickle on my left forearm revealed an inch of blue thread that hung loose from inside the three-quarter sleeve of my home-sewn black silk dress. I controlled the temptation to bite it off because, as Sergio would have said, "People are watching."

A rush of wind. Frida.

"Jesus, where the hell have you been?" I murmured.

"I forgot I had a parent-teacher conference at my children's school," Frida whispered. "I came straight here after it."

"I assumed maybe you didn't want to be seen with me."

"You're such an idiot."

"Do you know those people?" My eyes swept over a wavy group of unfamiliar faces who stood by a bench inside the Parque Domodosola, staring straight at me.

"They're from Sergio's work. That's what Carlos told me."

I panicked, seeing them head in my direction. "What am I supposed to say? I don't know them."

"Hey, they're not here because they cared for Sergio. They're here because they're diplomats and *he* was a diplomat." Frida's quick squeeze on the tickling forearm was supportive. "Say 'thank you' to whatever they say. It can't last long, because the crematorium has a limited time slot. The body has to get there half an hour ahead."

The body. I shook an unknown diplomat's hand, said a courteous *"Gracias." Yesterday's father, brother-in-law, son, and husband is today's body.*

In the distance, Xenobia Santander and company got into cars. *Is it over already?* My eyes searched for Frida, but she hovered yards away, talking to Carlos. So I stood there, lost, not sure of what to do until Frida came back for me.

"Come on. You're coming with us."

"To where?"

"To the crematorium."

The Via Expresa freeway, the business district of San Isidro, blazoned highway signs, the circular national stadium, the Avenida España, the Clínica Internacional, each whizzed past at the speed of memories while all I saw was Sergio lying dead inside a satin-lined coffin, padded and silky, white-cushioned and segregated from the terrifying reality of life. No dust would ever accumulate on Sergio's desk again. No geraniums would bloom by his windowsill, and no house of his would need repairs. A thin stream of tears blurred the outlines of pretty new buildings and unsightly, aged ones as I recollected the ride to Didima's funeral by the River Jamuna ghat in Old Delhi.

Would Sergio's family have let me ride in the funeral van with him? Unlikely. And soon, Sergio's body, too, would be reduced to ashes, like Didima's.

66

THE CORTEGE OF TWO CARS and the funeral van arrived at the Centro Funerario, located past the city on the Panamericana del Sur highway. The funeral parlor's drab concrete exterior defeated me as I exited Frida's car.

"Go on in," she said. "I'll join you in a minute."

Inside, a chapel that smelled of varnished wood and wax polish greeted me in silence. Designed to seat at least a hundred, it had more than a dozen pews. I sat on a back one and crossed my feet on cream tile flooring. *How much longer will this circus continue?*

In front of a nondenominational altar painted with blue-and-beige divine flames, Carlos talked to a crematorium worker.

Frida hurried in to sit beside me. "This is it." She pointed to Carlos and Nila, who walked in. "No one else is coming."

"¿Y la vieja?" I referred to our mother-in-law.

"*No viene.* Carlos persuaded her to go home with her pals."

My whole body relaxed. Four crematorium workers brought in Sergio's casket and placed it on a stand in front of the spot Carlos indicated with an index finger. A part of me wanted to rush up and bid Sergio a last farewell, but my body wouldn't move. It was Carlos who came and walked me to Sergio, giving me a last moment of privacy with him. But at the sight of Sergio, I felt my face crumple knowing I would never see him again, neither alive nor dead. Observing my state, Carlos called out to Frida and requested her to take me away.

Frida looped her arm through mine. "Come on. Let's walk." She pulled me toward the narrow garden path around the chapel.

On the way out, Nila, sitting on a pew, bestowed me with a disdainful glance. "I'll contact you about the will sometime."

As if she had struck me, I experienced an adrenaline rush. "No, you won't. You're not the executor anymore, so stay away from me."

"Yes, I am. Sergio showed me his will." Her smug expression made me want to slap her, but instead I punched her with, "Did he tell you I asked him to change it and he did? I can see from your face that he didn't. And you won't inherit our house or my kids if I die. So forget about lording over me or meddling in my life anymore. Serg and I had our differences, but in the end, he was well aware of exactly who cared for him and who didn't, and you were one of those who didn't."

I walked on, taller and straighter. But outside, my bravery fizzled out as fast as it had come to my rescue, and I fell to the paved path. I looked up, longing for a crackling New Delhi monsoon thunderstorm that would cry for me, cleanse the air, tear a hole in the hazy sky. But it was just a wish, similar to so many other wishes, because it never rained hard in Lima, and if it ever did, it was a major disaster.

Frida pulled me back to my feet, holding my hands. "Listen. The Santanders can hate you, but they can't beat you. You've got this, okay?"

Her words pitched me into feverish talk so I wouldn't have to face my fear. I talked of Didima's funeral and how Sergio had loved the Peruvian sea, of his love and hate for India and for Japan and the Eastern cultures versus the Western ones, of the polarities of hara-kiris, ikebanas, tea ceremonies, and the corpses of dead children floating in the Ganges River at the foot of Hindu temples, of how the East had changed Sergio's view of the West, and how, for him, it had reduced European Renaissance to the stature of a domestic animal when likened to the superior spirituality of Buddhism and Hinduism.

I talked of truths, lies, and appearances while Frida let me ramble. Finally, I said, "Sergio loved the Peruvian sea. I'll scatter a part of his ashes there, but he has to go to India too. His children are Indian. Yet it doesn't matter, does it? Eventually, his ashes from the Pacific will reach India anyway because all the seas are one, aren't they?"

Hours later, on the car ride home, I sat in the back seat of Frida's station wagon, quiet at last, as the heat from Sergio's ashes in a wooden urn warmed my lap. From time to time, weak sunlight swept in like a spotlight to illuminate Sergio's latest status, his new collocation in the scheme of the world.

From behind the wheel, Carlos asked, "Any ideas, anybody, on how to break it to Pia and Abril?"

Immediately I saw myself in our Jodpur Park townhouse in Calcutta, sitting by Baba's side on the white sheet-covered floor of Dadu's flower-filled wake. I saw Didima's middle sister, Auntie Shukhi, walk in with her five-year-old son, brushing past the petals of white lotus blooms. Auntie Shukhi had said, "Hassan, take the children to the New Market for ice cream. They shouldn't be here to see Vasant like this."

"Can we buy ice cream?" I heard myself ask.

"That's a great idea." Frida outstretched a hand for me to grasp.

Carlos swung the steering wheel to head toward the Quatro D Italian delicatessen on Avenida Angamos.

In Valle Hermoso, the formal attire of Carlos, Frida, and me was in strident contrast to Pia's and Abril's disheveled gray-and-white school uniforms.

"Hola, Mamá," Pia said. "Is Papá better after the operation?"

"When will he come home?" Abril asked.

I handed Frida the wooden urn and hugged the children hard. *Why haven't I ever noticed what an unbelievable resemblance to Sergio each child has?* He stared at me through Abril's eyes, tense and alert, and smiled at me through Pia's lips to show those large, square teeth. Self-conscious in my retrieval of the warm urn from Frida's hands, I motioned the children to sit at the dining table. From the kitchen, we heard Frida fuss and supervise Dulci on how she wanted the ice cream served.

Once Frida placed the porcelain dishes in front of each of us, Carlos cleared his throat. "*Niñitas—*"

"Wait a minute, Carlos," I interrupted, heart beating so hard I felt like it was knocking against my ribs. "Let me do this." Taut as a guitar string, I held each child by one hand. "Your *papito* didn't recover from that operation yesterday. He died in the hospital." I imagined Sergio lying on an autopsy table, his thorax bolt-cut open.

Pia's eyes shuttled to her sister, as if to check on a floating soap bubble, but Abril twirled a strand of golden-black hair with her free index finger, her Sergio-eyes shuttered, waiting for some adult to tell her it was a lie, waiting, waiting.

In that stillness, I saw myself by Jodpur Park Lake, looking up at Baba, the three-o'clock sun shadowing his face so I couldn't tell the expression in his eyes.

"Shona mona." Baba took my face in his palms. "You're a big girl now. You have to understand your dadu is no more. He has become the wind and the rain and the flowers you love so much. Think of him as a part of our garden. It won't hurt so badly if you picture seeing him all around you, just not in the ways you're used to."

At last, Abril stopped twirling her hair. "Can I see him?"

That guitar-string feeling inside me snapped. "No, amor." I dropped the children's hands and jumped up. "You see this box?" I picked up the wooden urn, my voice unnatural even to my own ears. "It contains your father's ashes."

Abril began to cry. "But why can't I see him? I want to see him."

My chair scraped back, resisting the woolly surface of a Kashan rug. I took Abril into my arms and hugged her. "You can't, amor," I whispered. "The hospital people cremated him. All they gave me of him are these ashes. Let's go to the garden and scatter the ash at the base of the rose bush. That way, each time a rose blooms, we'll know Papá is saying hello to us from heaven."

We headed out the main door and into the garden.

In front of the largest rose bush, I opened the urn for Pia and Abril to dip their hands into what was left of their father.

Abril lifted a fistful of the sandy gray powder and glanced at me, her huge brown eyes tear blotched. "It's warm," she said as I took the child's face in my hands and wiped Abril's tears with my thumbs. Abril raised the ashes to her nose. "It doesn't smell like my *papito*."

Triggered by that remark, I looked at Pia, but her eyes were dazed as she observed her sister.

We gathered under the dappling shade of a ficus tree while the little girls dispersed Sergio's ashes in heartbreaking silence on a half-opened pink rose. Disturbed by the activity, out scrambled a furry bumblebee, making the bloom quiver as Abril spilled the grainy dust on the rose petals.

Afterward, we filed back into the dining room to eat melting lúcuma ice cream, a Peruvian tropical fruit flavor Sergio had loved.

Late at night, hours after the children went to bed with the knowledge of their father's death a paralyzed lump inside them, I wandered the silent house, each second swelling around me until my feet walked into the empty study.

In the shadowy night, Sergio's vacant bed stood neatly tended. A lone ray from the streetlamp drew an oblique white line on the wall above its headboard.

Sergio's absence, more powerful than his presence, beckoned me from every corner. I groped for a bookshelf. *Had he felt as alone in here as I do tonight?* How cruel I had been to him, when it had been Nila, and not he, who had told me to leave the country. *Why did I assume those were his words and not Nila's?* Instead, I had shouted at him, insulted him, weak and suffering as he was. The regret ate me alive.

How petty it all seemed in the face of his departure. Never again would Sergio smile or cry or cook incomparable meals. Neither would anyone ever see to my needs as Sergio had because we shared two children. For the rest of my life, if I wanted chocolate cookies, I would have to go buy them myself. Sergio, steadfast in that seemingly innocuous gesture through the rollercoaster of our marriage, didn't exist anymore to buy them for me.

Rubbing the aching, hollow feeling inside my chest, I left the study to go to the porch. I slid the dining room French door open with effort and was greeted by the scent of jasmine. My breath and my heartbeats melded as I wilted on a porch chair. I laid my head back on the cushion behind me. Tomorrow. I would face real life tomorrow, phone Dick McBee at the Roosevelt and inform him I was available. But just for the night, I needed the absolution to acknowledge how much I missed Sergio already, accept who he had been in my life, admit that with him gone, I had no one left to obey or defy. At last, my dragonfly was as untethered as I had always wished it to be, but freedom terrified me a hundred times more than my life of captivity. *What will I do in a world without Sergio to answer my every question?*

My eyes blinked at the dark shapes in my garden, outlined against the inky sky dotted with a cold dusting of stars. Perversely, those stars brought back another night when Sergio had shown me the constellations in Machu Picchu during our honeymoon. Wrapped in the flimsy gauze of happiness, on that night, those faraway stars had appeared so near, we had both felt lightheaded. How appropriate the waning moon should be no more than a sliver to mourn Sergio's flight.

In agreement, a fitful breeze rustled the colorless leaves in my garden, each one a fluttering question mark. The wind brushed my exposed arms and brought back an old folklore Didima had once told me, reclined in her wood-and-canvas easy chair on our back patio in South Extension. "Hindus," Didima had said in her thready voice, "always light a candle on the night of a loved one's death, as a torch, you know, in case their soul is trapped on earth. I lit one for your dadu too…"

In the blackness, I groped my way to the kitchen and dug out a candle, a candle stand, and matches from a drawer beside the kitchen sink. A lone matchstick flared upon my utter solitude as I put fire to the candlewick. The flame danced, burnished yellow tinged with green, drawing a nosy flour moth to come wing with death. My chest tightened with trapped emotions.

I retraced my steps in the penumbral darkness, watching my solitary candle burn pure blue at the base, glow warm and heart shaped in the center and yellow-orange around the edges. The candle flame wavered wildly in another stray gust of wind, and its phantom did likewise on the patterned glass below it. I placed the candle on the porch table and cupped its glow.

In that moment, I finally understood I had not lost Sergio. He lived on inside Pia and Abril, like Dadu, Didima, and Baba lived on inside me, shaping who I was. I still had the chance to express to Pia and Abril the love I had never been able to express to Sergio while he was alive. My children would not depend on others to find happiness and stability. They would both grow up, finish college, and stand on their own two feet. Their fulfillment would come from within themselves, guided by their own actions. And no matter what the obstacles, I would never fail them in their quest. Honoring our daughters would be my deepest acknowledgement of who Sergio had been in my life.

***

DRAGONFLY HUNTING
NEVER SURRENDER

SNEAK PEEK

Noor's Story
◆ BOOK TWO ◆

RAYA KHEDKER

MAGENTA BOUGAINVILLEA

1

Lima, November 1992

FIND A JOB OR FOLD. That was what it boiled down to. Twenty days since Sergio had died, and I was already caving—jobless and moneyless until I received my pension of three hundred dollars in Peruvian currency from the foreign office of Peru because Serg had been a Peruvian diplomat. Only I couldn't get a job in the country without the degree or certificate I lacked. And jobless, I was an unfit mother to support my children.

I had paid the electric bill, the water bill, but food and gas money was running scarce when the Villa Maria School sent me a letter to collapse my world. It stated I owed the school a total of three hundred dollars in school fees for my two daughters along with a fine for the late payment. And I had assumed my biggest problem was the headache I had woken up with the day after the cremation that had never stopped. *Why didn't someone warn me that widowhood came with a permanent headache, intermittent vomiting, plus horrifying nightmares?* They were of Serg lying on the floor with his chest cut open in a pool of AIDS-tainted blood, Serg crying with his liver pulsating in his hands, Serg in a hundred predicaments that hadn't happened in real life.

"Señora, can I help you any further?" The brown-haired lady at the Villa

Maria School's business office held out a yellow receipt in place of the last two hundred dollars I had had to my name, though the solicited amount had been three hundred.

My eyes burned and watered, making the finance office glow white-hot under fluorescent lighting. I voiced the question that had kept me awake despite four antianxiety tablets and seven Advil last night. "Señora, isn't there a law in Peru that specifies how children who lose their wage-earning parent automatically receive a hardship scholarship from the school they attend? My children lost their father twenty days ago."

The finance lady touched her brown curls. "Let me fetch the treasurer. She might know the answer."

A few minutes later, a white-haired, bespectacled lady hurried out of an inner door. "I'm sorry for your loss, señora. Let me explain the death-related scholarship to you. To activate it, bring me Señor Santander's death certificate. You haven't done that yet."

Relief grayed the edges of my eyesight. "Where would I find his death certificate?" I wiped wet palms on the sides of my jeans.

"In the municipality of the neighborhood where he was born. On what day did he die?"

"October 6." Serg had been born in the older section of Jesus Maria near the center of Lima. I had no clue how to find its municipality. *How many other pitfalls await me?* Yet I couldn't hunt down the municipality that day if I meant to do the afternoon school carpool on time. The death certificate would be the next day's mountain to climb.

"Let's see. Today is October 26. Give it another week. They should have the certificate by then. When you bring it in, we'll refund the portion of school fees you just paid."

"Are you serious?" The refund would save the month of October. *Is this Serg saving the day?* Yes, in the Villa Maria, my children would never learn the English I wanted them to know—*yet right now, can I argue with a free education?*

Pia's and Abril's education was my crowning goal in life since, without it, they would be like me—basically unemployable in a country where I couldn't find a job without the credentials I didn't have. Someday, I would address the alarming dearth of English in my children's lives, since English was my comfort language besides being the most important language in the world, but it was not the day to face that fight.

Villa Maria business office transaction concluded, I hobbled to my car, officially penniless. I lost it once I inserted the key in the ignition. Without warning, I bashed my aching head on the steering wheel and let forth an animal cry. Shaking both fists at the sky, I screamed, "You bastard! You've given me a job I can't tackle. I want you to know I hate you! I will never ever believe in you again. Every hardship you've piled on my head I bore without question, but this time, you've maxed your quota. This time you've fucked with me one time too many. Go screw yourself, God!" I broke into sobs, but my sobs were of rage—sheer, panicked rage. A long time later, I turned the key in the ignition. I didn't have the luxury to break down with two children to take care of.

Once Sergio died, too soon, life forced Pia, Abril, and me to assimilate the fact and continue as if he had never existed. Each day, the children attended school while none of us mentioned the topic of their dead father. On the days I did the school carpool, I stared at Pia's and Abril's faces in the rearview mirror—Pia, blond, with her hair in a tight ponytail, had a stony face, her gray-green eyes focused on the cityscape racing by. Abril, brown haired, brown eyed, had an unfathomable gaze. *What are they thinking? Feeling? Are they both as overwhelmed as I?* At least neither one had complained of the nonstop headache I had, boom, boom, boom, clobbering the left half of my head, day and night.

A week into the crucifying pain, I had called Dick McBee, assistant headmaster of the Roosevelt School, to inform him I was available to work per diem as a substitute teacher. The Roosevelt administration knew me since I had briefly worked there as a substitute teacher several years ago—a time when Sergio had already been diagnosed with AIDS but was still alive to take care of the children and me, a time when I had no idea what "being alone" meant.

"We'll call you soon, I'm sure," Dick had said, but he'd never called.

Meanwhile, another week passed, and my nonstop headache didn't abate, convincing me I had a brain tumor. However, I refused to go see Dr. Ritter because his consult would cost forty dollars, and I didn't have health insurance.

I called him on day fifteen.

"What are you taking for it?" Dr. Ritter didn't sound happy.

"Advil. But it doesn't help." I rubbed my aching eye.

"It isn't a tumor. It's stress, so stop the Advil or you'll give yourself a nice big ulcer."

Upon reaching home after resolving the Villa Maria school-fee conundrum, against Dr. Ritter's warnings, I popped four Advil because the temptation to hope perhaps *that* time they might work defeated the logic of evidence.

Then I called Dick McBee again. "Dick, I know I'm supposed to wait for your call, but I'm desperate. Do you have any work for me?"

"We need a sub for two weeks from November 15. Can you do it?"

I felt like screaming, *Then, why didn't you call me?* Instead, I said, "I'll be there at seven thirty in the morning, sharp." *Please, dear God. Please let the two weeks of pay from the Roosevelt and the Villa Maria refund save November for me.*

To distract myself, I asked Dulci, our live-in maid, who substituted as my younger sister, to make me six toasts and layer them thick with butter and sugar. Eating to cope was a childhood habit I had never beaten. Whenever my grandma, Didima, who had been my primary caretaker, fell sick, I ate to overcome the threat of her dying and leaving me stranded.

The shrill of the phone ringing shattered the relief of my last bite of toast. From New Delhi, my mother said, "*Shona*, how are you and the children holding up? Come home. Robu and I will take care of you." Shona meant "darling" in Bengali.

I dug the heel of one palm into my throbbing left eye. "Thanks, Ma, but no. I'm never coming back to you or India."

"Ma shona, why are you so stubborn? Here, Robu will take care of us all."

Robu Chatterjee, my stepfather, had been unable to control his temptation to molest me at six years old, the first time I had visited the couple for a potential sleepover at their home.

"Ma, we've had this conversation a thousand times. I will never expose Pia and Abril to your pedophile husband."

"Shona, he's *not* a pedophile, and he never molested you! You're stuck on a childhood perception—" My mother's voice shrilled to defend her husband.

"Fine, he's not a pedophile, but I'm never returning home!" I slammed the phone back in its cradle, too angry to cry as I headed to the bathroom.

With manic urgency, I shoved two fingers down my throat. Only vomiting the toast, butter, and sugar I had eaten would afford me relief, give me a temporary sense of control. The phone rang again, but I ignored it. Instead, I heaved and retched the fresh taste of all I had eaten, hurling until nothing more came up. Panting like I had run a mile, I gagged as I washed up and brushed my teeth, head pounding so hard I felt it would burst unless I lay back and calmed my breathing.

I crashed onto my bed, face up. I had to find a job—a real one. Only, in Peru, as in India, by law, my chances of securing a job were slim without completed qualifications. That was why Dick McBee of the Roosevelt School couldn't hire me as a full-time teacher, overqualified as I was when measured in college credits. And if I didn't find a job, and the money ran out, my only asset was our house. I would have to sell it. When Serg had lost his health insurance in early 1992, it had automatically terminated the fifty thousand dollars of life insurance money I would have received upon his death. Right then, I didn't have a single penny until I either received my pension from the foreign office or the Villa Maria School refunded me the two hundred dollars I had given them.

Tears pooled in my eyes. Serg and I had struggled so hard, sacrificed so much to build a mortgage-free house, and I would have to sell it anyway. It would *start* the beginning of the end, and "the end" might well terminate in India, in my parents' home. *So much for telling my mother off.*

I was crying into my pillow when Dulci rushed up the stairwell.

"Señora Noor?" She shook her head at the sight of me crying because, during the past twenty days, sometimes I cried nonstop when the children were in school. Dulci understood stress since she was the oldest child of a farming couple on a remote mountain farm. As such, it had been her special burden to support her mother when her father had raped his wife's only daughter from a former marriage. The resultant child had become Dulci's fourth "brother" after Dulci's half sister had been committed to a mental institution. Like me, Dulci had aged young.

I wiped my eyes and nose with the corner of the bed cover. "Did you pick up the phone downstairs? Tell my mother I don't want to speak to her—"

"It's not your mother. The foreign office wants to speak to you."

ACKNOWLEDGEMENTS

My most fervent thanks to Lynn McNamee, owner of Red Adept Editing, who introduced me to my content editor, Alyssa Hall, and subsequently, line editor, Amanda Kruse. Without them I wouldn't have a book to publish—it's that simple.

Very special thanks to my graphic designer, Glendon Haddix, whose patience to accommodate my adamance knows no bounds.

Heartfelt thanks also to my two greatest writing teachers whom I have never met:

Gary Provost, whose book, *Make Your Words Work*, taught me how to write, and post mortem at that. Gary, your books make you immortal. You will forever be a master!! Thank you.

And Lisa Cron, whose two books, *Wired For Story*, and *Story Genius*, taught me how to first think in story, then tell a story. Cron's prose forced me to face that after twelve years of slog…all I had written were "a bunch of events that happened." A story is not a bunch of events. It is what happens inside the head of the protagonist living those bunch of events, and how they change her. It was a tough lesson…but without learning it, I would still be no closer to my dream of being a storyteller…

Others who helped me during an incredible sixteen year journey are: Terri Goral, Abby Smith, Judy Stolfo, Penny Loucas, Michael Breton, Marlene Adelstein, Judy Roth, Olivia Khedker, Jennifer Johnson, Constanza Ontaneda, Marty

Shiel, Steve Bernstein, Cathi Powers, Mert Camp, Mary Camp, Ash Knuteson, Ellen Cain, Heber Sanchez, Sara Rider, Patty Richard, Rita Rice, Mary Ellen Gaffney, Kelly Morgan, Luis Alberto Riva, Nadia Valdemoro, Wanda Vargas Quintanilla, Gino Arciniega, William Hoyos, Jyoti Gulati, Augusto Arzubiaga, Oscar Gonzalez, Aldo Arciniega, Sara Rider, Meneca Alvariño, Andrew McNeill, Roberto Villaran, Luis Alberto Riva Gonzalez, Hernan Couturier, Christine Adler, William Belevan, Harold Belevan, Jorge Armas, Sarah Mueller, Renato Blain, Courtney Olds, Polina, Eugenia Sokol, Lisa Kende, Sarah O'Donnell, Oswaldo Sandoval, Felix Denegri Luna, Takki Patsias, Liliana Cino, Luis Alberto León, Luis Elguera, Eugenia Quesada, Rocio Tudela, Fortuna Calvo-Roth, Elisabeth Jones, Eleanor Eckett, Ana Maria Vega, Alicia Shorthill, Victor Fernandez-Davila, Peg Cowen, Mari Shiel, Immer Cook, Kathryn Kothe, Sun Graham, Rose Kerlyne.

My most sincere apologies to those whom I might have missed. The omission is unintentional.

ABOUT THE AUTHOR

Raya Khedker was only three years old when she received her first writing inspiration, watching her father tie a thread to a dragonfly's tail in the garden of their Calcutta home, then handing her the ensemble to fly like a live kite. Too young to discern the cruelty of this practice, Raya flew those dragonflies, mesmerized by the beauty and iridescence of their gossamer wings shining like precious jewels under the Indian sun, delighted by how those magical dragonflies were always within her control.

Decades later, those trapped dragonflies would become the heart of Raya's debut novel, *Dragonfly Escaping*. Her biggest dream is to inspire women to recognize their untapped power, give it their all, and fulfill any goal they want.

When she isn't writing, Raya has worked as an interpreter, translator, teacher, private tutor, jail guard, and a seasonal farm laborer on different continents. At present, she lives in Massachusetts.

twitter.com/RayaKhedker
facebook.com/khedker.raya
instagram.com/rayakhedker

**Join Raya's Ray of Light
at
rayakhedker.com**

and please leave a review on Amazon!

Printed in Poland
by Amazon Fulfillment
Poland Sp. z o.o., Wrocław
15 December 2023

d5ebf901-a5a7-4513-b7ae-5c4c3a7d4805R01